Praise for
Beneath a Marble Sky

"[A] spirited debut novel. . . .With infectious enthusiasm and just enough careful attention to detail, Shors gives a real sense of the times, bringing the world of imperial Hindustan and its royal inhabitants to vivid life."
—*Publishers Weekly*

"Jahanara is a beguiling heroine whom readers will come to love; none of today's chick-lit heroines can match her dignity, fortitude, and cunning. . . . Elegant, often lyrical writing distinguishes this literary fiction from the genre known as historical romance. It is truly a work of art, rare in a debut novel."
—*The Des Moines Register*

"Agreeably colorful . . . [with] lively period detail and a surfeit of villains."
—*Kirkus Reviews*

"An exceptional work of fiction . . . a gripping account."
—*India Post*

"Highly recommended . . . a thrilling tale [that] will appeal to a wide audience."
—*Library Journal*

"Evocative of the fantastical stories and sensual descriptions of *One Thousand and One Nights*, *Beneath a Marble Sky* is the story of Jahanara, the daughter of the seventeenth-century Mughal emperor who built India's Taj Mahal. What sets this novel apart is its description of Muslim–Hindu politics, which continue to plague the subcontinent today."
—*National Geographic Traveler*

"A passionate, lush, and dramatic novel, rich with a sense of place. John Shors is an author of sweeping imaginative force."
—Sandra Gulland, author of the Josephine B. Trilogy

continued . . .

ALSO BY JOHN SHORS

Beneath a Marble Sky

Beside
A Burning Sea

JOHN SHORS

 NEW AMERICAN LIBRARY

New American Library
Published by New American Library, a division of
Penguin Group (USA) Inc., 375 Hudson Street,
New York, New York 10014, USA
Penguin Group (Canada), 90 Eglinton Avenue East, Suite 700, Toronto,
Ontario M4P 2Y3, Canada (a division of Pearson Penguin Canada Inc.)
Penguin Books Ltd., 80 Strand, London WC2R 0RL, England
Penguin Ireland, 25 St. Stephen's Green, Dublin 2,
Ireland (a division of Penguin Books Ltd.)
Penguin Group (Australia), 250 Camberwell Road, Camberwell, Victoria 3124,
Australia (a division of Pearson Australia Group Pty. Ltd.)
Penguin Books India Pvt. Ltd., 11 Community Centre, Panchsheel Park,
New Delhi - 110 017, India
Penguin Group (NZ), 67 Apollo Drive, Rosedale, North Shore 0632,
New Zealand (a division of Pearson New Zealand Ltd.)
Penguin Books (South Africa) (Pty.) Ltd., 24 Sturdee Avenue,
Rosebank, Johannesburg 2196, South Africa

Penguin Books Ltd., Registered Offices: 80 Strand, London WC2R 0RL, England

First published by New American Library, a division of Penguin Group (USA) Inc.

First Printing, September 2008
1   3   5   7   9   10   8   6   4   2

Copyright © John Shors, 2008
Readers Guide copyright © Penguin Group (USA) Inc., 2008
All rights reserved

 REGISTERED TRADEMARK—MARCA REGISTRADA

LIBRARY OF CONGRESS CATALOGING-IN-PUBLICATION DATA
Shors, John, 1969–
Beside a burning sea / John Shors.
p. cm.
ISBN: 978-0-451-22492-7
1. World War, 1939–1945—Pacific Area—Fiction. 2. United States. Navy—Hospital ships—Fiction.
3. Survival after airplane accidents, shipwrecks, etc.—Fiction. 4. Soldiers—Japan—Fiction. 5. Nurses—
Fiction. 6. Solomon Islands—Fiction. I. Title.
PS3619.H668B47 2008
813'.6—dc22   2008009398

Set in Adobe Garamond
Designed by Ginger Legato

Printed in the United States of America

For my family—

Allison, thank you for the gift of always believing.
I love you.

Sophie and Jack, nothing else compares.

Through the misery of war, love is lost and love is found.
Like all things of green and flesh,
Love dies when republics collide.
Yet amid the wreckage of minds and memories,
Love can quickly emerge,
As if a fresh rain that tries to wipe clean a field of battle.

—ANONYMOUS

Beside
A Burning Sea

DAY ONE

Warm winds bear old scents.
I ask why I have fallen
And how I may rise.

Benevolence

Ten minutes before a torpedo sliced through the sea and slammed into steel, most everything was normal aboard the U.S. hospital ship *Benevolence*.

Parting the temperate waves of the South Pacific at a speed of twelve knots, *Benevolence* more closely resembled a transatlantic passenger liner than the handiwork of the U.S. Navy. The five-story vessel spanned four hundred feet and boasted engines that generated four thousand horsepower. The ship was coated in white paint, with giant red crosses dominating its sides and smokestack. From a distance, *Benevolence* looked far more majestic than a massive chunk of floating steel had any right to. The ship radiated comfort and security and solace.

Below deck, reality was far different. *Benevolence* held nearly five hundred hospital beds, which were filled with soldiers who suffered everything from chest wounds to lost appendages to malaria and psychiatric maladies. Attending to these patients were several dozen navy doctors and nurses. Though few of these healers had been on the front lines, during the course of the war most had been shot at by snipers, lifted off the ground by bomb blasts, and contracted a tropical illness. Moreover, the mental toll of trying to cure the often incurable had pushed many of the staff to and beyond the breaking point.

Benevolence was designed to linger on the outskirts of battle, to swiftly enter burning waters, and to provide aid to the men who'd been maimed by bombs and bullets. International law mandated that hospital ships save both friend and foe, and *Benevolence* was filled with torn American and Japanese soldiers. The ship stank of unwashed bodies and disinfectants and bleach. Much worse, depending on one's location, the stench of burnt flesh could be as oppressive as the humid air that kept everything in an eternal state of dampness. Though the drone of *Benevolence's* engines drowned out the moans of the dying, the screams of the burn patients often pierced the air.

Ten minutes before his ship was split in two, Captain Joshua Collins absently studied the chart before him, wondering how his wife, Isabelle, was faring with the fresh batch of wounded. He knew that she'd be darting from soldier to soldier, creating order and sanity where no such havens should have existed. During this frenzied dance she'd act as a mother or lover or sister to the men who suffered and died before her. As far as he was concerned, she was able to almost magically transform into whoever these suffering men so desperately needed her to be.

Though Joshua and Isabelle had been together for almost a decade, and though he recognized that she wasn't perfect, he still marveled at her. He hoped that the men she saved understood the extraordinary measures she took to save them—for to do so she'd left a trail of herself from North Africa to Midway. This trail was filled with her laughter and youth, her faith and strength. Painfully aware of her sacrifices, Joshua often prayed that she wouldn't be an empty shell by the time the war ended. He'd seen too many such shells, and the fear of her becoming one was a burden that weighed heavily upon him. Unfortunately, despite this fear and his consequent longing to mend her as she mended others, he had his own demons, and such monsters rarely set him free.

Still absently gazing at the chart, Joshua reflected on what he worried was a growing chasm between Isabelle and him. For as much as he admired and loved her, over the past few months he hadn't felt as compelled to spend time at her side. As he saw it, the two of them inhabited different realms. After all, his complete focus centered on the safe and effective operation of *Benevolence*, and her duty was to ensure the best possible medical care for her patients. Neither task left much room for anything else. And the less time they spent together, the less inclined they were to seek each other out. It was as if, having left the overwhelming demands of the helm or the patients, neither spouse had energy for the other. And so they drifted apart, like kites released into a storm.

Saddened by the recent unraveling of his marriage, Joshua turned from the chart and, looking through a window, studied the calm waters surrounding *Benevolence*. The nearby sea had already witnessed enormous conflicts between American and Japanese warships, and Joshua knew that more such battles were coming. The Japanese, as he'd been briefed many times, needed possession of the nearby islands to protect their recent conquests, and the allied forces were desperate to stop further Japanese expansion. *Benevolence* had been sent to these waters because of the looming battles that so often stole his sleep.

Downwind from where Joshua stood and stared, a young officer hid in the shadows of the stern. Eyeing a distant island—which was bathed in amber by the dropping sun—he flicked a cigarette into the sea and checked his wristwatch. Knowing that a plane would arrive soon and release its torpedo, he stayed hidden. Though unafraid of bullets and soldiers, he didn't like the thought of plunging thirty feet into the water below, of being sucked deeply under that water, of having to swim a half mile to an empty island. He consoled himself with the knowledge that if he lived, he'd spend the rest of his life enjoying the vast wealth that a series of betrayals had brought him. He'd have his fill of women and possessions and power, and, best of all, he would never have to obey orders again.

The officer cared nothing for those he had killed or for those aboard *Benevolence*—the men and women whom he'd soon send to death. Occasionally, ruined faces haunted his dreams, but such torments weren't tangible enough to change his actions. People died in war, he reasoned, and if they died at his hand, so be it. He had ample cause to hate both

Americans and Japanese, and over the past nine months, he'd happily killed people on each side of the conflict. Killing had become his greatest joy.

Though his past deeds had led to the deaths of many, tonight his betrayal would destroy an entire ship. He eagerly awaited watching *Benevolence* burn, for he despised those who operated the vessel, and the thought of its commanding officers being forever silenced made him clench his fists with anticipation. Of course, he'd miss watching the nurses—miss the sights and scents and fantasies that they brought into his world. But the money and influence that his treachery would produce far outweighed anything that the opposite sex could offer.

He'd been told there would be no survivors, and worried for his own safety, he fidgeted and quietly swore. He increasingly felt as if he were entombed within his own casket. Continuing to curse, he looked skyward, wishing that the bomber would come. He knew it would, for the belly of *Benevolence* had been secretly filled with aviation fuel, antiaircraft guns, and stockpiles of ammunition. Once he'd discovered this development and alerted the Japanese to its presence, they couldn't have been more intent on sinking the ship.

As far as he knew, only one other person aboard *Benevolence* was aware of this cargo. Like everyone else, the navy intelligence officer would perish in a few minutes. He'd die with the doctors, the nurses, the sailors, the patients. They'd die in flames or in the sea, and their deaths would not be short of suffering.

When the officer heard the distant drone of an aircraft engine, he removed a life jacket from beneath a bench and quickly secured it about his torso. He then pulled a wooden box into the retreating light. The waterproof box contained a radio, a pistol, rations, cigarettes, and everything else he'd need to survive for several weeks on the island. With a grunt, he heaved it overboard. An ever-increasing hum filled his ears, and knowing that the plane would soon drop its torpedo, he inhaled deeply and vaulted over the railing. Just before he hit the water, his vision passed through an open hatch and he glimpsed a pair of nurses bent over a patient. Then the sea rose up to strike him, and his world went black.

The nurses heard the splash and paused in their work. One of them—whose eyes mirrored a clear sky and whose teak-colored hair had been cut short by her own hand—turned from the three-day-old wound before her, glancing at the hatch. "Did you hear that?" she asked her older sister, Isabelle.

"The splash?"

"It sounded louder than a wave."

"So?"

"I wonder what it could have been. Maybe a jumping dolphin?"

"You wonder about a lot of things, Annie."

"Well, I . . . I think it's good to ask questions," the younger sibling replied, returning to the wound. "It keeps everything fresh."

The Japanese soldier watched Annie study the stitches in his thigh. Though most of the Japanese patients were uncomfortable in her presence, this soldier took interest in her work. In fact, the sight of her diminutive frame and soft, almost girlish face intrigued him greatly. To him, her features and movements resembled those of a young deer—a gentle forest creature that was more intent on its immediate surroundings than the world around it. Her wide eyes, unblemished skin, and full lips seemed ill suited for the harsh, artificial light of the cramped room.

Annie started to tenderly clean the soldier's wound, surprised that a passing bullet could tear out so much flesh. This man may always limp, she thought, redressing the wound. Of course, a limp was a much better outcome than could be expected for most of the men she saw.

"When is Joshua off duty?" Annie asked, finishing up with her patient. She thought the foreigner might have nodded in appreciation but wasn't sure, as *Benevolence* incessantly swayed.

"Is he ever off duty?" Isabelle replied, methodically scanning a series of charts before her.

"I'd say that's the pot calling the kettle black."

"You would?"

"How many patients, Izzy, have you seen today? Forty? Fifty?"

"Oh, not that many. I should have seen more."

"Really? Did you eat lunch?"

"No, but I—"

"Will you eat dinner? Or faint like you did last week?"

"Enough," Isabelle replied. "You're beginning to sound an awful lot like Mother."

Annie paused from tidying the patient's bedding. "Don't say that," she replied, rolling her eyes.

"Well, it's true."

"Well, maybe she's right."

The patient heard the noise first. Annie saw him cock his head toward the hatch. He squinted, as if improved eyesight could somehow help his ears. Annie soon recognized the hum as the distant drone of an airplane. She was used to such noises and didn't think anything of it. "You never answered my question," she said.

"About what?"

"About Joshua."

"I don't know when he's off duty," Isabelle replied, making rapid notations on the charts. "For all we see each other, we might as well be on different continents."

"I'm not sure about that. At least you know where to find him."

Isabelle started to respond, but stopped herself and nodded. She understood that Annie was thinking of her fiancé—who fought Germans somewhere in Europe—and she put her hand on Annie's slender shoulder. "He'll make it through this," she said. "We all will."

Annie shifted on her aching feet, wondering where Ted was, why she didn't miss him more, why she hadn't called his name when the delirium of malaria had recently gripped her. Shouldn't she be writing him love letters and gazing longingly at his photo each night? Weren't such things what lovers did? What was wrong with her?

As the silence between the sisters lingered, the drone of the airplane strengthened. It soon grew from the hum of a motorboat to a metallic, violent roar that assaulted their ears. Annie was about to speak again when the Japanese soldier abruptly sat up, shaking his head in bewilderment. "Nakajima . . . Nakajima bomber," he said, his English surprising both nurses.

Isabelle was the first to comprehend his words. "It's . . . a Japanese bomber?"

The plane must have passed very low over the ship, for the deafening wail of its engine seemed to penetrate their skulls. For a heartbeat or two, the wail diminished. Then an incomprehensibly loud and powerful explosion knocked Annie and Isabelle off their feet. Both nurses were hurled so high that they struck the ceiling. Along with charts and instruments and patients, Annie and Isabelle fell to the floor. Landing awkwardly on bedding and steel, they were too stunned to cry out. They simply grunted with the impact and tried to draw breath into their throbbing lungs. Somehow time froze and rushed forward all at once.

Annie thought she saw Izzy's mouth move, but the younger sister couldn't hear anything. Her ears hummed as if they housed scores of mosquitoes. Her mind didn't work properly. She felt as if she'd drunk a bottle of wine, and found it impossible to comprehend what had happened. The world spun and tilted and swayed. It groaned and boomed. The lights had gone out. Water covered the floor. Where was she? Why did fires rage and why were so many bodies unmoving about her?

Annie spat through her bloodied lips as Isabelle reached for her hand. The strength of Isabelle's grip slowly shook such questions from her mind. She smelled smoke, heard distant screams, and saw that the room was slanting and filling with water. She still didn't fully understand the scene before her, but Isabelle seemed unhurt, and Annie could make enough sense of the situation to take solace in that fact. She started to hug her sister, but Isabelle turned and crawled toward the bodies around them. Annie did likewise, instinctively checking pulses as she had ten thousand times before. She felt the beat of several hearts, but seeing the gaping wounds before her, knew these hearts would soon quiet.

Suddenly, the Japanese soldier with the leg wound gripped her arm and tried to pull her to her feet. Failing to do that, he shouted something and dragged her toward the hatch. Annie screamed—certain he was bent on harming her. However, the soldier let go of her arm and pointed at her waist. Though the water was almost to her stomach, Annie's mind still reeled and she didn't realize that *Benevolence* was sinking. She desperately pushed her patient away and started to attend to the injured again, wading to where Isabelle tried to save a dying doctor.

The soldier, whose name was Akira but who hadn't been called that name for several years, glanced at the hatch, which was already halfway underwater. Whoever stayed any longer in the room would die. Grabbing the small, brown-haired nurse, Akira dragged her toward the hatch. She tried to fight him, but she wasn't strong and he hurriedly pushed her through the opening. The older and larger nurse must have heard her sister's screams, for abruptly she left the doctor and struggled through the now chest-deep water toward the hatch. She shouted something at Akira, but secondary explosions ripped through the ship, obscuring her words. He gestured frantically toward the hatch. Water poured through it, and he had to use his shoulder to push the nurse beyond the opening. It took all of his strength to drag himself through the violent water and into the emptiness beyond the steel.

Outside, the two nurses shrieked and held onto the ship's side. Above them, *Benevolence* burned and boomed as additional explosions gutted her innards. The center of the ship was unrecognizable. Fire billowed from an immense fissure that was partly underwater. "Swim!" Akira shouted at them in English. "Swim or you will drown!"

Remembering Joshua, Isabelle frantically spun in the water, looking for him, repeatedly screaming his name. *Benevolence* was quickly dying beside her, and she felt the sea try to suck her down with the ship. Despite her overwhelming fear for her husband, she didn't want to get yanked into the blackness below, didn't want to drown in that blackness. And so she kicked away from the steel.

"Good!" Akira shouted. "You both follow me! You understand, yes? Now please follow me!"

Isabelle wept as she swam after the soldier. Though the nearby fires dominated much of her world, she saw the brilliance of the stars and, prompted by this sight, she began to pray for her beloved. She begged God as she had never begged him—for she knew Joshua well and understood that he'd be the last to leave his ship.

WITHIN THE BURNING INFERNO that had once been *Benevolence*, the assistant engineer struggled up the tilting deck. By pressing his bare feet against either side of the narrow passageway, he was able to propel himself upward. Though he heard many screams and many voices needed saving, he ignored these pleas for help—for he desperately needed to rescue the boy.

Though Jake had only known the young Fijian for two weeks, he treated Ratu almost as if he were the son he'd never had. Jake had found the stowaway hidden deep within the engine room. And Jake had listened to his pleas, seen him holding back his tears, and decided that the boy should be looked after. Why Jake had subsequently related so powerfully to Ratu was somewhat of a mystery to the big engineer. Perhaps this attachment initially formed because Ratu's face was almost the same color as Jake's—a shade of mahogany that seemed so out of place aboard a ship where almost everything and everyone was white. Moreover, Ratu had left Fiji to search for his father, who led American forces as they battled Japanese from island to island across the South Pacific. And seeing how Ratu so yearned for his father, Jake had decided to help and comfort him during his ill-conceived journey.

As Jake propelled himself up the passageway, he shouted Ratu's name. The boy liked to watch sunsets from the bow, and if Ratu had been on the bow when the torpedo struck, he'd likely be alive. Jake knew that the ship would float only for another minute or two. He could tell by the ever-increasing angle of his climb that *Benevolence* would soon go under. Most of her already had.

Shouts emerged from far below him, and Jake saw that people were struggling to climb up the passageway. He looked for a rope to throw to them but, seeing nothing, screamed at them to climb as he was. They pleaded with him to help, but the rising sea quickly silenced them. Jake cursed, redoubling his efforts to reach the bow. Finally arriving at a door that led to the deck, he pulled himself through the opening. Objects of every sort slid down the deck toward where he clung. "Ratu!" he shouted. "Ratu, where you at?"

A stranger's voice answered, and Jake yelled at the man to leave the ship. He then tried to climb higher, but *Benevolence* was almost vertical in the water. "If you hear me, Ratu, slide down to me!" he yelled, his voice smooth and deep and possessing a slight drawl. "There ain't time for nothing else!"

A wooden crate tumbled down the deck and struck a steel girder not far from Jake, splintering into scores of jagged pieces. He grabbed a long plank as it slid past. Screaming with effort, he threw the plank into the nearby water. "Come, Ratu! Come!" he shouted frantically.

Jake wanted to remain on board longer, but such inaction would swiftly bring his death. Dragging himself to the railing, he managed to leap a few feet into the swirling water. He was immediately sucked under, twisting and spinning in the blackness. The fires above painted the surface orange, and Jake kicked and clawed toward this glow. His shirt snagged on a railing, and for a terrifying moment he was yanked deeper as *Benevolence* sank. Mercifully, his shirt ripped and once again he swam upward, desperate to exhale.

When Jake finally met the surface he burst through it as if he were leaping for the stars. He breathed in the night with vast shudders, trying to swim from *Benevolence*. "Ratu!" he shouted. "I'm here!"

Just as Jake began to lose hope, two men and a boy leapt off the side of *Benevolence*. They were sucked under as well. Jake filled his lungs and dove toward where Ratu had disappeared. He saw him tumbling in the darkness, and he wrapped his arm around Ratu's slender waist and kicked upward with all his might. The pressure to breathe soon became unbearable, and Jake sucked in seawater just before they reached the surface. He choked on the water, fighting to draw in air. He coughed and retched until his aching lungs finally emptied of the sea.

"Can you . . . can you breathe?" Ratu asked, his faint British accent obscured by nearby explosions. He shuddered as sobs wracked his small frame. "Please breathe, Big Jake! Please!"

Before Jake could nod, a man broke the water's surface. His uniform bore stripes, and Jake reached for him. "Cap-Captain?" he sputtered, somewhat incredulously.

Joshua didn't reply. "Isabelle!" he screamed, spinning in the water, peering into the flames and darkness. "Where are you? Please tell me where you are!"

When Joshua started to swim toward what remained of *Benevolence*, Jake was forced to grab his leg. "We gotta swim away, Captain!"

"No!" Joshua shouted, kicking fiercely.

"We—"

"Isabelle!"

"There ain't time!"

"Let go of me, damn you! Let go—"

"I spied two nurses! Swimming!"

Joshua stopped trying to free his leg and turned to Jake. "My wife?"

"I don't rightly know, Captain. Maybe."

"Maybe?"

"Captain, we gotta leave here. If we don't, we'll be sucked under like apples in a river. And then you ain't ever gonna know if she lived."

Joshua turned toward *Benevolence*, which burned like a funeral pyre and swiftly dropped under the surface. "God help anyone aboard her," he said miserably, making the sign of the cross. "God help us all."

Jake put his face into the water, looking for the other man who'd leapt alongside Ratu. Peering into the gloom and twisting all the way around, he saw no one. After wiping the sea from his eyes, he spied the plank that he'd thrown overboard and swam toward it. Ratu and Joshua followed his lead.

Soon the three survivors held the plank against their chests and swam backward, toward an island, their eyes still searching *Benevolence* for signs of life. Each survivor mourned the night in his own way. Jake often looked above to spare himself from the hideous sight before him. Ratu wept and shuddered, moving as close to his big friend as possible. And Joshua continued to scream Isabelle's name. He was besieged with grief and terror, for he was responsible for everyone aboard *Benevolence*. He had failed them. He had failed his wife. And the thought of her in pain or dying at that very moment caused him to tumble within himself. He plunged into a black abyss the likes of which he'd never known. Its walls closed around him, drowning him as he envisioned the horrors that she could be enduring. The suffocating blackness engulfed him, and even when he opened his eyes and saw the figures beside him, he was still entombed within this abyss. Sobs wracked him. "Isabelle!" he screamed, his world spinning, his lungs struggling to draw in air. "Where are you? Tell me where you are and I'll come to you! Please!"

After *Benevolence* disappeared, only the sound of Joshua weeping permeated the night.

A QUARTER MILE FROM JOSHUA, a trio of other survivors swam toward the same island. Knowing that they still had a long way to go, Akira worriedly watched the two women beside him. Though she cried and often shouted a man's name, the older nurse seemed to be doing as well as could be expected. Akira had seen enough strength and weakness to know that she was strong. She would make it to the island. Unfortunately, he wasn't so sure about the younger nurse. Her breaths were too quick and desperate, her pace too slow, her movements too erratic.

Though he had killed many during the war, and though parts of him were hardened to sorrow, Akira didn't want this woman to drown. For three days she'd treated him with kindness, and for three days he'd listened to her chatter with her sister. During the past five years, Akira had seen very little kindness and had listened to almost no such friendly banter. He'd fought from country to country, island to island, and he'd heard little but explosions and screams and misery, and was weary of such sounds.

"Are you tired?" he asked the nurse in English. When she made no response, he swam closer to her. "So sorry, but, Annie, are you tired?"

Isabelle stopped calling Joshua's name and moved protectively to her sister's side. "How do you . . . how do you know her name?" she asked, a wave rolling into her mouth as she spoke.

Akira turned toward the older sister. "I can speak English. And I listened to you."

"But how . . . how can you speak English?"

Akira glanced toward the island, worried that they weren't swimming directly toward it. He adjusted his course, lifting his head above the sea so that he could speak. "A long, long time ago, I was a university professor," he replied, even though that man was dead. "I taught advanced English and Western history."

"Western history?"

He spat out a mouthful of water. "Yes. It is true."

An unusually large wave lifted and dropped them fast enough that they went underwater. "It's so . . . so far," Annie said miserably after resurfacing. "It's too far. I can't . . . I just won't make it!"

"You'll make it, Annie," Isabelle replied, trying to stay calm for her sister's sake.

"I won't!"

"You will! I promise that you will."

"I'm so tired."

"You've always been tested, Annie, and you've always made it. Tonight won't be any different."

"But I'm still weak. I feel so weak!"

Reeling with worry over her loved ones, Isabelle prayed for Joshua and Annie, all too aware that her sister hadn't completely recovered from her bout with malaria. The island was still far away, and despite her best efforts to stay calm, Isabelle felt a mounting sense of panic grip her. "Look for some kind of debris!" she said desperately. "There must be . . . something has to be floating out here," she added between gulps of air. "Please, dear God, let there be something floating out here!"

Akira moved farther away from them. "You should take off your dress," he said, turning his back to them. "It will be easier, yes, to swim in your . . . undergarments?"

Isabelle started to protest but quickly changed her mind. "He's right, Annie. Let's get that off you." Before Annie could say anything, Isabelle helped unbutton and remove her long and cumbersome outfit. Isabelle undressed as well, immediately feeling more buoyant in her undergarments. "Don't you hurt my sister," she said, glaring at Akira. "When we're ashore, you will not touch my sister. You hear me? You won't touch her. You won't so much as look at her. Not if you want help with your leg."

Akira nodded, not blaming her for the hostility. He was sure that the nurses had heard rumors—stories of atrocities against women by Japanese soldiers. To his profound shame, Akira knew that many of the rumors were true. In fact, he'd been in Nanking, and for six weeks witnessed sights that he wouldn't have thought possible. How many Chinese girls and women had he seen raped and killed? A hundred? A thousand?

Akira had done his best to stop the madness. He'd moved his unit to the outskirts of the city and made his men dig trenches until they were too weak to stand. He'd warned them that if anyone hurt a civilian he'd kill that man on the spot. He'd been tested twice, he'd killed twice, and after the second death his men had dug trenches and done little else. But the rest of the Japanese army had mutated into some monstrous being—some fire-breathing dragon of the past. This dragon had raped and tortured and killed until few of the victims even bothered to scream.

As he swam in the warm water, Akira relived those terrible days as he had so many times before. He'd wanted to save the women, but everyone he saved was soon killed by someone else. He himself had almost been shot when he'd tried to intervene one time too many, stepping between a group of murderous soldiers and a young girl. If Akira had been brave and noble like his father, he'd have helped the girl to her feet and he'd have died holding her hand. He'd have never seen his mother again, never watched cherry blossoms tumble down the tile roof of his home. Yet how infinitely better that death would have been to the alternative he chose—turning his back on the girl to save himself.

Her face haunted him now as it often did. He tried to watch the stars, tried to remember that something of solace remained before him. But the stars were only beautiful when they illuminated a beautiful world. And Akira's world was hideous, and the stars only reminded him of that ugliness. To him they were the tears of those he'd seen murdered.

Willing himself to focus on the present, Akira kicked harder and lifted his head from the water. The island was closer, but not close enough. He knew that Annie wouldn't make it. She was sobbing—aware that death was coming for her and that she could do nothing to stop it. Her weeping sister tried to drag her through the waves, which often rose and then buried them. Annie started to beg Isabelle to let her drown so that they both wouldn't die. "One of us . . . has to live," she muttered, "for Mother . . . and Father."

"Swim, Annie! For the love of God, please swim! You can't . . . you just can't leave me."

"Don't . . . tell them . . . about this. I didn't die . . . like this."

"No! Please, God. Oh, please help us."

Annie dropped beneath the surface. When she reappeared, she glanced toward Isabelle. "I love you," she said weakly, her lips trembling.

"No! No, Annie, no! You need to fight!"

"It's . . . too . . . far."

"Oh, God, please don't let this happen! Please, please, please! Please don't take my sister!"

Akira kicked to them. "I am a strong swimmer. Very strong. Please put your arms around my neck and lie on my back." Annie hesitated only for a heartbeat, and Akira felt her weight press him into the water. "We will swim now, yes?" he said. "No more talking."

And so they swam. At first it wasn't hard for Akira to carry Annie. At first she tried to kick with him and he felt the strength of her kicks. But then she had nothing left to offer and the weight of her nearly naked body bore him down. Akira had spent his childhood near a mountain-fed river and knew how to swim with tired legs, knew how to conserve his energy and air. Alone, he could have swum in this sea all night. But with the nurse atop him, he wasn't sure if he could reach the island.

As time slowed and then seemed to stop, Akira continued to weaken. He tried to remember the little girl he had failed. Her face filled him with sorrow and misery and rage, and the rage prompted him to kick harder. How he wanted to run back into time and save her. He'd gladly give his life to again be offered the chance to lift her up into his arms and let the bullet take them both. She'd have felt no pain. She'd have known that he was there to protect her. And her terror would have fled and her death would have been merciful.

Thinking of her precious face—which had been battered and swollen and tormented with her sufferings—Akira began to cry. The sea mixed with his tears and stung his eyes, though he didn't bother to wipe them. Instead, he asked the little girl for forgiveness. He'd never asked for her mercy before, because he knew his cowardice was unforgivable. Yet at that moment, with the nurse pressing him deeper into the water and his wounded and weakening leg bleeding his life away into the sea, he begged for the girl's forgiveness. As his stitches ripped from his flesh and all warmth drained from him, he beseeched her to listen to him say that he was sorry.

And a miracle happened then—for he saw her. And she was not in torn and disheveled rags, but in a lovely white dress. Her hair, long and sinuous, bore several flowers above her ear. She stood next to a stone bridge, picking flowers and carefully positioning them within her tresses. She smiled and spoke with someone he could not see. Was she speaking to him? Was she saying his name? Though he failed to understand her words, the way in which her mouth moved comforted him. She was happy. She was happy and safe and her face was at peace.

The little girl's eyes met his and she reached out to him—and in her hand was one of the flowers she had found. Weeping like a child, Akira opened his palm and let her place the flower in it. She smiled when he took her gift, nodding to him. He told her that he was so terribly sorry, and she placed a small finger to her lips. She then pointed behind her and he saw a land of immense, enchanting beauty. He wanted to follow her into this lush land, and so he kicked harder as she drew back. He did not want her to leave him. And she did not leave him.

When his feet struck sand, he started to sob. The little girl moved closer to him, and as his body convulsed, he reached for her. And then there were others. Women were suddenly shouting and three figures rushed through the shallows to drag him toward a beach. The figures were embracing and crying and Akira wondered if they saw the little girl too. Had she saved them as well? Had she told them that she was safe and sheltered and that she did not fear?

Akira crawled toward her, wanting to hold her against his heart, wanting to feel the warmth and joy and hope of her. He felt her for a moment, felt all of those things he so longed to feel. And when she told him of her forgiveness, he went limp in her arms and for the first time in years he was at peace.

DAY TWO

Waves march like soldiers,
To bleed upon sun-bleached shores.
I long for old moss.

Friends and Foes

As far as could be discerned, nine survivors had endured the sinking of *Benevolence* and made it to the island. At first light, those able had made a simple shelter beneath a massive banyan tree, which rose from a tank-sized boulder that looked to have been thrown inland by a god of the sea. The trunk of the tree rested atop the boulder, with scores of thick roots following the contours of the stone into the ground below. The boulder was trapped within the roots in the same way that a dead wasp is cocooned in a spider's web. Other roots fell vertically from the tree's giant branches. These roots, which resembled slender saplings, were so frequent and spread apart that the one tree almost seemed like its own forest.

The banyan tree emerged from the border between the sand and the jungle. The sand comprised a curved beach that might take ten minutes to walk from end to end. Beyond the beach, which resembled a half-moon, stretched a protected and docile harbor. From the beach, it almost looked as if the harbor was a lake surrounded on three sides by land. Only a slice of the sea was visible, waves pounding against distant reefs.

Unconscious atop a bed of palm fronds was Akira. His wound had completely opened during the swim, and the loss of blood had almost killed him. Kneeling above their patient were Isabelle and Annie. The nurses, who now wore the shirts of Joshua and Jake, had bound his wound with fabric they'd torn from Joshua's pants. They'd spent the night lying on either side of Akira in an effort to keep him warm.

Talking a few feet away were the other survivors, who all had minor cuts and burns but were otherwise unharmed. Joshua squinted toward the sea, believing that his eyes were passing over *Benevolence's* grave. Jake and Ratu had been inseparable since the attack and now shared the milk of a coconut. Standing next to them was a middle-aged nurse, Scarlet, whose name was apt, as even the sand and salt couldn't dull her crimson hair. Beside her were Nathan and Roger—two of *Benevolence's* officers. Though Nathan didn't look like a sailor, Roger did. In fact, his features seemed to have been chiseled out of stone by the sea and wind. His face was gaunt, his gray eyes restless, his arms as muscled and bulging as a thick rope. Though Roger was only in his early twenties, he already looked as if he'd seen the worst that life had to offer.

"No matter what anyone else believes, I still don't see how the pilot could have mistaken our ship," Scarlet said, looking from face to face. "I don't think that the setting sun blinded him. I don't—"

"It doesn't matter what any of us think," Joshua quietly interrupted, trying to will himself to lead, knowing that he had to lead no matter how much he wanted to be led. Though grateful that Isabelle and Annie had survived, he felt terribly betrayed—by both God and his own shortcomings. "We're here," he continued wearily, "and now that we're here, we'd better do something about it. We'd better improve our shelter. And collect food and water. And we should walk the beach and see if anything floated here from *Benevolence*."

"There's an empty lifeboat, Captain," Ratu said, pointing far down the beach to where the sea had a direct passage to land. "Stuck on some rocks. Big Jake and I were going to move it but decided to come here first."

Joshua looked at Jake, who was broad chested and half a head taller than anyone else. His eyes and short hair were a shade darker than his skin. His face seemed as wide and round as a bowling ball. Despite a large gap between his front teeth, a smile seemed to be an almost permanent fixture on the oversized engineer. "Is it empty?" Joshua asked.

"Just of people, Captain," Jake replied. "Looks like someone chucked some supplies into it. A few life jackets. Some other odds and ends. Ain't much rhyme or reason to it."

Joshua glanced at the sea, wishing the lifeboat had been filled with survivors, wondering why God had let so many good men and women die. "Can you two bring it ashore?" he finally asked Jake.

"I reckon, Captain, that another set of hands would be mighty helpful."

Joshua nodded toward Roger. "Please give them that extra set of hands. And bring everything in the boat back here. I'd like a detailed accounting."

The burly sailor nodded. "You'll get it."

"Do you have orders for me, Captain?" Ratu asked, his slightly British accent making him sound older than his eleven years. He held his hands against his hips, standing as tall as his small frame permitted.

Though his horror at the loss of *Benevolence* made him want to disappear from the world, to walk out into the water and not return, Joshua forced himself to consider the boy. "Again, tell me, Ratu, how you got aboard *Benevolence*," he said, the fingers of his right hand rubbing together as if he held his favorite rosary.

"It wasn't bloody hard, Captain. I swam out and climbed up the anchor chain."

"Climbed up the anchor chain?"

"Yes, Captain. As I already said, you should have put another guard at the top. The bloke up there was half asleep."

Behind Ratu, Jake cleared his throat. "Well, Ratu," Joshua replied, "why don't you put those climbing skills of yours to work? After you help with the lifeboat, please go with Jake and gather as many coconuts and fruits as you can."

"I'm a cracking good fisherman, too."

"Let's start with the coconuts, Ratu. We can all live without meat for a day."

"Yes, Captain," Ratu said. "Thank you, my captain."

Joshua edged past Scarlet, knelt beside his wife, and eyed the Japanese patient. "What does he need, Izzy?"

"If his wound becomes infected, he'll die," Isabelle said, swatting away flies from the bloody cloth about Akira's leg. "We need medical supplies."

"Well, let's find some," he said, rising to address the group again. His bloodshot eyes darted uneasily from face to face. His fingers continued to move as if they twirled the rosary beads that once brought him peace of mind—the solace that he so desperately needed now. "A lot of those bottles float," he said, "and there are bound to be some ashore. We're going to look for them. We're going to look for everything we'll need, and then we'll get a good shelter built." Joshua paused, pointing inland toward a surprisingly large and steep hill that was dominated by what seemed to be an infinite number of trees. "For the next hour, I'll be up on that rise. I want to get the lay of the land and to see if other ships are about."

After Joshua gave each survivor specific instructions, he strode from the beach, fleeing the stares of those he'd so miserably failed. Beyond the beach, the island was extremely dense with vegetation. Trees twisted and reached skyward, fighting for sunlight. Vines dropped from the canopy above and spread atop the soil. Ferns and flowers and knee-high grass seemed to cover every inch of the jungle floor.

Unfamiliar sounds rose and lingered in the jungle, reverberating eerily, as if trying to escape the labyrinth of trees. A recurring hoot seemed to follow Joshua's footsteps. Insects of all colors, shapes, and sizes buzzed in the canopy. Birds fled his approach, while rustling leaves revealed lizards and hermit crabs as they scurried about.

Heat and humidity dominated the unmoving air. Sweat glistened on Joshua's bare chest as he climbed the rise before him. Though he'd grown up exploring the Rocky Mountains, he felt insecure in the jungle. He was used to either open spaces or the comforting steel of ships. He was a stranger to this land, and though he felt no malice from it, he sensed its overwhelming indifference.

Joshua climbed to the top of the hill, which provided him with an unrestricted view of every direction but north. As far as he could tell, the island was shaped like a fishhook. The beach on which they'd landed was located on the inside part of the hook. The large harbor bordering their camp appeared to be deep.

The blue-green water of the harbor faded into a darker blue that ultimately merged with the sky. Not a single cloud hung above the sea, and its waters were unblemished by shadows or waves. In another life, Joshua would have appreciated the beauty of the scene. Instead, he looked to where *Benevolence* sank, and once his eyes settled upon the area he shook his head in profound sadness and made no effort to wipe away his sudden tears. On the evening that she'd been torpedoed, *Benevolence* carried five hundred and sixteen souls. And Joshua had failed all of these people—even the very few who managed to survive. As he thought about the unburied corpses at sea, he leaned against a tree, trying to steady himself.

"Why, Lord, did you . . . did you take them?" he whispered, feeling nauseous and empty. He closed his eyes as memories of their deaths flooded into his mind much the way the sea had consumed *Benevolence*. He had tried to save those unable to save themselves, but his ship had sunk too swiftly.

"It wasn't your fault."

The voice caused Joshua's heart to skip, and he turned toward its source. "You . . . you followed me?"

Isabelle stepped forward, wrapping her arms around him. "I'm so sorry."

His tears began anew as she drew him closer. He was reminded of the previous night, of running through the shallows to pull her from the water, of his body trembling with relief at the feel of her against him. The elation of discovering her alive had been the only thing that had kept him from swimming out into the blackness and never returning. "I was . . . I was their captain," he finally replied. "I was supposed to take care of them."

"And you did, Josh. You did." When he only shook his head, she placed a hand against his face, which was thin but bore a somewhat oversized nose and ears that protruded slightly too far from his head. His curly brown hair was damp with sweat and stuck against his long forehead. Isabelle wiped his brow. "You did take care of them," she repeated, all too familiar with the vacant look of his eyes. She'd seen such looks on hundreds of her patients—soldiers who'd been numbed to the present by memories of the past.

"No," he softly replied. "No, I didn't."

"Don't be—"

"I didn't . . . take care of them, Izzy. Please . . . please don't tell me that I did. Don't tell me that."

"But how could you have known?"

He pulled away from her, shaking his head, unwilling to meet her gaze. "How could I have known? It's my job to know."

"But you can't see the future. How could you possibly have—"

"Scarlet's right," he said, looking again to where *Benevolence* rested. "She was on deck and she saw what I saw. We were sunk deliberately."

"Sunk deliberately? But that doesn't make any sense. Why would the Japanese sink a hospital ship?"

"I don't know. Something in our hold, maybe. Something that was there that shouldn't have been. Ammunition or fuel. Probably fuel. That explosion was far, far too massive to have come from a single torpedo. For the love of God, it ripped *Benevolence* in two. That's why she went down so fast, why hardly anyone survived."

"But we're a hospital ship. We can't carry ammunition or extra fuel."

"And why not? You think things like that haven't been done in this godforsaken war? The Germans and Japanese and Italians have done them. So have the Russians and the British. We're not above it. Not by a long shot. I promise you, something other than hospital beds and a single torpedo caused *Benevolence* to blow up like that."

Isabelle tried to recall the explosion. "It was large," she admitted, unconsciously rubbing the side of her sore hip.

"We're at the end of our supply lines out here," Joshua said softly, almost as if talking with himself. "We're thousands of miles from home or even Pearl Harbor. And I'm not surprised that some fool decided to have *Benevolence* loaded with . . . whatever blew her up. Maybe that same fool betrayed us to the Japs. Someone did."

"But wouldn't you have been told about the cargo? You're the captain, for goodness' sake."

"Which is why I was kept in the dark. I wouldn't have let it on board."

Isabelle shook her head in disgust. "What a horrible, tragic waste. Of people. Of skills."

"God help me for that."

"It's not—"

"I should have looked," he interrupted, continuing to stare at the sea, unaware that a mosquito drew blood from his bare back. "I should have walked every inch of her before we sailed. I should have operated *Benevolence* like any other ship—running emergency drills until everyone knew them by heart. Until people hated me. I didn't, and now . . . and now five hundred and seven bodies are out there because of me."

"You've saved a lot more men than that, Josh. A lot. And you didn't kill anyone aboard *Benevolence*."

"I killed *Benevolence*. She's out there. Torn in two and full of the dead."

Isabelle realized nothing she could say would comfort him, and so she pulled him closer. At first she felt him lean away from her, but she gripped him tightly. She'd lost enough patients to understand what he was going through. Was he seeing their faces? Could she hear them crying out to him?

"I love you," she finally said. "And I need you. Annie needs you. And I know that this hole . . . this awful hole will never leave you, but you have to remember that we need you."

"You don't need me, Izzy," he replied softly. "You're the strongest of us all."

"I'm strong . . . when I have to be. Just as you have to be now."

"I don't want to be strong."

"But you have to be. You have to lead. You were born to do it, and you can't quit now."

"I'm so tired."

"I know. But you can't rest. Not now."

Joshua nodded reluctantly, understanding that she was right, knowing that eight people still depended on him. She depended on him. Though he wanted nothing more than to sit motionless and mourn the dead, lament the demise of his world and almost everything in it, he knew that he could help the survivors. Once he helped them, once he ensured that Isabelle survived, he could mourn as much as he wanted. I'll pray for the dead later, he promised himself. I'll remember as many of their names as I can and I'll pray for each soul.

"What do we need to be doing?" Isabelle asked. He made no response, and she gently squeezed his arm. "Joshua, what do we need to do to survive?"

He willed himself to address the present, the needs of the living. Sighing, he gestured toward the harbor. "What's out there?"

She studied the sand and sea. "Nothing extraordinary."

"Nothing? Look at the harbor, and then the land behind the beach."

She did as he asked, her eyes sweeping about. "It's a nice harbor. And . . . and there's some flat ground behind the beach."

Joshua nodded. "The harbor is perfect. It's deep and big and amazingly protected. And the land behind the beach is suitable for a runway."

"So?"

An image of *Benevolence's* helm flashed before him—piles of broken steel and glass and bodies. He remembered stepping outside to watch the bomber soar toward his ship. By the time he realized that it had dropped a torpedo, and that the weapon was gliding through the water toward *Benevolence,* all he could do was shout a series of futile commands.

"Joshua? What does the harbor matter to us? The land?"

He dragged himself away from visions of the dead in the same manner that a car is towed from an accident. "This island won't be ours for long," he finally replied. "It's too perfect. Too strategic. Both navies are in these waters and both navies will slug it out here or near here. Whoever controls the Solomon Islands will put airfields on them and will control the skies of the South Pacific, will have the airpower to maybe win the war. And because of that someone's going to claim this island. Maybe us. Maybe them. If it's them we're going to have to hide. Hide for as long as we can. That's what we need to be doing. Figuring out how and where to hide. Because if the Japs come here and find us . . ."

"What? What, Josh?"

"We don't want them to find us. You. Your sister. Me. We'd all be in great danger."

She felt her heart quicken its pace. "Where will we hide?" she asked, glancing about the island.

"I don't know. But we'll find someplace. We'll find someplace and we'll wait. And no matter who comes here, we'll be ready."

"But . . . but couldn't we take the lifeboat? Take it and find another island?"

"Another island could already be full of Japs. Or we could easily be captured at sea."

She tugged at his hand. "Then let's get ready. We need to organize everyone and start searching."

He took a half step with her and then stopped. "Could we spend another few minutes here? I want to say good-bye. I . . . I need to say good-bye."

Isabelle nodded and then gazed toward the sea, which shimmered as the strengthening sun beat down upon it. She wondered what lay beneath the waves inside *Benevolence*. She cringed at the memories that quickly invaded her—visions of the doctor she'd tried to save, of Annie almost drowning. Like other such memories, she forced them from her, turning her attention to Joshua. She watched a tear drop from his lashes. She saw his lips move, and when no sound came forth she knew that he was praying.

Her husband was a strong man, Isabelle knew. In that way, they were quite alike. In that way, she was drawn to him. But she couldn't help but ask herself if she was right for him now. Could she best support him when she herself only knew how to press on, how to endure? Wouldn't he be better off with a woman who could cradle his head on her lap and simply listen? A woman like Annie?

A year ago, Isabelle could have been that woman. But not now. Not after seeing so many die such hideous deaths. Not after smelling the foul stench known as war. She couldn't sit and whisper that everything would be fine, because if truth be told, she'd said such words to boys who had needed to hear them. And she'd lied to those boys, because they had died before her eyes—died pleading for their mothers or lovers, morphine suppressing their pain but not their memories, not their tears.

Isabelle couldn't lie to Joshua. As much as she wanted to comfort him, as much as she yearned to make him feel whole, she couldn't be that woman. She couldn't be that woman because she didn't know if the end would be what he and she wanted, what they struggled and suffered to achieve. How could anything end well when an entire world was at war? When millions of men, women, and children were already dead and mostly unburied?

Isabelle put her head against his shoulder and cried with him. She cried for those aboard *Benevolence*. She cried for her husband. And she felt so very alone until he turned and kissed her lightly upon the brow.

SEEING THAT HER rescuer was asleep, Annie decided that the time was right to inspect his wound, and carefully untied his soiled bandages. Her patient's thigh was swollen—the torn flesh red and oozing blood. Afraid of infection, Annie leaned forward and smelled the wound, which, had it gone bad, would have likely emitted a pungent odor. To her relief, she couldn't detect any sign of decay. Of course, she needed to clean the wound properly and restitch it—otherwise an infection was almost inevitable. But she needed supplies for such a procedure.

Hoping the boy and the engineer would find what she needed, Annie carefully rebandaged the wound. As she worked, she looked at her patient's face, wondering why he'd saved her. Though his face was the color of an old newspaper and though it was the face of the enemy, she found his features to be strong and likable. His skin was smooth and almost flawless—marred only by faint lines near his eyes and on his forehead. His cheekbones and chin were prominent, hinting at the strength she knew he harbored. She'd never seen hair as straight and black as his. Not even on any of the other Japanese patients. His hair reminded her of a cloudy night—thick, dark, and dominant.

Annie studied him for a few more minutes before rising. She then looked for others in their party but could see no one. She hoped people were discovering the supplies they'd need, that medicine would be found. It certainly needed to be. If it wasn't, she'd have to simply boil water, clean her rescuer's wound, and hope.

A large white bird dropped into the water before her, diving for an unseen fish. Annie looked toward the gap in the harbor, which revealed the azure vastness that was the sea. She couldn't believe that something so beautiful was the surface upon which so many men died such bloody deaths. Even though she knew that the Germans and Japanese desperately needed to be defeated, she also knew that war was repulsive and she wondered why it wasn't fought upon something equally unsightly. After all, war turned beautiful things—whether men or forests or cities—into scarred remnants of what they once were. How was the sea alone able to resist this change?

"Thank you."

She turned toward the voice, surprised to see that her patient had rolled to his uninjured side and was looking at her. "For what?" she replied.

"My leg."

Annie wasn't sure what to say and so she said nothing. Finally, she glanced at his eyes. "In the water . . . you knew my name. May I ask yours?"

"Of course," he answered, bowing his head. "I am Akira."

She tried to silently repeat his name and found that it was easy. "May I ask another question?"

"Please do."

"What . . . were you reaching for? At the end, when we made it to the beach. You were reaching for something."

Akira turned toward the water. He suddenly remembered his vision of the little girl. He felt chilled without her before him and longed to see her again. "So sorry, but I do not know for certain," he replied quietly. "But perhaps . . . perhaps I saw a spirit. Or as you might say . . . an angel."

"An angel?"

"*Hai.* I . . . I mean, yes."

Annie had spoken to many dying men and had heard many such things. She'd been told of angels and darkness and tunnels of light, and believed in these visions. "Did she . . . did this angel save us?"

Akira nodded. "She saved me."

"And why . . . why did you save me?"

He smiled briefly. "You ask many questions, yes?"

"I'm sorry. I don't mean to pry."

"Please do not worry," he said kindly. Though once highly proficient in English, Akira spoke slowly, as more than five years had passed since he'd tried to think in the language he adored—to him the language of

Shakespeare and Dickens and Yeats. "I like questions," he added. "Very much. But no one has asked me such things for a long time." He paused to stretch his leg, grimacing in pain.

"Don't move it. You should keep it still until I restitch it."

He bowed slightly. "A pity that . . . they broke. You did an excellent job on your first attempt."

"Thank you," Annie replied, looking around, wondering when the others would return, nervous about being alone with the prisoner. She wished she had something to give him for his pain, which she knew must be considerable. "And thank you for saving me," she added. "Thank you very much for that, and for being so . . . brave. I'm sorry I was weak. Sorry that you had to carry me."

"There is no need to be sorry."

"I wanted to swim. I tried. I really did. But I'm still recovering from malaria. And I just . . . I just didn't have the strength."

"I did not carry you far. And you do not have to thank me. You helped me, yes? I merely helped you."

"You almost died helping me."

He shrugged. "Such a death . . . would have been honorable."

Annie wasn't sure what to think of his words. "So why . . . why did you do it? Why didn't you just save yourself?"

Akira looked upward, searching for a trace of the little girl. Finally, he replied, "Once, I saved myself. And once was . . . a mistake. A terrible mistake. It is much better to save others."

"Are you a doctor? How do you save people?"

"A doctor? No. Once I was teacher. But . . . so sorry to say, not now. I have fought in this war for five years. Five years too long."

Annie wondered if he'd killed Americans. She wondered if she should be talking to him in this manner. Perhaps she should simply leave him alone. He was a prisoner, after all. He was Japanese and foreign and seemed so different from anyone she knew. However, in light of the fact that he'd almost died saving her, she decided that leaving him would be an act of betrayal. Also, as a nurse she was accustomed to chatting with her patients and believed that such conversations did them a great deal of good. "Sorry," she finally replied, "I think you told me that before."

"I think you were almost drowning at that time."

"And what was it you taught?" she asked, no longer wanting to speak about the previous night.

He smiled, happy that he'd saved this kind nurse who had treated him so gently. "I was most fortunate," he said. "I taught Western history and advanced English to university students. And, of course, haiku."

"Haiku? What's that?"

Akira wanted to ask her to sit and, after hesitating for a moment, politely motioned for her to do so. Though his leg ached, the sudden thought of teaching someone something other than the art of war was immensely appealing. For the first time in five years, he didn't have soldiers to direct, didn't have to focus his mind on creating plans that would maim and kill. And not thinking of death, even for this single moment, was completely liberating. "Do you like poems?" he asked.

She shrugged, wiping sweat from her eye. "I don't know, really. I suppose so."

"In Japan, haikus have been told for centuries. They are our most famous kind of poems."

"Isn't a poem . . . a poem?"

Akira smiled again, pleased by what he sensed was her growing interest in the subject. "You would like, yes, to know more?"

Unsure, she looked around and saw no one. Her eyes drifted back to his ugly wound. Certain that it ached, and believing that he wanted to talk and presumably take his mind off the pain, she nodded. "Yes, please."

He bowed slightly. "I am honored to tell you." When she didn't respond, he continued, "Though many different forms of haikus exist, usually a haiku has three lines. And usually the first line has five syllables. The second has seven. And the third has five."

"Why in that form?"

"A haiku poem has a rhythm—five, seven, five."

"A rhythm like a song?"

"Sometimes yes. Sometimes no."

"What else?"

Not used to being so quickly questioned but enjoying her inquisitiveness, he smiled. "A haiku often has one word that describes a season. That way, the listener can imagine what the scene looks like."

"So many rules," Annie replied. "I didn't know that poems had so many rules."

"Yes. And one more. A haiku has two lines that are connected, and one that is . . . how do you say? . . . independent. But each thought gives the other deeper meaning."

"Can you . . . it's all so confusing. Do you have an example?"

Akira studied her, the conversation reminding him of his teaching days. Had he really spent years talking like this? Teaching bright minds and watching them bloom? How fortunate he had been. How utterly foolish to have not realized his profound blessing. "One moment, please," he replied, trying to quickly conjure a haiku. "Maybe something like this, yes? 'No end to the sea, / But a beginning spreads west. / Warm her face will be.'"

Annie smiled for the first time since *Benevolence* sank. "I like it. And another? Can you talk about people?"

He nodded, closing his eyes to remember someone from his past, someone free from the taint of recent memories. He thought of his mother. He saw her slide open the door to his room. She wore a kimono and had brought him a sweet from the city. She'd always brought him sweets. He smiled at the memory and said, "She wore red that day, / A day of ice and limp trees. / I so miss such sweets."

Annie repeated the little poem in her mind, counting out the syllables. As she was counting, she noticed figures in the distance. They carried wood and other objects. Standing up, she said, "I should help them. It looks like they've got more than they can handle."

"I think so."

She started to leave but then stopped. "Thank you, Akira. Thank you for teaching me about the poems."

He nodded, pleased to have shared his old passion. "Tonight," he said, "before you sleep, please think of one. Better to think of one, yes, than to ponder these times?"

Annie nodded and then hurried off to help the others. Watching her run, Akira contemplated the ways in which to describe how her feet took flight.

LESS THAN A HUNDRED feet away, Roger also watched Annie run. He'd returned from pulling the lifeboat ashore and, crouched in some underbrush, had been observing Annie chat with her patient. As she now hurried to help the others, she approached Roger's hiding position, passing close enough that he could hear her feet kicking up sand. The long shirt that Annie wore rose and fell as she ran, exposing most of her legs.

Roger had scrutinized Annie off and on since he'd first seen her on the island. Though he usually preferred women to be tall and contoured, he was drawn to Annie. She was petite and beautiful, and without question he craved her. As she now ran past and he glimpsed her thighs, he felt himself growing aroused. Clenching his fists, he imagined her naked body held still beneath him.

Roger watched her until she reached the other survivors. He then blended deeper into the jungle, quietly backtracking until he arrived at a coconut tree that seemed to loom above all else. He looked to where he'd buried the box in the darkness and was pleased to discern almost no trace of his efforts. Roger hadn't expected any survivors from the attack, and the past night upon hearing voices he had been forced to quickly hide his supplies. He'd considered using his pistol to kill the newcomers, but had decided that too many unknowns faced him.

Comforted by the knowledge that his pistol and radio were nearby, Roger moved even deeper into the jungle, looking for a break in the canopy that would provide him with a glimpse of the hills above. He'd need a high, secure, and secluded place to radio the Japanese. His contact, Edo, would be awaiting his call.

As Roger quietly made his way through the underbrush, he pictured Annie and her patient. They'd spoken at length and, amazingly, had even seemed to smile at each other. Roger had been immediately jealous of their rapport. Though he'd sought out many women in many lands, he'd never cared to actually talk to them. In fact, he'd thought such talk beneath him. And yet the sight of Annie and the Japanese soldier chatting so contentedly had perturbed him. Perhaps this displeasure stemmed from memories—visions of being the son of a missionary, of living in humiliating conditions in Tokyo, of being tormented by a boy who'd vaguely resembled Annie's patient.

That boy had been the leader of the first group to follow Roger from school. Unbeknownst to him, they'd watched him enter the cinder block room that his parents rented a few feet from the train tracks. As trains rumbled past, Roger's mother had soon ushered him outside to the cement steps rising to their room. She'd put a small cooking pot atop his head and proceeded to cut away any hair that emerged from beneath the pot. Her own prematurely gray tresses had twisted in the drafts of wind made by the passing trains. Her dress was not only dirty—for they could never keep dust from seeping into the room— but seemed to be held together by a variety of patches. The scene had greatly amused Roger's classmates, who were rich and pampered and eager to ridicule someone of a different ilk. Over the next few weeks, the boy had led many groups to Roger's home, and though the trains obscured much of their laughter, the tracks hadn't rumbled nearly often enough.

Continuing to move deeper into the jungle, Roger promised himself that he'd put Annie's patient in his rightful place—just as he had the boy so long ago. He'd waited for that joyous day for more than a year, preparing for it in secret. When he'd finally been paired against his tormentor in a kendo match, he'd experienced his first taste of what it was like to see someone terrified of his presence. Roger had often since recalled the stunned silence among the students of the dojo. They'd watched, utterly transfixed, as he had wielded his wooden sword with such skill that within a matter of seconds his adversary was bloody and begging.

Ever since that day thirteen years before, Roger had coveted the power that he'd first felt in the dojo. When his family had returned to America, he had to establish himself once more, and again he saw fear in the eyes of his enemies. He'd reveled in such moments, for when he was feared no one could question him, no one could laugh at his oddities. Japanese couldn't snicker at the self-conscious foreigner, and Americans couldn't mock his awkwardness on the football field or basketball court. More important, no one could deny him what he had wanted. And he had wanted so many things.

Progressing stealthily through the jungle, sweat oozing from seemingly every pore, Roger reflected on the fact that only a few men had survived the sinking of *Benevolence*. The temptation to shoot them was quite powerful, for with the men gone, he could do as he wished. He could be the king of the island, the lord to whom all others would kneel and obey. He believed that such a lord could push painful memories aside, that the present could overwhelm and obscure the past.

Roger envisioned killing the captain first—forever silencing his infuriating demands. He'd then take care of the burly engineer. And the rest could fall into whatever order the situation dictated.

Ultimately, Roger decided not to use the gun—at least not for the time being. No, it would be better to call Edo and have the Japanese take the island. They would kill the others—everyone, that is, but Annie. Roger wanted Annie for himself and would claim her when the Japanese landed. The little nurse would be his and his alone.

Wishing that he could return to his precious box and remove and enjoy a cigarette, Roger continued to advance deeper into the jungle—which was dark and thick and omnipotent and much to his liking.

THE SWELLING SUN momentarily lingered above the sea, bleeding into the sky, infusing the clouds with its hues until they themselves glowed with a rich luminescence. The clouds were long and graceful and resembled rust-colored serpents that slept above the sea. As the sun dropped below the horizon, the serpents slowly darkened—as if they blended into the night to confuse predators above. For a few heartbeats the clouds continued to smolder with memories of the sun. Then the sky merged into the sea.

Beneath the banyan tree that served as their shelter, the survivors gathered around a small fire. Palm fronds had been lashed to the branches above and to a makeshift wall toward the water. These fronds ensured that no eyes aboard passing planes or ships would see the fire. Though some debate had occurred on the subject, ultimately Joshua had said that more Japanese than American vessels patrolled these waters, and so the group would stay hidden for the time being.

The banyan tree provided a seemingly infinite supply of branches, and it hadn't been terribly difficult to weave palm fronds around these branches until a ceiling of sorts had been fashioned. If the banyan tree were an umbrella, and its haphazard branches the spines that supported this umbrella, the palm fronds had been woven around the spines until a second layer of foliage was created. This ten-foot-high layer was relatively square and parallel to the ground.

The survivors had dragged the lifeboat to the rear of the shelter. Upside down, the craft now served to protect everything that they'd found inside it or on the beach. And they'd found plenty—life jackets, medicine, clothes, and canteens. Perhaps most important, the lifeboat had carried a machete. Ratu had thus been able to climb palm trees and cut down scores of the fronds that now served to protect them from the elements.

Exhausted from a day of hard labor, the survivors encircled the fire, eating bananas but doing little else. Aside from the distant crashing of waves, the air was alive with the sounds of the jungle—hoots and screeches and buzzes and the occasional flutter of unseen wings. Logs had been positioned around the fire and, for the most part, people sat silently atop the logs, staring into the flames before them.

Suddenly Scarlet slapped at her neck. "Will they ever leave me alone?" she said angrily, scratching herself.

"You need smoke," Ratu proclaimed, pointing downwind of the fire.

"Smoke?"

"No animal likes smoke. If you give an animal smoke he'll run from you like he kissed your little sister. Bloody mosquitoes run the fastest. Stand in the smoke for a while and they won't bother you again."

Scarlet rose from her log. "You're sure?"

"Am I getting bitten? Not once, I tell you. And it's because I smell like smoke. You . . . you probably smell like flowers or something."

Still scratching, Scarlet moved into the smoke. As she did, Annie looked at Ratu and then nodded toward Akira, who was asleep nearby on a bed of fronds. "The bugs must be devouring him," she said. "Could we do the same for him?"

"A stick," he replied. "A burning stick will do the trick. I'll see to it."

As she thanked him, Ratu removed a branch from the fire and hurried over to Akira. Ratu held the branch upwind of Akira so that smoke drifted onto him. As he covered her patient in smoke, Annie wondered about him. "Do you have sisters?" she asked quietly, thinking of his earlier words.

"Five!" he replied, trying to whisper, pleased to have stepped from the silence that seemed to oppressively surround the fire. "Can you believe such a thing? It's bollix, I tell you. Five little sisters. And she thinks mosquitoes are bad!"

"Oh, they can't be that bad."

"Well, I tell you, Miss Annie, it's a cracking good thing that I like talking so much. If I let them do all the talking, my head would spin faster than a . . . than something very, very fast."

"Why on earth would your head spin?" Annie asked, smiling faintly.

Ratu turned to look at her, his small face tightening in consternation. "All the talk of dresses? Of pretend weddings? Of cooking and sewing and boys? You don't think such talk makes your head spin?"

"Is that . . . is that why you snuck onto *Benevolence*? Too much talk?"

Continuing to move the burning branch in small circles, he nodded. Her words reminded him of his search for his father, and the night abruptly seemed to darken. Was his father lonely? Ratu asked himself. Was he being careful? Had he been hurt? Such questions scared Ratu so much that he suddenly needed to speak. Turning to Annie, he said, "My father is a guide for you Yanks. He fights with them, island to island. He takes them through jungles and leads them to Japanese."

"And . . . you wanted to find him? That's why you came aboard?"

Ratu nodded slightly. "I wanted . . . to see him. And I thought that I . . . that I could find him. I left my mother a note . . . and . . . and I snuck onto your ship."

The pauses between his words made Annie think that she shouldn't further pursue the topic. She wondered what it was like for a boy to have a father at war. Did Ratu want to be beside his father, leading soldiers into the jungle? Or would he rather have his father home, doing whatever it was that fathers and sons did?

Annie pondered such questions until the fire on Ratu's branch vanished. The branch smoked for another minute before he tossed it into the darkness. He was about to leave when she touched his arm. Wanting to make him feel important, and seeking his help, she pointed to Akira's leg. "His wound needs to be restitched," she said softly, "and I've nothing to restitch it with. All day I've tried to think of something. You found the medicine. And you probably saved him by finding that little bottle. But can you find something else? Something that I can stitch with?"

Ratu looked at Akira, remembering how ugly the wound had looked. "Not bloody likely," he replied. "Do you need a needle?"

"Something like that. Something strong and sharp."

"A piece of wire? A splinter of bamboo?"

"Maybe. Yes, maybe the bamboo would work." Annie looked into the jungle, recalling that she'd seen groves of bamboo. "If you can get me a needle, I'll think of the thread. Could you do that? Could you please do that?"

Ratu nodded. "You'll like my needle. It will be strong and sharp and you'll wish you always had one."

"That would be wonderful. Just wonderful, Ratu."

She'd said his name for the first time, and he smiled at the sound of her saying it. He missed the way in which a female voice gave life to his name. And the mere sound of his name on Annie's tongue made him feel warm. He was about to reply when Akira groaned in his sleep. Not wanting to wake the injured man, Ratu whispered good night and proceeded to move back to the fire. Looking into its restless flames, he was again reminded of his father, for he wondered if his father was also sharing a fire with strangers. Ratu hadn't seen his father in almost six months. He missed the smell of him, the touch of his scratchy face. He longed for the stories his father told him—stories of great fish and great chiefs.

His father had taught Ratu about the importance of bravery, and as he cast twigs into the fire, he hoped that his father wasn't being too brave. Ratu didn't want to be without the stories, without the man who carried him on his shoulders, whom he loved so much. The thought of not seeing his father again caused Ratu to tremble, to move nearer to the fire—as if it could somehow bring him closer to his father, as if sitting next to it would draw him into the memory of sharing his father's warmth.

DAY THREE

In times of such woe,
Dreams are friends and
thoughts are fiends.
Sleet obscures the sky.

Fresh Wounds

An hour after dawn, aside from the breaking of waves on its reefs and beaches, the island still slept. It slept as a child might—unmoving and untroubled and unknowing of the world around it. The jungle that had creaked and hooted all night was now strangely silent. Even the wind was somehow rendered motionless. The giant, pillow-sized leaves that had been ready to take flight throughout the previous day and night now hung limp in the thick, salt-laden air.

Clad in men's shorts and shirts, Annie and Isabelle walked along the beach, occasionally bumping into each other because of the slope toward the sea. Here at the far end of the harbor, where the sea had open access to the shore, waves reached high enough to snatch their footprints from the sand. Both women had worn men's shoes for much of the previous day and now enjoyed being barefoot. The beach seemed to press between their toes and travel up their calves to massage their aching bodies. The warm waves embraced their ankles, tempting them to move deeper into the water.

The two sisters had been walking for some time. Annie had spent much of the night contemplating how she could stitch up Akira's wound. She'd wondered about thread from their clothing, plant fibers, and anything else the island might offer. When she could think of no substance that wouldn't quickly rot, she'd asked Isabelle to join her on a walk.

Perhaps the two of them could find some fishing line or additional medical supplies that she could put to use. Already they'd discovered a battered bottle of disinfectant and an assortment of crutches and splints.

As Annie scanned the sea and the sand, she wondered what Ted was doing. Earlier that morning, she had watched Nathan as he lay on the beach and looked at a photo that he'd carefully withdrawn from his wallet. Nathan—who had a rather owlish appearance, with a rotund body and face, short brown hair, and a broad nose—had gazed at the photo as if it revealed all the treasures of the world. Her curiosity overpowering her, Annie had finally sat beside him and asked to see the photo, which he'd been eager to share. The colorless, water-stained image was a simple one—Nathan and his wife standing behind a teenage boy and girl. The children smiled and leaned against their parents, as if intent on toppling them backward.

Annie had been happy for Nathan, happy for the obvious and powerful love he felt for his family. Of course, her pleasure had been tempered by the fact that they likely thought he was dead. And she could tell by the way that he looked at his loved ones that this fact was as hard on him as it surely was on them.

Wishing she had a photo of Ted, Annie glanced at Isabelle. "Did you see Nathan this morning?"

"I saw the photo, if that's what you mean," Isabelle replied, methodically scanning the sand before them.

"It touched me. . . . How he looked at them."

Isabelle nodded, her mind so used to moving in a thousand different directions that she felt slightly disconcerted by the simple experience of walking down the beach. "He's a good man," she finally replied, her eyes continuing to relentlessly seek items that had washed ashore. "Joshua told me all about him. Not the most decorated officer, but as a husband and a father, well, that's another story."

"Maybe he's not decorated because he doesn't want to be in the war. Maybe . . . maybe he's really still with them."

"I don't think any of us wants to be in the war, Annie."

"And yet we volunteered for it."

"Did we have a choice? How couldn't we?"

Annie shrugged, disagreeing. Certainly she'd faced a choice. In fact, the way she saw it, many of those aboard *Benevolence* could have remained civilians. Most had enlisted to help right the terrible wrong that was befalling the world. Annie had joined for that reason, but also because of Ted, who had once called her a coward and who wielded valid reasons for uttering that word. But still, it was easy to call someone a coward when you'd been a hero your whole life, easy to be strong when you were born strong—both in mind and body.

After spying and pocketing a vial of morphine, Annie continued to look for something that might be useful to restitch Akira's wound. "I'm sorry, Izzy," she said quietly. "That I was so . . . so weak the other night."

Isabelle heard the tremble in Annie's voice and took her sister's hand. "You weren't weak. And there's nothing to be sorry about."

"I almost killed him."

"Well, yes, he almost died. But it was his own awful country that almost killed him. Not you."

"But why . . . why is it always me?"

Isabelle turned toward the sea. She remembered Annie's early struggle with diphtheria—how fever had wracked her little frame, how terror consumed her as she struggled to breathe. Isabelle had overheard the doctor informing her parents that Annie would likely die, and later, her mother telling her father that if Annie died, she wanted to die with her so that Annie would never be alone. From that day forward, their mother had slept next to Annie, lying as close to her as possible. She'd cared for Annie with what Isabelle now recognized as an almost superhuman display of strength, compassion, and determination. When Annie had finally recovered, Isabelle and her mother had danced around her bed, and Isabelle had decided that she'd someday be a nurse.

"I don't know why it's always you," Isabelle finally replied. "But there must be a reason."

"A reason? People always say that. But only people who haven't really suffered talk about reasons. Because that's so much easier to say than to hear. What's the reason that our patients die? That they'll never walk again? That we've treated children whose limbs have been blown off? For that matter, what's the reason for this hideous war?"

Isabelle briefly closed her eyes at her sister's mention of the children. "I wish I had those answers, Annie. That might . . . somehow make things easier. Maybe you're right. Maybe there aren't reasons. Maybe things . . . evil things just happen."

Annie didn't reply, her own words about death reminding her of the terror that had consumed her when she dropped beneath the waves. In that blackness, she hadn't thought about those she loved, or of all that she'd done. On the contrary, she'd been reminded of what she hadn't done. And the fear of never doing such things had filled her with a longing she hadn't known. Before *Benevolence* sunk, Annie wasn't completely aware of this longing—this wish to see what had not been seen, to feel what had not been felt.

Of course, Annie also remembered the terror of her childhood illness, remembered how very alone she'd felt, even with her mother at her side. And that terror had left a scar within her, a scar that ultimately made her more interested in questions than answers. Ted had seen this side of her and called her a coward for being uncertain, for not knowing her path. And even though a part of her loved him, she also resented him for those words, for they represented her darkest fears.

"How do you always stay so strong?" Annie asked, stopping near a broken shell.

Isabelle scanned the undulating sea for floating debris. "I've never had a choice."

Annie nodded, resting against her sister the way Nathan's son leaned against him in the photo. "I could never ask for more than you, Izzy. You know that?"

"I know that I could say the same," Isabelle said, the intimate and timeless way in which Annie touched her making her want to share a secret. They'd always traded secrets, and Isabelle felt a sudden desire to tell Annie what she'd told no one else.

A bottle rolled up the beach toward them, and Annie reached down to retrieve it. "Maybe there's a message inside," she said, plucking it from the sea.

"Maybe Ted's sent you a rescue note."

"Sent me a rescue note?" Annie replied, smiling at the thought. "Now, that's something I'd like to see." She pocketed the empty bottle. "It would be nice to rescue someone else for a change. I'm tired of being the one who's always saved."

Isabelle decided that she'd tell Annie later, that this moment wasn't quite right. "Well," she said, "we'd better get back to camp if we want to do any rescuing."

"But what about his wound? We need to keep looking. We need to find something."

Isabelle gazed down the beach. The tide was coming in and she could discern several objects floating in the distance. Even though she wanted to return to Joshua, she also needed to help Annie and the man who'd saved her. "Fine," she said. "But let's walk with a purpose. We can leave the talking for later."

As they strode through the rising water, Annie was reminded of a distant time when they'd seen the sea and had rushed, holding hands, into its vastness—a time when they'd been intent on nothing other than exploring the wonderful new world before them.

WHILE HE ATE his second banana of the morning, Joshua watched his fellow survivors, studying each face. The Japanese patient lay atop his bed of palm fronds, and though he was awake, only his eyelids stirred as he stared at the sea. Nearby, Scarlet used her fingers to try to brush sand from her tangled hair—a process that greatly frustrated her. Ratu and Jake had tossed a coconut into the harbor and were throwing rocks at it. Nathan had his photo out again and alternated his gaze from his loved ones to the rock-throwing game. Closest to Joshua, Roger used the machete to sharpen several spears. After their tips were as deadly as he could get them, he hardened their points in a small fire before him. Roger's face reminded Joshua of a wind-filled sail—his skin seemed taut, his lips stretched too thin. Everything from his gray eyes to his short, dark hair to his ears appeared to be pressed tightly against his head, as if a bizarre gravity pulled these features toward the center of his skull.

As he often did, Joshua thought of *Benevolence*, said a prayer for those killed, and then forced himself to face the challenges of the moment. "We need to get a much better feel for the island," he said to Roger. "And to look for places where we can hide. I think we should have a couple of different options. That way, if the Japs land, we can hurry to whichever hideaway is farthest from them."

Roger turned toward Akira. "That monkey can speak English," he said, pointing a spear at Annie's patient, hating him for the memories he stirred. "You listen to our every word, don't you, Japper?" When Akira didn't alter his gaze from the sea, Roger stood up angrily and started to move toward him. "I asked you a—"

"That's enough, Lieutenant."

"But he's not—"

"I said that's enough."

Roger stopped a few paces from Akira, though he continued to menacingly hold his spear. "He sits here, pretending to be peaceful. But remember how the Japs acted like they wanted peace before Pearl Harbor? Well, this one here's no different."

"This one saved my sister-in-law. And probably my wife."

"Says who?"

"And I was at Pearl Harbor. I watched *Arizona* burn. So don't tell me what I already know."

As Akira continued to gaze at the sea, Roger silently seethed. He wanted the prisoner to be afraid of him, and yet Akira showed no such inclination. The monkey will learn to fear me, Roger promised himself.

A headache throbbed above his eyes, and wishing that he held a cigarette, Roger spat contemptuously into the sand.

Joshua stepped toward Nathan. Motioning for Roger to join them, Joshua moved farther from Akira. When both officers were near him, Joshua looked at Nathan. "We need to explore the island," he said, wondering what his officers thought of him, aware that everyone must consider him a failure. "The lieutenant and I are going to be gone for a few hours. While we're gone, you're in charge, Nathan. Please see that people stay close to camp. Watch the prisoner carefully. And for Pete's sake, keep out of sight if a ship or plane should come by."

"Do you want us off the beach, Captain?" Nathan asked, wanting his orders to be as exact as possible.

Joshua looked into the jungle, his gaze pausing on a trio of sand flies that feasted on a banana peel. "No, I don't think that's necessary. Just keep everyone nearby, and be ready to run if you have to."

"Yes, sir. And the prisoner? Do you want him bound?"

"Oh, he can't even walk on that gimpy leg of his. I don't think he's a threat. But you and Jake tie him up if he gives you any reason to. Better safe than sorry."

"Yes, sir."

Noting the photo in Nathan's shirt pocket, Joshua said, "I want you to get home to them, Nathan. To get home soon. If we're all careful, if we all work as one, you'll see them again."

The older officer nodded. "Thank you, Captain. I'll certainly do my best."

Joshua studied Nathan, wondering how many fathers had died aboard *Benevolence*. The thought of grieving wives and children abruptly assaulted him, made him want to flee this place and his memories. A part of him wished that he'd died alongside everyone else. In many ways, that should have been his fate. Why, Lord, did they die and I live? he silently asked, his fingers twisting beads that weren't there. Why, by all that is holy, did you take them from me?

Reminding himself that he needed to look after Isabelle, that he could protect her, Joshua picked up the machete and handed Roger another spear. Within a few minutes, the two of them were deep in the jungle. Wanting to find a good water supply, additional sources of food, and hiding places, Joshua moved slowly through the dense underbrush. Thirty feet above, a seemingly endless canopy of treetops blotted out the sun. Brightly colored birds protested the presence of the two men below. The birds' screeches mingled with the softer symphony of the millions of nearby insects, creating a discordant and primeval reverberation of sound.

As Joshua parted the ferns and vines before him, he wondered if anyone had ever stepped where he was stepping. Aboard *Benevolence*, he'd studied charts of this island, as he did for every landmass he navigated around. The charts had proclaimed the island to be uninhabited by humans, but Joshua couldn't help but ask himself if the charts were accurate. His uncertainty caused him to proceed with care and to keep his machete raised defensively. Mosquitoes assaulted his exposed flesh, and he silently derided himself for not standing in the campfire's smoke before they left. Moving faster to flee the flying devils, he headed toward the hilly interior of the island. Sweat dropped from his face as if it were a water pouch that had sprung several small leaks.

When Joshua paused to remove a thorn from his ankle, Roger swept past him. The underbrush quickly consumed Roger, and Joshua had to hurry to catch up. As he followed the younger officer, Joshua watched how he navigated the jungle. Though Joshua had grown up outdoors and knew how to traverse its obstacles, he quickly realized that Roger moved with stealth and fluidity that he himself could never replicate. The man didn't walk around fallen trees or boulders, but seemed to glide over them. He didn't push branches aside but ducked under them. Very few twigs cracked beneath his feet, and even fewer stones tumbled from below him when they began to climb a hill.

Joshua's breath became ragged. After being aboard *Benevolence* for the past nine weeks, he wasn't used to such physical exertion. And yet

Roger seemed completely unaffected by the heat and humidity and the steep rise of the land. Joshua saw the sharply outlined muscles in the calves before him, the effortless way in which Roger's legs propelled him upward. Even when they came upon a stream that trickled from above, Roger paused only long enough for Joshua to strip bark from a tree with his machete in an effort to mark the spot. Before he'd even finished gulping the cool water, Roger was once again headed up the hill.

What point is he trying to make? Joshua asked himself as he struggled to keep up. That he's stronger? That on *Benevolence* I might have been his superior, but in the jungle he's more powerful? Joshua had read Roger's files, and knew that he was gifted—both physically and mentally. And though at first Joshua had been glad to have Roger on the island, he sensed his hostility and uncomfortably pondered its origin.

Deciding to try to befriend the lieutenant, Joshua hurried to catch up to him. When he finally did, he tapped Roger on the shoulder and handed him the machete. "If you're . . . if you're going to lead, you should have this," Joshua said, his chest heaving.

Roger nodded, took the machete, and handed Joshua one of the spears. Though he pretended not to notice, Joshua saw that it was obviously inferior to the other. Seeing the stronger and better armed and somewhat intimidating man before him, Joshua suddenly felt vulnerable in a way that he hadn't for many years. For so long, his subordinates had tried to please him. For so long he had been in control.

And now things seemed quite different.

"WHO WANTS TO GO FISHING?" Ratu asked, looking from Jake to Nathan to Scarlet to Akira. After Jake nodded, Ratu picked up several spears. "And who else?" he added, assuming that everyone would be eager to fish. "You'll most certainly want to join us. You'll be able to eat whatever you catch—tuna and snapper and crab and maybe even some shark. I've watched these waters and they're full of delicious fish."

Nathan smiled at Ratu's enthusiasm, reminded of his own son's eagerness. "It sounds tempting, but I should stay here with the prisoner," he replied, musing over how much he loved fatherhood, longing to see his family.

"He's only got one good leg," Ratu replied. "And I tell you, he's not going bloody far on one leg. Have you ever tried to hop through a jungle on one leg? You'd get farther by crawling."

Nathan shook his head. "You go. And Scarlet, you should go as well. I'll stay and watch."

"I've never fished," Scarlet said as she rearranged a pile of firewood. "I wouldn't even know what to do."

"Big Jake and I will show you," Ratu promised. "It's not hard, trust me. If Big Jake can do it, anyone can do it."

Jake pretended to reach for Ratu, who giggled and sidestepped him. Scarlet smiled at their antics, dropping the firewood. "Why not?"

As Scarlet moved toward Ratu, Akira raised his head off his make-shift bed. "I hope that you have excellent luck," he said, bowing slightly to show his appreciation.

Ratu hesitated in replying, torn by the fact that he liked this man and that his father was fighting the Japanese. Finally he asked, "What's your favorite fish to eat?"

"I enjoy *maguro* the most."

"*Maguro*? I've never heard of that. It sounds like a bloody monster."

"So sorry. I mean . . . tuna. Tuna is wonderful."

Ratu nodded. "Then I'll catch you a fat *maguro*." As Akira thanked him, Ratu picked up another spear and started toward the beach. Jake walked before him, and Ratu feigned stabbing the big man with his spear. "What a cracking good catch you'd be," he said. "You'd feed us for weeks!"

Jake grabbed Ratu's spear and held it firmly as Ratu tried to pull it from him. "I reckon you're about to bite off more than you can chew," he said, repositioning a large blade of grass between his teeth.

"You and those bloody sayings," Ratu replied. "I never know what you're talking about. Bite off more than I can chew? How would it be possible to bite off more than I could chew?"

Scarlet smiled. Ratu's British accent and slang, coupled with Jake's slightly southern drawl and slow way of speaking, made for a lively conversation. Though they both spoke English, to Scarlet it seemed as if they often conversed in different languages.

Jake let go of Ratu's spear and hurried toward a distant collection of large, dark boulders that were partially submerged by the rising water. The rocks were at the far side of the beach, where the shore was exposed to the sea. When Jake spied a fist-sized crab atop one of the boulders, he immediately stopped. Ratu moved beside him, raising his spear. The crab was about ten paces from them, its blue-black legs holding it in place as waves pounded against the rock. Ratu switched his grip on the spear so that he held it like a baseball bat. "I've heard about your Babe Ruth," he whispered. "How many big slams did the Babe hit?"

"Grand slams," Jake softly replied. "Ain't no such thing as a big slam. But the Babe, he hit a bunch of grand slams."

Ratu turned toward his friend. "Grand slams? Not bloody likely. That makes no sense, Big Jake. I tell you, no sense at all."

Jake smiled, momentarily removing the blade of grass. "You ever played baseball?"

"No, but I'm a cracking good cricket player."

Ratu was about to move closer to the crab when Scarlet tapped him on the shoulder. "Look," she said quietly, pointing to another rock. Toward the middle of this rock a much bigger crab glistened in the sun.

"Brilliant spot, Miss Scarlet!" Ratu whispered excitedly. When the next wave rolled in to envelop the crab, Ratu hurried ahead, swinging his spear downward as soon as the wave started to withdraw. The almost-wrist-thick end of the spear struck the crab squarely in the middle of its shell, caving in the shell and sending the crab into the swirling water. As Ratu lunged to retrieve his catch, Jake swung his spear at the smaller crab. His blow wasn't quite so precise, but he was able to finish off the crab with a second swing.

Scarlet clapped. "Throw them here," she said, jumping backward when the two crabs landed by her feet.

A wave rolled in and caught Ratu squarely in the face. He coughed, simultaneously wiping his eyes and struggling to draw air. Jake moved to him, grabbing his arm so that the receding water didn't pull him out to sea. As Jake held Ratu, he noticed something wedged between a pair of rocks that were deeper in the water. At first he thought that perhaps a life jacket had floated ashore, but when the water dropped he realized that the life jacket held a body that was lodged between the boulders. The body was dressed in what had once been white clothes. Knowing that the deceased was either a doctor or nurse from *Benevolence*, Jake turned Ratu toward the beach. "Come," he said, pointing farther down the shore. "As sure as a puppy piddles, them big rocks are full of fat crabs."

Ratu continued to cough until they were beyond the reach of the waves. When his lungs finally stopped aching, he thanked Jake for pulling him from the sea. Jake picked up the two crabs and started walking to the distant rocks. Taking a quick glance toward where the body lay, he decided that at dawn the next day he'd return to bury the deceased. He would dig a proper grave, create a tombstone of sorts, and say some prayers. But he'd tell no one about his discovery. His fellow castaways had enough to worry about without carrying the additional burden of wondering whether bodies would float ashore.

"Might you want, miss, to try your hand at hitting one of them critters?" Jake asked when Scarlet glanced in the direction of the deceased.

"Me?" Scarlet asked, clearly surprised by the question.

Ratu pressed a spear against the palm of her hand. "Take this," he said. "I know that a beautiful woman like you has never held a spear before. But, I tell you, the more spears we have, the better."

Scarlet started to give the spear back to Ratu but decided to hold on to it. She might not kill anything with the weapon, but had to admit that she liked the feel of it in her hand. "Thank you, Ratu."

"For what?"

She looked closely at him, studying his expressive face, recalling how his dark eyes often darted about, and how his nose flared and his mouth opened wide when he was trying to make a point. No one had called Scarlet beautiful in a long time. People occasionally told her that she had beautiful hair, but this comment was the extent of the praise that she attracted. In her experience, strangers didn't call an overweight, middle-aged woman beautiful. "Thank you for being you," she finally replied, smiling.

"For being me? Who else would I bloody be?"

"I think, Ratu, that a lot of people . . . a lot of people pretend to be people they're not."

Ratu slapped at a troublesome fly. "Oh, my village is full of such people. Just full of them, I tell you. Our priest thinks he's Jesus Christ himself. And the bloke next door tells us that he's been to New York City. Can you imagine such a thing? A poor sugarcane farmer from Fiji traveling to New York City? Of course, I pretend to believe him."

"And why is that?"

"Because I fancy his stories. And I don't care if they're true or not." Ratu wiped sweat from his eye. "And because my father is a storyteller. And I've missed . . . I've really missed his stories for a long time."

Jake moved closer to Ratu. "Well, you can soon tell your daddy the darndest story of your own."

"What do you mean, Big Jake?"

"Tell him how you helped us live on this here island. How you taught a farmer and a beautiful woman to smash crabs."

"He won't bloody believe me!"

"Well, now, ain't you got a point there?" Jake teased, the grass between his teeth bobbing up and down. "Yup, I reckon you're as right as rain. Too bad you ain't got a photograph."

"Bugger off," Ratu said, punching his friend in the arm. He then scratched at his hair, which was black and curly and cut quite close to his scalp. Numerous chicken pox scars dotted his forehead. "Do you tell your father stories, Big Jake?" he asked.

"Does a dog have fleas?"

"Does he listen?"

"I expect so."

"Good. I'm glad he listens." Ratu grinned, increasing his pace. "Now let's go find some crabs and fish. Whoever gets the biggest crab or fish wins the game."

As Ratu raced ahead, Scarlet caught Jake's eyes. She smiled, nodding to him as if they shared a secret. Almost unconsciously, they slowed their steps—giving Ratu more time to hunt on his own and themselves a chance to enjoy the companionable silence that had suddenly dawned between them.

As THEY DREW nearer to camp, Annie was surprised at how familiar it looked. Though they'd only been on the island for a day and a half, the banyan tree that sheltered them was strangely reassuring. This surprised Annie greatly, as she'd never really felt at home anywhere. Even her childhood home—complete with its tire swing and sunny rooms and flowered wallpaper—had never put her totally at ease. Perhaps her disquiet had stemmed from the fact that she carried frightful memories of her home in addition to recollections of happiness. After all, she'd almost died in her perfect little room—a room that otherwise she would have treasured all her life.

When Annie and Isabelle approached, Nathan strode toward them. He wasn't wearing a hat, and his plump face was the color of a ripe peach. "Hello, ladies," he said, reaching out to help them with the things they'd collected. He tried to carry too much, and ended up dropping almost half of what he'd taken from them. Annie and Isabelle picked up their findings, then walked with him back to camp.

"Nathan, you need to stay in the shade today," Isabelle said.

He self-consciously touched his face. "I know. It already hurts." He dropped a crutch and hastily picked it up. "Rachel's always laughing at my pale skin. She calls me her ghost. So I thought I'd surprise her."

Annie wondered why Nathan wasn't already tan the way most every-one else had been aboard *Benevolence*. "Didn't you spend any off-duty hours on deck?"

"Not many. I read a lot and I wrote a lot. Letters and postcards mostly."

"You never . . . ran out of things to say?" Annie asked.

"Ran out? No, never."

Annie mused over his words as they approached their camp. Beyond the battles that she'd witnessed, Ted was interested in little of her life at sea. He pretended otherwise, of course, but his questions on such mat-ters tended to be superficial. And if truth be told, Annie wasn't particu-larly interested in telling him about her time aboard *Benevolence*. As she wondered why they could be getting married and talk so little, she saw Akira rise to a sitting position. Immediately, guilt swept through her, for she'd found nothing with which she could restitch his wound.

While Nathan and Isabelle started to arrange their findings beneath the banyan tree, Annie knelt on the sand next to where Akira rested. He greeted her politely and started to ask about her morning. "I've been everywhere," she interrupted, "and didn't find anything. Not fishing line or a spool of dental floss or even some strong string."

Akira shrugged. "Perhaps it could heal without your stitching?"

Leaning forward, Annie carefully removed his bandage. The wound was swollen and about half an inch wide. She needed to close it soon. "A needle. Did Ratu bring by a needle?"

Akira held up a thin sliver of bamboo. A small hole had been carved into its thick end. "He presented it to me soon after you left," he said, handing it to her. "He told me that you asked him to make it."

She inspected the needle, which was strong and sharp and would serve her purposes nicely. "What a great little boy," she said softly.

"I think so."

"What about a spool of dental floss? Have you seen anything like that at camp?"

He shook his head. "Cleaning string for your teeth? So sorry, but no. However, I was thinking. May I tell you my idea?"

"Of course."

"Thank you," he said, bowing slightly. "I am pleased that you want to hear my suggestion."

"What is it?"

"So sorry. Well, as you say . . . to cut a long story short, when I was seven or eight years old, I visited a castle. In this castle existed a special glass case, which held a thick rope of hair. I asked my mother about the hair and she told me that the castle . . . beams were too heavy to lift with a normal rope. This was a terrible problem as war was coming and the castle needed to be completed. So women cut off their long hair and . . . weaved it into a rope. This rope was strong enough that men could raise the heavy beams. And so the women saved everyone. And you can still see the rope made of their hair."

Her pulse quickening, Annie rose and hurried to Isabelle. Without a word she plucked several hairs from her sister's head. As Isabelle protested, Annie tested the strength of the strands. Akira was right—hair was surprisingly strong. Better yet, it wouldn't rot. "I think it will work!" she said excitedly. "I see no reason why it won't!"

"For thread?" Isabelle asked.

"Yes, yes!"

Annie started to reach for Isabelle's head again, and her sister backed away. "For heaven's sake, Annie, I can pull out my own hair."

"Oh, sorry. Mine's too short."

Isabelle ran her hands through her hair, plucking individual strands. She handed several to Annie and studied one herself. "How many hairs thick should the thread be?" she wondered aloud.

"I don't know," Annie replied as she held the hairs together and twisted them around each other until they became one. "Maybe five or six?"

Isabelle created a similar strand and wrapped it about her fingers.

She pulled until the tips of her fingers whitened. Finally, the strand broke. "I'd say maybe use a few more. Maybe eight."

"Isn't that a lucky number?"

"Is Scarlet's hair longer than mine?"

Annie thought. "Hers might be a bit longer. But hers is curly and yours is as straight as a post. Let's use yours."

Isabelle walked to where Akira sat watching them. He'd heard their conversation and bowed politely to Isabelle. "Thank you for your . . . " He paused, smiling. "Thank you for sharing your hair."

"It's the least I can do," she replied, pulling more hairs from her head. "Sorry, but I never properly thanked you for saving me. If you hadn't pushed Annie out of that room, we'd have both died in there."

"You were trying to save the doctor, yes?" Akira said softly and slowly. "Even then, as your ship sank, you tried to help him."

"I wish I could have," Isabelle replied, remembering the doctor's hearty laugh. Earlier that day he'd happily told her about his granddaughter—a four-year-old in whom he took great pride, but who would now grow up without him.

Annie stepped close to Akira. After studying the wound, she poured an entire canteen of fresh water onto the injury in an effort to rid it of sand and dirt. She'd found a large bottle of hydrogen peroxide, with which she dampened a cloth and prepared to further clean his wound. "This will hurt," she said. "But it will also kill most any germ." Annie poured some of the liquid onto her hands, and then dabbed at his wound with the cloth. Akira grimaced but was silent. "Izzy," Annie said, "can you thread—"

Isabelle handed her the bamboo needle with hair threaded through it. She'd used four hairs but had looped them through the needle's eye, tying them together at one end. Isabelle even had a second strand of woven hair ready.

"Perfect," Annie said, inspecting the needle and then dousing it with hydrogen peroxide. Isabelle didn't respond, nor did Annie talk further. Instead she examined the wound once more, determining where she'd place each stitch.

As Annie started to work, Akira watched her face, her hands. He noticed how she pierced his flesh swiftly so as to minimize his pain. Still, he grunted, and when he did, he saw her jaw tighten. Annie drew the needle through the other side of the wound. Akira was no medical man, but he realized that she was highly skilled. Her small fingers were confident and precise. Her hands were as steady as stone. When he bit his bottom lip in pain and held his breath as she pulled his flesh together, she leaned even closer to him, so close that her shoulder rested against his arm. Her touch didn't drive his agony away, but instead of focusing on his suffering, he was acutely aware of the sensation of her against him. A sense of warmth grew between them, and though he'd been touched by several women before, he didn't recall feeling warmth such as this. He realized to his amazement that Annie was trying to protect him with her touch, sheltering him as she pierced and pulled his inflamed flesh.

The thought of her protecting him caused her warmth to spread like hot sake throughout his body. He watched her shoulder as it touched his arm, deciding that her skin was the color of a late-afternoon sun. Tiny blond hairs emerged from her skin to lean against him. To his immense surprise, Akira felt a sudden urge to lean down and press his lips on her shoulder, to see if it was as soft as he imagined.

"Do you mind if I ask your age?" Annie said, drawing a section of his torn flesh together.

"I . . . I am thirty-four years old."

"Really? Your skin looks younger. It feels younger."

"And may I ask your age?"

"Twenty-four. Though soon I'll be twenty-five."

He nodded absently, still watching her shoulder. "So new to the world."

"There," she said, moving away from him. "It's done."

Akira looked at his wound, which was now closed. Annie's stitches were tidy and organized, like a row of tiles on a temple's roof. With her shoulder no longer against him, he was aware of the burning in his thigh. She gently dabbed at her work with the disinfectant, and his pain increased.

"I'm sorry," she said. "But I need to make sure it's clean."

"You are very skilled," he replied, wishing that her shoulder was still against him.

"Yes, you certainly are," Isabelle added, somewhat taken aback at how Akira had looked at her sister. Isabelle had seen hundreds of patients gaze at nurses with hope or longing or desperation in their eyes. And she'd come to expect such looks from the young men she aided. But still, Akira's gaze had seemed to contain something different. What it was, she couldn't discern. In any case, after glancing again at Akira, Isabelle walked toward Nathan, who'd been watching them from afar.

Annie tightly wrapped a fresh bandage around Akira's thigh. "If you're careful, the stitches should hold."

"I am honored to have you as my doctor," he said, bowing to her.

"Oh, no. I'm just a nurse."

He nodded toward the sea. "Is that just water?"

Smiling, Annie stood. She started to move toward her sister, but thinking of Akira's words, she walked down the beach toward the less tranquil side of the harbor. There she washed her hands in the waves that lapped at her feet. They were warm and welcoming and she moved deeper into the water. Impulsively, she sat down and let the waves roll against her. The sound of their tumbles was rhythmic and comforting. And though Annie did not have the courage to go deeper into the sea, she found solace in the gentle waves and the hope that Akira was right.

As THE DAY AGED, the wind gathered force, rushing past the island as if late to reach the other side of the world. The jungle that dominated much of the island swayed like sea grass. Coconuts fell with large gusts, thudding into soil or sand. Though the water of the harbor remained fairly smooth, beyond its protective shoreline, whitecaps rolled into the island. The sky was, surprisingly, almost free of clouds. No storm was imminent. No squall from which to flee. The wind was merely showing its strength to the island, which, aside from the unhappy trees, seemed rather unimpressed.

Dusk was near, and the survivors were busy improving the wall they'd built around their fire. Its flames danced wildly in the wind, and if anybody was going to cook the two dozen crabs that Ratu, Jake, and Scarlet had killed, the fire would need to be corralled. No one had eaten meat for two days, and each was excited about enjoying the crabs. Ratu and Jake had cut several saplings and would place a web of green wood above the fire so that the crabs could be properly cooked.

Roger and Joshua had returned from surveying the island. Joshua had reported the discovery of a nearby stream and a variety of fruit-bearing trees. Several more steel canteens had washed up on the beach, and these had been filled with fresh water. The finding of water and food had been welcome news, because with plenty of resources available, no one was in danger of dying from hunger or thirst.

When the fire was contained, Jake and Ratu hurried to the sea. They had laid the saplings underwater beneath some rocks and now pulled the wood from the sand. Once back at the fire, they carefully placed the saplings across the flames. Scarlet then used the machete as a spatula, depositing the crabs on the makeshift grill. "I think we found our hunters," Joshua said, watching the crabs sizzle over the fire, trying to be upbeat for the sake of the group. "If we were at sea, I'd grant you each three days of shore leave."

Jake chuckled at the joke. "Why, thank you, Captain."

"Big Jake told me you could be a funny bloke," Ratu added. "But I didn't believe him."

The crabs were turning red, and the delightful smell of their dinner prompted Scarlet to hand everyone a thick leaf. "Use these as plates," she said, swatting repeatedly at a mosquito. As the sun began its desent toward the horizon, she used the machete to scoop up the crabs. She gave everyone a crab before placing a second batch above the fire.

Though Roger took his crab and settled within distant shadows, everyone else stayed near the fire. "What's the island like, my captain?" Ratu asked, unsure if he'd rather fish or explore.

Joshua saw that Isabelle's crab was smaller than his, and took her leaf and gave her his own. "Roger and I climbed high," he replied. "My legs—"

"What did you see?"

"Hold them horses, Ratu," Jake interjected. "The captain will tell you."

With a pair of smooth stones, Joshua smashed the claw of his crab, then used the stones on Isabelle's crab. "The island is shaped like . . . oh, kind of like a giant fishing hook, I'd say. Where we are here in the harbor is where the curve of the hook is. We're on the inside part. The rest of the island is long and skinny. And though there are plenty of other beaches, they aren't nearly as protected as ours."

"And the middle?" Ratu asked.

"The middle has most of the high ground," Joshua replied, liking the boy. "Very tough terrain there. We climbed hills that were a few hundred feet high, and could see some other islands to the west and east of us. Maybe eight or ten miles away."

As Scarlet gave her a second crab, Isabelle asked, "Did you find anywhere for us to hide in case the Japanese land?"

Joshua shook his head. "Not yet. But she's a big, wild island. And I bet we'll find some caves."

"Look by the shore," Ratu suggested. "At home, the best caves are where the water hits the land."

"Good idea, Ratu."

"Thank you, my captain. I'm glad you think so."

The fire popped, sparks exploding into the darkening night. An ember landed near Akira, and he used a stick to cover it in soil. When

Scarlet brought him another crab, he thanked her. He broke into his crab and then watched Annie and her sister talking, leaning close together as they conversed through words and gestures and animated expressions. Suddenly, Akira thought of Nanking, for he'd seen many sisters die together. Memories of such heinousness invaded him the way oil from a dying battleship fouls the sea's surface. "May I say something, Captain?" he asked quietly, feeling compelled to speak, to protect the woman who'd so tenderly stitched his leg.

Joshua started to reply but stopped, weighing the pros and cons of letting an enemy soldier participate in the discussion. After all, the Japanese couldn't be trusted. Like most American naval officers, Joshua would never forget that while Japanese diplomats were negotiating a treaty in Washington, their carrier fleet was secretly heading toward Hawaii. However, he didn't perceive Akira to be a threat. And so he nodded.

"Thank you," Akira replied somewhat uncomfortably.

"What would you like to say?" Joshua asked.

"Captain, I am certain that Tokyo wants these islands."

"And why is that?"

"For the reason that after Midway, with most of our aircraft carriers destroyed, it is . . . imperative that we have airbases here to control the South Pacific."

"Yes," Joshua replied, "I think Uncle Sam believes as much."

"And if my countrymen come to this island, they will land on this beach. This harbor is perfect, yes?"

"It's not bad."

"So sorry for stating what you already know, but you must leave this place at once, Captain. Please find another camp immediately."

Joshua nodded and thanked Akira for his words. Though he still wasn't ready to trust the foreigner, he appreciated his concern. Normally, he might have questioned the legitimacy of such concern, but Joshua had seen Akira drag himself through the shallows with Annie on his back. The man had almost died saving a woman he hardly knew.

And Joshua's instincts told him that Akira had just spoken because he didn't want any harm to befall Annie and Isabelle.

Setting down the last of his crab, Joshua rose from the fire and stared at the harbor. The responsibility of the group's well-being suddenly weighing upon him, he walked closer to the water. Away from the fire and the smoke it was easier for him to think. He knew that Annie's patient was right. The sooner they moved, the better. But where to move? The Japanese would survey the entire island. Relocating to another beach would buy the survivors a day or two, but nothing more. No, they'd have to find someplace secret, someplace where they could hide for weeks.

As Joshua wondered where that place could be, Isabelle and Annie walked up behind him. Isabelle brought him a banana that she'd cooked over some embers. Joshua had always enjoyed fried bananas, and though this one wasn't drenched in butter and sugar, it still tasted sweet. As Isabelle and Annie quietly stood next to him, Joshua reflected on how fortunate he was to have met the sisters. Of course, he loved Isabelle, but a part of him also loved Annie, for she was like the little sister he'd never had.

"I think you can trust him," Annie said, her words soft but rather abrupt.

"Who?" he asked, his mind elsewhere.

"Akira. I don't think you have anything to fear from him. If you did, he would have let Izzy and I drown in that room."

Joshua nodded, having put more thought toward the subject than he'd care to admit. "Well, I'm certainly in his debt for saving you. But if the Japanese land, where will his loyalty rest? Probably not with a group of Americans he'd have killed a few weeks ago."

"I doubt he wants to kill anyone."

Shrugging, Joshua was about to change the subject when he heard a distant drone. "Aircraft!" he shouted, running back toward the fire. Though the wall they'd built over the fire was solid, Joshua threw several palm fronds on the flames. The sound of the planes grew louder, soon becoming a buzz that seemed to echo off everything around them. It was as if they were standing atop a honeycomb, and thousands of bees were about to enter a massive hive.

The last time that Annie had listened to such a drone they had been attacked, and she took Isabelle's hand within her own. The planes were very loud now. If Annie listened carefully, she could hear one engine misfiring among the steady hum of its companions.

Joshua looked toward Akira. "Zeros?"

"Hai."

"Hai?"

"So sorry. I mean, yes. I think so."

Staring upward, Joshua scanned for the source of the noise. The unseen sun still faintly illuminated the sky, but locating the planes was difficult, and Joshua gazed from clouds to solitary stars.

"There!" Nathan shouted, pointing.

The ever-so-faint outlines of fighter planes passed almost directly above. Leaning closer to Isabelle, Annie wondered how such small things could wreak such destruction. Had these planes just killed and were returning to their base, or were they just setting out? The sputtering plane made her think that they were returning from battle. How many Americans had they killed? How many boys from Texas and Oregon and Iowa had been maimed tonight?

As Annie avoided Akira's eyes and imagined the suffering of the burn victims, Joshua did his best to count the fighters. He estimated that at least a dozen planes flew westward. With a range of well over a thousand miles, the Zeros could be headed anywhere. And yet Joshua had a sense that the pilots' destination wasn't far. The formation was simply too compact for a long journey at night.

When the drone of the planes had passed, Jake and Ratu piled more wood on the fire. In the absence of the Zeros, sounds of the waves and the wind and the insects once again infiltrated their world. Still shuddering and reliving the night of the bombing, Annie looked for someone to talk with. But Isabelle spoke quietly with Joshua, and most everyone else seemed to be staring skyward. Akira appeared to be watching her, but she didn't feel like his company. And so she walked down to the sea and put her feet in the cool water, which not long ago had seemed so very warm.

DAY FOUR

In a stranger's shoes,
I once watered my garden.
Rain makes leaves tumble.

Discoveries

Dawn came at a leisurely pace. Since the sun rose on the other side of the island, the world around their camp transitioned subtly from darkness to indigo to amber rays of light. The sea had quieted, and shimmered as if thousands of mirrors sparkled in the sun. Near the shore, a school of miniature fish broke the surface as the creatures fled a determined predator. Gulls hovered above the water, and when the little fish swam too shallowly the birds plummeted from the sky to consume them.

Ratu stood knee-deep in the harbor, a long spear held aloft, watching the water for signs of the big fish. He'd seen it twice and thought it to be a yellowfin tuna. His father had taught him how to spear such fish. They had often worked together, with Ratu driving large fish toward his father, who was usually able to deliver a killing blow. Sometimes a fish, upon seeing his father, would swim back toward Ratu. Striking a fast-moving target was quite difficult, and more often than not, his spear had penetrated only sand. But instead of displaying frustration of any sort, his father had patiently explained to him how fish thought—how they usually darted toward deeper water, how a hungry fish most likely wouldn't stop chasing its prey even if threatened.

Once a shark had come between the two of them, and Ratu had watched in awe as his father flung his spear so forcefully that it went

through the shark's head and pinned the thrashing creature to the sea-
bed. Later, after they'd gutted and cleaned it, his father had made a
necklace for Ratu. From a leather cord he'd hung the shark's largest
tooth. As far as Ratu had been concerned, the necklace possessed near
magical properties, and he didn't take it off until one day when he lost
it in the jungle. That night, upon seeing Ratu's tears, his father had
promised to find him a new tooth. But two weeks later, he'd left with
the Americans.

After his father was gone, Ratu had hunted alone. He caught fewer
fish, and even though he desperately wanted to kill a shark and make a
necklace for his father, the one time a shark had turned in his direction,
Ratu had fled toward shallower waters. Over the long and lonely
months, he'd tried to ease his misery by bringing beautiful shells home
to his sisters. And for a time their smiles had warmed him. But at night,
sleeping on the floor of their hut, longing for his father's stories, his
tears had tended to be many.

As Ratu now hunted the yellowfin tuna, he thought of his sisters
and mother, wondering what they were doing. He missed his siblings
far more than he cared to admit. He even missed watching them pretend to be mothers. They'd always made him be the father, and as he
now stalked the big fish, he wished that he was talking in a deep voice
and laughing as his sisters brought him tea or kava.

Thirty paces up the beach from Ratu, the rest of the camp's members
had gathered around the fire. Joshua had brought everyone together—
after he'd risen early to pray for the dead and beseech God to grant him
strength. He had been telling the group what he thought about the
planes they'd seen the night before, about how he believed that either a
Japanese base or an aircraft carrier was near. "We need to explore every
last inch of this island," he said, reminding himself that most of the
survivors weren't trained in war and would need specific instructions.
"Where is there more water? Are there caves? Other places to hide? Because within a few days, we should leave this spot."

"But isn't the harbor the best place for us?" Scarlet asked.

"Well, yes and no," he answered. "It's great for us, but it would also be great for the Japs. And that's why we have to move."

Joshua proceeded to split up the group. Jake, Ratu, and Scarlet would explore the nearby beaches on the west side of the island. Roger would climb more of the many hills. Nathan and Annie would stay at camp with the patient while Joshua and Isabelle investigated the island's eastern side.

Roger was delighted to hear that he'd be free to travel alone. His plan had worked perfectly. The captain had realized that no one could keep up with him, and so the fool had sent him off alone. How easy it is to manipulate people, Roger thought, pleased with himself. How utterly predictable and pathetic people are.

As the camp disbanded, Roger grabbed a spear, a canteen, and two bananas. He also rubbed some soot from the fire on himself to ward off the ever-present insects. Without saying a word to anyone, he started walking toward the island's interior. Once within the jungle, Roger became a part of it, his movements even quieter than those of the previous day. He'd learned to look for brightly colored birds, and to circumvent them, as they always protested his presence. And he'd discovered that it was best to walk on ground that he could see, for leaves often hid dry twigs that snapped underfoot. Such precautions convinced Roger that being in the jungle was akin to being a spy, for awareness of all of his surroundings was crucial to remaining undetected.

Once he reached the location where his radio was buried, Roger knelt in the underbrush and waited—needing to ensure that no one had followed him or stumbled upon the spot. After about five minutes, he began to dig. Soon the wooden box was in his hands, its presence comforting and powerful. The pistol inside gave him the power of life or death, and he basked in that power the way a dictator presides over a terrified populace.

"I can kill any of you maggots," he whispered, longing to feel the gun, hating his fellow survivors for the smiles that came so easily to them. "I can put a barrel in your mouth and make you do whatever I want."

Though carrying the box and spear was difficult, Roger relished the challenge. He was never tempted to leave the spear, as it was always possible that he'd be forced to kill in silence. And so he walked through the jungle with the spear held parallel to the ground. The deeper he penetrated into the island's interior, the larger the foliage became. Impossibly massive banyan trees created their own forests, their trunks and limbs home to seemingly every species of frog and lizard, snake and butterfly. Under such behemoths, only thin shafts of sunlight struck the ground, and moss and ferns dominated the damp soil.

Eyeing the tallest rise within his field of vision, Roger continued to move quickly. To make certain that he couldn't be followed, he found a creek bed and walked upon a series of worn boulders. He soon leapt as far from the creek as possible, landing amid chest-high ferns. His feet struck something hard and he was surprised to see thick bones beneath him. Leaning down, he inspected the bones and decided they were remnants of a wild boar. Hoping that he'd have a chance to hunt such game with his spear, he continued onward.

The hill that he soon climbed would have winded the captain, but Roger made his way up easily. As he rose, the rich soil vanished and only rocks and bushes surrounded him. Toward the top of the hill, the ground beneath him became much steeper. He was climbing now, struggling up rock faces and slippery slopes. As he came upon a stone outcropping, he noticed a bird's nest that had been fashioned of driftwood. Two large, brown eggs lay in the nest. Knowing that he needed as much sustenance as possible, Roger broke the eggs open and quickly drank their contents.

Near the top of the hill, Roger found almost exactly what he'd hoped to discover—a bathtub-shaped depression surrounded by shoulder-high rocks and shrubbery. Setting his spear aside and carefully cradling the box, he jumped into the depression and immediately opened the clasps of the box. For a moment, he was tempted to light a cigarette. In fact, he held his teeth tightly together at the prospect, imagining the warm sensation of smoke as it traveled deeply into him. The smoke would dispatch the headache that surged from behind his eyes and would put him at peace. And yet the smoke could betray him, for the other survivors might smell its scent on him and wonder how he'd gotten cigarettes to the island. Angrily cursing his fellow castaways for causing this predicament, Roger vowed not to give in to temptation.

After briefly caressing the pistol, Roger withdrew the green radio. Flicking a switch, he was relieved to see that the radio had power. He turned up the volume and twisted the dial until he hit a frequency that he'd memorized. He then placed the headset over his ears. Static greeted him.

"Ronin to Edo," he said softly in Japanese into the mouthpiece. "Repeat, Ronin to Edo." The static continued, and Roger gently turned the dial to make sure he had the proper frequency. "Repeat, Ronin to Edo. Over."

"Edo here," a metallic voice that Roger recognized replied. "How are the cherry blossoms?"

"Always best at dawn." The code complete, Roger continued, "Operation White Crane successful. Eight surviving chicks with me in nest. Over."

A brief moment of static preempted Edo's reply. "Understood," the voice said. "Leave chicks in nest. Mother coming to roost in twelve to fifteen days. Report again in six days."

"Understood. Over."

Roger removed his headset, wiped his sweat from it, carefully placed the radio back into the box, and wondered what he'd do with the vast amount of money that would soon be his. With such wealth he could buy his own island. He could buy cars and women and guns. Best of all, he could savor the power that his wealth created. Of course, he was too important to the Japs for him to disappear for any length of time. They would arrive and kill or imprison the other survivors, and somehow he'd ultimately find himself once again with American forces. And once again he'd betray them.

Twelve to fifteen days, he thought excitedly, watching an immense beetle climb up a rock. Imagining that the creature was Joshua, Roger pressed the tip of his spear into the beetle's back until the insect was impaled. He then held the beetle near him, so that he could closely watch it struggle. The insect tried to free itself for a surprisingly long time, its head and mandibles and legs twisting this way and that. Finally, the beetle began to twitch and tremble.

Yes, Roger thought, everything will happen in twelve to fifteen days. People will die and people will suffer. And I'll get to decide who does what. And whoever so much as looks at me the wrong way when I get back to camp will be the first to get a spear in the back.

His mind churning with possibilities, Roger longingly touched the gun and the cigarettes. They spoke to him, and their words were as powerful as love or religion or drugs were to others. Reluctantly, he put both temptations away and started to bury his box. Once it was safely hidden, he smashed the beetle between his thumb and forefinger, lifted his spear, and returned to the jungle.

"WHAT ELSE DO YOU LOVE ABOUT YOUR WIFE?" Annie asked Nathan. The pair sat close together under the limited shade of a coconut tree. Less than ten paces away, Akira used a stick to write in the sand.

"She understands me," he replied, shielding his eyes from the sun. "She understands me and she doesn't ask me to do things that I'm incapable of doing."

"Like what?"

"Like . . . like pretending that I know all the answers. Like being able to buy her expensive things."

Annie watched an ant struggle up a rise in the sand. She'd never realized that sand was the landscape upon which so many creatures traveled. "And what do you give her?"

He turned away from the bright sun so that he no longer faced her.

"Two things, I think. I try to be a good husband and a good father. I try to keep her and the children happy. I'm not really interested in anything beyond that. I don't see how I can do more than that."

"I don't think you need to."

"You don't? I don't need a big car and more stripes on my uniform?"

"No, of course not."

Nathan smiled and looked across the sea, as if he could somehow gaze into his distant home and watch his loved ones. Knowing where his thoughts lay, Annie glanced toward Akira, wondering what he was drawing in the sand. Feeling somewhat guilty for ignoring him the past night, she turned to Nathan. "I'll be back."

"Sure, take your time."

Annie moved toward Akira. The sand was already warm under her feet, as if the earth were running a temperature. When Annie's shadow fell upon him, Akira looked up and said good morning. She made no immediate reply, as her first thought was of his wound. She didn't see any blood on the bandage and knew that her stitches had held. "It is a nice morning, isn't it?" she finally concurred.

He nodded slowly, his head rising and falling like the swells beyond the harbor. "Strange, yes, to war in paradise?"

"You made us fight here," Annie said, somewhat instinctively, remembering the previous night. "Your country brought the war to these islands. Just like it did to Singapore and China and Thailand and Malaya."

Akira took a deep breath, and she thought he was going to debate the matter. Instead he said, "So sorry for the Zeros. Even for me, a terrible sound."

She hadn't expected such an apology and wasn't sure how to respond. Finally, she said, "I don't like . . . the sounds of war."

"Neither do I."

"I've had too many patients cry at such noises."

He closed his eyes for a moment, as if her words stirred something deep within him. "Will you please sit?" he asked, politely gesturing to the sand beside him. Once Annie settled onto the beach, he said, "The sound of Zeros is—"

"I'm sorry," she interrupted, "but could we please talk about something else?"

He brought his hands together and bowed. "So sorry. Please forgive me."

"I just think that we should . . . talk about something other than war. Besides, the morning's too beautiful for such talk."

"Yes, yes, you are right. We should talk of something else."

Annie looked at the sand before him. "What were you writing?"

He cleared his throat. "These are Japanese characters."

"Characters?"

"Yes. Each character is its own word," he replied, tracing his work. "I was writing a haiku."

"Do you mind if I ask what it says?"

Akira looked at his poem, shaking his head with mild frustration. "It is unfinished, as the words are not right. They feel . . . awkward. Unfortunately, it has been three years since I last wrote."

"So long?"

"Yes. If my mother knew of this, she would be most unhappy."

"Do you miss her?" Annie asked, still musing over the characters, thinking that they were both foreign and beautiful.

He started to speak and then stopped, unused to being questioned on such personal matters. "I do miss her," he said. "She is very wise, and taught me so many wonderful things, including haikus. She creates them every day."

Annie smiled. "Perhaps you can write her the perfect poem. Here on this beach."

"That would be most agreeable." An unseen bird squawked behind them, interrupting his next thought. "Might . . . might you think of one?" he asked uncertainly, wondering if this woman who'd so tenderly cared for him was truly interested in poetry or if he'd imagined their earlier conversation. "Might you describe this morning?"

"This moment? Right now?"

"If you would like."

"But how?"

Akira remembered his students asking similar questions, and the memory warmed him. "Can you take . . . take your feelings and . . . blend them with what you see?"

"Oh, I don't think so. Not me."

"So sorry, but I am sure that you could do it."

"Why?"

"Because . . . because you said the morning was beautiful. And you meant what you said, yes?"

She looked at his mouth, which had formed into a half smile. "Blend them, you say?"

"Blending is what poets do, I think. Take what you see and put your emotions into that . . . vision."

Annie didn't reply. She knew that she was no poet. And yet it seemed that he wanted her to be one. How did he see her? As a student? A friend? As someone who'd helped him and he felt indebted to? Perhaps more important, was there anything wrong with her talking to him?

Unable to answer her own questions, but conjuring no reason why she shouldn't try to create a poem, Annie turned toward the sea. The day, for all its beauty, was strangely quiet. Not a single whitecap dotted the water. The palm trees lining the beach stood so still that they seemed devoid of life. The sky was unblemished and infinite. Though the world before her was striking, to Annie it appeared expressionless, more like an old postcard than something warm and wet and wonderful.

Words churned within her as she sought to do what Akira had asked, to mix her emotions with what she looked upon. But how could words, which often seemed so limiting to her, describe what she now saw and felt? As usual, Annie's emotions were cluttered and confused.

She felt both safe and fearful, content and utterly bereft of hope. How could she give life to her feelings when even she did not understand them?

Annie glanced at Akira and was surprised to see that his eyes were closed. He was obviously in no hurry for her to finish. And so she thought. She imagined her place in the world, and through that imagining, words slowly began to unfold. She spoke them to herself, listening to the sounds, the syllables, the deeper meaning that she strove to create.

"I'm not a poet," Annie finally said. "I can paint—flowers and even faces. But I can't write." His half smile returned, and she glanced at the sea. "Still, I do have . . . I've thought of something."

"Might you be so kind as to share it with an old teacher? It would be a gift to these lonely ears."

Annie started to speak but giggled softly, feeling foolish. "My words aren't any good. And I do feel like I'm in school. Like I'm twelve again and worried what the boys will say."

"Is that such a terrible thing? To feel young again?"

She shook her head, nervously running her hands through her short hair. "You won't laugh?"

"Not unless it is funny."

"Promise?"

"As you say . . . I will cross my heart and hope to die."

Annie's grin lingered. "Well, then, I suppose I have nothing to lose," she said, unsure what to think of this man. "So here's my first . . . haiku."

"Please."

"Is the wind silent? / Or am I deaf to such sound? / Waves melt on warm sand."

For a moment, Akira's face was blank. But then he smiled, bowing deeply to her. He held his bow low and finally rose to face her. "You do honor to yourself," he said. "And to me. Thank you."

"You like it? Really?"

"Yes, yes, I do. Very much."

"Why?"

"Because I think . . . I think you are being true. And most people are afraid of truth."

She started to reply but stopped, her good mood quickly departing. "No. You don't understand. I've been afraid my whole life."

"So sorry, but may I ask of what?"

Annie wondered again if she should be speaking to him in such a manner. What would Ted think? "Of the future," she finally replied. "Of my path. I've . . . I've been afraid of so many things."

"And yet, look at you, talking with a prisoner of war. Telling me your poem. How can such a woman be afraid?" She didn't answer, and he smiled. "Perhaps . . . perhaps your days of being afraid are done."

Her eyes began to water at his words, for they were welcome thoughts. She was tired of being afraid, so impossibly weary of her own fears that a part of her wanted to sit on the quiet beach forever. If she sat in the sand forever, she wouldn't have to face the troubles that often seemed to define her life. As a tear descended her cheek, she wiped it away, turning toward the sea.

"Your poem was lovely, Annie," he said, encouraging her as he so often had his favorite students. "It made me . . ."

His voice trailed off, and she turned back to him. "What? It made you what?"

"It pleased me very much. And I was . . . most proud."

"Proud? Why on earth were you proud?"

Akira glanced at the sea, thinking of the wonderful young minds he had encountered, thinking of his former life. "Because your poem . . . it reminded me of another time. A far better time."

As much as she enjoyed his words, Annie was reluctant to continue the conversation. And so she nodded and stood. The sun felt comforting against her face, as if she'd been awaiting its caress. She thanked him and then began to slowly walk down the beach. She wanted to believe him—believe that her days of being afraid were done. And she wanted to believe that he was proud of her. When was the last time, she asked herself, that anyone outside her family was proud of her?

As she continued to walk, Annie couldn't help but wonder how Akira seemed to know her. Was it because of that night, the night he saved her? Had that night somehow bound him to her? Does that happen when you almost die to save someone else? When a stranger's heart beats against you as you feel yourself slipping away? When your blood and tears wash over her? Annie had spent three days with Akira and a thousand days with Ted. And yet this stranger, this Japanese soldier, seemed to understand her more deeply than did her fiancé.

"He liked my poem," she whispered, as if she wished to share a secret with the sea.

Though the sea stayed silent, Annie didn't mind. And though she was alone, she didn't feel alone. She knew that his eyes were upon her, and strangely, this knowledge warmed her as much as the sun.

SITTING ON A FALLEN TREE, Isabelle and Joshua took turns sipping from an army canteen. The water they'd taken from a nearby stream possessed a slightly metallic taste but otherwise seemed clear and fresh. Above them soared the jungle's canopy, which was so thick that they might as well have been living within some sort of infinite greenhouse or cave. The usual noises—hoots and screeches and chirps—seemed to echo off this canopy, strengthening the sounds.

"Wouldn't some fresh-ground coffee taste good right now?" Isabelle asked, wiping sweat from her brow.

Joshua unconsciously licked his lips. "Even stale coffee would be good," he somewhat absently replied. "Stale, two-day-old coffee with cigarette ashes in it."

"Let's not get too carried away. We haven't been here that long."

"True enough."

Isabelle moved closer to her husband, putting her hand on his leg. She looked into his eyes, and he almost immediately glanced at the trees above. She knew that he avoided her stare when something troubled him—almost as if he feared that she'd peer into his eyes, see his pain, ask him about it, and demand answers that he didn't have. This habit of his had always annoyed her. After all, she didn't want him to interpret her questions and concerns as things to avoid.

Joshua's obvious misery prompted Isabelle to consider sharing her secret. For days she'd been tempted to tell him, tempted to tell Annie. But she'd told no one. The time had never felt quite right, and besides, Isabelle was someone who liked to deal in certainties, and when it came to her secret she was certain of very little. Moreover, though she longed to share her thoughts with Joshua, she didn't want to raise his hopes and then later dash them. And she didn't want him to feel that she was manipulating the situation to make him happier.

"What's on your mind?" she finally asked, once they'd started to walk again.

"Oh, nothing really."

"Joshua, don't say that when I know it's not true."

He pushed a flowering vine aside and held it at bay so she could pass. "You know what's bothering me, Isabelle. So why do you ask? I lost my ship. Almost my entire crew is dead. What the hell do you think is on my mind?"

"That tone isn't necessary. Don't take it with me again."

He swatted at a mosquito, and when the jungle cleared slightly he moved beside her. "I'm trying," he said, his voice softening. "I'm trying, God help me, to lead, to do what needs to be done. But it's not easy. It's awful, in fact. I'm a fraud. And I don't want to lead anyone. I don't deserve to. I'm only trying to because of you. Because of Annie."

"You're not a fraud. Not by—"

"You, more than anyone else, should understand where I'm coming from."

"I do understand."

"Then why are you asking me about it? Can't you see that I want to be left alone?"

"Why? Because maybe I can help. Because this island isn't a ship, and you don't have to lead alone. You're not standing on the bridge with men looking to you for orders."

"I don't know—"

"I want to help. That's all. To help you. Is that so wrong?"

He unbuttoned his sweat-drenched shirt almost to his belly. "No, it's not," he admitted, slowing his pace. "And I'm sorry . . . for snapping at you. For pushing you away. I don't mean to. And you don't deserve it. But I am used to being on my own, to standing on my bridge. Remember that for most of this war I haven't had you around."

"I'm here, Josh. Right next to you. Right where I'm supposed to be."

They came to a fallen sandalwood tree and he helped her over it. Nearby a green and yellow parrot suddenly took flight, leaves dropping in its wake. "I don't know," he said, "if I'll ever get over what happened to *Benevolence*. I paid more attention to my crew than I did to my own life, to you. And now they're gone forever."

"They didn't die in vain."

He shrugged. "I'm not sure about that. But . . ."

"But what?"

"But I'm sure that I'll try . . . I'll really try to let you in."

"I want to be in."

"I just . . . I think about everything I could have done differently. Checking the cargo. Having another lookout. Running more emergency drills. If I'd done things differently, so many good people wouldn't have died." He closed his eyes. "But I was a fool."

Isabelle knew that nothing she could ever say about his handling of *Benevolence* would ease his guilt. And so she replied, "Just remember that we're at war. And things like this happen in war. That's why millions are dead already."

He nodded but said nothing, continuing to trudge through the jungle. Though they used to take many walks together, she'd never seen him move so—with his shoulders slouched and his eyes oblivious to the world around him. Despite his just having angered her, it hurt her to sense the depth of his sorrow, to know that while he was doing his best to lead, he was nearly a broken man. And though she didn't want to manipulate the moment by sharing her news, she eased closer to his side and prepared to tell him her secret.

"We should be nearing the eastern beaches," he said. "There can't be much more of this jungle. I just don't—"

"Josh?"

He turned to her. "What? What's wrong?"

"Nothing's wrong. But I do have something . . . something to share with you."

"What is it?"

Isabelle stopped walking and brushed her long, damp hair from her face. "I think . . . I'm fairly confident that I'm pregnant." Joshua didn't say anything, but almost immediately dropped his gaze to her belly. "It's too early for me to show," she added. "But all the signs are there."

"When . . . when are you due?" he said slowly, as if awaking from a dream.

"Probably in just under seven months."

"So you've known for a month? And said nothing?"

She moved closer to him, tilting her head back so that she could look into his eyes. "I wanted to wait until we were ashore. Until we could go out and do something fun. To surprise you that way."

"And why not here? On the hill?"

"Because you needed to mourn the dead. And I didn't want to cheat you, or them, of that."

"And Annie? Does she know?"

"No, no. Not yet. I wanted to tell you first."

He put his hands on her shoulders, concern suddenly softening his face. "How are you feeling, Izzy?"

"Just fine. Good, in fact."

"Here I am . . . feeling sorry for myself, snapping at you. And you're—"

"It's alright."

"Are you sleeping well? Are you getting enough food?"

"Oh, with all the fresh fish and fruit here, I'm eating better than I would back home. And there's plenty of time to sleep. So don't worry yourself. Just think about being a father by springtime."

Joshua shook his head in wonder and smiled. Without warning, he dropped to his knees and placed his right hand against her belly. When her oversized shirt got in the way, he eased his hand under the fabric, so that his palm rested against her flesh. He held his hand against her, moving it slowly around her belly as if searching for something he'd lost in the darkness. "Are you sure you don't show? You feel . . . different. Your sides seem thicker."

"I don't know for sure that I'm pregnant. And my sides aren't thicker."

"You're a woman and a nurse. You know." Joshua wrapped his arms around her and leaned his face against her belly. "We've tried for so long," he said, his voice suddenly stronger and happier than she recalled it having been for quite some time. "I wonder why now?"

"That's a good question. But somehow . . . being here, with you, it seems right."

He stroked her skin with his thumb. He started to speak but then stopped, instead pausing to thank God for this gift. Finally, he said, "I love you, Isabelle. I don't say it nearly enough, I know. But I'd be lost without you."

"You've never been lost, Josh."

"Neither have you."

She smiled. "We haven't had time for it."

"You'll be a wonderful mother. You'll teach our child so much."

Isabelle ran her hands through his hair. He hadn't held her like this in many months, and she was in no hurry for the moment to end. She felt him press his ear against her belly, and smiled. "You won't hear a heartbeat yet. But soon."

"I used to be a submariner, you know. I have a good ear."

"Well, submariner, what do you hear?"

"The two of you," he replied, grinning. "I definitely hear something. And it must be the two of you."

"What does it sound like?"

"Water."

"Water?"

"Doesn't all life come from water?"

Isabelle smiled, dropping to her knees so that she faced him. "I love you too," she said, kissing him. "And I don't say it enough either. I think we're the same in that way. We kind of close ourselves up."

"War does that."

"I know. But we don't have to let it."

"You're right," he said, and then kissed her gently. His hand once again fell to her belly, his thumb stroking her flesh.

"Are you going to walk around camp with your hand under my shirt?"

"Maybe. I don't have a bridge, but I'm still in charge." He kissed her forehead, happily offering another quick prayer of gratitude. "I'd . . . almost lost hope about being a father. I wanted it so much, but . . . but I'd lost hope."

"You deserve this," she replied, finding his eyes. "No one deserves it more."

Joshua didn't avoid her gaze, and Isabelle saw the joy in his face—a joy that had been lacking since long before *Benevolence* sank. She hadn't been certain how he'd react to her news, and now as she looked at him, she felt as close to him as she ever had. He was a good man, and he loved her. And though she was strong and sure of the steps before her, she would be stronger and surer and happier with him at her side.

MUCH LATER IN THE DAY, when the sun had just dropped from the sky, Ratu made his way to Nathan. As he hurried over the cooling sand, Ratu kicked a sea sponge in front of him. Pretending that he was a famous soccer player, he kicked the sponge until he neared the jungle. He then launched it forward, cheering after it struck the middle of the banyan tree.

"Good shot, lad," Nathan said, applauding.

"It was bloody good, wasn't it?" Ratu replied happily. Before Nathan could respond, Ratu asked, "Since the captain is gone, you're the boss, right?"

"I suppose so. But not really."

"Well, since you're the boss, I was wondering if I could take some old palm fronds, light them on fire, and spear all the fish that come to investigate."

Nathan rose from a log. "Fish come to fire?"

"Of course. I tell you, they're just like us—full of curiosity. My father and I used to spear them by the boatload. If you let Big Jake and me light the fronds, everyone could eat delicious fish tonight."

Glancing into the jungle behind him, Nathan wondered about the whereabouts of the captain and his wife. "I don't know. Maybe we should wait until—"

"Oh, you can decide. You won't get into trouble. It's only a few palm fronds. If we hear a plane or see a boat, we'll just throw them in the water."

"Can you keep the fires small?"

"Of course. As small as necessary. Don't worry, Mr. Nathan. Everything will be fine."

"You sure?"

"Sure I'm sure. Now you go back to your photo and just leave the fishing to Big Jake and me."

Despite his reservations, Nathan smiled at Ratu's obvious excitement. "My son would get along with you so well. He's about your age, and loves getting into mischief."

"We'd be great mates, then."

"Mates?"

"Friends. We'd be great friends."

"Ah, yes, you certainly would."

Ratu thanked Nathan again and ran into the jungle, collecting almost as many dried palm fronds as he could carry. He then grabbed a burning stick from the fire, and shuffled down the beach to where Jake sat beside a barnacle-encrusted boulder. Ten spears were stuck in the sand.

"Bloody marvelous work with the spears, Big Jake," Ratu said.

"It was hardly hard, my little friend. Now tell me how we get them fish."

Ratu pointed to a pair of boulders that stood in waist-deep water. "Easy enough. We put the fronds on the smaller rock. And we light them on fire. And then we just wait. The fish will come. Like they're coming to a party or something. And when they do, we need to only spear the big ones. Don't worry about the little ones. Hit the big ones."

"Hit the little ones, you say?"

"Get stuffed, Big Jake!"

Jake took the fronds and the smoking stick and moved into the sea. After no more than a dozen paces, he came to the smaller boulder. As he started to lay down the fronds, Ratu climbed up the nearby rock. "If this doesn't work," he said, "we'll use the lifeboat. But I think this will work. Now come, light the fronds."

When a fire was consuming the fronds, Jake hurried to the other boulder, which was the size of a car. He picked up a spear and stood next to Ratu. The fronds burned quickly, and in the darkening sky cast light in all directions.

"I reckon we should have brought some logs," Jake said, an immense blade of grass trembling between his lips as he spoke.

"Shhh. A fisherman never talks," Ratu replied. "That's the first rule of fishing."

"I expect that's a mighty hard rule for you."

"It is, Big Jake. It is. Now be quiet and let the fish come."

Jake was beginning to doubt the wisdom of the expedition when a fish suddenly broke the surface next to the other boulder. The fish was small, and he didn't bother to use his spear. Seeing into the dark water was difficult, but the fire certainly helped. Soon another fin sprouted from the sea. Then another and another. Ratu and Jake threw their spears almost simultaneously at a two-foot fish that rose beside the boulder. Both spears hit the fish and it only thrashed for a few heartbeats. Instead of retrieving their catch, they waited for another big fish to arrive. When it did, it also died. This process repeated itself three more times before the flames died out.

After climbing down from the boulder, they picked up four of the five fish they'd struck. One fish had managed to swim off. Ratu wanted to look for it, but seeing how big the other fish were, Jake promised him that they had more than enough to feed everyone. Jake had also fished as a boy, though the ponds near his family's farm were filled with bluegill, carp, and bass. And so after he stuck their catch on the stoutest spear, he asked Ratu what they'd soon eat.

"Two yellowfin tuna," Ratu replied, "and a dolphin fish and . . . I don't know what that big-eyed, ugly one is. I've never seen it before. You can eat him."

"Why, ain't that real neighborly of you?"

"Oh, put a sock in it, Big Jake."

Jake chuckled, pleased by the weight of their catch. "Did your daddy teach you to toss a spear like that?"

"My father could throw a spear across this harbor. Even you, Big Jake, are not as strong as my father."

Jake's foot struck something hard and he grunted. "Darn coconuts."

"Just watch where you put those giant feet of yours."

"Simpler said than done."

A strong fire burned at camp, and they walked toward it. As they approached the massive banyan tree, Joshua and Nathan strode in their direction. Both men smiled when they saw the catch. "And how did you manage that?" Joshua asked, still thinking about Isabelle's news.

"Easy enough, Captain," Ratu replied. "It's not hard to throw a spear. I could teach you, if you wanted."

"Thanks, but I don't think we need any more hunters with you and Jake around."

"Well, that's certainly true."

The four of them walked to the fire, and Jake set the fish down on some fresh palm fronds. As other members of the group congratulated them on their catch, Jake used the machete to clean the fish. Before long, strips of fish were cooking atop saplings. The smell of the fish permeated the air, and people gathered around the fire, eager to fill their bellies. Jake was proud of Ratu and was quick to tell everyone how good he was with a spear.

Soon each survivor had a sizable piece of fish. And though mosquitoes still bothered them, they still lamented *Benevolence*'s dead, and their fear of the unknown remained strong, for the moment spirits rose. Ratu's excitement about the catch was infectious, and as he spoke of the lobster and tuna and crab that they'd eat each night, the mosquitoes seemed a bit less troublesome, and the sadness and fear were momentarily pushed away. For the first time since *Benevolence* sank, quiet laughter mingled with the crack of the fire and the crash of distant waves.

Pleased with how the night was unfolding, and aware that Ratu's enthusiasm had affected the group, Annie made her way toward him. He was in the midst of telling Nathan about the fish of Fiji. When Annie was a few paces away from them, Isabelle moved toward her and asked with a twist of her head if Annie would follow her to a somewhat distant log. Wordlessly, Annie did just that, brushing some sand from the log and taking a seat. Isabelle grinned, prompting Annie to lean close. "What?" Annie asked. "What on earth are you so aching to tell me about?"

Isabelle playfully put her finger to her lips. "What do you think?" she whispered.

"I have no idea. I don't even—"

"I think I'm pregnant," Isabelle quietly interrupted. "I don't know for sure, but I think it's true."

Annie leaned closer to her sister and tightly hugged her. "Really? That's wonderful! Just wonderful, Izzy! When? When are you due?"

"Seven—"

"And how does it feel? How are you doing?"

"I'm fine. Great, in fact."

"No morning sickness?"

"Not at all. Just a bit tired."

"You've been trying for so long," Annie said excitedly, taking Isabelle's hands in her own. "I'm so, so happy for you. I couldn't be any happier!"

"We're happy too."

"What did Joshua say?"

Isabelle smiled. "He couldn't keep his hands off my belly."

"He couldn't? You're not showing, are you? I don't see anything."

"Oh, maybe just a bit."

Annie put her arm around Isabelle, pulling her closer, hugging her again. "I'm so ready to be an aunt! I wonder if you'll have a girl. There are so many girls in our family. I bet you'll have a girl and I'll . . . I'll teach her to paint. I'm not good, as you know, but I'll teach her anyway. We'll paint with our fingers and make fabulous messes."

"That would be lovely, Annie."

"There's so much that I'll want to show her. Or him."

Isabelle kissed her sister on the cheek. "Let's keep it quiet for now. Joshua isn't sure how he wants to handle it. And I'm not either. I like . . . most of these people. But I'm not ready to tell them about my private life."

"Well, you don't have to share anything you don't want to. Unless we're here for a few more months, of course. Then people might start to wonder about that belly of yours."

Isabelle smiled, pleased that Annie seemed to be in such good spirits. After all, she worried about Annie a great deal. Ever since they were young girls, she'd tried to protect her. And little had changed through the years. "I should go back to Joshua," Isabelle said. "He's watching me and waiting for me."

"Then go. We'll talk later. But can we start thinking of names? That's going to be such fun."

"You think I haven't started already?" Isabelle asked, grinning, making her way back to Joshua.

Annie brushed sand from her legs and walked to Jake, who was handing out more pieces of cooked fish. Seeing that Akira had finished his first portion, Annie took a piece to him. As usual, she looked at his leg first. The bandage bore no blood, and she felt relieved. "Hello," she said warmly, thinking of Isabelle's news, buoyed by her sister's good fortune. She knelt beside Akira on his bed of palm fronds. He was about ten paces from the fire and everyone else, and Annie couldn't help but wonder if he felt this distance. "Would you like to be closer to the fire?" she asked.

"No, this location is suitable for me. But thank you."

"I brought you some fish."

Akira eyed the tuna, wishing that it were raw. How he loved raw tuna. "Thank you," he said politely.

She smiled. "It wasn't terribly difficult."

He watched a spark from the fire travel up into the night, flickering as if it had metamorphosed into a firefly. "May I tell you something?" he asked, prompted by her obvious good cheer. "Something about you?"

Suddenly self-conscious, Annie brushed sand from her cheek. "About me?"

"Yes."

"Well, I suppose if you'd like to."

He nodded, noticing how the blue had faded from her eyes now that the sun had departed. Her eyes are like the sea, he thought to himself. He then wondered why he continued to seek her out, why he so wanted to talk with her. Before answers emerged, he heard himself say, "I do not think, Annie, that you are unable to hear."

"What?"

"Your poem. In it you said that you are unable to hear. I do not think this is true."

"But you . . . you don't really know me."

He blew an ant from his shoulder. "Of course, I agree. But still. I think you hear very well."

"Why?"

"Because you listen. And people who listen are able to hear."

Annie glanced at Ratu, who ran into her view as he chased something in the sand. She then looked for Isabelle and smiled when she saw her sister laugh. "I listen . . . because I don't have any answers," she finally replied. "And so I ask questions. Lots of them. And sometimes I'm impatient for answers."

Akira stretched his wounded leg. "Would you like to hear an old Japanese saying?"

"Please."

"It says that patience is the art of letting life carry you."

Annie let the words echo in her mind. "That's nice. Beautiful, really. But maybe easier to say than to do. For me, at least."

"For most people, I think."

She smiled. "Thank you, Akira, for teaching me about the poems. Maybe I'll come to you tomorrow with another."

He bowed slightly. "I would most enjoy that."

Still buoyed by the thought of the new life within Isabelle, Annie reached out to gently touch his knee. "Sleep well tonight."

Akira said good night and watched as she walked back toward her sister. Much to his surprise, he suddenly felt alone in her absence. It was as if a present had been stolen from him—something beautiful and wondrous and enchanting. Though he'd coveted this gift for so very long, and though now he could almost touch it, he felt as if it lay beyond his outstretched fingers and was impossibly outside his reach.

DAY FIVE

A silk flower seeks
To rise from a hardened ground.
Light falls on gold skin.

Uncertain of Tomorrow

The city smoldered about him. He had seen cities die before, but something was different about these torn streets and buildings. It was the screams, of course. They should have ended long ago. Usually the screams stopped a few hours after the fighting stopped. But here in Nanking, a city that should never have been defended, screams rose from gardens and temples, homes and public squares. These miserable, often inhuman sounds made him wince as if they were bullets striking his flesh—small pieces of hot steel that pierced him from all angles.

He carried some rank and was known as a man of war. Thus he tried to walk the streets as often as possible. On this walk he'd already saved a pregnant woman from being bayoneted, and had also shot a soldier who refused his orders to untie a dying boy. Of course, even with his rank and reputation, he stayed far from the large concentrations of soldiers and civilians, as most of the screams came from such gatherings and the bloodlust could not be stopped by one man alone.

At the edge of the city, where a few families still hid and were still found, he walked with his hands on his pistol and sword. He moved past many sights known to him—piles of ruined armaments and animals and people. Houses had collapsed atop the street, and he often climbed over these stony, dismembered skeletons to continue on. High above, unchallenged Zeros darted to and from distant battles.

He heard them laugh before he saw her, heard her cry from within a group of boisterous soldiers. A booted foot rose and fell, and a female voice pleaded. His heart suddenly skipping, he hurried forward. Eight men surrounded her. They must have just discovered her, for her clothes were somewhat intact, though her face was bloodied. She likely had not seen ten years come and go. Her delicate hands clung to a toy horse that she protected rather than herself.

Though two of the men bore higher rank than he, his horror at her looming fate propelled him onward. Speaking forcefully, he used lost words—ancient sentiments of the samurai—to try to shame these men. They paused, and he moved between them. The little girl looked up at him, pleading with terror-stricken eyes and a quivering mouth. Her face was already swelling from their beating, and through bleeding lips she begged him to help her. She was young and innocent and desperate, and he leaned forward, reaching for her.

A pistol pressed hard against his temple. The barrel was still hot. He froze. She continued to beg him as his flesh burned. His assailant ordered him to rise. She frantically shook her head at these words, her fingers clinging to his hand, her toy horse caught between them. The gun pushed violently against his skull and he was given a choice—to stand or die. He did not want to die, and so as his tears dropped on her leg, he rose. Someone then took his weapons and roughly pushed him away. The little girl screamed. He heard fabric tear and he hurried forward like a beaten dog. As he started to run, her screams grew louder—screams that ravaged him until he blindly stumbled into a deep bomb crater and was knocked unconscious.

Akira awoke from his dream with her screams still reverberating within him. Silent sobs wracked him, and he put his balled fists against his eyes. He saw her precious face and he started to crawl, as if he could flee his dream, as if this past could be expunged from his memory. He crawled until his tears mixed with the sea. His fingers dug into the sand

and he squeezed fistfuls of this gritty wetness until his knuckles whitened and his hands shook. He wrung the sand with all his might—each granule a demon to be smothered, each ounce of the earth he held something upon which he could thrust his horror and grief and rage.

"I'm so . . . so . . . so very sorry," he whispered in Japanese, bowing until his forehead touched the sea, his hands finally unfurling and clumps of compressed sand dropping. "I . . . I should have stopped . . . those beasts. They should not . . . I should not have let them touch you. Oh, how lovely and pure and good you were. How beautiful. And how . . . how terribly I failed you."

Akira remained on his hands and knees for some time. When he finally ceased to tremble, he sat up. He remembered the girl's fingers against his and, moaning, he looked to the stars for her. To his dismay, no trace of her was present. In fact, nothing of any solace existed at that moment. No girl. No peace. No religion. No hope. In this void he saw her pleading eyes, saw himself turn away. He cursed himself then, cursed his entire being. How he hated who he had become.

Gradually, Akira's tears subsided and his heart slowed. His thoughts wandered. He realized that if he were alone on the island, he'd do the only honorable thing left to him and end his life. He'd read the death poems of samurai—haikus written just before noble men forced their own swords into their own bellies. Beauty dwelled in those words, and were he alone, he'd write a haiku in the sand for the little girl and then begin his journey toward rebirth.

But Akira was not alone. And though he cared nothing for the men nearby, he felt strangely linked to Annie. She had somehow briefly brought him back into his former life, into a place that once gave him the peace and religion and hope that he so lacked now. Without question, she reminded him of his past—when he helped people instead of hunted them—but she also kindled a part of him that he'd not known.

Akira had never believed in fate, but as gentle waves lapped at his flesh, he wondered if he was meant to be here. These nurses, who had saved so many, who had so compassionately taken care of him, could die soon. If his countrymen landed on this beach, they might well hurt these women. They might hurt Annie. She had told him that she'd always been afraid, and he couldn't endure the thought of what evil might befall her.

Rising to his feet, Akira closed his eyes and imagined his homeland. He saw pagodas and water lilies and white-faced geishas. And he saw his fate as he suddenly imagined it. *May my ancestors forgive me; I will betray my own people,* he thought, wiping his face of sand and tears. *I'll hide her. I'll hide her and pray that they will not find us. And if we are found, and if they seek to harm her, then I will fight them. I will be the warrior I was before Nanking, and I won't fail her as I did the little girl. And if they are too many, then I'll take her life and also end my own. And she won't die alone.*

Akira glanced toward camp, toward where Annie lay sleeping. *I won't let anyone hurt you,* he promised. *No matter what has to be done, or what may be done to me, I'll never see such hurt again.*

Dawn had recently unfolded when Joshua and Jake reached the top of one of the hills. Both men sweated heavily, and upon reaching the crest, removed their shirts. Though their camp was hidden by the thick foliage below, a tendril of smoke rose through the trees, dissipating into the heavy air. A trio of figures walked the beach—the women, perhaps. Beyond them, the sea looked like an endless sheet of gold. Past the confines of the harbor, this sheet shimmered with the movement of the bigger waves. No ships encroached upon the water—only a splattering of distant islands.

"Thanks for joining me," Joshua said, still slightly winded from the climb.

"It was a mighty fine walk, Captain," Jake replied, removing a leaf's stem from his teeth. "And there sure ain't no views like this back home."

"Missouri, isn't it?"

Jake smiled, pleased that the captain remembered. "Sure is, Captain. As the feathered friend flies, ain't but two hundred miles from Chicago."

Joshua nodded, liking Jake. "You must be wondering why I brought you here."

"Oh, I expect you'll tell me."

"I brought you here because I trust you. You've served me on two ships, and from the beginning I've felt that you were a man I could count on. You're an able, good man, Jake."

"You can trust me, sir. But as far as being able . . . well, it ain't easy to make a silk purse out of a sow's ear."

Joshua shook his head. "You're no sow's ear, Jake. I can't think of anyone I'd rather have with us on this beach."

"Thank you kindly, Captain."

"I'm going to tell you something, and I want you to do as I ask." Jake nodded but said nothing, and so Joshua continued, "Isabelle thinks she's pregnant."

Jake paused only for a moment before reaching out to grasp Joshua's hand. "Congratulations, Captain. That's mighty fine news."

"Thank you, Jake. It really is something." Joshua shook his head as if he still couldn't believe it. "In seven months I'll be a father. Imagine that."

"A darn good thing to imagine, I reckon."

"Yes, yes, it is." Joshua thought he heard a distant drone and scanned the sky for planes. Seeing nothing, he said, "If something should happen to me, I want you to watch over the women."

"Captain, ain't nothing gonna—"

"I want you to watch over them as if they were your own blood. Do you understand that? Your own blood."

Jake briefly closed his eyes. "Yes, sir. I do. But might you oblige me with a request?"

"That depends on the request."

"If any job's dodgy, I want it. I want that job, Captain."

"I can't do that. I can't give every dangerous detail to you."

"No offense, Captain, but I expect you can. You think of that sweet little baby and you give that darn detail to me."

Joshua took a deep breath and let out an equally long exhale. "Help me find some places to hide, and hopefully none of us will have to do anything dangerous. We can simply hide and wait for the cavalry to arrive. That's all I want. When it comes to this, I'm not afraid to be a coward."

"Better to be the beak of a chicken than the tail of an elephant."

Joshua smiled. "I believe you're right."

"Ain't no doubt about it."

A gust of wind buffeted them, and Joshua instinctively looked for signs of bad weather. His gaze drifted across the spot where *Benevolence* rested, and a sudden sense of loss surged within him. "I'm sorry, Jake," he said, shaking his head, his fingers again twisting beads that didn't exist.

"For what, Captain?"

Joshua gestured toward the sea. "For her being on the bottom. For you being stuck here."

Jake absently placed the stem in the corner of his mouth. "Them people on *Benevolence*, they saved a lot of soldiers, Captain. As sure as rain's wet they did. Better to have brought them all this way, to have saved as many as you did, than to have stayed home."

Joshua nodded slowly. "You're talking about . . . the greater good?"

"Yes, Captain. I suppose so."

"But . . . does much feel good to you?"

The engineer pursed his lips. "Ain't much that's good, Captain. But maybe enough. Maybe . . . things can begin again."

"If things . . . begin again, where will you go?"

"Home, I expect. To the farm."

"Do you miss it?"

Jake smiled. "Parts of it. I don't much miss manure. But I sure do miss my momma's cooking. And my daddy's pipe. And that soil. I reckon them's enough reasons to go home."

Joshua nodded, aware that Jake was one of those rare people who forever seemed content and happy. Even back on *Benevolence*, when he was covered in grease and nursing bloody fingers, he'd always seemed pleased. "Why, Jake, did you leave your momma's cooking and your daddy's pipe?" Joshua asked. "Why come to this war?"

"To do my part, Captain."

"As simple as that?"

"I suspect so. I didn't see how I could stay on the farm and shoo grasshoppers when the whole world was bleeding. I had to do something. They weren't real eager to let me fight, so I started fixing engines. I'd done such work on the farm, so it came natural to me."

Joshua looked at the man before him. Jake's face was proud, defined by sculpted cheekbones, sharp eyes, and a strong jaw. His coffee-colored skin was smooth and, bearing a glaze of sweat, seemed almost polished. Jake was well over six feet tall, and his body looked as if it could lift a house. More important, Joshua knew that Jake was bright and quick-witted. How utterly foolish, Joshua thought, not to let this man fight. "The world is bleeding, isn't it?" he finally replied.

"Yes, Captain. I do believe it is."

"Will you look after the women if something should happen to me?"

"As if they were my own kin."

Joshua extended his hand. "Thank you. I'll sleep better knowing that."

Jake glanced toward the jungle. "Let's go find a cave, Captain. A hidden cave that will be just right for us chickens."

"I like your thinking."

Joshua followed Jake down the hill. After almost a year of war, Joshua had seen enough men to know who was truly a man. And though Jake was humble and often overlooked, he was without question a man who Joshua was glad to have beside him. Men like Jake would win the war.

Isabelle and Annie walked toward Scarlet, who was in the process of tidying up camp. Aside from the flicker of the fire, Scarlet represented about the only nearby movement. Nathan and Ratu collected coconuts fifty feet down the beach, Roger was in the jungle, and Akira had sat by the sea's edge all morning. Annie had been surprised to awaken and see him there, with his feet in the water and his gaze fixed somewhere in the distance. She'd considered saying hello but decided that he must have wanted to be alone.

With some of the men gone, Annie had thought it would be a good time for a swim. She hadn't bathed in several days and was certain that she'd have to scrape the grime from her. Isabelle had immediately welcomed the idea, and now the two sisters trudged through the deep sand until Scarlet finally looked up.

"We're going swimming," Annie said. "Want to join us?"

Scarlet's gaze traveled up and down the beach. "Where?"

"A secluded spot not far from here. Near the big rocks where you caught the crabs."

Scarlet rolled a depleted coconut toward the water. "Why not?"

The three women walked in the opposite direction of Ratu and Nathan. The tide had been high the previous night, and the beach was littered with shells, driftwood, jellyfish, and even a few more bottles from *Benevolence*. The patches of sand free of such debris seemed to glow in the morning sun. The harbor appeared to be an even deeper turquoise than usual and, looking forward to getting wet, Annie increased her pace. Before long, they came to the gathering of barnacle-encrusted boulders. Walking twenty paces beyond the boulders, she was pleased to see that their camp disappeared behind the rocks. The sea here was quiet and dominated by soft sand. It would be an ideal place to swim.

"What are we waiting for?" Annie asked, stripping to her undergarments. She balled up her oversized clothes, set them in the shallows, and waded into the water. The sea was warm and gentle, and for a moment Annie had a hard time believing that it had almost killed her. A school of red-finned fish swam before her, darting into deeper and clearer water. She followed them until the sea reached her belly button. She didn't want to go any farther, and so she held her breath and dropped beneath the miniature waves. Once underwater, Annie scrubbed her scalp, then ran her fingers through her tangled hair. She opened her mouth and swished water through her teeth.

Rising to the surface, Annie closed her eyes and lay atop the waves, basking in the sun. She'd never experienced an ocean as warm as this one, and sighed contentedly. "Have you ever felt such water?" she asked, removing her bra and underwear.

"Not even close," Isabelle replied, vigorously scrubbing her naked body with sand.

Annie spied something white below and reached down into the clear water to grasp a sand dollar. She studied her find before placing it back in the sand. "Why don't we just stay here?" she asked. "Why rush back into war?"

Isabelle stopped scrubbing. "People need us, Annie. We've work to do."

"I can't wait to get off this island," Scarlet added. "I'm already sick to death of bugs and bananas and the awful heat."

Annie followed her sister's lead and used sand to clean her body. "You think we're going to lose this war if you're stuck here for a few days?"

"Those boys need our help," Isabelle replied, rubbing her arms so hard that they turned red. "You know that as well as I do."

Annie started to respond but stopped, not wanting to admit that she was tired of seeing torn bodies, tired of watching boys die. A part of her agreed with Isabelle, and this part intended to return to the front lines. But she was also in no rush to leave the island. After all, on the island she could sleep without constantly worrying about her patients. She could breathe. She could walk the beach with her sister and write poetry with a gentle man.

"Don't you ever get tired, Izzy, or you, Scarlet?" Annie asked. "Sometimes . . . sometimes aboard *Benevolence* I just felt overwhelmed."

"I'm always tired," Scarlet replied. "I think I've aged ten years in the past six months."

Isabelle nodded. "And I'm tired too. But just think of those boys, Annie. Think of what they've been through. What they—"

"I always think of the boys," Annie interrupted, dropping two handfuls of sand. "Do you know how many nights I've cried myself to sleep thinking of them?"

Scarlet stripped off her undergarments. She then looked east. "Last I heard, my little brothers were headed to North Africa," she said quietly. "To help the Brits with Rommel. It's a big secret of course, but they told me. For all I know, they're already in the desert, fighting in some awful place . . . so far from home. Jimmy runs a tank crew, and Bobby defuses bombs. I still can't get over that . . . my baby brother drives a tank. He's only a boy. It seems like a few years ago I was teaching him to ride a bike. And he . . . he was so little. So happy and innocent." Scarlet's eyes watered at these words and she began to cry.

Isabelle and Annie moved closer to her. "I'm sorry," Isabelle said, putting an arm around her fellow nurse. "But I heard that Rommel's finally on the run."

Annie wondered what it was like to have two brothers fighting in the deserts of North Africa, facing a legendary man who'd rarely tasted defeat. She thought of her fiancé, Ted, who was battling Germans somewhere in Europe. Though she didn't miss Ted as much as she once thought she would, she worried for him all the same. "You'll see your brothers again, Scarlet," she said. "I realize I've no right to say that, but I believe it."

"Why?" Scarlet asked.

"Because this war can't go on forever. And if one of your brothers is a tank commander and the other is defusing bombs, then they're bright and they'll make it through this."

Scarlet wiped away her tears. "They are bright boys. Their marks at school were always much better than mine."

Annie was about to respond when she saw a trio of fins slicing through the water not far from them. Her immediate thought was that the newcomers were sharks, but as she grabbed her companions and pulled them toward shore, she realized that dolphins, not sharks, were paying them a visit. "Look," she said excitedly, pointing. "Three dolphins!"

"How do you know they're dolphins?" Isabelle asked, still moving toward shore.

"See their curved backs? And look at how they play!"

The trio of dolphins, which were about a hundred feet away, swam with great speed and with what Annie thought to be exuberance. They often rose above the sea's surface as if seeking to glance at the nearby island. One suddenly leapt out of the water, its gray body glistening in the sun. The dolphin reentered the sea with hardly a splash, darting underwater with exquisite grace. The same creature leapt again, its arching body stretching skyward.

Does he see us? Annie asked herself. She waved at the dolphins, wondering what they might think of her. For a moment she was tempted to swim out into the deeper water, but seeing how dark that region was, she remained motionless. As Isabelle and Scarlet renewed their conversation, Annie thought about what she'd witnessed. Impulsively, she decided to try to create a haiku. Her initial words were far too clumsy to bring life to the memory of the dolphins, but she lowered herself into the temperate water and continued to think. She patiently mixed words and feelings, remembering what Akira had told her. And a few minutes after the dolphins had vanished, she whispered, "Leaping from the sea, / Bright new sights are bound in blue. / Worlds so far and close."

As she scrubbed herself with sand, Annie wondered what Ted would say to such a poem. Would he smile or laugh? Would her words further convince him that she was forever lost in a land of fantasy? Or would he come to peace with the notion that she was different than he? That she enjoyed splicing together pleasing phrases and painting impossible scenes? Annie wished he was with her in the water, so that she could watch his face, repeat her poem, and have her questions answered.

Suddenly, Scarlet wiped her eyes and sniffed, and Annie chastised herself for being so self-indulgent. After finding the sand dollar that she'd discarded, she hurried to Scarlet, pressed the simple treasure into her hand, and tried once again to reassure her that her brothers would live through the war.

BACK AT HIS USUAL station at camp, Akira watched the three women walk toward him. Each was wearing a man's khaki-colored shirt and shorts, with belts fashioned of rope keeping the shorts from falling to the sand. Annie was between Isabelle and Scarlet and was a full head shorter than each. Otherwise, the two sisters looked very much alike. Akira knew from earlier encounters that the sun had already changed their appearance, transforming their former honey-colored skin into a deeper shade of brown. Several freckles had gained prominence on their cheeks and shoulders. The sun had even lightened their hair, slightly bleaching their bangs.

Akira's gaze lingered on Annie, who carried something, and twice dropped the object as she gestured to her sister. He smiled, realizing how often Annie used her hands to emphasize her points. Though the concept of doing so was foreign to him, he liked that her hands were often in motion. She was excitable and unique and utterly compelling.

When the women drew near, he pretended to be writing in the sand. To his delight, Annie walked straight toward him. "Did you get enough of the beach this morning?" she asked, sitting down near him.

A vision of the little girl flashed before him. "I . . . I needed to think," he said, forcing thoughts of Nanking away.

"Oh." Annie repositioned her body so that she also faced away from the sun, as he did. "We went for a swim."

"Was it a good swim?"

"Yes. Yes, it was." She looked at his leg. "May I inspect your wound?" He nodded, and she carefully removed his bandage, bringing her hands together in a brief clap when she saw that the stitches had held without exception. The skin on either side of the wound was already starting to bind together. No sign of infection was present, and though having to restitch the wound would ultimately make for a large scar, she felt lucky that he was healing so well.

After leaving Akira briefly to find some disinfectant, Annie returned and started to clean his wound. As she carefully worked, she wondered how he'd been hurt. Though she didn't like such thoughts, she almost always asked herself this question when attending to a wounded soldier. Akira's injury was obviously from a bullet and seemed large enough to have come from a high-caliber weapon at close range. But she knew little beyond that.

She put a fresh dressing and bandage on the wound, and then took a drink of coconut milk. He thanked her, and she said, "You should start to exercise that leg."

"What is best?"

"A bit of walking, I think." She wrapped up the old bandage in a palm frond. "Care to join me?" she asked, not ready to retire beneath the shade of the banyan tree, and believing that some company would lift his spirits.

Akira smiled. Wanting to please her, he tried to rise to his feet without appearing to be stiff or in pain. He almost succeeded. Glancing up and down the beach, he said, "So much beauty. Where is it best to start?"

Annie held him by the elbow and proceeded to lead him toward the water. Once the sea touched their feet they began to walk near the shoreline. Though the sun was far along in its journey across the sky, its touch was still fairly hot. Fortunately, a breeze kept the air refreshing. To Annie, the island seemed unusually alive. Crabs scurried about the sand, ivory-colored birds dove upon unsuspecting fish, butterflies added color to the sky, and trees danced in the wind.

"Tell me about where you lived as a boy," Annie said, holding his elbow tightly so that he wouldn't stumble.

Her directness pleased him, and he smiled. "My home was in the mountains near Kyoto, which is the old capital of Japan. The city sits within mountains, green mountains full of streams and forests and ancient temples."

"It sounds wonderful. Almost like . . . like another world."

"When I am in those mountains, it is another world."

"Can you tell me more?"

"Of course," he said, trying not to grimace at the tightness in his leg. "About what would you like to hear?"

"Oh, tell me about . . . about what you used to do, before you knew anything about poetry or . . . or homework."

He smiled. "As a boy . . . I did so many things. But mostly, I would climb mountainside trails made by monks two thousand years ago. In the springtime, cherry blossoms would fall like snow on the trails. And in the autumn, the leaves of maple trees were such a bright orange that the mountains looked to be on fire."

"How beautiful."

"It was. I would often climb a mountain and sit and watch the city. Many times I sat under my umbrella in the rain." Akira looked at her, noting that though she was small and thin, she tried her best to support him as he walked. "I sometimes think of myself as . . . as this boy . . . as if he were a different person than me," he added, speaking quite slowly. "After school, his mother would give him a sweet, and he would climb those green mountains. He would study ants. He would listen to crickets. He would read while atop a rock."

Annie helped Akira step over a weather-beaten tree trunk that had been marooned on the beach. "Do you miss this boy?" she asked, sensing that he did.

"Yes. I do miss him. Very much. In fact, I sometimes . . . sometimes I wonder where he has gone."

"Oh, I don't think such a boy changes that much. He may have grown into a man, and maybe being a man has brought him to different places. But I think he could still walk those trails and still climb those trees."

Akira paused, gazing at her face, her eyes. He had never experienced anyone speaking to him this way—telling him how he was perceived. In Japan, people might have found such a comment presumptuous. "I hope you are right," he finally said, pleased that she could so readily imagine him as a boy.

"Well, I don't think a man who writes poetry in the sand is that different from a boy who follows ants up a mountainside."

He smiled at her. "And what of you? May I hear of your childhood?"

She started walking again, leading him over the uneven sand. "My childhood was good and bad. My parents are wonderful. And my sister, as you know, is wonderful. The four of us lived in a cottage in California. We had a dog and a garden, and life was very good." Annie watched a miniature crab disappear into a nearby hole. "But when I was nine, I almost died from diphtheria. That was the bad. The terrible, really. It . . . changed my childhood. For two years afterward, I hardly left my house. I was afraid of everything. Cars. Strangers. Getting sick. I just . . . I just didn't want to be hurt again. I still don't."

He shook his head. "I am so sorry about that." She didn't reply, and he leaned closer. "May I ask you something?"

"Of course."

"If you were so afraid, why did you come to this war?"

Annie started to speak but stopped. She'd asked herself this same question dozens of times, and had never discovered the right answer. "To tell you the truth, I don't really know," she finally said. "I've never had any . . . direction. Never wanted to work to achieve a certain goal because I didn't want to dedicate my life to something and then not be around to enjoy it. Though you'd never believe it, I was like Isabelle when I was a little girl, working so hard to do everything right. But then I almost died, and everything changed."

"But the war . . . it is hard work, yes?"

"Exactly. I finally decided to stop running. But I'm not sure if I have. My . . . my fiancé once called me a coward, and I think that he was right."

"A coward?"

"He had a reason . . . a good reason for saying it."

"You are no coward," Akira replied. "I have seen many such people. In China, I saw terrible, terrible things. The men that did those things were cowards."

"I have no idea what it feels like to be brave," she confessed, her free hand swinging upward and opening as if to emphasize her point. "What does it feel like?"

He briefly thought of those he had saved and then the little girl. "For a time, I was brave. I was good. But then I was not."

Annie sensed sorrow creeping into his mood, and she did not want his first walk upon his mended leg to be a sad one. And so she said, "I thought of a poem this morning."

"You did? May I ask what it is?"

"We were swimming, and three dolphins came by. One leapt from the water, and to see it . . . well, I wish you had seen it."

"May I please hear your poem?"

"You promise once again that you won't laugh? That you won't think I'm a silly girl?"

"Yes. I give you my promise."

Annie briefly closed her eyes, reliving the memory, re-creating the words. Her heartbeat quickening, she told him her poem. After she finished, only the kiss of the waves upon the shore could be heard. "What do you think?" she finally asked.

"I think," he said, smiling, "that I may have saved a poet."

His words pleased her greatly, and a sudden and unexpected urge to pull him into her arms almost overcame her. Annie felt inexplicably drawn to him, as if he were a colorful flower and she had wings instead of legs. Though Ted was handsome and charming, she'd never been so enticed by him. In fact, she hadn't even known that she was capable of such powerful feelings.

"Thank you," she said finally, managing to resist pulling him closer. "You know, I'm glad it was you who saved me."

He looked into her eyes and smiled. "It was a good swim, yes?"

"A good swim," she replied, grinning. "Now, here," she said, pointing beyond the boulders, "is where we saw the dolphins. Let's look for them."

Though his leg was no longer so stiff and he could have easily walked on his own, Akira continued to gently lean against Annie. He sensed that she wanted him to need her, that helping him heal was somehow a part of the path she longed to follow. He wasn't certain, however, if she saw him as anyone more than a patient with whom she had developed an unforeseen friendship. He hoped she saw him as more. For a reason that he didn't altogether understand, he wanted to be special in her eyes, to be someone who provided her with solace and sanctuary. Akira had never been such a person, and to his immense surprise, as he walked along the beach with this foreigner who so inspired him, he wanted to do just that—to make her smile and feel as if she were not alone in the world.

DAY SIX

The earth is burning,
Blackened by machines and men.
Raindrops are lost tears.

Fire in the Sky

In the half-light of dawn, the drone of planes came first, a hum that rose in pitch and volume as engines neared. The pulse of numerous machine guns followed, the sound of airborne warfare strangely rhythmic. Thin orange lines raced across the blue-black air. The sky was suddenly illuminated by explosions of every shape and size. Flying shadows shuddered and burst. The screams of dying planes rose to earsplitting levels as the fragile machines tumbled from the sky. These lopsided fireballs cartwheeled into the sea and vanished.

On the beach, the nine survivors from *Benevolence* stumbled from their makeshift beds. Isabelle and Annie rushed to Joshua, Jake held Ratu against his chest, and Roger immediately climbed their banyan tree to get a better view. Following Joshua's orders, Nathan did his best to put out their campfire. And Akira and Scarlet hurried toward the water with their eyes fixated on the heavens.

The air battle continued. Joshua, Roger, and Akira understood it best—each able to discern an almost full squadron of bombers with a half-dozen fighter escorts. Another group of fighter planes was attacking the slower bombers. To Annie, guessing which force was American seemed impossible in the faint light. Joshua suspected that the attacking fighters were his comrades, but wasn't sure. Several of the bombers were destroyed in vast eruptions of fire, while two others slowly arched from the sky to disintegrate into the ocean. Many of the attacking fighters were so bent on annihilating the bombers that they themselves became ripe targets. Explosions illuminated the underbellies of clouds as if some sort of bizarre lightning storm assaulted the sky.

The battle—as ferocious as it was—lasted only a few minutes. As soon as the attacking fighters wheeled away, Joshua started hurriedly giving orders. He was certain he saw at least one parachute descend to the sea. "A survivor will likely be armed," he said, wondering how to best protect his wife and unborn child, far more worried about them than himself. "Nathan, conceal the camp and pull everyone back into the jungle. And please do it fast."

Roger, who'd dropped from the tree as soon as Joshua spoke, stepped to the lifeboat and quickly produced a coil of rope. "I'll tie up the monkey," he said, gesturing toward Akira, eager to humiliate him. "I'll gag him too."

Joshua nodded. "Better safe than sorry."

"I'll—"

"But, Roger, don't hurt him. You hear me?"

"He's a Nip. Not a—"

"I asked if you heard me. Did you, Lieutenant? Or do I have to repeat myself?"

Hating the fact that Joshua saw fit to order him around, Roger tried to suppress his sudden rage. "I heard plenty," he finally replied, his hands squeezing the rope, a relentless headache adding to his anger. "Now, if you don't mind, I'll tie up the yellow bastard."

Annie witnessed their exchange and hurried to stand before Akira. "You can't be serious!"

"Annie," Joshua replied, "he's with the enemy and we—"

"What's wrong with you? He saved my life and he's my patient! And I won't have him tied up and gagged!" Furious, Annie stuck her hands out, holding Roger at bay.

"It's for our protection!" Joshua said, concerned that they were losing valuable time, and in no mood for such a debate. "He'll stay tied and gagged until this is over."

"He's no threat!" Annie replied.

"I'll be the judge of that! It's my responsibility!"

"He's my patient and my responsibility!"

"We don't have time for this," Joshua said, thrusting his forefinger in her direction. "Not one bit."

"Then leave him be!"

"Annie, you're putting us all in danger. And you have no right to do that. Do you understand? Now let's get it over with."

"No. We don't—"

"We're going to do this. Right now!"

Roger stepped forward, roughly pushing her aside. "Get out of my way, you stupid little skirt."

Without thought, Annie slapped him. She didn't mean for her blow to be hard, but in the dim light Roger failed to see it coming, and it landed with some force upon his cheek. Cursing, he dropped the rope and reached for her.

"Enough!" Akira shouted, moving protectively in front of Annie. "Tie me up! Tie me up now!"

Roger threw Akira aside. "Shut your mouth, Jap! I'll break your—"

"You'll stand down!" Joshua shouted, grabbing Roger by the shoulders and yanking him backward. "You'll stand down and you'll do it now!"

Roger spun to face Joshua. He balled a fist, but suddenly Jake and Nathan stood beside their captain. His rage nearly overwhelming, Roger resisted the powerful urge to launch himself into the other seamen. He remained still, abruptly craving a cigarette to ease his throbbing head. Cursing again, he picked up the rope and thrust it into Joshua's hands. "You tie up your Nip."

"I will," Joshua replied. "And you will assist in concealing the camp. Do it well. Then I want you and Jake to meet me in the jungle fifty feet south of the banyan tree. Nathan, take everyone else back into the jungle. Wait there until I send for you." Joshua muttered something, glanced at the sea, and then started to tie up Akira.

Annie put her hand on Joshua's elbow. "We don't—"

"Stop it, Annie," Isabelle interrupted, stepping forward. "For the love of God, stop it right now and come with me. He'll be fine."

"We've never gagged or tied up a patient!" Annie said, ignoring Isabelle's outstretched hand. "It goes against everything we stand for!"

Isabelle grabbed Annie's elbow. "We've never been stuck on an island before either, have we? There could be Japanese coming ashore! And he could shout to them! Now, stop being so obstinate and come with me!"

Annie shook off her sister's grip and hurried into the jungle. After a few paces, she tripped on an unseen root and went sprawling to the dirt. Not bothering to rise, she hugged her knees to her chest and began to cry. She'd grown accustomed to not thinking of war upon the island, but war had once again found her, ripping her apart as it always did.

JOSHUA, JAKE, AND ROGER lay at the edge of the jungle, peering out over the harbor. The sun had started to rise, and the sand and sea glowed faintly. Joshua held the machete, while Roger and Jake each wielded a spear. "I saw a parachute," Joshua whispered, still furious about the confrontation but doing his best to face the situation at hand. "It would have fallen not far from here."

"Did it drop from that sputtering bomber, Captain?" Jake asked.

"Yes."

"Then I spied it too."

Joshua turned to Roger. "And you? What did you see?"

Roger had a sudden urge to thrust his spear into the captain's mouth, to listen to him scream. "The same as you," he heard himself reply, even as he continued to fantasize about what he could do with his fire-hardened spear.

"Jake," Joshua said, trying to slow his breath, "your eyes are younger and better than mine. What do you see?"

"My eyes, Captain, feel older than the hills and twice as dusty, but I do see something."

"What? What, Jake?"

"A man, I reckon." The engineer pointed far out into the harbor. "Do you spy him, Captain? I think he's . . . it sure looks like he's swimming."

"Yes, I see something." Joshua briefly closed his eyes to think. "But we're not going to do anything until we determine if he's American or Japanese. If he's a Jap, we're going to wait until the right moment to jump him. Let's not kill him, if we can help it. He might have some useful information." Joshua watched the man slowly draw nearer. "When I point my finger at him, we'll jump him. But for now, follow me."

Estimating where the man would come ashore, Joshua moved quietly through the underbrush. He periodically peered from the jungle to watch the man, who floated on his back and kicked awkwardly toward the beach. Content with their position, Joshua held up his fist, and the three Americans stopped. They then lay down, each positioning himself beneath the undergrowth so that he had a clear view of the harbor.

As the stranger approached, Joshua's heart began to race. When the airman neared the beach, he rolled to his stomach and slowly waded ashore. He must have been injured, for his movements were unsteady.

"He sure ain't from Arkansas," Jake whispered.

Disappointed that the airman was Japanese, Joshua quietly replied, "Remember, when I point, we go. If he draws a gun, kill him. But otherwise, let's take him alive. No words from here on out."

The airman crawled from the sea to the sand. He removed his life jacket, revealing a blue coat. He also wore some kind of hood and flight goggles. A holster hugged his waist. The man stood up slowly, took a few halting steps, and then collapsed. Immediately, Joshua thrust his finger forward, and the three Americans silently sprang from the jungle.

They ran beside one another, and by the time the airman heard the shift of sand, they were upon him. Roger and Jake each dove on one of his arms, and as he struggled, Joshua groped for the airman's holster, which happened to be empty. When their captive continued to fight, Roger hit him hard in the back of the neck. The man went limp.

Joshua used the airman's own belt to tie his hands. He then searched him for other weapons. A dagger was strapped to his calf. Joshua pocketed the blade and continued to look for anything of interest. Other than a compass, a pair of binoculars, a medal of some sort, and a pouch of once-dried squid, the airman carried nothing of value. "Jake, you stay here in case another Jap comes ashore," Joshua said as he stood. "If you see someone else come in, for Pete's sake hurry and get one of us. I don't want you facing anyone alone."

"Sure thing, Captain."

"Wait about an hour and then join us back at camp. An hour ought to be enough." Joshua handed Jake the machete and the airman's binoculars. He then watched the engineer vanish into the nearby jungle. Before Joshua could offer to help, Roger slung the unconscious flier over his shoulder, and without a word, headed toward the distant banyan tree. Joshua picked up the two spears and followed.

Not long after the airman began to moan, Roger dropped him behind the banyan tree, so that the tree shielded him from the beach. They hadn't cleared this space, and Joshua pulled ferns from the ground and pushed rocks aside to give them more room. He whistled loudly, and soon Nathan and the others emerged from deeper in the jungle. Upon seeing the unconscious man, the three nurses stepped forward to inspect him. Roger started to block their way, but Joshua told him to leave them be.

Isabelle found his head wound first—a quarter-sized contusion just above his hairline. "Did you do this?" she asked.

"No," Joshua replied. "He was dazed when he came ashore."

"We'll have to keep a close eye on it," she said, looking for other wounds, pausing only when the injured man groaned.

Joshua was about to ask Annie to remove Akira's gag when he noticed that it was nowhere to be seen. Stifling his frustration toward Nathan for not ensuring that his orders were carried out, he lifted the airman so that his back was against the massive boulder that supported the banyan tree. The man muttered, and Joshua looked to Akira. "What did he say?"

Akira frowned, shaking his head. "Untie my hands first, yes? Then I will tell you what he says."

Joshua swore to himself, aware that he needed to lead for the sake of his family, and feeling that his authority was being usurped on multiple fronts. He moved behind Akira and quickly untied him. "Now, what did he say?"

Akira rubbed his wrists. "A woman's name. All he said was a woman's name."

Away from the gentle breeze of the beach, the air was hot and teemed with bugs. Joshua slapped at a mosquito. He didn't want to be unnecessarily hard on Annie, or even Akira, but he knew that he had to be careful. Two Japanese were now among them, and others could be swimming ashore.

The airman opened his eyes. He blinked repeatedly, swinging his gaze from person to person. Finally, he looked at Akira and spoke in Japanese. Akira answered him, and the two briefly conversed.

"What are you talking about?" Joshua asked.

Akira noted how Roger was perched near the airman, a spear in hand. The American looked as if he hoped the prisoner would try to escape. "He asked me why you removed my bonds," Akira replied.

"Can you tell him," Joshua asked, "that we haven't harmed you? That we'll treat him well if he answers a few simple questions?"

Akira moved toward the prisoner, kneeling on the ground before him. Switching to Japanese, he said, "These people are from an American hospital ship. They are not bad people. But they'd like to ask you several questions."

The man grimaced, shifting against his bonds. "Tell them . . . tell them that my urine's sweet and that they may wet their tongues with it."

"You're unwise to—"

"Tell them that yesterday I put a bomb through the deck of an American destroyer. It was a beautiful sight—more stirring than Mount Fuji. The cowards jumped off that burning ship faster than the sea would take them."

Akira straightened. "And yet you are here. Their prisoner."

"But my bonds are loose. Give me a moment and I'll be ready. You surprise the leader and I'll handle the one with the spear. We must act now, before the big black one returns."

"No," Akira said quickly. "There's no need for anyone to die."

The airman seemed surprised. "No need? Why not? Are you afraid?"

"Not of death."

"Then help me. It's pathetic to be a prisoner. Unforgivable. I'd rather die than live with the shame." The airman's tone was growing sharper and more menacing. "Do you hear me?" he asked harshly. "I'd rather die a thousand deaths than sit here in shame! Where is your honor?"

"My honor is—"

"You shame the emperor!"

"I have been fighting the—"

"We must move now!"

"Wait!"

"The spear! I'll take the spear! And you do the rest!"

In spite of himself, Akira glanced at the spear. And at that moment, he saw Roger's fingers tighten about it, almost as if he understood what might happen. "The American's ready for your move!" Akira said to the prisoner. "Please! There's no need to die!"

"We must all die someday," the airman retorted angrily. "And today is as good as any and better than most."

"Wait!"

"Attack now!" the prisoner said, leaning toward Roger.

"His bonds are loose!" Akira suddenly shouted in English, stepping back.

The airman tried to strike Roger but only managed to free his hands before Roger, Joshua, and Nathan jumped on him. He struggled mightily, screaming at Akira to help. But Akira only stepped away, positioning himself between those involved in the melee and Annie.

Soon the prisoner was completely immobilized by ropes and belts. His hands and feet were bound tightly together and he was tied to a nearby tree. At some point during the fight, he'd managed to bloody Joshua's lip and leave four scratches down the side of Roger's face. As Joshua wiped his lip and spat blood, Roger walked over and viciously kicked the prone airman in the stomach.

"Enough!" Joshua shouted.

"I'm not done—"

"By God, that's enough!"

Roger cursed and strode away from the unconscious man, vanishing into the jungle. Isabelle hurried to Joshua, looking at his lip. "We need to wash this out," she said, eyeing the deep gash. "We'd better cool it off or it's going to swell up like a balloon."

Annie nodded toward the beach. "Go. Wash it in the sea."

Joshua started to protest but suddenly felt inordinately weary and was almost relieved when Isabelle took him by the hand and led him toward the water. With Roger and Joshua gone, the area behind the banyan tree was silent. Scarlet took the prisoner's pulse and nodded to Annie, then handed Nathan a spear and told him to watch over the fallen man.

Annie moved forward to touch Akira's shoulder. "I'm sorry about the gag, sorry that—"

Akira's gaze abruptly left her, and Annie saw that Roger had returned. The four scratches on his face were red and inflamed, and without question he was enraged. "I'm going to bind you now, monkey. Bind you like the animal you are. And if you so much as twitch, I'll spear you straight through. You got that?"

"There's no need to insult—"

"Shut your mouth, fat man," Roger said, interrupting Nathan. "I'll deal with the Nip. I'll nail his yellow hide to a tree."

"Get out of here!" Annie shouted as Roger stepped toward her patient. She tried to get in front of Akira, but he wouldn't let her.

Though Akira had recently grown used to the sound of waves and the rhythm of words, and though he felt reincarnated in such a world, he'd survived five years of ferocious fighting and was unafraid of Roger. As Nathan tried to convince Roger to leave, Akira watched the tip of Roger's spear while simultaneously keeping his peripheral vision on his adversary's face. "If you had a gun, you would shoot me, yes?" Akira asked. "But the airman had no gun, and so you will have to use your spear. So do your best with it, coward."

Roger dropped the spear and lunged at Akira. The big man's speed surprised Akira, and he was barely able to deflect an open-fisted thrust meant to shatter his nose. Even as Roger's attack was being blocked, he swept his foot toward Akira's injured leg. Akira sensed rather than saw the kick coming and managed to twist his body so that Roger's foot struck his knee. The blow caused him to stumble, and Roger pressed forward with his attack, chopping at him with a series of powerful and precise strikes. Akira blocked the blows with his forearms, looking for an opening through which to counterattack. Though Annie and Scarlet screamed for help, and Nathan tried to intervene, Akira was aware only of Roger.

Suddenly, Jake and Joshua burst through the underbrush. Jake tackled Roger while Joshua grabbed Akira. When Akira made no effort to resist, Joshua helped subdue Roger. "It's over!" he yelled, wrapping himself around Roger's legs so that Jake was no longer in danger of being kicked. "Do you hear me? It's over!"

As deadly as he was, Roger couldn't possibly throw two strong men from him, and ceased his efforts to do so. His chest heaving, he tried to slow his breath, tried to suppress his fury. "The Jap tried to kill me!"

"That's a lie!" Annie retorted, furious that Roger had attempted to kick Akira's wound.

Jake relaxed against Roger, and Joshua said, "Don't move, Jake. Not yet."

"Sure, Captain."

Joshua started to swear and then stopped himself, slapping his open palm against his thigh. "What's wrong with you?" he yelled, glaring at Roger and then Akira. "Don't you think we have enough problems without you two at each other's throats? You obviously don't, so I'll spell it out for you. The next person who breaks the peace on this island will be put in the lifeboat and set adrift! I'll give him food and water, but so help me God, I'll set him adrift with no oars and he'll have to make do at sea!" Joshua paused to spit out some blood. "Is that understood?" When no one answered, he shouted, "I asked if that was understood!"

Only after a series of affirmative responses did Joshua allow Roger to be released. "We're done here," he said, his voice hoarse. "No one else is coming, so there's no reason to stay off the beach. Jake, kindly bring the airman into our camp. Scarlet, please see to it that he has food and medical care. And, Akira, join me by the water."

The group quickly dispersed. Limping, Akira followed Joshua to the sea. He watched the captain lean down and rinse his mouth out with salt water. Covered in sweat and grime, Akira knelt and began to splash himself. The water, though warm, felt refreshing in the rising heat. Not a single cloud floated above. The day was still—bereft of wind or pulse. Even the sea was little more than an endless blue mirror.

"If you give him a reason to kill you, he will kill you," Joshua said. "Isn't that obvious?"

"I have given him no reason," Akira replied. "But he looks for one, yes?"

Joshua nodded, rinsing out his mouth once again, wincing as salt water cleansed his cut. He took a deep breath, rising to his full height and studying the distant sea. He was still angry and made no reply, letting his emotions slowly settle. Eyeing *Benevolence's* grave, he suddenly missed his rosary, missed how his fingers caressed its beads as he whispered Hail Marys.

Finally, he turned to Akira. "I have no ill feelings toward you. None whatsoever. You saved Annie and Isabelle, and I don't consider you an enemy."

"I am not your enemy, Captain."

"You are and you aren't." When it was clear that Akira didn't understand him, Joshua continued, "My country is at war with yours, and you're my prisoner. But I don't want to bind you, don't want to treat you poorly." He glanced toward the banyan tree, ensuring that his orders were being carried out. "Isabelle tells me that you were a teacher," he said, wishing that he was alone with her.

"Yes. In another life."

Joshua turned to face Akira. "Do I have your word, your word upon all that's sacred to you, that you'll do nothing to harm or endanger any of my people?"

"So sorry, but what of that man? He will cause trouble for me."

"That man I will handle. I've handled his kind before."

"Thank you."

"Now do I have your word? My wife is here. And her sister. Do I have your word that you'll never endanger them?"

"I want them to live, Captain. They have been good to me, and I want them to live. That is why I warned you about the airman."

"Then you'll remain untied, and you'll have free reign of camp. But don't go out of sight."

Akira bowed slightly. "May I say something?"

"Please speak freely."

"Our countries war. And as you say, we cannot change this unfortunate truth. But we do not have to war. There can be a peace between us, yes?"

"I'd like that. I see no reason why there can't."

Akira studied Joshua's face, which was long and narrow. The sun had left his skin the color of sand, and wrinkles gathered near the corners of his mouth and eyes. His curly, dark hair was receding. His blue eyes could be hard, Akira knew, but they could also emanate friendliness. He found it unsettling that two weeks ago he'd have killed the American had they met upon the battlefield.

Realizing that Joshua was staring at the spot where *Benevolence* disappeared, Akira said softly, "I also know of guilt."

"You . . . you do?"

"I know how one moment you believe that you are free of it, and how the next moment you are reminded of your failings, and how those failings can almost . . . suffocate you. This cycle goes on and on. Like the rise and fall of the tide. And then one day you discover that you will never be free of the guilt."

"It becomes a part of you, doesn't it?" Joshua asked, thinking of his dead crew.

"Yes, so sorry."

"How big a part?"

Akira gazed at the sea. "I used to think it was most of me. But recently, other parts of me have grown."

Joshua thought of his unborn child. Would his child mark a new beginning? "I hope the war ends soon," he finally said.

"It will. And you will win. After Midway, the emperor can only dream of victory."

"Were you there?"

Akira nodded slowly. "They told us that Americans were soft. That you were spoiled by fast cars and easy lives and that you would flee at the first sight of blood." He shook his head, pursing his lips. "But . . . wave after wave of your torpedo pilots came at our carriers. Came toward their certain deaths. They fell from the sky like snow and yet they still came."

Joshua thought about the dead of that battle, of how the unimaginable heroics of the doomed pilots might have turned the war. "And they finally got through," he replied, saying a silent prayer for the airmen.

Akira turned from the sea to look at Joshua. "I also want this war to end. Too long has it raged already."

Joshua watched a gull glide about the beach. "Isabelle told me about that night. The night you saved them. And more than you'll ever know, I'm grateful for what you did."

"It was my honor."

"You . . . you saved my family. Which means that you also saved me. And because of that I'm going to trust you."

Akira turned back to the sea. "What, may I ask, will you do with the prisoner?"

"I don't know," Joshua said, sighing. "Nothing, I suppose. Just keep him tied up and hope that he doesn't cause any more trouble."

"He will not tell you anything."

"I agree. I'm through asking him questions."

Straightening his wrinkled shirt, Akira said, "I wonder what the emperor would think of this."

"Of what?"

"An officer of the Imperial Army talking with an American naval captain." Akira smiled, adding, "He would fall from his throne."

"Maybe we should send him a picture."

"Ah, I would like that. A picture, yes?" Akira grinned. "Thank you for that thought."

Joshua turned from *Benevolence*. "It was my pleasure," he replied, his swollen lip forming a smile. "I like the thought as well."

WAIST DEEP IN THEIR swimming hole, Annie scrubbed her arms with sand. During the past few minutes she'd also tried seaweed and the husk from a coconut. She'd ultimately decided that sand worked best, that it actually removed the island's grime from her skin. A few feet away, Isabelle had come to the same conclusion. The sisters scrubbed in silence, each angry about the morning's events.

Not surprisingly, Annie was the first to speak. "It was wrong to gag him, Isabelle. You know that as well as I do."

Isabelle dropped the sand from her hands. "What was wrong was for you to openly debate Joshua."

"Debate him? Is he a king and I'm his subject? I was only trying to protect our patient. I was—"

"Do you have to be so naïve? Is it really necessary, Annie? We're at war, remember? We're not on vacation in a tropical paradise, but at war. And in war unpleasant things happen."

Annie stepped toward her sister. "He saved us! He carried me on his back and almost died in the process!"

Isabelle picked up a handful of sand and began to scrub her legs. "I know that. For goodness' sake, don't you think I know that? I'm grateful for what he did, but it still doesn't change the fact that we're at war. Joshua was just playing it safe."

"If Akira had played it safe we'd both be dead!"

"Annie, that's not—"

"He'd be free on this island and we'd still be in *Benevolence*."

"Fine. I'll grant you that. But would you rather that Joshua not play it safe? That he jeopardize lives just so a man's feelings don't get hurt?"

"Of course not!"

"He loves me. He loves you. He loves his unborn child. So he's going to do his best to protect us. Just like you're protecting Akira—a man, I should remind you, who you hardly know. Think about what you'd do if you were about to become a mother. Who would you protect then? What lengths would you go to so that no harm came to your child?"

Annie started to speak, then stopped. "I'm not . . . I'm not angry at Joshua for protecting us. I just . . . I'm just not pleased with how it happened. Akira didn't deserve that."

"He's a soldier, Annie. He understands."

Sighing, Annie sank deeper into the water. Though irritated that Isabelle couldn't see her point, Annie was mostly unnerved by the fight between Roger and Akira. "If Josh and Jake hadn't returned, Roger would have killed him," she said, glancing back toward camp. "That man's a monster."

Isabelle nodded, starting to scrub herself again. "Akira moved just as fast. But I agree; something's not right with Roger."

"He's crazy and evil; that's what's not right."

"But we've seen that before. We know how war turns good men into great men and bad men into villains. How many times have we spoken about that?"

"I don't trust him," Annie replied uneasily. "I've caught him watching me. And . . . and I didn't like what I saw."

Reaching for more sand, Isabelle resolved to keep a closer eye on Roger. She hated the thought of him watching Annie. "I'll talk to Joshua about him. I'll get him sent off to look for caves, and we can wash our hands of him. But just to be safe, stay close to someone, because I don't trust him either."

"I will."

"You hear me, Annie? Stay close to someone and you'll have nothing to fear."

Annie spotted a strand of seaweed in her sister's hair and leaned forward to remove it. The strand was tangled in Isabelle's locks, and as Annie pulled it out, she was reminded of untying her sister's braids in the bath. "I don't know . . . I don't know why I'm so protective of Akira," she said softly.

"You're a nurse, Annie. He's your patient. And he did save you."

"I know. But . . . he's more than a patient to me."

"What exactly is he?"

"I don't know exactly. But he's teaching me about poetry, and I . . . and I like spending time with him."

Isabelle flinched as a fish bumped into her calf. "Why?"

"Because he doesn't judge me. And I . . . seem to please him."

"And he pleases you?"

"He does."

"And you don't feel guilty about Ted?"

"Why would I? I haven't done anything wrong. Can't I be friends with my patient?"

Isabelle shrugged. Though she didn't agree, she wasn't interested in further debating the point. "Well, I'm happy that he's put a smile on your face, that he's teaching you poetry. I'm sure it helps to pass the time."

"It's wonderful. It's . . . taught me to think in different ways. Kind of like painting did."

"He certainly seems to enjoy teaching you."

Annie plucked the last of the seaweed from Isabelle's hair. "As you know better than anyone, I'm unsure of almost everything. But his presence . . . it makes me less unsure."

"How?"

"Is that how you feel with Joshua? More sure of yourself? Of course, I know that's never been one of your bigger problems."

Isabelle swished seawater through her teeth. "You're right. I've always been confident. At least, ever since you got sick. So that's not why I'm with Josh. I don't need his . . . validation. But still, his company makes me happy. Sometimes I stop worrying about all that I have to do and instead, believe it or not, simply enjoy the moment. That's why I'm with him, I think. Because it's possible for me to relax in his presence. Because he lets me know that I'm not alone."

"But you've never been alone."

"Never? No, that's not true. There are degrees to everything."

"What do you mean?"

Isabelle smiled faintly, accustomed to Annie's questions, which at times seemed endless. "The love of a good man makes you feel less alone, Annie. Ted doesn't . . . he doesn't make you feel that way?"

Annie picked up a shell, bringing it into a light it had never seen. "He has a good heart. He makes me laugh. But at the end of the day, Ted is mostly concerned about Ted. And he has little faith in me."

Isabelle nodded, knowing that one of the reasons Annie became a nurse was to prove her fiancé wrong. "No one else sees that in him."

"I know. To everyone else, he's the sports hero, the homecoming king, the future governor. And I'm just the lucky girl who will someday bear his children."

"Maybe the war will change him for the better. Maybe he'll see things differently."

"I'd like that, Izzy. I really would. But I think . . . I think people are less capable of change than we want to believe."

Isabelle sighed, taking Annie's hand. "We should go. We've been gone too long as it is."

Annie followed Isabelle out of the water, glad that their argument was over. She hadn't gone far when she wondered why her sister's footsteps were so easy to follow and her fiancé's sometimes so difficult. Where did Isabelle lead her that Ted didn't?

DEEP WITHIN THE JUNGLE, Roger seethed. To release his fury, he threw rocks at geckos on a tree branch until he struck one and it fell to the ground. Grabbing the stunned creature, he crunched its skull between his thumbs and then leaned back against a boulder. Furious that he'd tightened his grip on the spear when the prisoner had spoken of attacking, and that he'd so completely lost his temper during the ensuing confrontation, he pressed his sweaty palms against his eyes, craving a cigarette. "Goddamn Japs," he muttered, picking up the gecko's body and hurling it into the jungle.

Roger had long known that his temper could undermine his missions, and yet until landing on the island, his rage had never created problems. But here, with the relentless headaches and heat, his rage had become almost unmanageable. His hate of the other survivors further fueled his fury, and sometimes it took all his mental fortitude to not lash out at everyone around him. To not punish those who offended him was entirely contrary to his convictions. He felt helpless, painfully aware that his strength had somehow been stolen, that circumstances had reduced him once again to the young boy who was unable to silence his tormentors.

As if he didn't have enough pressure on him, Roger now had to worry about whether Akira had seen him tighten his grip on the spear. "Did the monkey notice?" he asked himself, slapping at a mosquito, his voice raw with fury. Roger didn't think that Annie's patient had seen him prepare to be attacked. But still, giving any hint whatsoever that he understood Japanese had been a colossal mistake—a mistake almost bound to be repeated, as with the two prisoners together, he'd be forced to endure more such conversations.

Roger debated the merits of killing either or both men. Even though he reviled Akira, he hesitated dispatching him immediately because the others would know that he'd done so. No, it would be better to kill him later, during or after the Japanese landing. He could then kill him in his own way—taking his time and savoring the moment. He could bury him neck deep in the sand and watch the tide rise over his pleading face.

Killing the airman first made more sense. The man was bound and already injured, after all. How hard would it be to suffocate him in the dead of night? And how could anyone suspect treachery when the Jap already had a head wound and could easily have died naturally?

His pulse quickening, Roger continued to plot. He could wait to kill the airman until the moon was hidden by clouds and the wind masked his sounds. Fortunately, the wind was often loud at night, flapping the giant leaves about them.

Or he could do the opposite. He could whisper to the airman of who he was. He could somehow set him free and rendezvous with him later. An ally could certainly be useful in the days ahead. With such an ally, he could easily kill all of *Benevolence's* survivors.

Though intrigued by the possibilities of letting the airman go, the four scratches on Roger's face still burned, and because of those scratches, he decided that the prisoner would perish.

The Nip will die tonight, he promised himself. And though he'll die without a sound, he'll see me, and I'll make it hurt like hellfire, and he'll know of my revenge. That goddamn monkey will know I won.

DAY SEVEN

As Plato once said,
Just the dead will see war's end.
Young flowers fear frost.

False Dawn

B eyond the harbor, beneath the swells to the west of the island,
Benevolence rested. After sinking, the ship had broken in two
and each part had settled upon a virgin reef. For three days, oil
had leaked from *Benevolence's* torn stern, fouling the pristine waters.
The oil had kept sea life away, but once the water cleared, turtles and
sharks and dozens of varieties of fish ventured into the ruined infra-
structure of the ship. Some of the turtles became trapped within *Benevolence*, and soon their bodies mingled with hundreds of human
corpses.

Scavengers now explored the lifeless ship, cleaning it of the dead.
Already miniature barnacles had affixed themselves to massive iron
walls. And lobsters and moray eels had made homes within man-made
caves. The bridge of *Benevolence* was still intact, and a leopard shark had
taken up residence beneath the table where Joshua once studied maps.

Not far from *Benevolence*, scores of planes and smaller boats also
littered the seafloor. These were burial grounds for men and homes to
all forms of sea life. Soon other objects would sink from the world
above—tanks, rifles, bombs, and ships that dwarfed *Benevolence*. Thousands of soldiers would also fall beneath the surface—their bodies and
memories forever lost at sea.

Staring out over the waves, Joshua was aware only of his ship. As he kneeled on the beach in the early morning light, he prayed for the dead. He offered such prayers every morning, praying that the dead were in heaven and that their families would someday again know peace. Though he believed strongly in God, his belief was not unshakable, and he often looked skyward as if seeking a reminder of a higher power.

After praying for the safety of his family and making a sign of the cross, Joshua returned to camp. Everyone was still asleep, or at least content to have their eyes closed—perhaps enjoying the coolness of the morning. Over the past few days, people had started to sleep farther from the banyan tree. Thus palm fronds, banana peels, and coconut husks were scattered about. Joshua began to collect such items and quietly place them into the fire. When he neared Isabelle, he paused, watching her sleep. Though her skin was speckled with sand and lined with grime, the sight of her sleeping was a beautiful thing, and he beheld her face as the sun climbed higher. He thought about the child she carried, and he marveled that a new life grew within her. Though he wasn't prone to such thoughts, Joshua wondered what it would be like to have life develop within him. Would men be so quick to kill each other if they experienced such creation?

Joshua licked his swollen lip and continued to tidy the camp. He would have never let *Benevolence* fall into such disarray, but here he didn't want to order people around unnecessarily. After all, everyone was tired and hot and covered in bug bites, and yesterday's events proved that people were also on edge. Morale needed to be raised, he realized, though he was uncertain what to do to lift their spirits. Of course, Roger would be sent away, he knew that much. And without Roger sulking about, the mood around camp should improve.

Nearing the airman, Joshua was surprised to see that he hadn't changed positions all morning. The prisoner's hands and feet were bound and a rope connected him to the banyan tree. He still lay on his side and rested his hands beside his belly. A cup of water and some nearby bananas were untouched. A fly landed on the man's face, and instinctively Joshua leaned down to chase it away. Only then did he realize that the airman's chest wasn't moving.

Joshua dropped to his knees and felt for a pulse. The man's flesh was cool and unmoving against him. "Oh, no," he whispered, placing the back of his hand before the airman's mouth. No breath came forward. Muttering to himself, Joshua ran his hands through his hair. He rose, moving quietly toward where Scarlet lay some two dozen paces away. She rested on her back and her eyes were open.

"I need you," he whispered. Wordlessly, she followed him to the airman. Joshua knelt and said, "I think . . . I think he's dead. I don't understand it, but I think he's dead."

Scarlet moved forward, checking the man's vitals. She turned to Joshua. "He's been dead for some time," she said quietly. "By the look of him, probably for hours."

"For hours? How?" he asked, untying the man so that she could more easily examine him.

She sighed and carefully moved his head. Blood trickled from his ears and his nose. The skin around his wound was bruised and swollen. "He must . . . he hemorrhaged in the night."

"Hemorrhaged? I didn't think his wound was life threatening. I thought—"

"Head wounds are always dangerous," she interrupted. "He must have been bleeding internally and we never realized it."

"Didn't you look for that?"

"Of course we did. And if we'd been aboard *Benevolence*, with proper equipment, I'm sure that he'd still be alive. But we're not. We're on a beach and we've no doctors and there's no bringing him back."

He rubbed his temples, as if his head suddenly ached. He was responsible for this man's safety, and had utterly failed him. "I'm going . . . I need to bury him," he whispered, glancing skyward. "When the others wake up, can you please tell them what's happened?"

"I'll tell them."

Joshua lifted the airman, putting him over his shoulder. He took a few paces toward the jungle and then noticed Akira asleep. Impulsively, Joshua strode to Annie's patient. Grunting with effort, he leaned down and tapped him on the shoulder. Akira's eyes opened, but he didn't move. "Can you come with me?" Joshua whispered.

Gazing at the lifeless body, Akira nodded. The two men stepped into the jungle, which in the half-light of the morning seemed to consume them as if it were a vast mouth swallowing a pair of ants. "How did he die?" Akira asked quietly, walking before Joshua to clear a path.

"I didn't want this to happen. I wanted to treat him fairly."

"What did happen?"

"His head wound. His brain bled during the night and he died in his sleep. Scarlet checked on him several times, but . . . but a few hours ago he died." Joshua sidestepped a fallen log, the weight of the dead man pressing him down upon the earth. "I'm sorry."

"Why am I with you now?"

"Because I want . . . because he needs a proper burial. And I know nothing of your religions. I'm hoping that you can help me."

Akira stopped. He turned around to study the dead man. "Most Japanese," he said softly, "believe in Buddhism or Shinto. Both groups . . . cremate their dead."

"Then I'd like . . . then we need to do that."

"Please find an open space and gather wood. I will soon return." Akira disappeared into the jungle.

Joshua moved forward. Vines obscured his path, and with his one free arm he pushed them aside. Though he longed to rest, to put the body down beside him, he continued on. His mind was overburdened with conflicting emotions about what had befallen his prisoner. The airman had been without question a dangerous addition to their group, a fanatic who'd have either escaped or died trying. And from that perspective, Joshua didn't mind the man's death. His death, after all, meant one fewer threat that could endanger Isabelle or anyone else. On the other hand, Joshua had been responsible for the airman's well-being, and letting any man, even a man bent on destruction, die while tied to a tree was unforgivable.

A clearing revealed itself, and Joshua moved forward, gently setting the airman down among a group of knee-high ferns. Nearby, a dead and emaciated tree leaned against a sapling that struggled to reach the light above. He pulled the dead tree from its resting place and began breaking it into smaller pieces. Bugs attacked him as he worked, and he often slapped at his back and legs in an effort to keep them at bay.

Soon Joshua had a cot-sized bundle of wood piled in the center of the clearing. He lifted the airman, carefully placed him in the middle of the pile, and crossed the man's arms over his chest. He straightened the flier's clothing. He then closed his eyes, made the sign of the cross, and prayed.

After a few minutes passed, Akira arrived with a burning branch. Seeing the funeral pyre, he nodded in appreciation, then eyed the jungle that rose above and about them. "A good place, yes, to continue a journey?"

Joshua glanced around, noting the trees and birds and a pair of giant butterflies that fluttered about a violet orchid. "I think it's a fine place. As fine as any."

Akira set the burning branch beneath the pile of timber. At first only smoke rose, which was white and slender and altogether unlike the smoke that had billowed up from *Benevolence*. But the fire quickly spread, consuming the dry wood and the man atop it. Soon unable to watch, Joshua sat among the ferns, closed his eyes, and silently confessed his sins.

Akira continued to stand. When the fire finally wavered, he added more wood. Then he sat next to Joshua and listened carefully to the sound of rebirth.

AFTER SCARLET FINISHED telling everyone of the airman's death, people went in opposite directions. Before Roger vanished into the jungle, he let Annie know that he was glad one fewer Jap existed in the world, and she replied by turning her back to him. Nathan—who hoped to redeem himself for his failures of the previous day—also ventured inland, seeking the cave that Joshua so desperately wanted. Each of the three nurses felt guilty for not paying more attention to the airman's head wound, and each reflected on his passing.

Ratu, who'd been relegated to the periphery of the group by the violent events, slowly built a new fire pit. The airman's demise had shaken Ratu. He hadn't expected to find death on the island, and he obsessed about his father being captured by the Japanese and dying in such a manner. Ratu had always believed his father to be invincible. But now, as he dug in the sand, he remembered the numerous times that his father had been injured during their adventures, and how his legs and hands bore as many scars as an old turtle's shell. Also, his father's eyes weren't as sharp as they once were, and he worried about him walking into an ambush.

Thinking of himself on the island, so far from his family, Ratu began to panic. What would happen to his mother and sisters if his father died? Who'd feed them? Who'd tell his sisters that their dreams were only dreams and that they had nothing to fear from the night?

Breaking out in a sweat, Ratu hurried from the fire pit, anxiously following Jake's deep footprints down the beach. He needed to talk to his friend, and with each passing step he felt this urgency increase. By the time he reached Jake, Ratu's face was streaked with tears.

"Big Jake!" he sobbed, running into the engineer's arms.

Jake dropped his spear and the three fish he'd caught. "What? What ain't right?"

Ratu clung to Jake as if only he could pull him from a swirling sea, could stop him from drowning. "I'm scared . . . so bloody scared for my father," Ratu stammered. "I want to see him. What if he's tied to a tree with no one to protect him? What . . . what if he's hurt?"

Stroking Ratu's cheek, Jake held him tight. Ratu shuddered against him. For not the first time, Jake realized how slender and small and young Ratu was. "How many sharks has your daddy killed?" Jake asked, his cigarlike fingers still moving against Ratu's tear-stained face.

"I don't . . . I don't know. Why?"

"How about a guess?"

"Fifteen or . . . maybe twenty."

"Twenty sharks," Jake replied, shaking his head as if in wonder. "You reckon a man who's killed twenty sharks is gonna go and get himself captured? Get himself captured when he's got such a fine boy to go home to? No, sir. I don't expect that such a shark killer has much to worry about. You'd sooner see a fish drown."

"But his eyes aren't good and . . . and he's not as strong as I told you. He couldn't really throw his spear across the harbor. He couldn't—"

"Shhh," Jake said, trying to calm Ratu. "It'll rattle right. You'll see. No shark killer is gonna get himself captured or shot."

"But what . . . what if he doesn't come home? What will happen to my mother? My little sisters?" Before Jake could answer, Ratu continued miserably, "They're not strong, I tell you. They get scared at night. I should never have left them. Oh, why . . . why did I ever leave them?"

"You'll be with them real soon."

Ratu shook his head, a trail of mucus stretching from his nose to Jake's shoulder. "You can't . . . you can't promise that, Big Jake."

Jake wiped the tears from Ratu's face. "Well, I can promise you that we've both got bones in our backs and we'll escape this darn island. You'll be home before the crickets cry."

"And my father?"

"Why, the war's almost over."

"It is?"

"Well, them Japs ain't gonna quit. And they'll ride their horse until they get knocked off. But they'll eat dirt soon enough. Their horse is plumb dead already. They just don't know it."

Ratu nodded, leaning into his friend. "I'm just so bloody afraid. I don't want anyone else to die."

Jake continued to stroke Ratu's face. He'd never held a child in such a manner, and found that he'd be happy to embrace Ratu for as long as he needed him. "You should fetch each one of them sisters something," Jake finally said. "Something from your adventure."

"Like what?"

"What do they like? What makes them smile?"

Sniffing, Ratu thought about his siblings. "Sometimes . . . sometimes I bring them seashells."

"Then let's gather up some seashells. The prettiest seashells on the island."

"And I collect . . . I've found fourteen heart-shaped stones for my mother."

"Then let's get her a fifteenth."

Ratu nodded. "And my father? I could bring him a shark's tooth. That would be wonderful, Big Jake. Oh, Big Jake, would you help me get a shark's tooth?"

"Just tell me how to do it. I'm a farmer, remember?"

Wiping his tears away, Ratu replied, "I taught you how to fish, didn't I?"

"I reckon so."

"Well, I tell you, if I can teach you how to fish, then I can teach you how to spear a shark. It's really no different."

"Except that sharks have teeth. Lots of them. And I don't fancy—"

"Sharks are dumb. Probably as dumb as the pigs you're used to. You shouldn't have any problems."

"Pigs ain't able to eat people. You forget that little-known fact?"

"I forgot what a baby you could be."

Jake smiled, pulling Ratu closer to him. "It's good to see the old you."

"I'm not old, Big Jake."

Chuckling, Jake ruffled Ratu's hair. "I have an idea. Care to hear it?"

Ratu wiped his face. "You're a good mate, Big Jake. A cracking good mate. Sure, what's your idea?"

"The way I see it, these last two days have been real hard on everyone. As hard as hail on crops. And I reckon we should do something about it."

"What should we do?"

"Fish. Fish like your daddy taught you. Let's catch tuna and crab and lobster. And one of them big, ugly fish that tastes like chicken. We'll cook it all tonight. And then people will fill their bellies and something real fine will have happened today."

Ratu rose from his friend's lap. "Let's keep it a secret. Let's surprise everyone."

"A secret it is," Jake replied, handing Ratu a spear. "And if a shark happens to amble our way, well, then, we'll just make a meal of him too."

Once the funeral pyre had quieted, Joshua asked Akira to return to camp. The captain had said that he was going to spend the day looking for a cave, that he wasn't going to return until he found them a hiding place. He'd told Akira to stay clear of Roger and had thanked him for helping with the airman.

As the fire had burned, Joshua came to the realization that it was up to him to find a hiding place. He'd asked Roger to do it, but the man, despite his obvious talents, had found nothing. Nathan was incapable of such tasks, and Jake, though capable, was providing most of their food. The women could search, of course, but Joshua didn't like the thought of them in the jungle, as it was an unforgiving place and posed all sorts of dangers.

The air battle had reminded Joshua that the war was coming to them, that they'd need a secret refuge. If his wife and unborn child were to live, it was up to him to protect them, to ensure that their beauty could not be stolen from the world. And so he hurried through the underbrush, determined to make it to the other side of the island. Perhaps Ratu was right. Perhaps along the far shore a cave would exist.

Thorns tore at his flesh and birds protested his passing. He moved with haste, wanting to cover as much territory as possible before the day was done. Whenever he grew tired, he thought of his child, and pressed forward with renewed strength. He imagined Isabelle running into the jungle and having nowhere to hide when the Japanese came. Troops would pour onto the island, and though his group might be able to disappear for a few hours, or even a day, they'd ultimately be discovered. And at that point anything was possible. They could be treated well or he could be shot and Isabelle ravaged. The thought of her helpless in the hands of cruel men profoundly motivated him, and he saw more of the island than he ever had. He climbed rises and crossed streams and moved so fast that mosquitoes couldn't keep up.

Joshua debated the pros and cons of the possible hiding spots that he discovered. Piles of boulders were pondered. Dense vegetation inspected from every angle. Within a particularly thick part of the jungle, a trio of large trees had fallen against one another. Saplings had emerged around the larger trees, and the result was an almost tepeelike structure that could hide a handful of people. Though the shelter wasn't what he sought, he'd used the airman's compass to get a feel for the location.

His shirt and shorts and even shoes damp with sweat, Joshua continued on. As midday approached, he finally reached the other side of the island. Though a long beach was present, no harbor existed, and the waves were much larger here. Piles of driftwood lined the beach. He noticed some cliffs to the north and, eating a breadfruit, headed toward them. As he walked, he scrutinized the beach for valuable items. After all, untold ships navigated these waters, and anything could have washed ashore.

Though the beach contained mostly driftwood, shells, bloated jellyfish, and rotting seaweed, he discovered a few things fashioned in distant worlds—wooden fishing buoys, a small bottle with Japanese or Chinese markings, and an empty crate. He pocketed the bottle and kept walking.

Not far ahead, Joshua noticed a large number of gulls circling and dropping to the beach. He quickened his pace and was surprised to see that the gulls were feasting on small, slow crabs that emerged from a hole in the sand. After a few more steps, he realized that the gulls weren't eating crabs, but baby sea turtles. Instinctively, he hurried toward the nest, waving his arms in an effort to scare the birds away. A dozen half-eaten turtles lay beyond the nest. Several scores of hatchlings were in the process of breaking free from their eggs or methodically crawling toward the surf. Joshua scooped up as many of the babies as possible and, with gulls darting about him, ran toward the sea. He waited for a wave to recede and dropped the turtles into the water.

Numerous gulls had returned to the nest, and Joshua ran at them as fast as possible. He yelled, waving his arms. The gulls shrieked, rising to circle above the nest. All of the eggs had either been destroyed by the gulls or had hatched. At least another twenty turtles scurried toward the sea. Joshua held his shirt out before him, using it like a bag in which to collect the remaining hatchlings. This time he walked deeper into the water, and when he sat in the sea, he watched the babies swim away. They immediately headed toward darker water, and he couldn't help but wonder how many finned predators awaited them. One turtle, which had lost part of a flipper to a gull, struggled to make headway. Joshua picked it up and waded into the surf. Once he was up to his chest, he gently placed the turtle into the water and watched it swim into the mysterious beyond.

After he returned to shore and ensured that no other turtles remained, Joshua continued to walk toward the cliffs. His encounter with the hatchlings reminded him of his unborn child. He and Isabelle had been trying to conceive for several years, and after failing to do so, a part of him had sadly concluded that he'd never be a father. Over the past year, as the war and his responsibilities increasingly weighed upon him, he'd thought less and less about fatherhood. In fact, once he'd been given control of *Benevolence*, such musings had almost completely disappeared. To make matters worse, even after he managed to get Isabelle assigned to his ship, he'd hardly seen her. They'd both worked endless hours, and the work that might have bonded them actually served to push them apart. He had his responsibilities and so did she. Little time existed for anything else.

As Joshua walked in his wet clothes toward the cliffs, he realized that Isabelle's pregnancy had prompted him to think more of her in the past few days than he had in the past few months. Without question, he felt closer to her than he had in a long time. And even though she was strong and sure and capable, he knew that she needed his encouragement more than ever. He'd sensed this need over the past several days. Being who she was, Isabelle tried to hide this want, but he wasn't fooled. She'd tended to others for years, and for the moment, a part of her wanted to be looked after.

While pleased that their child had already brought them closer together, Joshua worried about how he'd fare as a father. He owned more than his share of demons and disappointments, and how could he be a good father, a good teacher, when he'd failed at the most important mission ever given to him?

He was soon at the cliffs, which were set back thirty or forty feet from the water. The beach before the cliffs was littered with rocks of all sizes. The sea pounded against the land here, spray erupting into the sky. With care, Joshua circumvented tide pools and barnacle-encrusted rocks. Parts of the cliffs had fallen, and he looked into piles of massive boulders, seeking hiding places.

Joshua hadn't walked more than a few hundred paces in front of the cliffs when, to his utter amazement, he found what he was looking for. Between a break in the cliffs, where the land opened up and the jungle managed to creep forward, an overhang of rock seemed to obscure a hollow or a cave. His heartbeat quickening, he hurried forward. His feet fell upon rocks, then sand, then the tentacles of vines and plants that crept forward from the jungle.

At one point waves must have crashed against this spot, for what had once been a cliff had collapsed. And at the bottom of that cliff was a cave, a hollow that had been carved into the stone by the assault of billions of waves over thousands of years. Joshua rushed into the cave, which was shoulder high at its entrance, but at least twenty feet tall inside. The cave was as big as a small house. Sand comprised its floor, and in one corner, the sand sloped into a bus-sized body of water. "Please, dear Lord," Joshua whispered, rushing toward the pool. He knelt in the sand, cupped his hand into the water, drew some into his mouth, and whooped in joy when he knew that it was fresh and pure.

With the thrill of a child stepping onto a Ferris wheel, Joshua explored the cave. Aside from the body of water, it seemed dry. The sand was deep and soft. Coolness prevailed. The light cast through the opening was enough to at least partially illuminate the entire area.

Joshua looked up, overwhelmed with relief. "Thank you, Lord," he said emotionally, not believing his good fortune. "Thank you so very, very much."

With an endless supply of water and piles of driftwood nearby, enough resources existed here that Joshua thought the cave could support the entire party. His only uncertainly had to do with food. Could Jake and Ratu catch fish here, as they did in the harbor? Hurrying to the cave's entrance to eye the raging surf, he had his doubts. Deciding that they'd simply have to dry fish caught in the harbor and bring food here, he clapped his hands together. Isabelle would be safe in the cave. Everyone would be safe. Even if a large force of Japanese landed on the island, the cave was so well hidden and far removed from the harbor that it would likely never be discovered. And if the survivors camouflaged its entrance, the cave would be all but invisible.

Twice since *Benevolence* sank, Joshua had felt hope. The first time was when Isabelle told him that she was pregnant, and the second was now, as he looked into the cave and his dread of discovery lessened into something much more tolerable. Within the cave, they could hide from the war. They could hide and they could hope. And they could think of the future—a future infinitely more alluring than the present.

BACK AT THE HARBOR, Annie had finished collecting coconuts and now sat against a palm tree, watching clouds drift above the sea. A gentle breeze caressed the clouds and her face, keeping the day's heat at bay. After seven days on the island, Annie realized that such breezes made life bearable. When the wind didn't stir, the heat often became a living thing—an omnipotent force that could render her almost powerless. She'd never experienced such heat, never known how it felt to breathe air that seemed too hot and heavy to draw into her lungs. Fortunately, most of her days on the island had been accompanied by breezes similar to what touched her now. And in the shade, with such a breeze upon her, the sun seemed more a friend than a foe.

As usual for this time, camp was quiet and barren. Annie looked down the beach to where Akira sat on a rock with his feet in the sea. He had his shirt off and was washing himself. Normally, Annie would have left him in peace, but still feeling guilty about recent events, she decided to seek him out.

The sand was hot against her feet. She quickly headed to the water and then started to move in Akira's direction. When he glanced up, she waved. His return greeting was pleasant, which was a relief, as she had been afraid that he'd be resentful about his treatment.

Akira sat on a fairly flat rock that rose just above the water's edge. With his legs dangling off the rock, he'd been in the process of cleaning his feet. Pleased that he was keeping his wound dry, Annie waded through the shallows until she stood near him. Turning toward the shore, away from the glaring sun, she said, "I never got to finish apologizing for what happened."

"With the gag, yes?"

"With the gag, the ropes, Roger, and now . . . and now for the death this morning."

Akira set aside the coconut husk that he'd been scrubbing his toes with. "You did none of these things to me, Annie." Before she could reply, he added, "So please do not worry about them. Besides, I do not blame your captain for what happened. He did what he should have done."

"But Roger?"

"Roger does not trouble me. I have met his kind before."

Annie had never seen Akira shirtless, and was surprised at how muscular his compact torso was. His chest, which was almost free of hair, looked hard and lean. Dropping her gaze to his leg, she said, "Your wound is healing wonderfully."

"I have a wonderful doctor, yes?"

She smiled. "I'm a nurse, Akira. A nurse."

"Ah, but better than a doctor, I think." He politely motioned to an empty spot on the rock beside him. "Would you care to sit?"

Annie nodded, taking his hand as he helped her climb atop the rock. She put her feet into the water and felt the sun against her back. "This morning, why did you go with Joshua?"

"He was going to bury the airman. But he needed to burn him."

"Is that what . . . what Hindus do?"

"Yes, though I am Buddhist."

"Oh," she muttered, putting her hand in front of her mouth as if to keep it from revealing any more of her ignorance. "I'm sorry."

"Please do not be. We have never spoken of this before."

She took his coconut husk and began to absently scrub the back of her calf. "Can you tell me something of Buddhism? Enough so that when I meet another Buddhist I don't sound like a complete fool?"

Akira put his hands in the water and splashed his face. "The sea feels good, yes?"

"It feels perfect."

He smiled, remembering how it felt to be a young boy and to dangle his feet in the Kamo River. "Buddhists believe that life is reborn. Like a tree that goes through the seasons. Each leaf on the tree is a new life, and each life is reborn with the spring."

"You're talking about reincarnation?"

"Yes. Or rebirth. We believe that once someone experiences enough rebirths, and once they release their . . . attachment to desire, to themselves, that they will go to Nirvana."

"And Nirvana is like heaven?"

"Yes, in a way."

Annie rinsed his coconut husk in the water and handed it back to him. "Sorry," she said sheepishly. "I should have asked if I could borrow it. You'd never take anything from me like that."

He handed her back the husk. "I am glad that you do not feel the need to ask."

"What else do Buddhists believe?"

"You truly want to know? I would not want to bore you."

"I do."

Akira smiled and said, "Buddha's four noble truths are quite simple. One, suffering exists. Two, a cause for suffering exists. Three, an end to suffering exists. Four, only by accepting suffering, by releasing desire, can one end suffering and ultimately reach Nirvana."

Annie pondered his words as she watched fish swim about their rock. "Can you . . . do that? Accept suffering and . . . and release desire?"

"No, I cannot. I still have desires, and I would rather not suffer."

"So you're not anywhere near Nirvana, are you?"

He grinned. "I am not near Nirvana. Although with the water on my feet, the sun on my back, and . . . and with my wonderful nurse beside me, this is a good day. Yes?"

Nodding, she replied, "A good day."

Akira noticed Nathan emerge from the distant jungle. Shielding his eyes from the sun, he headed toward camp. "I like him," Akira said. "A simple man. But simple men are fine men."

"He misses his family so much. He must constantly think about his wife, because he's called me by her name more than once."

"I hope he gets home to her soon."

Annie's gaze followed a manta ray that glided over the sand below. "May I ask you something, Akira? Something personal?"

"Of course."

"Do you have a wife? Children?"

He turned to her. "In Japan, the oldest son takes care of his parents.

When my father died, maybe seven years ago, I moved into his house. I have lived with my mother ever since."

"And you've never met someone?"

"No. I was a teacher, so I only met young people. And I had to take care of my mother."

"And you're alright with that?"

He shrugged. "I have no choice. It is my duty and . . . and my honor."

Annie shifted atop the rock. She watched as he gently stirred his feet in the water. Something in the way he moved intrigued her. It was almost as if he took great pleasure from the feel of the sea against his skin.

"Now may I ask something of you?" he questioned, the movement of his feet pausing slightly.

"If you're brave."

"I am being brave right now, I think."

"Well, then, ask away."

"What of your fiancé? He makes you happy, yes?"

Annie started to reply but stopped. She'd asked herself that same question a thousand times and was still unsure how to answer it. "Ted makes everyone happy," she finally said, wondering why it was so easy to share her thoughts with Akira. "And for a while, that made me happy. But now . . . now sometimes I think that I'd rather be with someone who only made me happy."

"Does—"

"I know that makes me sound terribly selfish, and I'm sorry for that. But it's true. I'd rather have him be more concerned about me than everyone else."

Akira looked at her feet beneath the water, noting how small and slender her toes were. He experienced a sudden impulse to touch those toes, to see if they were as supple as he imagined. He also wanted to tell her that she deserved all of her fiancé's attention, that the man didn't understand the gift that had been bestowed upon him. He wanted to tell her so many things. Instead he asked, "May I share a story with you?"

"By all means."

"I am sorry?"

"Yes, yes. Please tell me."

Akira looked from her toes toward the horizon. "In Japan, beautiful gardens have existed for several thousand years. These gardens are full of stones, of ponds, of red maple trees. In the springtime, cherry blossoms cover the ground, and moss turns a deeper shade of green."

"How wonderful."

"Yes, very much so," he said, wishing she could see such sights. "As a young man, I used to often visit a garden near my father's house. There the same tree had shed cherry blossoms since the time of the shoguns. I would sit beneath this tree and write poems. And when words escaped me, I would watch the gardener. After many months, I noticed that he spent most of his time attending to a single bonsai tree. It stood on a small island within his pond, and each day he would cross a stone bridge and inspect this tree with great care. He would remove a leaf or twig or insect from it. He would brush it with a damp cloth. For many weeks, I did not understand why this man spent so much time on this one miniature tree when so much other beauty existed around him."

Annie leaned closer to Akira. "Why did he?"

"Because, I think . . . I think he understood that life is precious and lovely and fleeting. And I think that this bonsai tree, with its imperfections and frailty, reminded him of these things, reminded him of the good in the world. And because of that . . . I think because of that he loved the bonsai tree. He loved it because it inspired him."

Annie noticed that his feet had stopped moving. "Why, Akira, why are you telling me this?" she quietly asked.

He sighed. "Because precious things are sometimes . . . overlooked. But such things should be cherished. Poems should be written about them and they should not be forgotten. And . . . and . . ."

"And what?"

"And though I know so little of the love between a man and a woman, it seems to me that it should be like the love between that man and his miniature tree."

"And you think . . . you think that's the kind of love I should have?"

He paused to consider his response. "I think you deserve such a gardener," he finally replied. "And I do not think you are selfish for wanting one."

She smiled, and beneath the water her foot touched his.

DAY EIGHT

She came from the sea
Like a pearl forged from the deep.
Light melts an old snow.

Confronting the Past and Present

I t's almost as big as a house," Joshua said excitedly, addressing the group. The nine survivors of *Benevolence* had gathered on the beach near the banyan tree to talk about his discovery. For the first time since they'd been on the island, he looked people in the eye and tried to truly lead. Though he still didn't feel as comfortable in this position as he once had, he didn't have to force himself to speak either. "And it's got more fresh water than we'll ever need," he added.

"How do you know the little monkeys won't find it?" Roger asked, though he realized it must be well hidden, since he hadn't discovered it.

"If the Japs come," Joshua answered, "they'll land in the harbor. Their base will be right where we're standing. They're not going to waste much manpower on the other parts of the island. And the cave is almost impossible to notice from the sea. Even from the beach it's awfully tough to spot. And if we camouflage the entrance, no one will ever know it's there."

"What about food, Captain?" Jake asked. "Fishing this harbor is easier than shucking corn. It ain't gonna be good to leave them fish."

Joshua nodded. "You and Ratu can spend a few more days fishing here. Catch as much as you can. Dry the meat in the sun and we'll bring it to the cave. That way we'll have extra food in case . . . the fishing over there isn't like shucking corn." As if a teacher in the classroom, Joshua studied the faces before him, trying to discern where thoughts lay. Isabelle followed his every word. Annie was with him one moment and gone the next. "We should leave in a few days," he continued. "That will give us enough time to collect food, erase any trace of our presence here, and row the lifeboat to the other side of the island."

"Can I ride in the boat, my captain?" Ratu asked. "I can help you row."

Smiling, Joshua replied, "Of course. You can lead us to the other shore."

"And, sir, the dried fish and the other supplies, they'll go in the boat?" Nathan wondered.

"Exactly. We'll transport most everything in the boat. Much easier to get it to the cave that way than lugging it through the jungle."

Jake put a fresh blade of grass in his mouth, savoring the faint taste of mint. "The goose sure honks high, don't he, Captain?"

"I'm sorry?"

"Oh, that's just something my daddy used to say. It means that everything's rattling right."

Joshua repeated the line and grinned. "Let's make this simple," he said. "Simple for everyone over the next few days. Jake and Ratu, kindly catch as many fish as you can and dry the meat. Cut it as thin as possible. Nathan, you're in charge of getting the lifeboat ready. Our lovely nurses can erase our existence from this spot, erase it so well that the Japs will never know we were here." Joshua turned to Roger. "Could you continue to scout the island? Two caves would be better than one. And, Akira, I'd like you to walk the beach, to look for things that washed ashore from *Benevolence*. If any new arrivals find items from our ship, they may wonder if survivors made it here too."

Roger twisted his spear butt deeper into the sand, hating the way that the captain was once again in control. "You trust the Nip?"

"Obviously, I do."

"But he'll leave some sort of message. He'll scratch a message on a rock and tell his fellow Japs all about your great cave."

Joshua glanced at Akira, who was standing like everyone else, no longer favoring his wounded leg. "And risk getting himself hung by us?" Joshua asked. "Besides, he's earned my trust. He's earned it several times over. And so he'll walk the beach."

"If I had such a pretty wife, I wouldn't be so quick to trust the monkey. He sure hasn't earned my trust. He—"

Waving Roger to silence, Joshua said, "Someday, Lieutenant, when you're in charge, you can give the orders. Understand?"

Roger spat and walked back toward the banyan tree. Though frustrated by Roger's increasing and almost intolerable insubordination, Joshua's spirits were buoyed enough by the discovery of the cave that he quickly turned back to the group. "Please, if anyone has ideas about the cave, let me know. Let's talk them through."

"Are there bugs?" Scarlet asked. "I've had my fill of bugs already."

Joshua held up his arms. "See? Not a single new bite. So you won't have to worry about any more bugs."

"Then let's get to that cave," she replied melodramatically.

As several people laughed and the group dispersed, Joshua stepped toward Isabelle, wanting her to be the first to see his discovery.

THE JUNGLE, AS ALWAYS, met them with complete indifference. Carrying the machete, Joshua walked ahead of Isabelle. Though he'd have liked to clear a path for the others to follow, he was afraid that the Japanese would stumble upon such a trail and be led directly to the cave. And so he memorized the way, noting the number of streams that needed to be crossed as well as a variety of landmarks. He'd later explain the route to everyone and ensure that each could find the cave on her or his own.

At first, Isabelle hadn't wanted to make the long walk, but upon seeing the look in her husband's eyes, which hinted of a newfound self-respect, she agreed to come. She'd never experienced the jungle, and now, as she eyed the foreign trees and birds, she felt like an explorer. Isabelle had studied Darwin in school, and imagined that an expedition of his might have been similar to what she experienced now. Though aware that she lacked the necessary patience to study animals and plants, she'd have enjoyed organizing and overseeing such an expedition. And Annie could certainly have drawn the wildlife and mused over the strange creatures that abounded within the jungle.

Moving through a maze of flowering sandalwood trees, she asked, "Do you like it here?"

Joshua pointed out a bright-green snake and made certain that she passed well clear of it. "I'm not sure. I think I like parts of it. But sometimes I feel like . . . like I'm being watched."

"Is that why you carry the machete?"

"Probably." He held her hand as they moved down a ravine, toward a thin stream. "Is this too much for you?" he asked, concerned when she grunted slightly.

"Don't be silly."

"We can go back if—"

"I want to see the cave, Joshua. I'd like to know where I'll be spending the next bit of my life."

"Speaking of that, did I tell you about the bathtub? And the fresh linen? And the piles of books and chocolates?"

She grinned, hitting him on the shoulder. "Don't tease a pregnant woman about chocolate."

The canopy above them parted and rays of sunlight angled down to strike moss and ferns. "It can be beautiful here, don't you think?"

Isabelle nodded, pleased to have heard him once again say something in jest. "We could honeymoon here," she said, taking mental notes of the landmarks they passed. "In fact, I think Annie and Akira just might."

"You've noticed too?"

"How couldn't I? I don't know how or why it happened, but she seems to be drawn to him."

"And he to her. That's one of the reasons I trust him." Joshua switched his grip on the machete, his hand slick with sweat. "If Americans land here, I'll make sure he's treated well. He deserves to be."

"Yes, he does. But I still worry for her. What about Ted? Her life back home?"

"Oh, Ted's not so wonderful. I think Annie, of all people, would be better off without him."

Isabelle sighed. "He really doesn't get her, does he? Even though he tries."

"No."

"But what future could there possibly be with a Japanese soldier? For goodness' sake, he'd probably be locked up in one of those awful camps."

Joshua paused before a steep climb, handing her a canteen. An immense hermit crab scurried toward her, and he edged it away with his foot. The creature patiently dragged its weather-beaten shell over a branch and headed down the hill. "Can I tell you something?" he said, wanting to be honest with her, to open up to her as she'd asked him to. "Something serious? Something not altogether pleasant?"

"You can tell me anything you want, Joshua. You know that."

"You might not like all of it. But it's been on my mind and I want to—"

"I can handle it, whatever it is," she interrupted, trying to sound convincing.

Joshua took back the canteen from her and attached it to his belt. He licked his swollen lip, unsure of exactly what he wanted to say and how he wanted to say it. "I didn't think . . . I never expected to truly return from *Benevolence*."

"What do you mean?"

"I mean, to be honest . . . perhaps too honest . . . I didn't think I'd ever get back to who I was." He glanced at the canopy above, briefly avoiding her eyes. "Getting back to that person seemed impossible. Even . . . even with you beside me it seemed impossible."

An enormous fly landed on her arm, but she made no move to sweep it away. "Even with me beside you?"

"But I was wrong, Izzy," he said, his fingers reaching out to touch her cheek. "So very wrong."

"How?"

"A part of me . . . will always be on that ship. A part of me won't return."

"I know."

"But there's another part of me that will always be with you."

"The bigger part?"

"Yes, the bigger part."

"Then why do you suddenly look so lost?"

He absently batted the fly from her arm. "Because . . . even as happy as I am to become a father, I worry."

"About what?"

"About how much of me is left."

"There's plenty of you left."

"But you understand me, Isabelle. You know that a part of me is gone and you're strong enough not to suffer for it. And you have your own life. But what about our daughter? Or son? What if I can't be the father I want to be because I'm . . . I'm not whole? Won't our child suffer? Won't he recognize that I have less to offer than I should?"

Isabelle saw the sadness and concern in his eyes, and she squeezed his arm. "But, Joshua, you can still teach him about what it means to be good. To be noble. To laugh. That part of you . . . the part that I still know and see, can teach those things and a lot more."

"But I'm a failure. And how can a teacher be a failure?"

"You think teachers don't make mistakes? How can you learn if you've never made mistakes?"

He glanced at a leaf that dropped from the canopy above. "I just . . . I just want to be a good father, and sometimes I wonder if I'll be able."

"Will you love our child?"

"Of course."

"Then our child will be lucky. How could he not be lucky to have your love?"

"You think?"

"I don't think any of us are perfect. I probably won't be as . . . entertaining a mother as, say, Annie might. She'll teach her children to finger paint, to stomp in puddles, to chase pirates. I don't do those sorts of things. Those fun things. But I like to think I'll still be a good mother."

"You'll be a wonderful mother."

"Well, I feel the same about you. And if a year from now you're having a tough day, then go spend the day by yourself. You won't always need to offer our child every bit of your heart and soul. No one can do that."

Joshua pulled her closer to him, hugging her. "I'm sorry. I don't mean to be such a . . . handful. I just don't want to shortchange our little one. And I worry about that."

"And I love you for worrying. But don't. You're not one to shortchange anything, Josh. If you were, I wouldn't have married you." She smiled, adding, "Believe me, the life of a navy wife isn't that grand."

He studied her face, thinking that the years had passed too quickly. "How am I so lucky to have you?"

"Isn't it obvious? You made a wise choice."

"I did. I really did." He pressed his lips against hers and then took her hand. "I have something to show you."

"Something other than bugs and birds?"

"Trust me."

Joshua led her through what remained of the jungle. As they neared the eastern beach, they heard the restless surf. Upon reaching the rocky beach, Isabelle was surprised at what a different world existed on this side of the island. Gone was the peaceful enchantment that seemed to hang over the harbor. Instead, waves hurled themselves upon rocks and spray erupted skyward.

Continuing to hold her hand, Joshua led her past tide pools and boulders. Once, when they moved too close to the sea, a wave struck nearby, drenching them in its froth. As they walked, crabs and lizards scurried out of their way. Tiny fish darted about in transitory pools that were destined to forever change and forever remain the same.

"Do you see it?" he asked, when they reached the break in the cliffs.

Isabelle studied the rock and foliage before her. After a few seconds, she replied, "I wouldn't have."

"Let me show you."

They hurried into the cave, and she marveled at its size, the softness of the sand, the freshness of the water. The cave reminded her of an old cathedral. Muted light reached almost every part of it. Echoes abounded. An almost intoxicating coolness prevailed. Though the air was damp, the dampness wasn't nearly as insufferable as the heat outside.

"How wonderful," she said, not believing their good fortune, and excited to finally get the chance to organize a proper camp. "What a magnificent—"

Joshua gently lifted her chin, kissing her, savoring the fullness of her lips. "I'm glad you like it," he whispered.

"Is that, Captain Collins, why you brought me here? To seduce me?"

"It's been far too long since I've seduced you."

She kissed him leisurely, her hands sliding beneath his shirt to trace the contours of his shoulders. His lips moved to her neck. She arched her head backward to expose more of her flesh, and he eagerly exploited this invitation. As he savored the softness of her throat, he slowly unbuttoned her shirt. When each button was unmoored, he spread her shirt farther apart and kissed the flesh that had been hidden. He kissed her collarbone, her freckles, the small mole near the middle of her chest. He kissed all of her, delighting in the unfamiliar taste of salt on her skin. Her breasts seemed slightly larger than normal, and he explored this new element of her with his lips.

When Joshua finished removing her shirt, he laid it on the sand. He took off his own clothes and added them to the bed he fashioned. He carefully helped her to this bed, and she sighed at the soft sand beneath her. When she was naked, he traced the slopes of her with his fingers. "You're changing," he said reflectively, in wonder at the transition within her.

"Is it . . . is it a good change?"

"It's a beautiful change, Izzy."

He kissed her lips, her eyes, her forehead. His mouth moved to her belly, and as he kissed it she ran her fingers through his hair and whispered of her love for him.

ON THE OTHER SIDE of the island, Annie and Akira sat under a palm tree and watched the breeze pull clouds across the sky. Akira had told her that he thought the clouds looked like giant white whales. Annie had said they could have been waves breaking upon a distant shore. The two castaways had been speaking of how poets looked at everyday images through eyes that didn't take such things for granted. Eyes that tended to see the world as if it were being observed for the first or last time.

"I think poets examine things as children do," Akira said softly. "And sometimes the way you do."

Annie moved her toes into and out of the sand. "How so?"

"Because children see more than most adults, yes? Sometime, watch a child looking curiously at . . . something very ordinary. I believe that child is not seeing what you and I see, but something else. And that is how poets . . . interpret their surroundings."

"And me?"

"You ask questions like a child. And you seek experiences like a poet."

"So, I'm a child poet?"

He smiled. "You said this, not me. But, yes, that is an excellent term for you."

She playfully kicked him in the calf. "Well, I'll just have to think of one for you."

Akira was about to respond when he noticed several fins in the harbor. "Sharks," he said, pointing toward the water.

Standing up, Annie replied, "No, not sharks. Dolphins. Like the ones I saw the other day."

As Annie and Akira watched, the fins came closer to shore. There must have been at least six dolphins, each of which seemed to want to lead the group. Suddenly, one of the dolphins leapt high, slicing through the air and then the water.

"Let's get closer," Annie said, hurrying forward.

Though the dolphins were several hundred feet from shore, each dorsal fin was visible when the creatures rose into the world above. The dolphins appeared to be playing—almost as if they were a group of children enjoying a game of tag. Circling, twisting, and speeding through the sea, they frolicked in the gentle waves, often leaping far from the water.

Akira touched Annie's elbow. "You should swim to them, yes?"

"What do you mean?"

"You should swim out there and get close to them. What a fine memory that would be."

"I can't do that."

"May I ask why not?"

She stepped from him. "Look how far out they are. That water's deep. And the last time I was in deep water, I almost died. And I don't want to go out there. It's too deep and there could be sharks and I don't even think I could see the bottom."

Akira turned to her, noting that her face suddenly seemed flushed. "May I . . . may I take your hand and tell you something?"

"I don't want to go out there."

"May I, Annie? May I, please?"

She sighed. "What?"

Akira reached for her hand, cradling it in his own. "The dolphins are having fun, yes?"

"It looks that way."

"Do you think they would be having such fun if sharks were nearby?"

"I'm not an expert on dolphins, Akira. I have no idea."

He paused, as if not expecting such a response. After a dolphin leapt, he said, "I know that bad things have happened to you. Terrible things. But I think now . . . I think that right now you are like a caged bird. And even when the door to your cage is opened, you do not fly free. You are drawn to the dolphins yet you do not fly free."

Annie's face tightened. "You're judging me."

"So sorry, but no, I am not. I only see something beautiful that I want to watch set free. If my words are not right, then please accept my apology. I will not repeat them."

She started to speak but stopped, seeing that he had lowered his head as if suddenly ashamed of advising her, of causing her pain. "I'm not angry at you, Akira," she said, wondering if he was right, if she really was like a caged bird. "It's just that I'm afraid of that water."

"Then please do not swim. We will sit here and observe."

Annie nodded, noticing in her peripheral vision that Jake and Ratu were also standing on the shore, presumably watching the dolphins. Earlier in the day, when Jake had been talking at length with Joshua, Annie had seen Ratu crying by the sea. She'd started to walk over to him, but upon seeing her advance, he'd stood up and run down the beach. Annie could only guess at the source of his pain, and for much of the morning had wondered how she could bring a smile to his face. She'd longed to do just that—to make him laugh and forget about whatever ailed him.

An idea dawning within her, Annie turned to Akira. "Thank you," she said simply. She then started walking toward Ratu. Walking quickly. Soon she was running. She hurried with a sudden desperation, a desperation born of fear that the dolphins would leave, or worse, that her anxiety would again overcome her and she'd change her mind. When she finally reached Ratu, she took his hand. "Will . . . will you . . . will you please swim with me?" she asked, winded.

"With the dolphins, Miss Annie?"

"With the dolphins. With me."

"Brilliant," he said, removing his shirt with a sudden exuberance.

Annie turned to Jake. "Would you mind, Jake, closing your eyes for a moment?"

Jake withdrew a blade of grass from his mouth. "Happily done, miss," he replied, turning toward the jungle, pleased that she was taking Ratu for such a swim.

Annie stripped to her undergarments. She took Ratu's hand. "Will you lead me?"

"I'll bloody well try," he said excitedly, pulling her into the harbor.

The water was warm against her calves, her thighs, her belly. Soon she was swimming. At first she put her head above the water and tried to see the bottom. At first she felt a fear of the unknown. But then, something somehow changed. Her arms and legs seemed surprisingly strong. Her ears filled with Ratu's laughter. And the sea didn't seem to pull her under, but to caress and carry her.

"They aren't leaving!" Ratu shouted. "I tell you, Miss Annie, they aren't bloody leaving!"

Annie glanced toward the deeper water and saw that the dolphins didn't seem concerned by the approaching swimmers. The creatures continued their playful antics—circling one another and leaping above the turquoise water. Annie was now close enough to realize that several of the dolphins were much larger than their companions.

When Annie and Ratu were about thirty feet from the dolphins, the creatures stopped leaping from the sea and started to slowly circle their visitors. The dolphins stayed close together, the pod they formed reminding Annie of the military convoys she'd seen from the deck of *Benevolence.* However, within no more than a minute, the pod loosened. The dolphins circled closer. Soon Annie and Ratu could see bright eyes and old scars. Soon they could hear the creatures calling to each other through a chaotic mixture of whistles, clicks, and chirps. Annie thought that the whistles sounded similar to what she often heard in the jungle as birds screeched at each other.

The dolphins swam at the surface or near it. One of the larger creatures dove almost directly beneath the humans. Bubbles from its blowhole drifted into them, and the sensation of the bubbles bumping along his leg caused Ratu to laugh.

To Annie's surprise and delight, the dolphins continued to draw closer. Two of them were much smaller, and she wondered how old the babies were. The biggest dolphins seemed to be the most inquisitive and vocal. These animals, with their gray backs and white bellies, swam an arm's length away from Annie and Ratu.

"Let's look at them underwater!" Ratu suddenly said.

"Won't the salt sting our eyes?"

"So? A little stinging salt won't hurt you. Not a bloody bit, Miss Annie."

Annie laughed, took a deep breath, and dropped underwater. She opened her eyes. They immediately hurt, but she resisted the urge to close them. A dolphin was quite close to her, and she watched in wonder as it swam directly toward her. She reached out slowly, and though it didn't touch her, it swam beside her. Annie marveled at the beauty of the creature, as well as its grace and permanent smile. She'd listened to dying soldiers speak of angels, and of how such apparitions moved upon the air. To her, the dolphins were angels of sorts, for their grace was something that she'd never before beheld. The dolphins moved with an almost divine loveliness, floating through the water as if each had been doing so for thousands of years.

Annie surfaced, rubbed her aching eyes, and returned to the world below. The dolphins were very close now, circling Annie and Ratu in a manner suggesting that the animals were highly interested in their visitors. Annie was surprised to see Ratu dive deep and pretend to be a dolphin, arching his back and gliding through the water. A dolphin darted toward him, then stopped to float upward as he did. Annie instinctively clapped. Repeating Ratu's idea, she mimicked the movements of the sleek creatures, kicking downward with her legs together and her arms at her side. Two dolphins swam toward her, and she smiled as they bumped into each other, almost as if competing for her attention.

For the next few minutes, Annie was in awe of the scene before her. A marvelous intimacy seemed to exist between her and the dolphins. She felt as though they were honoring her, letting her into their world and asking for nothing in return. Watching the dolphins so unabashedly play, she resolved to not worry as much about the future. Akira was right. She'd been caged for far too long. Despite trying to step from her cage by volunteering for the war effort, she hadn't stepped far enough. And though she was still bound by her darkest fears and these binds were almost impossible to sever, she was going to try to break free.

At that moment, with the dolphins gliding about her, Annie realized that the sea could be dark and cold and unforgiving but could also be full of light and warmth and hope. And was life any different? Yes, she had almost died three times—once as a girl and twice as a woman. And those scars would never truly leave her. But a scar shows that a wound has mostly healed, and if something has mostly healed, why did she need to live in fear of it? Why shouldn't she venture into the jungle near camp, the water of the harbor, or her true feelings for Akira?

When the dolphins finally headed toward much deeper water, Annie and Ratu surfaced. Rubbing their bloodshot eyes, they laughed and spoke excitedly about what they'd seen. Ratu was convinced that he'd made friends with the largest one. "I tell you, Miss Annie," he said, "that big boy smiled at me many times. He opened his mouth and smiled at me."

"How do you know it was a he?"

"Because the other dolphins were all younger girls. Trust me, Miss Annie. I have five little sisters and I know how sisters can drive a brother crazy. My mate, Ratu Junior, was just trying to escape his sisters. That's why he fancied swimming with me."

Laughing, Annie splashed water into Ratu's face. "Did you ever think that Ratu Junior could have been a big sister with a lot of little brothers? Maybe she was trying to escape them!"

"You didn't see Ratu Junior, Miss Annie. You were too busy swimming with Spotted Sally."

"Spotted Sally? Did you name them all?"

"Of course. How can someone be your mate if you don't know his name? There was Ratu Junior; Spotted Sally; Blue-nose Beauty; Smiley; and the twins, Teeny and Tiny."

"Did you tell them your name?"

"Don't be silly, Miss Annie. I can't bloody well talk underwater. And I can't talk to dolphins. But I'm sure they came up with their own name for me."

Annie splashed him again and he laughed. He sprayed water her way, and before she knew it, he swam to her, pushed on her shoulders with his outstretched arms, and sent her underwater.

After Annie surfaced and had her revenge, she turned toward the shore, noticed the distant figure of Akira, and waved happily to him. He waved back, and feeling warm and invigorated, she asked Ratu if he'd like to swim deeper into the water and try to rediscover his newfound friends.

NEARLY ATOP A BANYAN tree on the far side of the beach, Roger peered through the airman's binoculars. When he saw Annie wave at Akira, he cursed and then spat in disgust. "That little bitch," he whispered, shaking his aching head in bewilderment. "She likes the goddamn Nip."

Though Roger was an agent of the Japanese, he despised them as much as he did everyone else. They simply paid him enough that he was able to set his hate aside and deal with the task at hand. If the Americans were as generous, he'd gladly kill Japanese.

The image of Annie waving to Akira reminded Roger of his elementary school days in Tokyo. He'd been allowed to attend a private school on the condition that he spend an hour each day speaking English with some of the teachers. At first, the new school had been fascinating. Like everyone else, he wore a uniform, so none of his classmates ever saw his worn and patched clothes. However, he'd been much taller than everyone else, had an early onset case of acne, and could barely understand Japanese. Consequently, the uniform hadn't mattered as much as he'd hoped. Under the navy blue fabric he'd still been a gaijin—a foreigner. And his odd ways and insecure manner had made him easy to ridicule.

Once, when Roger wasn't aware that he was being spied on by other boys, he'd waved to a girl he thought was curious about him. Instead of waving back, the girl had put her head down and run until she disappeared. The boys who'd been watching burst from their hiding place and laughed until Roger was forced to rush off as well. In the following days, the story of his wave permeated the school. The girl was so embarrassed that she never spoke to him again. The episode had increased Roger's anxiety, worsening his case of acne. Soon many of his classmates began to call him Mount Fuji because of the large pimples that dominated his forehead and chin.

Roger had lived with such taunts and smirks until he'd bested the boy in the kendo match. After that match, after realizing that through his strength he'd find salvation, Roger began to stalk and assault his tormentors. He'd faced them when they were alone, when his greater size and determination allowed him to overwhelm them. Knowing their shame would be so great that they'd never reveal him, he hurt them badly, bloodying them until they begged him to stop, until they happily handed him the coins in their pockets. After anyone who taunted him turned up at school with a black eye or a swollen lip, Roger was rarely ridiculed.

Once four boys had banded together to attack Roger and had managed to knock him unconscious with their kendo swords. Roger told no one about his attackers, but as soon as his strength returned, he hunted them down individually. After beating them into submission, he'd taken off their sandals and broken each of their big toes. The boys limped for the rest of the year and no one bothered him again.

Now, as Annie waded through the water, Roger focused his binoculars on her small figure. A rust-colored ant bit his knuckle, and cursing the island's insects, he smashed the ant against a branch. He put the binoculars again to his eyes and saw that Annie was only wearing undergarments. Quickly he became aroused. He clenched the binoculars hard, refocusing them constantly in order to maintain the best possible view of her. He swore silently as he remembered how she'd slapped him. The memory invaded him like an illness. No woman had ever slapped him, and no attack had ever felt so personal. She'd assaulted and humiliated him, and he'd do the same and much more to her.

Roger watched her put on her shirt and shorts. She hugged Ratu and then moved toward Akira, who walked in her direction, his limp barely noticeable. When they finally met she embraced him briefly. Roger wondered if the Jap was aware of her breasts against him. They were small breasts, Roger reflected, but still he must sense them. Did the monkey want to rip off her shirt and squeeze them tight?

Hating the two of them, Roger counted the days until he could feel her. Once the Japs landed, he'd lead them to the cave and then have his fill of her. He imagined breaking her toes, as he'd done to those boys so long ago. That way, she'd be unable to run from him. Or he could slap her repeatedly until she begged him to forgive her. Or he could do both.

Roger shifted his thoughts to Akira. He swore to himself that the Nip would suffer and that he'd see Annie suffer. How best to do that? he wondered. How can I ensure that he and his bitch share their misery?

As Roger descended the banyan tree, he debated such questions, ultimately not deciding upon anything until long after dusk had fallen. At that point, though he craved a cigarette and his head felt as if someone had driven a railroad spike into it, he clucked his tongue excitedly and went to sleep.

DAY NINE

The past comes to me
Like a shadow to its source.
Where is the monsoon?

Longing for Dreams

The tide was rising. Jake had noticed how the harbor swelled and the beach shrank each morning. To him, it seemed that the two entities were in a never-ending war over territory. The sea and beach fought the same way that night and day fought—a patient, hopeless struggle for domination of space.

Following Ratu into deeper water, Jake held his spear aloft. Despite their prowess as hunters, the two friends hadn't been able to spear many fish the previous day. The drying rack they'd built wasn't even halfway full. Knowing that Joshua depended on him, and that he was failing his commanding officer, Jake had asked Ratu if they could fish in deeper water, where bigger fish might linger.

"I tell you, Big Jake, it's much bloody harder to throw a spear into deep water," Ratu said. "Aim lower than you think you need to because water will lift the spear up."

"Ouch," Jake muttered, as his toe stubbed against something hard and sharp.

"What did you say?"

"Oh, ain't nothing worth repeating."

"If I'm going to tell you things, mate, you need to listen. I do think I'm interesting, but I don't just want to talk for myself. If I'm going to do that, I'll talk about sports. Maybe about the greatest cricket players or something like that."

"Don't you worry none. I'll aim lower. Or was it higher?"

"Bugger off, Big Jake. I don't know what to do with you. I really don't. Throw lower. Much lower."

The water was up to Ratu's belly and Jake's thighs. To their right, birds circled over a series of ripples. Believing that large fish were feasting upon something near the surface, Ratu and Jake waded toward the ripples. Sure enough, a school of thousands of inch-long fish was being chased by a handful of much larger predators.

"Barracuda!" Ratu exclaimed, pointing at the long and narrow fish. "Their mouths are full of teeth, Big Jake. Be careful when you spear them or you'll have an angry barracuda hanging from your leg. And the blood will bring his friends, and suddenly you'll be little more than barracuda dinner. Once I saw—"

Eyeing a large barracuda that rose to the surface, Jake threw his spear quickly and with great force. The spear struck the fish right behind the head and skewered it completely, pinning it to the sand.

"Brilliant!" Ratu shouted. "What a cracking good shot! Your teacher must have been fantastic!"

"My teacher fancies his voice a heap more than his spear. I ain't seen him hit a darn thing in two days."

"Teachers can't always do everything. And who'd do all the talking if I didn't? This island, I tell you, would be a dull place if I left all the talking up to you."

Jake chuckled, watching the bloody water for other barracuda. "Ever since those dolphins, you've been happier than a pigeon in a puddle."

"You should have come with us, Big Jake. You definitely need to next time. What bloody marvelous fun it was. And I want to introduce you to Ratu Junior."

"Does he prattle on as much as you?"

"Probably more."

"Then I'll pass, thank you kindly."

"Oh, put a sock in it, Big Jake. You'd bore him anyway."

"I reckon he'd—" Jake stopped, his words dying as a large shark swept into view, heading straight for the twitching barracuda. "Behind you!"

Ratu spun in the water, leaping out of the way of the shark, which tore into the fish. The water immediately turned a deeper shade of crimson. The shark's top fin and tail emerged from the sea as it consumed the barracuda. Ratu started to flee for the beach, but seeing that the shark was occupied with its meal, he stepped forward, raising his spear.

"No!" Jake shouted. "Head straight ashore. Now!"

Wishing that his father could see him, Ratu edged closer to the bloody water. The shark, which was about six feet long, was having a hard time consuming the part of the barracuda that was pinned to the seafloor.

"Leave him be!" Jake shouted.

Ratu didn't hear his friend. He wanted a tooth from the shark so much that his senses were entirely focused on the churning water. He saw the broad back of the shark's head emerge from the sea, and remembered where his father had told him to strike. The shark thrashed, banging the spear that held the barracuda in place. The spear started to fall. The shark turned in Ratu's direction. It came at him.

Ratu raised his arm back as far as possible and then stepped forward with his left foot, twisting his body to the left, heaving the spear with all his might. The spear struck the shark just behind its gills, driving deep into the creature. But the shark didn't die and swam madly in a circle, like a kitten chasing its own tail. Ratu stepped away from the predator, his heel striking a mass of coral, which sent him tumbling backward. The shark bumped into his legs, its rough skin scratching him. Ratu tried to crawl away but the red water seemed to boil over him. Then he saw Jake wrench his spear from the barracuda and drive it into the shark's head, drive it so hard and deep that the shark was suddenly pinned to the seafloor.

Jake grabbed Ratu's hand and pulled him toward the beach. About to shout at Ratu for being so rash, he had to stop himself when Ratu wrapped his arms around him. Jake carried him to the sand, where they sat and watched the shark slowly die. Though Ratu trembled, he didn't seem overwhelmed with terror, which surprised Jake.

"A coconut for them thoughts?" Jake finally asked, massaging an ache in his right shoulder.

Ratu slowly looked up from the water. "The shark. It didn't . . . it didn't want to die."

"No, I expect it didn't."

Ratu nodded absently. After a few dozen heartbeats of silence, he turned to Jake. "Have you ever killed a man?"

"No."

"Is it like that, you think?"

"I reckon it's something like that. And then some, I'm sure."

Ratu nodded again. "I don't ever want to kill a man, Jake. I won't have to, will I? No one will send me to kill a man?"

Jake sighed, unsure of how to respond. Finally, he said, "I expect when you're old enough to be sent for, you'll be old enough to decide. And if you don't want to do it, well, then, ain't no need to do it."

"I won't. I won't ever do it."

The shark finally stopped twitching. "That was one tough fellow," Jake said.

"Will we have enough food?"

"What?"

"After we cut him up, will we have enough food?"

"Yes, I suspect so."

"Good. Then I think . . . I think I'll take a break from fishing."

Jake put his arm around Ratu. "Now that we got a tooth for your father, we can get to finding them shells."

"That would be good, Big Jake."

Jake gently blew on Ratu's knee, which had been scraped raw by the shark's rough skin. "Maybe, Ratu, maybe that old shark done told you something."

"What do you mean?"

"I reckon you know."

Ratu moved Jake's arm aside and stood. "Big Jake?"

"Yes?"

"I still want the tooth. But it's not for me. It's for my father."

Jake rose, patted Ratu on the back, and then waded into the water. "Well, then, I reckon we'd best get busy."

LATER, WITH STRIP upon strip of shark meat drying in the sun, the survivors gathered at the base of the banyan tree. Eyeing all the food, Joshua nodded appreciatively toward Jake and Ratu. "We certainly picked the right hunters."

"Ratu gets the credit, Captain," Jake replied, nudging the boy. "It ain't healthy to have fins around these parts."

"Well, I'm awfully glad you got the shark instead of the other way around."

Jake removed a stem from his mouth. "That makes three of us, Captain."

"How long," Joshua asked, "do you think it will take to dry?"

"In this sun? I reckon three or four days should darn near do it."

Joshua glanced at the drying rack. "As soon as it's ready we'll wrap it in leaves, pile it in the lifeboat, and then all head toward the cave. Some of us will row, and others will walk."

Scarlet scratched at a fresh mosquito bite. "Is the cave really going to be better than the beach? Maybe we should just stay here. If we're here and one of our ships passes, we can easily signal it."

"We can signal a ship from almost anywhere," Joshua responded, stooping to pull a thorn from his ankle. "Believe me, the cave's not only safer, it's much more comfortable. Like I said before, there aren't many bugs, for starters."

"No bugs and built-in air-conditioning," Isabelle added.

"Really?" Scarlet asked.

"Like you're in some fancy hotel."

"Let's keep cleaning up this area," Joshua said. "When we leave, the place needs to look like no one's ever set foot here. Our charts are probably the same as the Japanese charts. And our charts say the island's deserted. No reason to give anyone any idea to think otherwise."

"So for three days, sir, we just do what we've been doing?" Nathan asked, standing deep in the shade, as he was still recovering from a bad case of sunburn.

"I don't see any reason why—" Joshua stopped talking when he saw Akira suddenly rise and step toward the beach. Akira said something in Japanese and pointed beyond the harbor. A gray dot marred the sea, breaking up the flat horizon. Joshua grabbed the binoculars from where they hung from a branch.

"Is it American?" Roger asked abruptly, his mind reeling with the problems that such a ship would pose to him.

"Yes, yes," Scarlet added. "Is it ours? Oh, please let it be one of ours!"

Joshua adjusted the binoculars until the ship came into focus. The vessel had two smokestacks and bristled with heavy guns. On its gray side were white markings of some kind. "A Jap destroyer," Joshua said, his heart racing. "But why . . . why is she all alone? She's a sitting duck."

Akira moved to Joshua and politely asked if he could use the binoculars. Joshua nodded, and Akira quickly located the destroyer. He looked at the name on the side and said, *"Akebono."*

"What?" Joshua asked.

"So sorry. *Daybreak* is the ship's name," Akira replied, handing back the binoculars.

"I wonder what she's doing here," Joshua said, again eyeing the ship, which wasn't under way and seemed to just sit atop the water. Though the destroyer was several miles away and didn't pose an imminent threat,

Joshua felt unnerved, as the Japanese often used destroyers to protect troop transport ships or aircraft carriers. Typically, Japanese destroyers traveled in groups of three or four and shielded more important ships from plane and submarine attacks. As far as Joshua knew, a lone destroyer was a highly unusual sight.

"Why is she all by herself?" he asked Akira. As Akira again looked through the binoculars, Joshua wondered if he was wise to trust Annie's rescuer.

"She has recently been fighting," Akira replied.

Joshua nodded. "I saw the damage to her superstructure."

"She could be conducting repairs, yes? Hiding in these islands and doing repairs?"

"Or she could be waiting to rendezvous with other ships. It just doesn't make sense for her to be so isolated out here." Joshua felt a tap on his shoulder and was surprised to see Annie beside him.

"May I look?" she asked.

"Of course."

Annie refocused the binoculars and let out a small gasp when she saw the ship in full detail. She was used to the innocuous lines of *Benevolence* and not the long guns that dominated the Japanese destroyer. The ship gave her the chills. "It's so . . . menacing," she said softly, handing the binoculars to Joshua.

Knowing that the Japanese had more than one hundred such ships, Joshua scanned the horizon for other visitors, but saw nothing else but the distant islands. "She's all alone," he said, still bewildered.

Roger asked for the binoculars and took in the full view of *Akebono*. He knew that the Japanese would take the island by force, and suspected that his foe was correct. The destroyer had arrived early and was repairing the damage to its superstructure while waiting to escort a troop ship through these shallow and dangerous waters. "The Nip's right about the repairs," he said, delighted that he'd soon be off the island, and envisioning the cigarettes he'd smoke and the women he'd dominate. "I bet she'll be gone in a few days."

By now the entire group had gathered around Joshua, and everyone took turns looking through the binoculars. Annie wondered how the Japanese could call the ship *Daybreak*, finding it incomprehensible that anyone would compare such a machine of war to dawn. Isabelle methodically counted the large guns, committing the destroyer's profile to memory. Nathan worried that the war would drag on until his son would someday be forced to fight such ships. And Ratu looked at *Akebono* so long that when he finally handed the binoculars back to Joshua, circles had formed around his eyes. "It looks like the shark," he said, stepping closer to Jake.

"I don't think this changes our plans," Joshua said finally, addressing the group. "They can't see us. Not if they don't come closer and we're careful with our fire."

"What if they come ashore?" Scarlet asked.

"That ship wasn't designed to carry large numbers of troops. Nobody is coming ashore." Joshua let the binoculars hang from his neck, and for the first time no one asked for them. "But we need to keep a better eye on the horizon," he said. "I think someone should stay put on one of the hills above us and watch to see if our visitor gets any companions."

"I'll do it," Scarlet said almost immediately. Unlike most everyone on the island, she didn't have anyone close to her with whom she could share her thoughts. For days she'd felt like an outsider, and she was tired of the feeling. She reasoned that at least if she were atop a hill she could be helpful.

"Are you sure?" Joshua asked.

She held out her hand, and he placed the binoculars within her grasp. "What do you want me to look for?"

"If that ships leaves, if she comes closer, people down here need to know. But we especially need to know if other ships appear. If that happens, please hurry down." Joshua pointed to the hill that he'd climbed during his first day on the island. "It's not a bad walk," he said, "and it's close."

"Then that's where I'll be."

After Joshua thanked her, Scarlet slung the binoculars around her neck and grabbed a full canteen and some bananas. She then headed into the jungle. Because of the bugs, she hadn't spent much time beyond the beach, but she'd heard Isabelle say that the higher one got, the more wind prevailed and the less one had to worry about such airborne pests.

For the first time in several days, Scarlet felt a pulse of happiness as she entered the jungle. Though she hated the mud and the insects and the damp heat, she was eager to climb the hill and have the binoculars to herself. With the binoculars, she could keep her eye out for ships and could also watch the island's colorful and varied birds. She'd been fascinated by these talkative creatures for several days, and they were about the only thing that prompted her to pause in obsessing about her brothers.

Scarlet had always enjoyed birds. One of her fondest memories was visiting Central Park with her grandmother and feeding pigeons. She'd participated in this ritual almost every Saturday afternoon for several years. Though hundreds of pigeons had always seemed to gather about them, Scarlet, like her grandmother, had her favorites and tried to give them extra bits of bread.

Wishing that her grandmother could see the island's birds, Scarlet continued through the jungle, eyeing parrots and cockatoos. Even on the beach Scarlet had never seen the brilliant and varied plumage that she did now, and she was certain her grandmother would have thought this place to be a small slice of heaven. She'd have watched birds from dawn to dusk.

Though her grandmother had been dead for many years, Scarlet missed her, and memories of the pigeons were suddenly bittersweet. Her mood soured, as it often did on the island. The stress of being stranded and unable to hear about her brothers had started to affect her. She incessantly worried about her siblings, imagining how Rommel's tanks might maim them. Such imaginings produced an anxiety that gripped her so tightly that the only way she could flee its grasp was to sleep. And even then, nightmares often plagued her—visions of her brothers' lifeless eyes and torn bodies. Scarlet hoped that atop the hill she'd at least be able to temporarily forget such visions as she focused her binoculars on distant ships and birds.

The jungle was hard to navigate, but she moved forward steadily, like a patient eager to be rid of crutches. She flinched as giant cockroaches scurried beneath her or bats stretched their wings within shadowed havens above. Her pulse started to race, and she had a sudden desire to see the sun. But to her dismay, she couldn't locate it through the jungle's canopy.

Fortunately, the hill wasn't far and she was soon climbing, soon free of the suffocating trees. Though the climb was relatively gentle, Scarlet continued to pace herself, pausing occasionally to wipe her sweaty brow. Upon reaching the summit, she sat atop a flat rock. The view felt liberating, as if she'd just been released from a cage and was gazing upon a world without bars. She could see most of the island and the sea beyond. The Japanese destroyer hadn't moved. Lifting the binoculars, she looked for other ships but saw none. She then sipped some water and started searching for birds. At first she saw nothing of interest, but after focusing on the treetops, her world came alive. Birds of seemingly every size, shape, and color darted about the verdant canopy.

For the first time in two days, Scarlet smiled. She'd been right about this place, right about coming here. Perhaps this hill would be the sanctuary that she so desperately needed. Perhaps here she'd experience a sense of serenity that had avoided her by the beach.

An immense gray-and-white-feathered bird suddenly sailed into view from the sea. Scarlet followed it with the binoculars, marveling at how the bird didn't even need to flap its wings to soar. She expected the creature to drop into the jungle, but instead it flew to a steep and rocky hill in the middle of the island. The bird landed amid a nest of driftwood, tucking its wings against its body.

Scarlet aimed the binoculars back and forth between the ship and the birds. And at least for this moment, with a breeze on her face and a new world to observe, she stopped thinking about Rommel and what his awful tanks might do to her brothers.

DEEP WITHIN THE JUNGLE, at the bottom of a gulley that ran between two rises, Roger carefully pushed his shovel into the earth. The shovel was his creation. He'd used the machete to chop a large tree branch until it somewhat resembled a canoe paddle. He'd then hardened the shovel with fire. Knowing that Joshua wanted him outside camp, Roger had said that he'd seen a wild boar and that he hoped to fashion a trap to catch it. Predictably, the captain had been delighted to send him away.

Roger had been digging for what he assumed to be several hours. His hands trembled as he dug, for he hadn't savored a cigarette in days, and his body was in turmoil. The headache that assailed him had been growing in intensity since not long after he'd set foot on the island. It radiated forward from the back of his skull, and his eyes felt as if they'd pop from his head. Moreover, his heart often raced and his feet tingled. His throat even ached.

These maddening symptoms reminded Roger of living alone in Philadelphia at the peak of the Great Depression. Like so many others, he'd been jobless. Unlike most others, he'd thought the soup lines beneath him, and stole what food he could. Still, very few coins had rubbed together in his pockets, and he'd no money to spend on luxuries. Limiting himself to one cigarette a day had led to his first experience with the headaches.

For many years, Roger had hated the Japanese. But it wasn't until returning to America and experiencing the Great Depression that his hate followed him across the ocean and spread like the plague within him. He quickly grew to detest America, to despise his country of birth for how it had failed him. He could still remember his father telling him and his mother that the banks had collapsed and what precious little money they'd saved was gone. His mother had wept quietly while his father shrugged and said that though the Devil was hard at work, God would see them through. Roger had thrown his father down at these words, sickened by his weakness and blind faith. He'd cursed the man and woman who'd brought him into the world. He'd screamed at them for all his pains and wants and memories. His spittle had struck his mother's face. His booted foot had caused his father to beg for mercy. And he had seen neither parent since.

Now, as Roger dug deeper into the black soil, the temptation to climb the hill, uncover his box, and smoke cigarettes all afternoon was frighteningly powerful. He hadn't felt so vulnerable since those unbearable months in Philadelphia, and his feebleness enraged him. If only he were alone on the island, as he was meant to be. Then he'd have a cigarette between his lips right now, drawing sweet smoke into his lungs and watching it disperse into the day.

Trying to ignore his cravings, Roger continued to work on his hole, pausing only to pull apart or smash insects that he uncovered. Such insects had tormented him during his stay on the island, and he found it gratifying to watch beetles try to walk with half their legs missing or centipedes writhe after he chopped them in two. These sights briefly obscured the ache behind his eyes, as they reminded him of how boys had struggled and squirmed after he'd hurt them.

The soil was quite soft, and if he labored with care he didn't think he'd break his shovel. The hole was already as deep as his chest and as long as his outstretched arms—bigger than it needed to be to catch a wild boar. Working with determination—for his discomfort and anger gave him immense resolve—he continued to widen and deepen the pit.

Finally satisfied, Roger climbed from the hole. He closed his eyes for a few heartbeats, trying to ignore the throbbing pulse in his head by listening to the jungle. Its familiar cadence filled his ears and, knowing that no one was looking, he picked up the machete. With a backhanded strike he cut a sapling in half. He then made two-foot spikes out of the young tree. He felled a second sapling and a third, cutting them low enough to the ground that ferns hid whatever remained of their trunks. More spikes followed, their tips as sharp as possible.

Roger tossed the spikes into the hole and carefully climbed down, drops of sweat striking the torn earth. He used both hands to press the dull ends of the spikes into the ground, set no more than six inches apart. Anyone who fell into the hole would likely be impaled by at least ten spikes. Though Roger didn't believe that he'd ever need the trap— after all, when the Japanese landed, he'd retrieve his gun—he liked having options. And if he was somehow forced to run, he could lead his adversary here.

As Roger worked, he held a slender, cigarette-shaped stick between his teeth and imagined Akira and Joshua chasing him through the jungle. He saw himself lead them into the gulley. He then jumped over the trap and, after rounding a nearby corner, grabbed a pair of spears. By the time he turned back to the trap, the Jap and the infuriating captain had already fallen into it. They were pierced in a dozen places and dying quickly. With no need to use his spears, he set them down, put his legs over the edge of the pit and listened to his enemies plead for mercy. He laughed, picked up several stones, and began to hurl the stones into their faces, killing them the same way criminals had been slain for thousands of years.

His breath quickening at the prospect of such a moment, Roger climbed from the pit and with his trembling fingers began to lay long and slender branches over it. Once he'd placed enough branches so that they were almost touching, he tossed leaves atop the branches. The gulley was covered in leaves and twigs, and Roger was easily able to replicate the look and feel of the jungle floor. Finally content with the concealment of his trap, he picked up a blood-colored boulder and set it next to his pitfall. He pretended to run and jump over the trap, repeating the sequence several times until he felt comfortable with how he'd recognize the rock and then leap over the hidden pit.

Carefully skirting the trap, Roger followed the gulley around a bend and hid a spear. Though this was the first such trap he'd created, he had already concealed a variety of weapons and supplies all over the island. Despite his assumption that it would be easy to find the Japanese once they'd landed and take them directly to the cave, he'd learned that in war anything was possible. Prudence demanded that he prepare for every contingency, and he believed he had.

Thinking about the cave, and how the idiot captain was convinced that it would protect everyone, Roger smiled for the first time all day. That cave will be the fool's tomb, he thought excitedly. He'll hide in it like a coward, hide with that annoying, know-it-all bitch of his. He'll think he's safe, but I'll lead Edo's men straight to his door. I'll tell him that the women can go free, and when the skirts come out, we'll open fire on the men. They'll burn and scream and they'll never leave that worthless cave. And when those maggots are dying, I'll let them know what will happen to their whores.

Pleased with his trap and by thoughts of the future, Roger decided that he'd reward himself with a cigarette. As he had several days before, he'd climb to his secret stash, strip off his clothes to keep them free of smoke, enjoy several cigarettes, and later swim in the ocean and remove all scents but salt from him. If smoking presented a small risk, so be it. It was far better, he reasoned, to take a slight chance at discovery than to continue to suffer from an intolerable headache and to have the trembling hands of an old man.

Making his way through the jungle, his mind euphoric over the prospect of his reward, Roger again thought about what the near future would bring. In less than a week, he said to himself, I'll have everything I want, everything I've worked for. I'll have it because I'm smarter and stronger than anyone else on the island. And though now they laugh at me and hate me and I can't do a goddamn thing about it, soon enough they'll know that I betrayed them, that I sold their souls, and they'll understand that I won. And when they look into my eyes before they die, when their pain's so great that they beg for an end, I'll drag them to the sea and let the waves wash them away.

ANNIE WASN'T USED to walking the beach alone, having spent most of her time on the island with Isabelle or Akira. And though she didn't need constant companionship or distractions—as she sometimes thought her sister did—creating poetry with Akira or talking with Isabelle about her baby had provided her with much-needed escapes. She'd initially told herself that she was fleeing nothing more than the horror of *Benevolence* sinking. But as the days passed, and she continued to seek diversions, she realized that she wasn't running from the past, but from the future.

The future, after all, had been almost determined for her. She'd return from the war, marry Ted, bear and raise children, and spend the rest of her life playing tennis and bridge. That was the future that Ted saw, that he wanted. And to be fair, at one time she'd wanted that future as well. It had seemed safe and decent. But not long after Ted had proposed, Annie started to have misgivings. She'd started to panic.

As Annie walked down the beach, she tried to remember the good times she'd experienced with Ted. Almost immediately, she reflected on how easily he could make her laugh. No one had ever prompted her laughter like Ted, and the many smiles he put on her face endeared her to him from their very first date. After the seriousness of her childhood, it felt so wonderful to laugh. And the discovery that laughter could temporarily obscure difficult memories had been extremely cathartic.

To Ted's credit, he clearly enjoyed provoking her laughter. Her smile made him smile, and he seemed happiest when she was grinning because of something he'd said. In this way, he did his best to encourage her to forget her past, to enjoy the present. In this way, he succeeded in giving her bliss. At times she laughed so hard with him that she felt as if she were once again a little girl, giggling at her puppy's antics.

Ted also treated her parents well. He smoked pipes with her father and complimented her mother on her cooking. And Ted came from money. He'd once shown Annie the house he had already purchased for them. Though she'd hoped for something quaint and cozy, he'd bought a large, ranch-style home on twenty acres of land. He'd get her a horse, he promised, so that she could ride alongside him.

Annie had slowly come to realize that to Ted, life was a series of great adventures. In some ways, he reminded her of Fitzgerald's Gatsby, for Ted loved to hunt, to fly, to host lavish parties, to buy the latest cars. He'd been a strong advocate of America joining the war in Europe, even while the vast majority of his countrymen argued that one world war was enough. When the Japanese had attacked Pearl Harbor, Annie thought Ted to be actually happy, for suddenly the nation had no choice but to join in the fight against fascism. Like Roosevelt, Ted would finally get his way.

The last time Annie had seen Ted was in New York. He'd been granted a week of leave, and with only a day's notice, she'd packed up and taken a train from California. They'd met in his hotel's bar, and he told her all that he'd done during his time in Europe. She'd heard of how he had been one of a handful of American pilots to help the Royal Air Force engage the Luftwaffe during the Battle of Britain. He'd flown mission after mission over a burning and shuddering London, attacking the Luftwaffe with great success. He'd been shot down once but was hardly scratched.

When Ted had finally finished regaling her with tales of his dogfights, Annie had applauded his bravery and given him a present. The silver flask bore his initials and was filled with fine bourbon—which she knew he loved. He'd smiled at her gift and though he hadn't meant to hurt her, had told her how impractical it was for someone at war to carry such a flask. He had handed it to her and asked that she keep it. He'd then apologized for having nothing for her. Of course, she hadn't minded the oversight. But she was bothered when a group of pilots he'd trained with stumbled into the hotel, sat down beside them, drank his bourbon, and took him by the arm and vanished from sight. When he'd returned four hours later, though she was already asleep in their room, her slumber hadn't kept him from telling her amusing stories from the war, and from later undressing her with clumsy fingers and making love to her as if he were in some sort of race.

Will it always be this way with Ted? Annie wondered as she stepped around the bloated body of a dead lionfish. Yes, he could make her smile and occasionally warm her heart, but his ability to touch her beyond his humor and charm was limited. Parts of her existed that he would never fully understand. And this gulf between them troubled her even though its presence wasn't his fault. She didn't blame him, because their experiences were so different. After all, how could he grasp her fears if he'd never felt fear himself? How could he appreciate her uncertainty if he'd always stepped firmly on a path of his making?

Though Annie knew from Isabelle that marriage wasn't perfect, she wanted more than laughter and children. She wanted true companionship. She wanted something beautiful.

Can Ted give me what I need? she asked herself as she walked back to camp. Yes, he can help me enjoy the moment. And he can please my parents and provide for me forever. But what can we teach each other? What's going to bind us together when life isn't so amusing?

Annie absently said hello to Nathan—who was using the airman's dagger to finish a wooden carving that he'd been making for his daughter—and walked toward the banyan tree. Akira was sitting at his usual spot, picking meat from the bones of a burnt fish. Seeing him grimace as he ate, Annie was reminded of how her Japanese patients had occasionally asked if any raw fish was available.

An idea quickly blossoming within her, she walked farther down the beach, where Jake was spearfishing. Annie was surprised that Ratu was nowhere to be seen, as he often seemed to be Jake's shadow. "Where's the namesake of Ratu Junior?" she asked, smiling at the memory of swimming with Ratu and the dolphins.

Jake set his spear next to a large tuna that he'd killed and removed a stem from between his teeth. "That darn shark spooked him, miss. Spooked him like a rattlesnake rattles a horse. I reckon he's looking for shells for his sisters. We already found a handful of them, but he wants an armful. I'd be with him, but the captain asked me to catch a few more fish in case people don't fancy shark. So here I am."

Glancing at the ocean, Annie saw that the Japanese destroyer hadn't moved. "Are we sure they can't see us?" she asked, suddenly frightened.

"Even with them binocs we can't see much of that big boat, miss. They sure ain't gonna be able to see us."

Annie nodded, turning her gaze to the fish that Jake had speared. "May I have a piece of that, Jake? Do you need it all?"

"A piece, miss?"

"A piece of meat. Believe it or not, Japanese like to eat raw fish, and I thought Akira might enjoy some."

Jake smiled, the gap between his front teeth somehow serving to make his other teeth appear even whiter. "I hear them Japs eat anything from the sea," he said, using the machete to cut away several strips of cherry-colored meat. "Snakes and slugs. Things like that. I reckon I'd sooner eat my own foot than a raw fish."

"Could you cut them even smaller?"

"I suspect so. Ain't only one way to skin a cat, or in this case, a fish."

"Perfect," Annie said, holding out her hands.

"You wanna put it on something? Maybe a rock? A big old leaf?"

"A leaf. Yes, that's a great idea, Jake." Annie hurried to the edge of the jungle and quickly returned with a leaf the size of a cookie sheet.

"That'll work real nice," Jake said, carefully placing the cuts of tuna on the leaf.

When he finished, Annie put her hand on his arm. "Thanks, Jake. Thanks for everything you do around here."

"Happy to help, miss. Ain't much else to do anyhow."

Annie thanked him again and, holding the leaf like a large platter, moved toward Akira. He'd risen and was stretching his muscles as he leaned against a palm tree. As usual, she instinctively glanced at his wound, which had completely closed up. Deciding that she'd remove the stitches the next day, she showed Akira the fish she'd brought. "You like raw fish, right?" she asked. "Don't Japanese like raw fish?"

Akira eyed the sliced tuna. "You did this? For me?"

"I can put it away if you don't want it. I didn't know if—"

"No, no, no," he said, bowing to her. He gestured for her to sit, carefully taking the leaf and lowering himself to the sand beside her. "A wonderful treat," he said. "A wonderful treat that you have prepared for me. Thank you for your kindness."

"Is this how you eat it? Just like this?"

He shook his head. "Usually we have some . . . sauce. But this is nearly the same. This is perfect, in fact." She smiled and he asked, "Will you taste it with me?"

"Me?"

"Only if you care to." Akira picked up one of the smallest pieces of fish and put it in his mouth. He closed his eyes, chewing slowly and methodically. "What delicious sashimi."

"Sashimi?"

"Yes. When it is so fresh like that, it . dissolves into your tongue."

Annie glanced at the platter before her. The meat was red and ragged, and the thought of eating it repulsed her. "I'll try . . . one bite," she said, selecting a sliver of fish. Before she could stop herself, she closed her eyes and set the meat in her mouth. At first she noticed the coolness of the fish, which felt surprisingly refreshing. She then bit, and though she didn't like the texture of the meat, the taste was pleasant enough and she ate the entire piece. "Not bad," she said, smiling. "Not bad at all."

He grinned. "Yesterday you swam with dolphins. Today you are eating sashimi. What will tomorrow bring?"

"It's your turn to do something brave tomorrow. I think I've done enough."

Akira took another piece of fish. "Yes, yes, I sincerely agree."

Annie watched him eat, noting how refined his movements were.

How differently Akira and Ted approach eating, she thought. While Ted seemed to attack his food, Akira appeared to savor and almost study the fish. "Can I ask you something?" she said softly, the comparison of the two men prompting her curiosity.

"Of course."

"It's kind of silly. Rather childish, actually."

"I think that today I have time for one silly question."

She smiled nervously, her gaze darting from him to the sea to a bug bite on her arm. "Do you really think . . . think that I'm like that little tree?"

"I think—"

"I just don't know if it's realistic for a man to pay that much attention to a woman. Or for that matter, for a woman to pay that much attention to a man. Who has time for such things?"

Akira looked out over the water. "I do not know what is realistic," he finally said. "But I do know what is possible. And is it possible for a man to pay such attention to a woman? Yes, I think so."

Annie's thoughts drifted back to Ted, and she wondered if he'd ever see her as the gardener had seen the tree. What would he do with her once they were reunited? "But anything is possible," she replied. "That doesn't make it probable."

"This morning," he said, setting a piece of tuna aside, "I found something."

"What?"

He pointed to her feet. "Beneath you. Please look beneath you."

She dug into the sand at her feet. Almost immediately, she uncovered a snail's shell, which was sculpted and blue and highlighted with white borders—almost as if the sky had somehow been painted onto the shell. "It's beautiful," she said.

Akira wanted to tell her how his discovery made him think of her, of how he had written a haiku about her after he'd found it. But she was engaged and American, and the impossibility of their union weighed so heavily upon him that he simply said, "I would be honored . . . if you would keep it."

Annie sensed that he wanted to say more. She was unsure, however, if she wanted him to. "Thank you," she said, continuing to hold the shell. "It's quite lovely."

He smiled, aware that he'd thought of little but her for the past three days. "The fish is delicious, yes?" he asked, picking up another piece.

"It's certainly simple to prepare," she replied, smiling. "Beats cooking all day over a hot stove."

"Simple is good."

Though a part of her wanted to leave, another part longed to know where his mind lay. Her heart beating quicker, she licked her salty lips and found his eyes. "What were you thinking about?" she asked, surprised by her brazenness and unsure what to think of it.

"When?"

"When I was . . . holding the shell. After you gave it to me."

Akira looked at the shell, which she held in her cupped hand. "The shell," he said quietly, uncertain what he should tell her, "reminded me of you."

"It did?"

"It made me . . ."

"What?"

He started to speak again and stopped. Though he'd always been honest with her, he wasn't sure if she should know the truth, as he was afraid that it might drive her from him. Nevertheless, despite his fears, he wanted to tell her what so heavily weighed upon his mind, what kept him awake at night long after the moon had risen. And so he took a slow breath and said, "The shell . . . inspired me to write a haiku about you."

"A haiku? What does it say?"

"It is unfinished. I am not . . . content with it yet."

"Why not?"

He sighed, setting the leaf next to him. The words of his poem flashed within him. "Because," he replied quietly, "to describe . . . the wonder of you with only three short phrases is a most difficult task."

Annie drew back, simultaneously thrilled and confused and scared. "I don't know what to think," she said, more aware of his gaze as it fell on her than she had ever been.

He immediately bowed, briefly closing his eyes. "Please forgive me. I should not have told you this."

She nodded absently, torn between longing to tell him that she felt the same and needing to be faithful to Ted. She looked at his hands, sensing that he yearned to touch her as much as she yearned to be touched. What would he do to me? she asked herself. How would he touch me, and what words would he share with me?

"Please forgive my foolishness," he said, bowing again to her.

"Don't . . . please don't do that," she replied, her voice and legs unsteady as she rose from the sand.

"I should not—"

"No. I put those words in your mouth. I wanted . . . I needed to hear them. And I'm sorry for that." She wiped her brow, which was suddenly damp with perspiration. "I'm glad you liked . . . the fish," she said, turning from him, the space between them suddenly too small. He said something to her, but she did not hear it, her mind reeling from conflicting emotions.

Annie's feet were heavy and the sun was hot and she couldn't get to the water fast enough.

DAY TEN

Some say love is dead.
But why do I feel such bliss?
Frogs shout in the rain.

A Choice Is Made

For the first time since *Benevolence* sank, the sky was rendered mute by clouds. A thick gray blanket hid the sun and tarnished the sea. Diminutive waves marched through the harbor and tossed themselves upon the shore, dying on the sand like soldiers trying to take a trench. The wind seemed restless, pressing on trees and faces from a variety of angles.

Stiff from a nearly sleepless night, Akira walked the beach alone, disgusted at himself for shaming Annie into running from him. He'd never said such a thing to a woman, and his words had backfired in exactly the manner that he'd most feared. He had betrayed her just as she was coming to truly know him, and this betrayal tormented him the way a bee sting assails a child.

Before being stranded on the island, Akira felt that he'd come to know most every emotion. He'd understood want and hope, hate and fear. He'd loved his mother and enjoyed his students. He had longed for nothing more than a simple life. Moreover, he had recognized his place in the world, and at least until Nanking, never sought to fight it.

But now, as he walked the beach, as he drearily placed one foot before the other, he was thoroughly confused. He didn't understand how one moment he and Annie had been coming closer together, and the next they'd leapt apart. He couldn't comprehend that with the utterance of a few words, his joy at her presence had turned to a sorrow at her loss. He'd never so quickly gone from ecstasy to agony, never seen such a beautiful world so rapidly turn gray.

Akira wanted to make amends with Annie, wanted to tell her that he'd never dishonor her again, that he knew she was engaged and that he had no right to tempt her with words. He'd been weak—so consumed by his own musings and fantasies that he hadn't thought of her. And that omission besieged him, for he felt that she'd given him the key to her and, instead of hiding that key in a safe place, he'd opened her up, violating her trust.

Cursing himself in Japanese, Akira kept walking. The wind strengthened against his face, and he thought it apt that the day mirrored his mood. Normally, he liked such days, enjoyed being reminded of his humble place in the world. But today the sky was the shade of tanks and ships and bombs, and no solace existed in such a colorless realm.

Akira came to the large boulders that marked the swimming hole. After calling out to ensure that no one was bathing, he rounded the rocks. Almost immediately, he noticed a wooden case on the beach. The case, which was made of a highly polished hardwood, had been stranded alongside seaweed and jellyfish by the high tide. Akira walked to it, and was surprised at its heaviness. He opened it. A trickle of water poured out, but the inside was fairly dry and was filled with bottles of pills and white powders, a stethoscope, syringes, needles, sutures, bars of soap, bandages, and a steel scalpel.

He'd been without a weapon since landing on the island, and so he contemplated the scalpel, picking it up and cutting the hairs of his forearm. The blade was sharp and deadly. Without additional thought, he wrapped a leaf of seaweed about the blade and carefully pocketed the item. Even though he was highly skilled at fighting with his hands and feet, he knew that such a weapon could be the difference between life and death. And with so many uncertainties abounding, he wanted any advantage he could get.

Closing the case, Akira started back to camp. For the first time all morning he had an excuse to talk with Annie, and was eager to share his discovery with her. Perhaps she'd find some use for the items, and perhaps she'd again look to him as someone she could trust. The wind was at Akira's back and seemed to propel him toward camp. Soon he approached the familiar banyan tree. Everyone but Jake and Ratu was gathered around a small fire. Joshua was pointing toward the distant ship, and noting, as Akira had earlier, that it was much farther from shore.

As Akira approached, eyes fell upon his discovery. "I found this case by the rocks," he said, giving it to Joshua.

After opening the case, Joshua showed its contents to the nurses. "Any special treasures?" he asked, hoping that the medical kit contained aspirin, as the dropping air pressure had given Isabelle a sinus headache.

Annie immediately recognized the monogrammed case. "It's Dr. Burton's kit," she said, recalling how meticulous he'd been about his instruments. Everything of his bore his initials and was kept in perfect order. "There's morphine and penicillin and sulfanilamide and quinine," she said excitedly. "And his stethoscope and sutures and scalpel and . . ."

"And what?" Joshua asked.

"Oh, his scalpel's gone," she replied. "But his stethoscope and syringes and dressings are all here. And everything's in good shape. We're really quite lucky to have this."

"Wonderful. Nicely done, Akira." Joshua closed the case. "Well, then, getting back to—"

"Wait," Roger interrupted, stepping into the circle. "What did you say was missing?"

"Nothing, really," Annie said. "His scalpel isn't here. But we've everything else we need. There's even—"

"Give it to me," Roger said, stepping toward Akira. "Give it to me now or I'll split your monkey skull."

"What are you talking about?" Annie asked, closing the case.

"The scalpel. I want it."

"Well, he doesn't have it," Annie said. "It's just not here."

"He found the case," Roger said, bunching his fists, his headache suddenly forgotten. "And if there's a scalpel missing, I bet it's that bulge in his pocket."

Annie looked to Akira's pocket. She shook her head. "He . . . he didn't take it." When Akira failed to respond, she stepped closer to him. "Please tell me you didn't take it."

Akira wanted to explain that he'd taken the blade to protect her, that he dreaded what would happen if his countrymen landed and found their cave. But he couldn't reveal his feelings for her in front of the others, and so he reached into his pocket and produced the scalpel.

Joshua took the instrument. "This shouldn't have happened," he said, shaking his head, his jaw tightening. "You had no reason to do this."

"Why?" Annie asked, stepping away from him. "Why betray our trust?"

Roger, who'd been ready to pounce upon Akira, decided that his adversary would suffer more if he wasn't attacked. And so Roger said, "Because he's a Jap. And betraying trust is what Japs do best."

Annie abruptly walked from the group toward the harbor. Though Akira desperately wanted to follow her, he remained still. Joshua swatted at a sand fly and then looked at the blade. "I don't know what to do about this. I just don't."

"Make him regret it," Roger replied, reveling in the moment.

"How?"

"Easy enough. Keep his hands bound. Put him on a leash like the dog he is. If he—"

"Won't you stop?" Isabelle asked. Though she'd always tried to remain silent when Joshua gave orders, she was furious that her husband was actually listening to Roger. "You have the scalpel and the dagger and the machete and dozens of spears. He's got nothing but a little limp.

What on earth is he going to do to you? What threat does he possibly pose?"

"He could escape," Roger countered, hating the nurse, wanting to squeeze her neck until her face turned purple. "Escape and tell all his Nipper friends where our cave is."

Isabelle shrugged, as if his words meant nothing to her. "Then tie him up if the Japanese come. But for goodness' sake, can't you leave him alone for the time being?"

"He'll run," Roger replied, his headache abruptly assaulting him, his rage like a beast within him that needed to be freed.

"He won't—"

"Ever see a monkey run? They're fast."

"He took a bullet in the leg ten days ago," she said angrily. "Ever see what a bullet does to a leg?"

"I've—"

"And he's no monkey, you lunatic."

Roger's nostrils flared. "You useless—"

"That's enough!" Joshua shouted, suddenly aware that he'd thoughtlessly left Isabelle alone in her fight, that he'd waited too long to intervene. "This isn't a democracy," he said, glaring at Roger. "We don't stand around and argue. I'm taking responsibility for him. He'll do as I say, and if he doesn't he'll pay dearly for it. Understood?" When no one responded, Joshua continued, "We're leaving this beach tomorrow. A storm's coming, and we'll be much happier in the cave. So let's get to work." As Akira started to turn away, Joshua grabbed his arm. "And you and I are taking a walk."

Akira nodded, glancing down the beach toward Annie, who sat with her back to them. The sight of her alone assailed him, and it took nearly all his strength to repress his desire to go to her. Stifling the urge to call out to her, he walked in the opposite direction. Joshua quickly caught up to him.

"You promised me that I could trust you," Joshua said, his voice sharp and resolute. "And yet the first chance you got, you betrayed that trust."

Akira continued to walk, slightly favoring his wounded leg. "You have much to protect, Captain, yes? I do also."

"What do you know of protection? Your country only invades. You don't protect. You destroy and plunder, and you're no better than the motherless Nazis you call friends."

Akira stopped. "I am no Nazi," he said simply, though he was deeply offended.

"You think you're different?" Joshua asked. "They butcher Jews and Poles. You butcher Chinese and Koreans."

"I—"

"Did you know that? Does your precious emperor tell you such things? Did he tell you about the Bataan death march? Where your countrymen forced ten thousand American and Filipino prisoners to walk until many of them died?"

"I was not there."

"Have you heard the rumors about Hitler's death camps in Poland? About what your noble ally is doing? While you plunder Asia, that . . . that devil moves thousands of Jews by trains to distant camps. The Jews are never seen again. The trains come back empty." Joshua shook his head, his jaw clenching. "You talk of protection, but you know nothing of protection. The only things Japan protects in this war are its own self-interests."

Akira briefly closed his eyes, trying to slow a sudden rage within him. "You know nothing of me."

"I know that I trusted you. That I've treated you far better than you'd any right to expect."

"Did you know, Captain, that I was at Nanking? That there I let a girl die? That I tried to protect her and failed? You Americans think you know so much. You speak of us plundering Asia. How long have your allies, the British, been the white lords of Asia? How much of the world have the British and French ruled and plundered through their military strength? Almost all of it, yes? Were they invited? Were they welcomed? No, they were not. We are only forcing them back to Europe where they belong, something that should have been done many years ago."

"And yet you attacked Pearl Harbor. You attacked America."

"You cut off our oil," Akira countered. "Your politicians knew that the emperor would see this as an act of war. And yet they did it. No one should have been surprised that we attacked. As you know, we are not a hard people to predict."

Joshua raised the scalpel into the light. "Pearl Harbor was a mistake. And this was a mistake. You've forced my hand. You've forced me to now treat you as a prisoner."

Though normally Akira would have allowed himself to be tied up, he knew that he couldn't protect Annie if he were bound. "I protected the sisters on the ship," he said, letting the anger fade from his voice. "When you could not. Why would I not do the same again?"

Joshua looked out at the sea to where *Benevolence* rested. He hadn't yet prayed today for his crew, and he experienced a brief pang of guilt. "Why did you save them?" he asked.

"Because they were good to me. Because I let a girl die. Because I am tired of war."

"But why . . . why, when I put my trust in you, did you betray me?"

"Because, Captain, I do not want to see them perish. I swear upon the honor of my ancestors that this is true."

"And you think you can protect them? That this little scalpel could save them?"

Akira remembered killing with his hands, with a helmet. "Yes," he said simply.

"And you were a teacher before all of this? A poet, even?"

"A teacher, yes."

Joshua sighed, still unsure if Akira's presence on the island was a blessing or a curse. "If you betray me again . . . if you do that I'll kill you," he said, his eyes meeting Akira's. "So help me God, I will."

"That is fine."

"Then go. And the next time you find a scalpel, tell me about it. Come to me before you try to save the world by yourself."

Akira started to leave but then stopped. "I am not trying to save the world, Captain. Much of it . . . much of it is not worth saving. But the sisters? I will protect them if I can."

AFTER LEAVING JOSHUA, Akira walked directly toward Annie. Though his upbringing told him to leave her in peace, to honor her wish to be alone, he had learned one thing from war—that leaving important words unsaid was a mistake that sometimes could never be undone. And so he sought her out, walking into the strengthening breeze. When Annie saw him, she turned away. Drawing a deep breath, he sat beside her—though respectfully distant—and for a time said nothing. He noticed that the shell he'd found was before her, overturned in the sand.

"I took the blade because . . . because I wanted . . . I needed to protect you," he finally said, forcing himself to talk. She made no reply and he watched her face, longing to touch it. He started to speak again and then stopped, unused to expressing his feelings so openly—after all, in Japan people rarely spoke in such ways. After mustering his courage, he said softly, "You cannot give someone . . . a treasure and expect them to not protect it."

"I didn't ask you to protect me."

"This is true. But you gave me a gift. And it is natural, yes, to protect a gift?"

She looked into his eyes. "What . . . what did I give you? What did I give you that's so important that you'd deceive us?"

"Yourself."

"And this . . . this is how you see me? As a gift? A treasure?"

"Yes."

"But why?"

"Because a treasure provides. It provides hope and beauty and comfort, yes? And this is what . . . this is what you do for me."

"I'm just . . . I'm really nothing special," she said unsteadily, still angry, but also wanting to believe him, wanting to hear more.

He craved to touch her hand but held himself motionless. "May I continue?" he asked.

"Only if doing so will explain your actions."

He sighed, glancing anxiously from the shell to her face. "You are special."

"What does this have to do with the scalpel?"

"You fill my world . . . with color. And how could that not be special?"

Despite her irritation, his words warmed her and she picked up the shell, holding it between her hands. "And so you took the scalpel because you wanted to protect me?"

"Yes."

"Nothing more?"

"No. But nothing less."

"But why didn't you tell me about it?"

"I should have. And I am sorry. I am so sorry for that mistake."

She nodded, twisting the shell, remembering the happiness on his face when he'd given it to her. "Would you mind telling me . . . of this color?" she asked, sensing that he yearned to say more and knowing that she needed to prompt him.

He paused. "I will not dishonor you if I tell you?"

"No. Of course not."

"Are you sure? I have already said too much, yes?"

"You can tell me."

"I—"

"You need to tell me. Because if you don't, I'll never understand why you took the scalpel or why I'm so confused or why on earth I feel so torn."

Akira noted the speed with which her voice had suddenly moved. She was also fidgeting—brushing sand from her shell, shifting this way and that. He watched the wind tug at her hair as he searched for the words to describe how he felt. He did not rush into trying to explain his feelings. Rather, he thought about what it was like to spend time with her, about how she opened a part of him that he hadn't known existed. "When I see you," he finally said, "when I talk with you . . . I am reminded of all that is good in the world, and of all that is good in me. Because you carry me to a place . . . to a wondrous place where I have never been. And in this place I feel as I have never felt. Everything is alive . . . almost singing . . . like a spring day. And this is how you fill my world with color."

A tear descended Annie's face and dropped to her lap. She put her hand on his knee. "Will you show me this place?" she asked, her voice thick with emotion. "Will you show me . . . tonight?"

"Yes."

"When the sun is down. Please show me when the sun is down and I can see all of the colors." She wiped a tear from her face, squeezed his knee, and left him by the sea.

THE CLIMB WAS even easier than Roger remembered. He attacked it like a leopard—staying low to the ground, moving up using his feet and hands, practically leaping to and from boulders. Despite his lingering headache and rage, he reveled in his strength, delighted in his taut muscles. Imagining himself as a samurai, he charged his foes above. He held an imaginary sword, a *katana*, and dispatched everyone who stood in his way. Heads and limbs tumbled to the bottom of the hill while he remained unscathed.

He leapt into the depression containing the radio. The earth was undisturbed, and he quickly uncovered his secret box. Within a few minutes, he was naked and his lips held a cigarette, which he sucked on as if it were the vessel of a magical elixir. As the wind bore ashes and smoke away, he set up the radio, placing the headset over his ears. A mosquito landed on his arm and he slapped at it so hard that his skin turned red. "Goddamn island," he muttered, readjusting his headset.

After taking a deep breath of smoke to steady himself, he said, "Ronin to Edo. Over."

Static greeted him for a few seconds. Then he heard the metallic voice of his contact. "Edo here. How are the cherry blossoms?"

"Always best at dusk."

"Agree."

"Still in nest with eight surviving chicks."

"Stay in nest. Mother coming to roost in five to eight days. Will rendezvous on highest ground near nest, then find chicks."

"Understood. Highest ground."

For a moment, static filled Roger's headset. Then the familiar voice was back. "Expect typhoon tomorrow."

Roger's heart skipped. "Repeat?"

"Typhoon headed in your direction. Expect direct hit. Find suitable shelter. Contact me after storm."

"Understood. Over."

The static returned, and Roger looked to the sky. It did seem ominous, full of gray clouds and restless winds. After lighting a second cigarette, he started to disassemble his radio, continuing to glance above. He thought of the captain's plans for the next day, thought of how the fool and a few others were going to take the lifeboat at first light and row to the cave. Knowing that a typhoon would pick up the lifeboat as if it were no more than a leaf, Roger clapped his hands. "You and your bitch are going to die tomorrow," he said gleefully, smoke seeping from his lips. "You couldn't save *Benevolence*, and you're sure as hell not going to save that little lifeboat."

Barely able to contain his enthusiasm for the chaos of the coming day, Roger buried his box. He then put his clothes back on and began to descend the hill. As he moved from rock to rock, he wondered what he should do with the party that journeyed overland to the cave. When the storm hit, he could lead them to the cave and would be a hero. Or he could get them lost and watch them die. Or, perhaps better yet, he could let some die and some live.

I'll have to make sure that the bastard captain leaves just before the storm strikes, he thought. But how can I do that? He'll read the weather and know that something is amiss. And the coward will want to play it safe.

His mind embracing and disregarding schemes, Roger continued down the hill, almost as excited as the day Edo told him that *Benevolence* would be sunk.

BACK AT CAMP, JOSHUA stood on the beach and studied the sky. He hadn't spent much time in the waters of the South Pacific, and couldn't interpret the weather as well as he'd have liked. The air—cool, gray, and agitated—seemed to be telling him something.

"What is it?" Isabelle asked, watching her husband.

"I don't know. Probably nothing."

"Is a storm coming?"

He turned about in a circle, looking at the sky from all directions, trying to interpret it as he might Isabelle's face. "I think so," he replied. "But I'm not sure what kind of storm. We might just get really wet."

"Do you want me to tell everyone that we'll leave at first light tomorrow?"

Joshua looked about the camp, wishing they could leave immediately, but knowing that the fish was still drying and that people were scattered and ill prepared. "You read my mind, as usual." She smiled and started to leave when he touched her shoulder. "Notice anything else?" he asked.

"Only that the destroyer left an hour or so ago."

"You don't miss much, do you?"

"Not when I can help it."

"I wonder why she left. So odd to come here for a few days and then leave. I should climb the hill and ask Scarlet some questions. She may have seen something we didn't."

"How about some company?"

"I'd love some. You can talk with the others later about our departure." Joshua glanced again at the spot where the destroyer had been lurking. He'd grown somewhat used to the sight of the ship, and with it gone the sea looked oddly barren. Wondering where she'd sailed, Joshua followed Isabelle into the trees. For the first time since he'd been on the island, he didn't feel as if the jungle was some kind of immense green oven he'd stepped into. The air was damp and cool. The birds and animals were silent and seemingly forlorn.

"It feels like a different place," Isabelle said, walking carefully so that she'd leave no sign of her passing.

Joshua noted his wife's precise steps and smiled. "Two weeks ago you were the best nurse on *Benevolence*. And now you're moving through the jungle as if you'd been born here."

"*Benevolence* had a lot of good nurses. We were very lucky in that department."

"But you were the best, Izzy. And everyone knew it. Why do you think all the doctors wanted you? Why couldn't you ever get a moment's peace?"

"I was happy to help," she said, knowing he was right but unwilling to admit as much.

"Still as stubborn as a mule," he said, half under his breath. Then he smiled. "Anyway, more important, how are you feeling?"

"Now you're my nurse?"

"No. Just a worried husband. Though you could probably use a nurse."

"Well, you needn't worry, Josh. I feel fine. A bit tired by the end of the afternoon, but that's to be expected."

"Maybe you should start taking naps."

"I've never napped. I wouldn't know how to—"

"Would you do that for me? Please?"

"But I'm getting plenty of sleep."

"Then just sit and rest." When she didn't respond, he thought of the past few days, of how Isabelle was often husking coconuts or washing clothes or collecting drinking water. She was used to doing more work than anyone, and he wondered how he could possibly slow her down.

"Please," he said, "for me, don't work so hard. I'll sleep better if you don't work so hard."

"Alright, Joshua," she replied, rolling her eyes. "I'll sleep more. I'll do it."

Deciding that he'd seek Annie's assistance on this front, he opted to let the matter rest. He swatted at a mosquito. The pest tumbled through the air, righted itself, and came at him again. "Why haven't we gotten malaria?" he asked, swinging a second time.

"Simple enough. The mosquitoes here don't seem to be infected."

"But what if they are?"

"Well, we've got plenty of quinine now that Dr. Burton's case has been found."

Joshua had seen more than enough malaria patients, including Annie, to understand the significance of having ample amounts of quinine. "That was a lucky break," he said. "Finding his kit, that is."

"What did you say to Akira anyway?"

Shaking his head, he replied, "I had a right to be angry. And he understood that."

A large bat hanging from the underside of a branch stretched its wings above them. Isabelle paused, leaned against the tree, and studied the bat. "Funny how they like to sleep upside down, isn't it?"

Joshua was tempted to ask her if she'd brought up the discovery of Dr. Burton's case because she thought he'd been too hard on Akira. But he quickly realized that Isabelle was direct enough that if she wanted to tell him that he'd mishandled the situation, she'd simply do so. Deciding that he was being too sensitive when it came to questions about his leadership, he forced away memories of the morning's confrontation. He sensed that she wanted to enjoy their walk, and he sought to lift her spirits. "How do they go to the bathroom like that?" he asked, nodding toward the bat. "Don't they foul themselves?"

She smiled. "Only you'd think of that. For all your prayers, you can still be quite the deviant."

"God doesn't mind a little deviance," he replied, grinning. "If you know where to look, you'll find it in the good book. And I'd say it's a fair question. Bats are either flying or hanging upside down. So one way or another, there's a lot of bat urine in the air."

"Joshua!"

"And bat poop, I should add."

"And I'm standing under it!" she said, quickly moving forward.

He hurried to catch her, taking her hand before she could walk too fast. Over the past few months they'd rarely held hands while walking, and, enjoying the link, he continued to slow their pace. He watched her as she confidently strode forward, and suddenly found himself surprised that such a talented, brilliant, and attractive woman would find him of interest. "How did I find you?" he asked.

She pointed out a thorn-filled bush for him to avoid. "I found you, Josh. It wasn't the other way around."

"You'll never let me forget that, will you?"

"Why would I?"

He smiled, recalling how she'd asked him to dance. That first night with her—a night of dancing and laughing and a good-night kiss—had been one of the most thrilling experiences of his life. "I'm glad," he said, "that I'm here with you now. Though no good will ever come of *Benevolence* sinking, at least . . . at least it brought us closer together."

Isabelle turned to him as they started to climb the hill that Scarlet was perched atop. "But why did we need to be brought together?" she asked somewhat abruptly. "How did we drift apart?"

He shrugged. "Too many responsibilities. We both had too many, and we took each other for granted."

"I don't want that to happen again."

"It won't."

"But how can you say that? Really, Joshua, how can you?"

"Because when this war's over, life will go back to normal. And it will be like this."

"Like you telling me about bat poop?"

Nodding, he pretended to nervously glance above. "We'll have to move somewhere with lots of bats. Just so we'll feel at home."

"So this island is home now?"

"Oh, I don't know about that," he said, smiling. "But I feel closer to you now than . . . than I think I ever have."

"Why now? Because of our child?"

He helped her up a fairly steep section of the hill. "I don't know, exactly. But just being here with you. There's no one in the world I'd rather be here with."

"And?"

"You need more?"

"Why wouldn't I?"

"I'm a naval captain. Not a poet like your sister or her new friend."

"So try, naval captain. Try to tell me how you feel."

He slipped, letting go of her hand so as not to pull her down with him. Brushing off his knees, he stood up. "Sometimes," he said, "when I look at my father and see him all shriveled up and in pain, lying in bed, I'm afraid of getting old."

"You are?"

"I think it's my biggest fear."

"Well, I think most people fear getting old. I wouldn't worry about worrying."

"I'm trying, Isabelle, to tell you how I feel."

"Oh," she said, smiling. "I wasn't sure where you were headed. By all means, please go on."

"Patience isn't your strong suit, you know."

"What can I say? I like to get to the end of the story as quickly as possible. Why waste time trying to figure everything out?"

He shook his head in pretend exasperation. "Well, despite your lack of patience, knowing that you'll be with me makes the fear subside. Because with you at my side, I don't feel alone. And if I end up like my father, prematurely old and run-down, I'll still have you. And I won't really need much more."

She took his hand. "I won't ever let you get run-down," she said, grinning. "I've too much invested in you."

He kissed her forehead. "Good."

"And do you know what?"

"What?"

"I'm glad I asked you to dance, my gallant naval captain."

"You are?"

"Yes," she replied. "And even though we were terrible dancers . . . the worst on the floor . . . it was still the best dance of my life."

"We've gotten better."

She started to slip, but he pulled her up. "You're right about *Benevolence*," she said. "No good will come of her sinking. But at least we've been brought back together." She stood on her tiptoes and kissed his forehead, just as he had hers. "At least I have you once again. And believe me, I'm not going to let you go."

They embraced briefly and began to climb again. Though the sun was still hidden and a breeze tugged at them, they each felt warm and were momentarily untroubled—a combination that both had rarely experienced for many months.

"How do you find them so darn easily?" Jake asked, eyeing the beautiful shell that Ratu had discovered in a few inches of water.

"I just look, Big Jake," Ratu replied. "Do you have sand in your eyes? Can't you see?"

"Everything I find needs fixing."

"Well, you have to look for unbroken ones. I tell you, you don't have to be a bloody genius to know that."

Jake splashed a handful of water at Ratu. "Show me a genius, and I'll show you a fool."

"What?"

"And didn't that daddy of yours tell you to respect your elders?"

"Almost everyone is my elder, Big Jake. I don't want to respect some silly bloke who couldn't walk and talk at the same time just because he's older than me."

"As I said before, I reckon not everyone likes to talk as much as you. If everyone liked to talk as much as you, the—"

"World would be a bloody interesting place."

Jake smiled, sifting through the sand. Suddenly wondering how their catch was drying, he turned to look at their rack, which was full of thin slices of fish and shark. Though he was too far away to discern much, the slices were definitely darkening, and several flapped in the wind. "It's about time," he said.

"Are you mumbling to yourself again?" Ratu asked, wiping sand from another small treasure. "I tell you, you'd better stop that habit or one of those pretty nurses will lock you up."

"I reckon that ain't a bad fate."

"What? Being locked up, or the pretty nurse part?"

"What do you think?"

"What is the bloody big deal about women? I don't understand it, Big Jake. Why do men act like children when pretty women are about?"

"Someday you'll understand. That is, if you can find someone who's deaf or odd enough to have a hankering for the sound of your voice."

Ratu splashed Jake. "Oh, put a sock in it, Big Jake. Why don't you find some shells instead of teaching me about women? I don't see any pretty women around you, by the way."

"They're all holding tight in Missouri. Ain't going nowhere until I get back."

"Waiting for you? Ha! They'd better bloody well find something else to do."

Jake chuckled, glad to finally be done with all of the fishing. His muscles ached, and the simple process of searching for shells was much more enjoyable than he'd have thought. It reminded him of being a child and looking for arrowheads while he helped till the farm. He'd found dozens and had filled his mother's canning jars with them. Where are them jars? he wondered, thinking he'd ship some arrowheads to Ratu.

Jake glanced at Ratu's necklace. Tying the shark's biggest tooth to a thin strip of leather cut from Jake's belt had been far from easy. But they'd managed the task, and Ratu hadn't taken off the necklace since he looped it over his head. Jake knew that Ratu was eager to give the necklace to his father, just as he was excited to find shells for his sisters and a stone of some sort for his mother.

"Tell me about them sisters," Jake said.

"See, there you go again."

"What?"

"You complain that I do too much talking, and then as soon as I stop you ask me a question. I tell you, Big Jake, I can't bloody well answer questions without talking."

"Well, now, ain't you got a point for a change?"

"You think I talk a lot? You should meet my sisters. Maybe someday you will. Anyway, they're always asking me to pretend to be a husband, a father, a doctor, or some bloke who they're in love with. They make necklaces out of sugarcane and ask that I put them around their necks. They do a lot of silly things like that."

Coming from a big family himself, Jake understood. "It sounds real nice," he said, avoiding a sea urchin as he continued to look for shells.

Ratu absently fingered his necklace. "It is nice, Big Jake. Cracking good, really. At night . . . at night we all sleep on the floor of our hut together. My mother and father are on one side, with my five sisters and me on the other. On some nights my father tells us stories. But if he's out drinking kava or something, then I tell the stories. Each night I tell a tale about our family, like we're on some great adventure. And each night one of my sisters is the hero. They all take turns being the hero, and if I don't make them do enough wonderful things, they ask for more."

Jake handed Ratu a spiral shell that had been cut in half. "This one sure is pretty."

"Oh yes. Brilliant. My baby sister, Bari, will fancy that. She likes to look inside things. Thanks, mate."

A gust of wind ruffled the surface of the harbor. Jake, who had spent so much of his life outside, knew that a storm was approaching. "Let's gather a few more shells, Ratu, and then wrap up all them fish. I expect we're gonna get wetter than muskrats tonight."

"Sure, sure. But first we must find a shell for Kesea. She's my oldest sister, and she's seen most everything."

Jake started to search the sea again, musing over how much he enjoyed Ratu's company. For a moment, Jake was jealous of Ratu's father. How wonderful it would be to have a son like Ratu, to be able to teach such a son what was worth teaching. Thinking of fatherhood, Jake couldn't help but wonder what kind of son he'd been. Mostly he'd done as was asked, though he hadn't stayed on the farm like his brothers, but had looked for a way to get into the war—a war that sometimes felt as if it had nothing to do with his people. Jake could still remember his mother asking him why he was going off to fight in a white man's war. He'd thought about his answer for the rest of the day, finally telling her that it was a war for freedom and that any such war was his war as well. She'd stopped peeling potatoes, nodded slowly to him, and never mentioned the subject again.

The wind continued to tug at the sea, and Jake wished that his parents could witness such a sight, if only for a moment. Neither had been outside Missouri, and he felt it unfair that they didn't even know such a world existed. Thinking that perhaps his mother would also enjoy a shell, Jake started to scan the sand with her in mind. He'd give her a pretty shell after the war was won, and she'd nod to him once again. And she'd understand what the shell meant and why he'd brought it all that way for her.

DUSK DID NOT ARRIVE that night with glowing colors. The gray sky merely got darker. As it became an infinite shadow, Akira labored deep in the jungle. His work focused on an area surrounding a small body of water that at one point had been connected to a nearby stream. The pool was roughly the size of a jeep and was several feet deep. Rising above it stood some of the most beautiful trees on the island. The trunks that ascended for seventy or eighty feet had no bark, but instead what seemed to be a pale, green skin. The leaves were broad and numerous and formed a thick ceiling.

Dragging old limbs from the nearby underbrush, Akira created a series of woodpiles that formed a large circle around the pool of water. He then carefully positioned fist-sized rocks within the piles. He created haikus as he worked, thinking of ways to describe the jungle, the trees, the noises around him. The words came easily, much to his surprise, for he was nervous about the evening.

Akira started to spread out small treasures that he'd collected earlier in the day. He outlined a path to the pool with sand dollars, and hung golden and lime and violet orchids from nearby branches. Orchids were plentiful in certain parts of the island, and he'd worked carefully to select ten of the most beautiful flowers that he could find.

As if whatever was within the circle was a part of his home, Akira methodically cleaned its interior. Any stray leaf or twig was carried beyond the circle. Any sharp rock was also removed. Using a branch dipped in the stream, he sprinkled water over the area, further purifying it. He tossed the branch far into the jungle and then slowly reexamined everything. Finally content, he began the walk to camp.

With the limited visibility brought by the approaching storm, there was no chance of detection from a plane or ship, and people were eating a fresh batch of fish around a fire they'd made near the sea. Annie was at the old fire pit, pretending to organize her medical supplies. Akira wordlessly emerged from the jungle, took a burning branch from the fire, and led her away from the sea. They didn't speak as they walked within the light cast by the torch. Each was anxious. Akira wasn't sure if what he'd prepared would be to her liking. Annie wondered why she was taking these steps and if she should stop and turn around. She thought of Ted, thought of how he loved her in his own way, and even though it wasn't a way of her choosing, she hesitated betraying him.

Deep within the jungle, they came upon the circle of woodpiles, and, entering it, Akira motioned for her to sit atop a smooth rock by the water. He then took his torch and began to light each of the piles. One by one the piles burned, and with the addition of each gathering of wood, the halo of light strengthened. Before long the collective light was strong enough to illuminate the trees and the flowers. Each tree seemed to come alive, its trunk painted gold by the fires. The orchids' shadows were almost as beautiful as the flowers themselves.

The fires grew, and soon Akira and Annie were sitting within a ring of flames. He'd placed the wood carefully, and the fire wasn't in danger of spreading. It swayed and moved as if it had always been a part of the jungle, as if it were no more perilous than the trees above.

Annie turned to him, taking his hands in her own. "It's perfect," she said, the beauty of what he'd created compelling her to touch him.

"Just wait," he replied softly. "Kindly sit and wait."

She nodded, gently moving her thumb against the back of his hand. Though only a small part of her touched a small part of him, Akira had never felt anything as intimate. It seemed as if all of her embraced all of him. Her touch, warm and light, echoed throughout his entire body. His skin tingled. His heartbeat quickened and suddenly felt too powerful for his chest. He edged closer to her so that their knees touched.

The treetops swayed in the wind that managed to penetrate the jungle. The flames twisted and consumed. Otherwise the night was still. Annie continued to move her thumb against the back of his hand. She'd never touched a man in such a way and found the firmness of his flesh comforting and alluring.

"It is almost ready," he whispered, longing to return her touch, but also wanting to move slowly.

"What's almost ready?"

"Your surprise."

Her thumb paused for a moment. "This isn't it?"

"Not all of it. Just ten more minutes, yes?"

Annie nodded and watched the flames around her. She guessed that he'd created the fires in part to keep the bugs away, but the way he studied them made her think that they also played another role. He looked from fire to fire, sometimes squinting to see better.

"What," he asked, "do you think the trees look like?"

She sensed the nervousness in his voice, which endeared him more to her. She gazed upward, wondering how she could describe the slender golden trunks and the thick canopies of leaves. "It's like they're dancing above us," she said. "As if . . . as if they're a part of some ancient play that we'll never understand."

"Ah, I like that," he replied. "Especially the second half."

"I want to remember what they look like, so that someday I can paint them."

"Then you must close your eyes and try to see them again."

Annie briefly did as he suggested, though she had a hard time concentrating on what the trees looked like while her flesh pressed against his. Acknowledging her touch with a slight nod and smile, Akira gently removed his hands from hers. He picked up a long bamboo pole that he'd leaned against a tree earlier. Placing the pole into the innards of the first fire he'd lit, he jostled the burning logs around, looking for embers. "This fire is hot," he said, mostly to himself. "Wonderfully hot."

Akira used the pole to push a mango-shaped stone from the fire. The stone, which had been painted black by smoke and flames, steamed as it rolled over the damp earth. He continued to push it with the pole until he sent it dropping with a hiss into the pool of water. Moving back to the same fire, he repeated the process a second and third and fourth time. He then walked to the next fire and again proceeded to move searing stones into the water. After moving about thirty stones, he felt the water with his fingers, and smiled. "Almost. You can wait another few minutes, yes?"

Mesmerized by the sight of him working with the long pole amid the fires, Annie nodded but didn't speak. Akira returned his attention to the stones, moving them with great care and patience, smiling as they hissed when entering the water. He checked the temperature again and set his pole down. "Are you ready?" he asked.

"For . . . for a bath?"

Taking care to move slowly, Akira knelt at the edge of the pool and removed a thick cloth from his pocket. He tied the cloth around his head so that he couldn't see. "In ancient Japan," he said, "the best masseuses were the blind masseuses. People would travel great distances to see a blind masseuse."

Annie felt her heart quicken. Though she wanted him, though she needed him, a part of her was afraid to move. Again she thought of Ted, wishing that he made her feel the way Akira did, wishing that she had the strength to control her longing. "Why . . . why were the blind so good?" she finally asked, her voice sounding unfamiliar to her.

"Because a blind masseuse proceeds by touch alone," he replied, trying to suppress his mounting anxiety. "A blind masseuse could do many things that someone with sight could not."

She didn't reply, but instead watched him. He continued to kneel with his back straight and his hands by his sides. Perched upon a nearby tree, a violet orchid fluttered gently in the wind. She realized that he'd placed the flowers so that each petal faced her. Even the patterns on the sand dollars seemed to be aligned in her direction. The thought that he'd taken such care to present her with as much beauty as possible warmed her. Better yet, he hadn't called any attention to what he'd done. He'd simply done it, knowing that she would notice.

"It's all . . . so beautiful," she said, yearning to touch him but remaining still. "It's almost like . . . you created a poem. A poem just for me."

"Do you . . . remember the gardener?"

"Yes."

"I have also been inspired. Like never before."

No longer able to remain motionless, Annie slowly undressed, setting her clothes aside. Soon she was standing in her undergarments.

Standing not free of guilt, but of indecision. Nervous and excited and trembling with emotion, she removed the last impediments to her flesh. She walked to the edge of the pool. Dipping her foot within it, she was surprised by the wonderful heat of the water. Carefully, she stepped into the pool, sighing in pleasure as the water rose to her thighs, then belly, then chest.

Akira reached to his left and handed her a smooth plank of wood, which he'd found on the beach. "Here," he said, holding it out for her, "please sit on this."

Annie took the plank and slid it beneath her. She then moved to the edge of the pool, so that she was as close to him as possible. The water was almost up to her neck, and again she sighed as the heat penetrated her muscles and bones. She'd never been in such a large bath, and she reached out into the water and stretched her arms. Taking a long and deep breath, she closed her eyes and tried to ignore her racing mind.

Still blindfolded, Akira gently touched the top of her head. He let his hands remain motionless for a moment, as if they needed to become acquainted with her skin. He moved his fingertips in small circles atop her scalp. He concentrated as he worked, not knowing how she liked to be touched. Soon he let his fingers go flat against her, using his palms to move and stroke her scalp. He gently pulled on her hair, and she groaned in pleasure at this unfamiliar sensation.

His fingers slowly descended, and he traced the contours of her ears, tugging tenderly on her earlobes. He then started to rub her neck, his hands caressing her flesh—as if it were the last time that he'd ever touch a woman and he wanted to commit the sensation to memory. He sought out her muscles and worked on them carefully—compressing and releasing, twisting and straightening. Annie gradually leaned back into him, for she wanted to feel more of his touch. He obliged her by moving so close to the pool that she could rest her head against his knees.

Akira started to explore her shoulders, running his forefingers atop the rise and fall of her flesh. He traced her collarbone, delighted in the hollow of her neck, felt the subtle edge of her breasts. His fingers began to massage the body beneath them, squeezing the tight muscles along her shoulder blades. Working in darkness, Akira was acutely aware of how her body responded to his touch. He applied more pressure when it was sought, less when it was not. Though his pulse raged like a mountain stream in springtime, he moved unhurriedly.

Reaching behind him, Akira felt for an orchid that he'd laid upon the ground. Finding it, he placed it in his hands and rolled it vigorously between his palms until the flower's fragrance seeped into his skin. He then reached around her to massage her face. His forefingers traced the curves of her eyes and nose and lips. Annie kissed his fingers as they passed, and suddenly unable to bear the distance between them, she turned around, her hands rising to remove his blindfold.

He opened his eyes and consumed the sight of her. She was precious and petite and beyond his imaginings. He saw her as living art and shook his head in wonder at the beauty of her creation.

No one had ever touched Annie as Akira had, and her eyes were drawn to his fingers. "I've been . . . I've searched for you so long," she whispered, simultaneously vulnerable and potent, intoxicated with newfound emotions. "I didn't think you existed."

He placed his hands on her face. She gripped his wrists and moved back, so that he was pulled into the water. He wanted to speak to her, but words had abandoned him. He was without thought, without direction, but alive with wonder. He eased against her and his arms encircled her, drawing her closer. His lips felt her mouth, her neck, her eyes. He tasted her. His hands journeyed about her, delighting in each discovery.

Soon he was naked. Soon the water began to cool, but they did not know it. No thoughts or discomforts or distractions existed—only the overwhelming feeling of a world of their making. A world that spun around them, engulfed them, lifted them a thousand feet in the air, and left them breathless and wanting more.

DAY ELEVEN

Man thinks himself strong,
Until the sky reminds him.
Ants explore green trees.

The Island

The rain came not long after dawn, dripping from a somber sky as if a trillion wet towels hung above. A schizophrenic wind started and stopped and changed directions. The wind's uncertainty seemed to infect every creature on the island with a similar sense of bewilderment. Birds flew toward distant horizons and then flew back. Frogs ceased to croak. Insects were suddenly nowhere to be seen. Even the fish that usually darted about the shallows sought deeper water.

Standing in the rain, Joshua scanned the sky, which perplexed him greatly. He'd seen such skies before and knew that they portended nothing good. But these conditions had arrived so fast. He'd gone to sleep with little more than a gentle wind and gray clouds, and had awoken to a world that seemed at odds with itself. Is this why the destroyer left? he anxiously asked himself. Was she seeking safer waters?

Roger stood next to Joshua, trying to read his face as hard as Joshua was trying to read the weather. He knew that his adversary was debating putting the lifeboat to sea. And he very much wanted the captain and his wife to drown. "What do you think?" he asked, feigning ignorance.

Joshua grimaced, not wanting Roger's company and in no mood for such a conversation. "That a storm is coming," he replied. "A big storm."

Recalling how the fool had tried to keep up with him in the jungle, and knowing that his failure to do so was a sore spot, Roger said, "Why don't I row the boat to the cave? I could make better time than anyone."

"I don't think you'd find it from the sea. It's almost impossible to spot."

"It can't be that hard. You found it easy enough."

Joshua pretended that Roger's words didn't register. Licking his finger, he held it aloft. After its temperamental start, the wind seemed to be mostly blowing from the southeast. Though he was tempted to turn the lifeboat upside down over the food and lash the boat down, Isabelle had awoken with a bad stomach ache, and he didn't want her making the difficult trek across the island. "If something develops," he said, "it's not going to happen for a few hours. That's plenty of time for me to row around the island."

Roger wanted to smile. Instead he said, "Well, you'd better get going."

Uncertain what to think of Roger's behavior, Joshua nodded and walked over to the lifeboat. The vessel was filled with all of their provisions. The slices of fish that were already dry had been carefully wrapped in leaves and shouldn't succumb to the elements. The medical supplies, a pile of fresh fruit, and several full canteens lay in the stern of the craft. Knowing that he'd occupy an entire seat to row the boat, and that their supplies consumed a great deal of space, Joshua figured that he could take two passengers. Ratu had already asked for a spot, so that meant that he, Isabelle, and Ratu would soon be leaving.

Joshua found his two traveling companions and Jake. He asked Jake to help launch the boat, and soon the two men pushed it toward the water. When the craft touched the sea, Joshua returned to camp. With Jake, Roger, and Nathan crowded around him, he said, "I want to leave before the storm gets any worse."

"That ain't an awful idea, Captain," Jake said.

Joshua glanced around camp and saw that Annie and Akira were huddled under the banyan tree. "Where's Scarlet?" he asked.

"Atop the hill, sir," Nathan said, worried for her, wishing that she hadn't insisted on going up alone.

Joshua sighed. "She's not going to spot a ship in this mess."

"Easier to spy a penny in a puddle," Jake replied. "Want me to fetch her?"

"Yes, please. And when you get back to camp, everyone immediately head to the cave. I don't like the looks of this storm. Not one bit."

Jake shook Joshua's hand. "Good luck, Captain. I reckon we'll see you in a few hours."

"Do you remember my instructions on how to find the cave?"

"I surely do."

Joshua nodded. "I've still got the matches from the lifeboat. And I'll have a good fire going by the time you arrive. Just get everyone there in one piece, and then this storm can do whatever God intends."

Jake and Nathan followed Joshua back to the lifeboat. They helped Isabelle climb over the high gunwale. Ratu had already seated himself at the bow. "Let's go!" he said excitedly. "I want to get out in those waves!"

About to launch the lifeboat, the men paused when Annie suddenly ran down from camp. She carried two giant leaves, which she handed to Ratu and Isabelle. "Try to stay dry," she said to her sister.

"I've been dry and hot for ten days," Isabelle replied, though she held the leaf above her. Smiling despite the ache in her stomach, she added, "You should get going, Annie. Don't forget to keep heading due east after you cross the third stream. And when you hit the beach, walk—"

"We've been over all this before," Annie said, putting her hands against the lifeboat. "Now off you go!"

Annie, Joshua, Nathan, and Jake pushed the lifeboat into the harbor. When the water was up to his thighs, Joshua put his hands atop the gunwale and hoisted himself aboard. He sat down, turning his back to the bow, so that he faced the shore. Taking an oar in each hand, he began to row into deeper water.

"Please be a dear and turn back the sheets for us!" Annie said melodramatically in a thick British accent. "And do get some music going. And a few cocktails, if I may say so!"

Knowing that something had made Annie quite happy, Isabelle laughed. "Shall I ring the maid and have her tidy up before we arrive?" she asked in a similar voice.

"Oh yes. Please do! That would be most lovely."

"What are you talking about?" Ratu wondered. "And why do you bloody sound like that? I tell you, women are crazy."

The sisters laughed as the boat pulled away. "I do so adore your umbrella," Annie shouted. "Did you encounter it in Paris?"

Isabelle lifted her giant green leaf. "Venice, my dear! Venice! It's the latest Italian fabric. Quite charming, isn't it?"

Annie held her sides and grinned, waving good-bye. "I love you all!"

Isabelle blew her sister a kiss and watched her grow smaller as the lifeboat continued into deeper water. She couldn't help but wonder why Annie was so happy, standing in the rain. What had happened? Had Akira done something for her? Or was she simply excited to be moving to the cave?

Pleased for Annie but not possessing any answers, Isabelle turned her thoughts elsewhere. The ache in her stomach wouldn't leave her in peace, though she didn't pay it much heed. Aches were a part of her life, after all. If she didn't hurt at the end of the day, that meant she hadn't worked hard enough, hadn't seen enough patients.

"How long will it take?" she asked Joshua, who appeared to be straining at the oars.

"I don't know. Two hours. Maybe three."

"Don't overdo it," she replied, noting his smile, but also that his knuckles were turning white on the oars, and that a vein bulged in his neck each time he leaned back and pulled.

BENEATH THE BANYAN TREE, the rain seemed less oppressive. Nathan, Annie, and Akira sat at its base, watching the distant lifeboat become fainter. Roger stood a few feet away, facing the trio. He said nothing, but stared at them as if he were a predator and they his prey. Jake had left to find Scarlet, and though Akira was at her side, Annie wished that Jake would return. Roger's eyes unnerved her, almost immediately spoiling her good mood.

"I'm taking a walk," she said suddenly, unable to bear Roger's presence. "Would anyone like to join me?"

"In the rain?" Nathan asked, wanting to accompany her but suspecting that she hoped Akira would rise.

Akira bowed slightly and stood. "I would most enjoy a walk."

Nathan smiled. He believed that Annie and Akira were falling in love, and was greatly pleased for them. Watching them reminded him of his own courtship. "Don't get washed away," he said, thinking of his wife.

Annie said good-bye and led Akira down the beach. They deviated briefly from their intended path to pull two immense leaves from a rambling bush. Strolling beneath the leaves, they edged closer to the water.

"Please do not let Roger bother you," Akira said, watching the rain roll off her leaf.

"That's impossible. I'm not a Buddhist, you know."

"Well—"

"But I can let other things occupy my mind."

"Like what, may I ask?"

"Like last night."

He saw a beautiful shell but didn't pause to pick it up. So intent was he on her words that he could consider nothing else. "You asked me to show you how I felt," he said, trying to keep his voice from revealing his anxiety. "Did I do this?"

Annie wanted to take his hand, but knowing that eyes were upon her, she merely walked closer to him. "I don't know . . . I don't have any idea how to describe it, but last night . . . last night I felt like a different person. Like I was reborn."

"Maybe you are a Buddhist after all," he replied, overjoyed with her answer.

She looked at him, her face tight with incredulity. "How did you do that to me? I had no idea . . . that someone could do that to me."

"Make you feel reborn?"

"Yes. That little thing."

Smiling, he watched a miniature wave plunge upon her toes. "You were not the only one who felt such things."

"What did you feel?"

"Alive. So very alive. And I felt a sort of . . . wonder at being so alive. I did not ever expect to feel that way."

"I'm glad, Akira. I'm so glad you felt that way."

A sudden and powerful gust of wind sent rain flying horizontally into their faces. "We should go back, yes?" he asked.

Annie shook her head. "I don't like that man."

"That is because he tries to frighten you."

"Why? Why does he do it?"

"Because he is a coward, and that is what cowards do best."

"He doesn't look like a coward. He's strong and cunning, and I don't think he enjoys seeing us together. And that scares me."

Akira stopped. "Please do not worry about him, Annie." He looked to the west, following the lifeboat as it disappeared, noting how the rain seemed to rise after striking the sea. "There is . . . a side of me that I have not shown you," he said, his voice reticent. "The side that war made. And although I . . . I despise this side, it can overcome a man like Roger."

Despite the strengthening storm, she dropped her leaf and took his hand in hers. "I just want to see the side that I saw last night."

He watched raindrops race down her face. She looked so exposed, as if her old fears of the future had suddenly resurfaced. He touched a tiny piece of the sky as it tumbled down her cheek. "You said you have been searching for me, yes?"

"I have been."

"Unlike you, I did not know that I was searching. But for a long time I have been jealous of that gardener. And now . . . now I no longer am."

"Why not?"

"Because I too have found something precious. Something that eclipses all else. And I will take care of it as best as I can."

Beyond the pleasant confines of the harbor, the sea's true passions were revealed. With the wind picking up substantially, three-foot waves slammed into the side of the boat, inundating Ratu, Isabelle, and Joshua with spray. His hands already blistering against the oars, Joshua rowed as hard as possible. At the bow of the boat, Ratu leaned forward, so that his head and chest were above the water. With each rise and fall of the craft, he let out a jubilant cry.

Though Isabelle felt nauseated, she tried to hide her discomfort from Joshua. She could tell that he was quite worried about the storm, and she didn't want to burden him with additional anxiety. Instead, she managed to catch his eye on occasion and give him a nod of encouragement. Each of them had put on a life jacket, and Isabelle constantly adjusted the straps of her vest, trying to get comfortable.

Looking at the island, Isabelle was surprised to see how morose it appeared in the rain. The vibrant jungle and sparkling beaches were rendered to near insignificance by the storm. The wind howled, and as she faced the island, Isabelle's back was struck by rain and spray that strong gusts drove against her.

Joshua had planned to round the southern end of the island and then head north to the eastern beach. Glancing south, Isabelle saw that the tip of the island was still fairly distant. They didn't seem to be making particularly good time, and she wondered how much stronger the storm would become.

"Another two hours to the cave?" she asked, shouting above the wind.

"Hopefully less," he replied, grimacing as he pulled on the oars. "If it gets too bad, we'll head ashore and walk."

"No, no, no!" Ratu interjected. "Why would we walk when we can ride these bloody waves? I tell you, that makes no sense. And this will be such a cracking good story!"

Joshua eyed the sea. "It certainly will."

"Are you knackered, Captain? Would you like me to help? I'm good at rowing."

"Knackered?"

"Are you tired, Captain? Do you need a break?"

"Oh. Well, maybe later, Ratu. But thank you for asking."

A large swell caught the starboard side of the boat, tilting it up, letting it roll into the trough. "Mother Mary," Isabelle whispered, fighting back the urge to vomit. Joshua glanced at her and then paused for a moment to look at his raw hands. Seeing her husband's discomfort, she tried to ignore her nausea. Opening the medical kit, she used the scalpel to cut two strips of cloth from her shirt. "Wrap these around your hands," she said, handing the strips to Joshua.

He did as she said. "Are you alright?" he asked worriedly. "You look awfully pale."

"I'm fine. Just a bit seasick."

Joshua strained to propel the lifeboat even faster. He now felt almost certain that a typhoon was on its way, as they were at the height of the storm season, and the elements that assaulted them were behaving so strangely. Already since they'd been at sea, the temperature had dropped considerably. And the wind was strengthening by the minute. Knowing that nowhere on the island would be safe but the cave, Joshua hoped that the rest of the group had started their walk. He debated putting the lifeboat ashore, but believed he could get Isabelle to the cave quicker by sea than by land.

"Is the worst over?" she asked when a sudden lull in the wind quieted the world about them.

He started to lie but realized that she always dealt in truths and always sought truths. "The worst is yet to come," he said simply.

"Oh."

"So we need to get to our cave. Everyone needs to get to our cave."

"What can I do to help?"

Despite his pain and fear, Joshua felt a sudden sense of pride at her strength. "Hand Ratu that canteen by your feet so that he can bail out the water we're taking on. It's slowing us up."

Within a minute, Ratu was ridding the lifeboat of water almost as fast as the storm was dumping it in. Seeing that Ratu couldn't keep up, Isabelle stuck a finger down her throat, made herself vomit over the side of the boat, and then picked up another canteen and started to help.

SCARLET AND JAKE finally appeared at the banyan tree. A few words were uttered, and the group headed into the jungle with Roger leading the way. The storm followed them into the foliage, beating against their backs. Trees writhed as if being tortured. Coconuts dropped like bombs. A parrot tried to fly into the wind and was sent backward, exploding in a burst of green feathers against a boulder.

"Watch out for them darn coconuts!" Jake shouted, after one narrowly missed Nathan's head.

The storm gathered its strength and truly began to assault the island. Trees bent like grass. Branches, nests, and animals tumbled from the jungle's canopy as if the world had been turned upside down. Streams that had been inches deep now flowed like small rivers, cascading over rocks and fallen branches. The ground was littered with debris or occasionally was nothing more than a deep layer of mud.

Scarlet had already climbed up and down the hill, and now moved slower than everyone else. Jake held her hand. He used his strength to pull her up rises, to lift her over obstacles. The deeper they got into the jungle, the harder it became to make progress. Storm-generated waterfalls tumbled from heights above. Rain and debris pelted them with alarming intensity.

Roger, who walked at the front of the group, debated leading everyone astray. They were blindly following him, and he doubted that any of them remembered the captain's instructions on how to find the cave.

How easy, he thought, to lead the pigs to the island's center and to leave them there. And how wonderful to watch them from afar and listen to the screams of the skirts as the typhoon descended upon them. They'd be scattered like insects.

Immediately behind Roger, Akira helped Annie forward. Though his leg was still slightly stiff, it didn't hamper him. Akira had survived typhoons while in the woods of Japan, and knew how to navigate the jungle, knew which trees were unduly stressed and would likely fall. He ushered Annie ahead, somehow simultaneously staying aware of dangers above their heads and at their feet.

Though such a scene would have once overwhelmed Annie with fear, she wasn't unreasonably afraid of the storm. On the contrary, with Akira leading and protecting her, she felt rather safe. She'd never felt so secure with a man, even with Ted and his seemingly infinite talents. The difference, she knew, was that some friends and loved ones would sacrifice her before themselves. Even Ted might. However, such self-preservation was not the case with Akira. He'd never leave her when she needed him, and that belief was of great solace to her.

At the rear of the group, Scarlet stumbled, banging her knee into a slick rock. Wiping blood and dirt from a deep cut in her flesh, she began to cry. Without a word, Jake picked her up and gently draped her over his shoulder. "It'll be fine, miss," he promised, carrying her as carefully as he could.

Though Jake was strong and sure, maintaining the pace of the rest of the group soon became impossible. He started to lag, which prompted Nathan, Annie, and Akira to slow. Seeing that everyone was falling behind him, Roger cursed and hurried back to the group. "What the hell's wrong with you?" he shouted at Scarlet, enraged that someone's weakness could put his life in danger.

"She's hurt—"

"That's nothing but a scratch!" he yelled, interrupting Nathan.

"She's already climbed to the lookout point and back," Annie replied, her fists on her hips. "She's tired and hurt!"

A tree groaned beside them, fighting the strength of the wind. "Don't you maggots see what's happening?" Roger shouted. "A typhoon's coming! If she can't keep up, dump her! We'll be better off without her anyway! She's a worthless old hag!"

Annie put her hand on Scarlet's back. "You leave her alone!"

"We all know it's true!"

"Get away from her!"

"Scarlet is coming with us," Akira said, lifting her from Jake's shoulder so that he and Jake could carry her between them. "We are much better off with her."

"You're a fool, monkey man," Roger said, roughly bumping into Akira. In a few seconds, Roger was back at the head of the column. Akira and Jake each put an arm around Scarlet and helped her move forward. Annie walked behind them, hating Roger, trying to protect Scarlet from falling limbs.

Still furious that their progress was being hampered by nothing more than a split knee, Roger continued to set a brisk pace. He decided that if the others couldn't keep up with him, so be it. He'd leave them to fend for themselves, and if they all died, he'd have to forgo the pleasure of Annie's company, but otherwise would be rid of five stones in his shoe. "I won't wait!" he shouted, not bothering to listen to their replies. "So you'd better start to drag the old hag!"

THE SEA HAD MUTATED into some kind of wet inferno. The wind whipped up waves that rocked the lifeboat to and fro. As the waves crested, their tops were gathered by the wind and sent flying horizontally. The sky was the shade of coal. The air was so laden with rain that it seemed a mere extension of the sea. Like the salt water, the rain sailed almost horizontally, pelting the side of the lifeboat so ferociously that the noise produced was almost as loud as the shrieking wind.

Turning to eye the distant shoreline, Joshua looked for the break in the cliffs that marked the entrance to the cave. Though visibility was too poor for him to see their destination, he knew he was headed in the right direction. Now that he'd rounded the tip of the island and was rowing toward the eastern shore, the wind was directly behind him and pushed the lifeboat forward as if it were a leaf.

"Ratu!" he shouted. "Ratu, get to the bow and warn me of any reefs!"

Ratu stumbled forward, the rain stinging his exposed flesh. "What do I do?"

"Tell me how far the reefs are ahead, and whether they're on the port or starboard side!"

"Starboard?"

"Right or left! Tell me if they're on the right or left!"

Lightning cracked overhead, and Joshua cursed himself for putting them in such danger. He'd been foolish to think he could outrun the storm. Wiping salt water from his eyes with a bloody hand, he continued to row, staring straight back behind the boat, watching the storm grow closer. Like most seamen, he considered storms to be living things. He knew that this one was feeding off the warm waters of the South Pacific, feeding and growing larger. How far away is the eye? he wondered, trying to fight his way through his panic. How much time do we have?

"What can I do?" Isabelle shouted.

"Watch for rocks! Help Ratu watch for rocks!"

Joshua tried to row as upright as possible, for with the wind blowing them straight into shore, his body acted as a sail. "Must be a sixty-knot wind," he muttered to himself, knowing that it would grow stronger. "Oh, Lord, please let me get them to safety. Please protect them."

"A rock to the right!" Ratu screamed.

Joshua stuck his right oar deeply into the sea and pulled his left oar from it. The lifeboat immediately turned from danger.

"Brilliant!" Ratu yelled. "Bloody good work, Captain!"

A new roar grew to fill his ears, and Joshua realized that they were approaching the surf. "Find a channel!" he shouted. "Find a channel free of rocks and get us to the beach!"

Thunder boomed, causing each of them to duck lower. "There's a way!" Isabelle announced. "When I tell you, go to the left!"

Joshua glanced at the bottom of the lifeboat and saw that it had a good four inches of water in it. He started to ask Ratu to bail once more, but decided that he didn't want him leaving the bow.

"Now!" Isabelle shouted. "Go left!"

Joshua did as she commanded and the lifeboat slowly changed course.

"And now straight!" she said.

He put his weight equally behind both oars, pulling hard.

"And now right! Right, Joshua, right!"

Hearing the panic in her voice, he furiously worked to get the boat to change direction again. The waves were growing larger as they approached the shore, and each swell rolled the boat forward. He knew that if a wave picked the boat up and dropped it on a reef, they'd be swimming for their lives.

"That's it!" Ratu yelled. "Ha! Good job, Captain! Cracking good job, I tell you!"

"Yes!" Isabelle added. "Yes, now just go forward! We've a straight shot to the beach!"

"Keep looking for rocks!" Joshua shouted, blood dripping from his palms. "Ratu, start bailing! Get that water out of here!"

Wishing that his father could see him, Ratu jumped to the floor of the lifeboat and began to dump out water as quickly as possible. The wind screamed in his ears and the rain stung his eyes. He looked behind and saw a large wave rolling toward them. "Captain!"

"Hold on!" Joshua yelled, frantically trying to keep in front of the wave. The lifeboat managed to for an instant. Then the wave lifted it up and carried it ahead. Joshua felt the bow of the lifeboat tipping too far forward and he instinctively leaned back to try to counter the movement under him. Miraculously, the bow didn't disappear beneath the sea, but struck sand. Everyone and everything was thrown forward. Fortunately, Isabelle and Ratu had been holding on to the benches and succeeded in remaining in place. Joshua's grip slipped from the wet oars and he tumbled toward the bow, careening into the bench beside Isabelle. The air was hammered from his lungs, and, struggling to breathe, he rolled out of the lifeboat and into the shallows. His chest still throbbing, he dragged the craft behind him toward the beach. Isabelle and Ratu joined him, and the three of them pulled the boat as far as possible out of the water.

"You two . . . take the food and supplies . . . inside the cave," Joshua said, still trying to catch his breath. Worried that the typhoon would destroy the lifeboat, he ran twenty paces to a boulder the size of a small pillow. He wrenched the boulder from the sand and carried it to the lifeboat, setting it on the floor of the vessel. He repeated the process at least ten more times. At that point, he felt he had enough weight in the boat that no wind could carry it away.

"Thank you, Lord," Joshua whispered, making a sign of the cross. He grabbed whatever supplies remained in the boat and followed Isabelle's tracks to the cave, flying sand stinging his exposed flesh as he moved ahead. He hoped that the rest of the party would already be there, but upon entering the cavern saw that it was empty save Isabelle and Ratu. Groaning, he said a quick prayer for their safety and hurried to Isabelle. Putting his hands against either side of her face, he asked anxiously, "Are you alright? Is the—"

"Shhh," she said, placing a finger against his lips. "Everything's fine."

"Are you sure?"

"I'm sure."

He hugged her tightly. "I'm sorry to have put you through that," he said, feeling her belly, weak with relief that she and their child were safe.

She kissed his cheek. "I'm fine, Joshua."

"I can't believe how bloody big this place is!" Ratu exclaimed, gazing about in wonder. "It's like the inside of an old church!"

Ratu's enthusiasm had a slightly calming affect on Joshua, who reached out and squeezed his shoulder. "You were a wonderful first lieutenant."

"I was?"

"You most certainly were," Isabelle added. "I don't think we'd have made it without you."

Ratu fingered the tooth on his necklace. "Would you . . . would you call me that, Captain?"

"First lieutenant?"

"Yes, please."

Despite his throbbing hands and fear for the other party, Joshua tried to smile. "I certainly will."

"Thank you, Captain, I tell you, my father will be so happy about that."

Joshua turned to Isabelle and shook his head. "I don't know why they're not here. They should be."

"You're going after them, aren't you?"

"Wouldn't you?"

Isabelle nodded reluctantly. "But come back. I need you. We need you. So for goodness' sake, don't do anything foolish out there."

He pulled a metal vial from his pocket. "Here are the matches," he said, attempting to slow his breath, to gather himself to again face the elements. "There's wood in the back. Get a nice fire going and get yourself warm."

"You promise to return?"

He kissed her. "I love you."

She reached for him as he stepped outside and was swallowed by the storm.

THE WIND HOWLED. It screeched and panted and wailed. Its fury bent trees to impossible angles and ripped branches from trunks the way a child pulls petals from a flower. Objects of every size and shape pelted the six figures as they stumbled through the jungle. Faces and arms bled from a variety of cuts and scrapes. Voices were strained from trying to shout above the storm. Visibility was almost nonexistent.

A coconut flew toward Roger and he spun away from it, so that it only grazed his shoulder instead of breaking it. Knowing that he could make it to the cave in a matter of minutes by himself, he took one final glance behind him and started to run. After he'd taken no more than a few strides, a tree split and fell before him. A small sliver of wood flew through the air and embedded itself in his thigh. The primeval scream of the wind assaulted his ears. He began to tremble in fear, his teeth chattering, his legs growing weak. He stumbled forward, fighting the wind.

Akira saw Roger leave but said nothing. Avoiding dead or dying trees that would surely fall, Akira led the party forward. He was unafraid. As long as he made no mistakes, no one would die. He could hear the distant surf, and knew they were close to the sea. Stopping next to a boulder, he looked for potential dangers and planned their route. A cluster of bent trees would be avoided. An open space that might draw lightning would be circumvented. A stream swollen to ten times its normal size would be forded, with everyone holding hands.

Akira thought about each obstacle ahead before he began to move again. He held Annie's hand, simultaneously pulling her forward and supporting her. He found it hard to believe how calm she seemed. Behind them, Nathan and Jake helped Scarlet. "Watch above!" Akira shouted, worried about flying debris. "I will watch the trail!"

The group proceeded to the stream, and after they all held hands as Akira suggested, he stepped forward. Soon he was knee-deep in the raging water. Branches and fruits and dead animals were carried toward the sea by the swollen stream, and these objects swept into Akira's legs. He paid them little heed, as he was much more worried about the danger of trees shattering above. Incredibly, the wind grew even stronger as they neared the shoreline. Akira realized that he was walking directly into the storm's fury. Each step soon became nothing less than a battle, a test of will.

"We are near!" he shouted, finally stepping from the stream. He peered ahead, trying to discern a path that would lead them safely to the beach.

"Watch out!" Annie shrieked, pulling on his arm.

Akira fell backward, toward her. A healthy-looking tree that he'd been standing next to suddenly split shoulder high from the ground. The upper part of the tree sailed for a few feet and then tumbled into a group of saplings. To his amazement, Akira saw a swarm of bees emerge from the hollow where the tree had split. The wind sucked up the bees and carried them away.

Akira wiped blood from a deep scratch on his cheek. Knowing that he might have died if Annie hadn't pulled him back, he struggled to his feet and yelled, "How did you know?"

"I saw part of the hive! And then the tree started to split!"

He squeezed her hand. Not wanting any bees to be thrown into their faces, he walked upwind of the shattered trunk. The storm's ferocity was suddenly appalling. He had to lean far forward to move. Through a break in the trees he glimpsed the surf. Akira knew the cave was close, but wasn't exactly sure how to find it.

Unexpectedly, he thought he saw someone waving up ahead. Had Roger returned? Akira took a few steps and realized that Joshua had found them. The American, with the storm behind him, quickly ran forward. In fact, he almost ran completely past Akira, and only when Akira extended his arm and the two locked hands did Joshua stumble to a stop.

"You made it!" Joshua yelled, thrilled that everyone seemed to be fine. "Well done!"

Akira bowed slightly. "It is good to see you!"

Seeing that the group was holding hands, Joshua took Akira's hand in his own and stepped into the wind. Sand flew from the beach, and he used his free arm to shield his eyes. He knew that if the typhoon further intensified, it would pick them off the ground and toss them to their deaths. And so he tried to walk low, tried to put all his strength behind each step.

When Joshua reached the beach, he turned to his left and was no longer walking directly into the storm. He started to half run, half stumble toward the cave. Still holding Akira's hand, he willed himself forward. Lightning cracked above, as if the storm, seeing the humans headed for safety, wanted to give one last show of its strength.

Joshua saw the cave, saw Isabelle, Ratu, and Roger at its mouth. He staggered ahead and then shouted in joy and triumph and, without further thought, leapt into Isabelle's outstretched arms.

DAY TWELVE

To touch her is grace,
To hear her laugh is rebirth.
Summer stars burn bright.

A Walk Through Time

Within the cave, the typhoon seemed almost harmless, like a cobra that had been liberated of its fangs. Though the wind howled and the distant surf pounded, the cave's interior was warm, dry, and quiet. A fire burned near the middle, casting uncertain light in all directions. The nine survivors had gathered around this fire and now ate dried fish and fresh mango. Everyone seemed exhausted by the previous day's events, and aside from several intense arguments about Roger separating from the group, little had been said.

Despite his exhaustion, Joshua had thought through how they'd live in the cave and had been talking about such logistics. Though he'd welcomed input, he had mostly spoken alone, the cave magnifying his words. It had been decided that Jake and Ratu would continue to catch fish. Joshua and Isabelle would locate fresh fruit, as well as camouflage the cave's entrance. Nathan would collect wood and keep a fire going at all times, as their supply of matches was limited. The detail of exploring the area outside the cave had been given to Akira and Annie, while Roger would probe the island's innards, and Scarlet would find a high place to watch for ships. As far as social niceties, no one would bathe in the cave's water supply, and people were expected to keep the area as clean as possible.

"The good news," Joshua said tiredly, "is that the storm will destroy any trace of our presence at the harbor." He glanced at his bandaged hands, which felt as if he'd held them in boiling oil. Though he wanted to do nothing more than lie down next to the water and soak his hands in its coolness, he continued to address the group. "Let's all promise not to go back to the harbor. Unless Scarlet sees an American warship drop anchor, I don't see why any of us should return. We're much, much safer here."

"Captain, what'll happen if we eat all them dried fish and can't catch a darn thing here?" Jake asked.

Joshua pointed toward Ratu and tried to smile. "With my first lieutenant leading the way, I doubt that will happen."

"Thank you, my captain," Ratu replied. "You won't have to worry about fish, I promise you. Big Jake is just being cautious as usual."

Joshua nodded, trying to think of anything but his throbbing hands. Addressing the group, shifting his gaze from person to person, he said, "We were lucky yesterday. All of us. Let's not rely on luck any longer. And for the love of God, let's get along. I don't want to hear any more arguments about how or why Roger separated from the group."

Roger glared at Akira. "The monkey needs glasses," he said, wishing he had a cigarette, already feeling claustrophobic within the cave. "It's not my fault he can't see through those slant eyes of his. If he could, he'd have followed me."

"I couldn't see you either," Nathan replied, surprising the group, for he rarely spoke during such conflicts. "And I tried to, believe me."

"Maybe if you didn't walk like a toad you'd—"

"I've heard it all," Joshua interrupted, smothering his desire to shout at Roger, to scream at him for abandoning the group. "And I don't want to hear it anymore. It doesn't do anyone any good. Understood?"

Seeing that her husband was struggling to contain his emotions, Isabelle stopped wrapping leaves about the leftover fish and said, "We're safe. We made it. Let's just be thankful for that and leave it at that. It could have been much worse."

As Akira nodded, he glanced at Roger, who glared at him. The glare contained the same sort of malevolence that Akira had seen on the field of battle and in Nanking. He'd never understood the sheer hatred that one human being could harbor for another, as if all the woes of one's life could be blamed on a fellow man. He'd certainly never encountered a more powerful emotion, for such hatred led people to do unspeakable things.

Akira didn't turn from Roger's glare but absorbed it, committing it to memory. He suddenly understood that at some point, Roger would try to kill him. The American would come during the night, or in the midst of some chaotic event. And when he came, Akira would have to be ready. He'd have to see the attack before it materialized. And then he'd have to end Roger's life.

THE BRANCH BURNED slowly in Ratu's hand. He'd wrapped dried coconut husks around the gnarled piece of wood, creating a torch. Pointing to the back of the cave, which was dark and unknown and dominated by piles of boulders, he said, "Who wants to be an explorer with me?"

Jake, Akira, and Annie looked up from their spot by the side of the underground pool. They'd been talking about what they would do the next day, once the weather cleared. Though the cave was quite large, the stale air and muted light made for somewhat confining conditions, and everyone was eager for the storm to end so that the area outside the cave could be investigated.

"I reckon I never met a boy with so many ants in his pants," Jake said, smiling at Annie. "They must be red ants, too. Them little black ones ain't nearly able to do the trick."

"What are you talking about?" Ratu asked. "Red ants? Black ants? Did a coconut hit that big head of yours yesterday?"

Jake splashed a handful of water at Ratu and got up. "I expect my legs could use a stretch. Sure, I'll explore with you."

"And you, Miss Annie?" Ratu questioned, handing Jake an unlit torch. "And you, Akira? Don't you get bored of sitting there looking at each other? Come with us."

Annie glanced at Akira, who actually wanted to explore the area for other reasons. Though the cave was wonderfully hidden, as Joshua had said, Akira didn't like the fact that only one entrance and exit existed. After all, a lone gunman standing outside could trap the entire group. And though a cave could be a refuge, it could also be a tomb. Hoping to find a hidden exit, Akira dusted the sand off his knees and rose. "I would like to explore with you."

"Can you lead us?" Annie asked Ratu, knowing that he enjoyed such adventures.

"Of course, Miss Annie. Just follow the light of my torch. And if you get scared, let me know and we'll turn around."

Annie smiled at Ratu. After allowing Jake to walk in the second position, she stepped forward. The remainder of the group was gathered much closer to the cave's entrance, and, seeing that no one was looking in their direction, Annie sought out Akira's hand and gave it a squeeze. The warmth and comfort of his flesh brought back memories of the earlier night. She remembered how the hand she now touched had stroked her face, the soles of her feet. She had kissed that hand. She had felt her heart beat against it.

Though Annie wanted to continue to hold Akira's hand, she needed to be a free woman to do that, and with her engagement looming over her, she did not feel free. She reluctantly released his hand, immediately feeling vulnerable from its absence, as if this one hand could somehow protect her from her own dark thoughts. And as preposterous as the notion sounded, she knew that Akira's touch was capable of just that. After all, she'd told him that he made her feel reborn, and those hadn't been idle words she'd shared with him. He'd somehow infused her with such passion and energy and life that she did feel like someone completely new. And this newness almost overwhelmed her at times. Even during the chaos of the storm, she'd felt a childlike giddiness as unfamiliar emotions enveloped her, as she realized that for the first time in her life, she was falling in love.

Stubbing her toe on an unseen rock, Annie grimaced. Glancing at her bare feet, and knowing that she could ill afford to cut herself, she vowed to pay more attention to her surroundings. The cave was much deeper than she'd realized. Looking toward the orb of light that marked the entrance, she guessed the opening to be at least two hundred feet away. Even this far from the entrance, the height of the cave was much taller than even Jake. The rock surrounding them, which she thought might be limestone, was the color of old ivory. Unlike the caves she'd read about in novels and magazines, this cave contained no giant stalactites. The walls and ceiling were fairly uniform.

Ratu approached the large slabs of rock at the cave's rear and started to navigate around them. The slabs had obviously fallen from the cave's ceiling, and Annie wondered if it was wise for them to be walking so far from the entrance. Another cave-in could leave them trapped without any chance at escape. Feeling a familiar sense of unease seep inside her, she again reached for Akira's hand. He reassuringly squeezed her fingers in the darkness, and she felt better.

Though the slabs lay in discordant piles, a path seemed to zigzag forward. Muttering to himself, Ratu continued ahead, holding the torch with one hand and his shark's tooth with the other. After spending the past ten days in a world where everything appeared to move, Annie felt odd to be walking in a realm where not even the air seemed to stir. She wondered about the age of the cave. Could someone else have stepped here? Searching for an answer, she followed Ratu, twisting far enough to their right that the cave's distant entrance disappeared.

"Please light another torch," Akira said softly, a few feet after the entrance had vanished.

Ratu held his torch against the one that Jake carried. The fire spread, and the halo of light that surrounded them swelled. Ratu walked slowly ahead. The cave seemed to be narrowing, its walls almost reaching each other.

"So this big snake does have an end," Jake said, peering about.

"Wait, Jake, wait," Ratu replied.

"You're eyeballing the tail, Ratu."

"No, I tell you, I'm not."

Ratu continued forward, feeling the presence of the others behind him, wondering if his father felt such a presence as he led Americans into the jungle. Though the cave appeared to end, Ratu sensed something ahead. He couldn't define it, but something did exist. Something new to his senses. "Do you smell anything strange?" he asked, filling his lungs.

Akira inhaled deeply. "Yes. But what?"

"Air," Annie said. "It's fresh air."

The four exchanged perplexed looks, and Ratu once again moved forward. The walls of the cave drew to within a few feet of each other. Remarkably, they then began to pull apart. The cave twisted again to the right, and to everyone's amazement, a barely visible shaft of muted light fell from far above. It almost seemed as if they were deep within the ocean, and a slice of the sun managed to penetrate the gloom just enough to faintly illuminate the seafloor.

"Blimey!" Ratu shouted, his voice sounding unnaturally loud. "What a brilliant discovery!"

A small, subdued cry escaped from Annie's lips as her gaze traveled to the walls that were so dimly illuminated, for as the torchlight fell on them, the walls suddenly seemed to come alive. They were covered in red-and-black images depicting ancient canoes and sailing ships. The vessels' hulls were curved like bananas. Some of the ships had masts and sails, while others were powered by oars alone. Several of the largest boats boasted ornate bows resembling what appeared to be birds with their wings outstretched. The vessels carried anywhere from three to ten human forms.

Annie's skin tingled. She felt as if she'd leapt back into time. Dozens of questions immediately surfaced within her. Who had created these astonishing paintings and when were they created? Who'd last seen them? Had this cave once been inhabited, or were these images left by passing travelers?

Stepping toward the most intricate of the paintings, Annie studied the ship and the people on it. The ship was elaborate and large and in some ways resembled the bird on its bow. The people, who were little more than stick figures, were bent forward as if performing some action, but had nothing in their hands.

"Look at this," Akira said, rising from the ground. In his hand he held what appeared to be a piece of charred wood. He twisted his discovery between his fingers, and black powder fell to the floor. "Once someone had a fire here. A long, long time ago."

"How long?" Ratu asked excitedly, dropping to his knees to search for an ancient fire pit.

"So sorry, but I do not know."

Gazing at the ships reminded Jake of what it felt like to discover arrowheads on his family's farm. He'd always experienced a sense of connection with the soil of his land, which was as black as the back of his hands. But the arrowheads had managed to deepen this bond. Eyeing the figures, he said, "They sure look mighty happy, don't they?"

Annie couldn't tell if the figures were meant to be happy, but replied, "Almost like they're celebrating."

Jake nodded. "They're traveling somewhere. They're free."

Akira gazed up at the crack through which the faint light descended. The crack—perhaps reachable if all four of them stood atop one another—looked to be a foot wide and maybe three feet long. "We should go above and locate that opening, yes?" he asked. "And secure a rope to a tree and drop it down."

"A secret exit?" Ratu asked.

"Yes."

Jake nodded. "I reckon the captain will want that done pronto."

"He'll love this place," Annie said, knowing that Joshua enjoyed everything about boats.

"Let's name it something," Ratu suggested, still digging through sand and soil. "I tell you, we should name it something."

Annie returned her gaze to the ships. "Name this place?"

"Of course."

"You should name it," she replied, "since you discovered it."

Ratu smiled, rolling a small piece of charred wood in his fingers. He thought for a long time, as everyone else continued to stare at the ships. Finally, he said, "Raja's Ships. Let's call it Raja's Ships."

"Raja's Ships?" Annie asked. "Why that?"

"Ratu. Annie. Jake. Akira. We found it. It should have our names. Aren't all great mountains and seas and lakes named after the explorers who found them?"

"It seems that way."

Ratu nodded, rising from the ground. "Raja's Ships," he said happily. "What a cracking good name. What a perfect name. I tell you, names are everything. Better to have a good name than a good nose."

Annie smiled. "It is a . . . cracking good name, Ratu. And you're sweet to include everyone."

"I bloody well should include everyone, because everyone helped. Big Jake held the torch, and Akira . . . Akira held your hand, and you smell nice, and I like the way you say my name."

SITTING ON A BOULDER that had fallen inside the cave's entrance, Joshua and Isabelle watched the storm. Though it had lessened in ferocity since the previous day, the storm still acted as if it wanted to drown the island. Rain continued to cascade from the sky, and water running down the hill behind them created a waterfall that obscured much of the cave's entrance. The roar of the waterfall partially masked the uninhibited wind and the pounding of the surf.

"I wonder if we lost any ships in this," Joshua said quietly, thinking that *Benevolence* would have handled the elements.

Isabelle paused from organizing their medical supplies. "I certainly hope not," she replied. After carefully setting aside the quinine, she located the medicinal cream she wanted and found some clean and dry bandages. "Now let me see those hands."

"They're fine."

"Joshua, you're going to let me see them this instant."

"I think we should save those supplies for something more important. We might—"

"I'll be the judge of how we're doing on medical supplies, thank you very much. Now put out your hands."

Reluctantly, Joshua held out his hands, unfurling his palms. Isabelle dropped to her knees and slowly began to remove the cloth that they'd wrapped around his fingers and palms. She was surprised at the size and severity of his blisters. Red and open, the flesh of his palms looked as if he'd grabbed a rope and slid a hundred feet down. She knew that he must be in significant pain, and yet he'd mentioned nothing of his discomfort all morning. "You're a mess," she said.

He tried to smile. "I thought nurses were supposed to paint a rosy picture."

"Well, your hands aren't going to fall off. That's about as rosy as I can get for now." She used a damp cloth to gently clean his wounds. He winced, several times pulling his hands away from her. "I have to get these clean, Joshua," she said, trying to hold him still.

"Sweet Mother Mary," he replied, exhaling deeply.

"Try to think of something else."

"Easy for you to say. You're not the one being tortured."

"Do you want infected hands? Here on this island?"

"No, but you shouldn't be on your knees, attending me." He glanced about to ensure that no one else was near. "I mean, with the baby? It doesn't seem right. I don't want—"

"That's it. Think of our baby. What should we name him?"

"Ouch!"

"What names, Joshua?"

He moved his gaze from his hands to her face. "Do you think it's a boy?" he asked, attempting to stay still.

"Does it matter to you? What the sex is?"

"Well, I always thought that . . . ouch . . . that I'd want a boy. But now it doesn't matter. Either would be wonderful."

"What about names?" she asked, beginning to spread the medicinal cream on his hands.

"If it's a girl, we could name her after your grandmother."

She paused. "Gertrude?"

He winked when she looked up from his injuries. "It has . . . a certain charm. And your grandmother certainly does."

"Don't be an ass," she replied, trying not to laugh. "It's not her fault that she's so . . . interesting."

"That's an interesting way to put it."

"You mustn't feel that bad. If you're going to sit there and poke fun at my family, maybe I should leave your hands alone. And for the record, your family is definitely odder than mine. At least my parents don't live in a tent."

"Now, that's just a few months out of the year. And it's not really a tent. More of a home on wheels."

"It's a tent, Joshua."

He smiled, thinking of his parents and how they liked to spend summers high in the Rockies. "What about Claire? Or Alice? Or maybe Catherine?"

"What about boys?"

"Well, I've always liked the name Owen."

"Owen?"

"That's right. A name you don't hear on every corner."

She started to apply fresh bandages to his blisters, covering the wounds with care and precision. "I'm surprised you wouldn't want to name him after some ship you saw in port."

"Now, there's a thought," he said, feigning excitement. "He could be . . . Barnes or Lexington or Casablanca or Hancock. Oh, and Saratoga would make a fine name. Saratoga Collins. Let's do that."

"Let's pretend that I never mentioned the idea." She finished wrapping his hands and started to tidy up the medical kit. Everything went into its proper place, and the kit was sealed shut. "You're not an easy patient," she said, moving closer to him.

"I'm a deviant, remember?" he replied, kissing her forehead.

Isabelle leaned against his knees and stroked his forearm with her thumb. Lightning flashed above the sea, followed by the groan of thunder. "It's good to hear . . . the old Josh make an appearance," she said.

"I like the sound of him too."

"Will I hear more of him in the days to come?"

"Undoubtedly. Probably more than you want."

"Promise?"

He nodded, though his smile soon wavered. He opened and closed his bandaged hands, listening to the storm howl. Its fury was such that he wasn't surprised that the ancient Greeks thought mighty gods lived atop a mountain in the sky. Turning his mind to the present, he said, "But we need to get off this island safely. And the war needs to end."

"It will."

"And we'd better win," he replied, his face and voice suddenly solemn. "We have to win. If we don't . . . everything will have been in vain. And a monster . . . a true monster . . . will rule the Earth."

Isabelle looked toward the sea. "Do you think the rumors are true?"

"Of the camps?"

"Yes."

"I pray that they aren't. But . . . but I hear that terrible photos are being smuggled out of Poland—unspeakable things, really. Pictures of mass graves and gassings and mountains of naked bodies. Some say Hitler's dream is to kill every Jew in Europe."

"It can't be. It just can't. How many people is that?"

"Something like eleven million."

Isabelle groaned, running her hands through her hair. "What can be done, Josh? What can we do to stop it?"

"Win the war. Win it as fast as possible. And hang Hitler and all of his kind."

"We're going to win, aren't we? You've told me that a hundred times."

"I ask the good Lord for victory every night," he replied. "And I start every day with the same prayer. But, yes, I think we'll win. Between us and the Russians, we'll strangle Germany."

"And Japan?"

"Japan is fighting a country twenty times its size. And Japan will fall, though it will be bloody."

Isabelle mused over his words. As a nurse, as one who'd devoted her life to healing others, it was hard for her to wish ill upon anyone. But she knew that if Hitler stood before her, she'd find the strength to pull any trigger. "When do you think it will be over?" she asked, wanting to somehow count down the days.

"Two years. Maybe three. We're just not ready to cross the Channel. And we can't invade France until we can get there."

Suddenly tired of her dark thoughts, she tried to bring herself back into a place of light. "So, in three years it will be done? All of it? The camps and the convoys and the buckets of amputated arms?"

"It ought to be."

"And we'll own a little house somewhere on the water, and you'll be teaching me to sail? And we'll have a baby who's learning to talk?"

Joshua closed his eyes, imagining such a world. "That sounds wonderful. Just wonderful, Izzy."

She kissed his hand, needing to believe in that future, needing for him to believe in it as well. "It will be wonderful," she said softly. "It's going to be our life."

"Can you find your way?" Akira asked, wanting her to make the journey, but afraid for her all the same.

Annie held a torch in one hand and another branch in the other. Two weeks earlier, she'd never have dreamt of venturing alone to the back of an immense cave. But over the past few days, such fears had weighed less upon her. "I'll be fine," she said, pleased that he seemed concerned for her.

Akira lifted a coil of rope and draped it over his neck and shoulder.

He glanced toward the campfire, around which everyone but Roger and Nathan was resting. Roger had left several hours earlier, disappearing into the rain. Nathan had recently departed. "Are you sure?" Akira asked, just to be certain.

"I'm sure."

"Then I will next see you at Raja's Ships, yes?"

"I'll get a little fire going."

"Please do not rush. It may be rather difficult for me to locate the opening."

"Take your time. I won't leave for a bit."

Akira smiled and stepped into the waterfall that covered the cave's entrance. A curtain of water cascaded upon him with considerable force, and even before he entered the storm, he was soaking wet. He was eager to explore the ground above their hideout, for the soldier in him knew that having an escape route at the cave's rear was essential. Otherwise, they could be trapped far too easily.

The hill behind the cave was dominated by rocks and foliage. At some point, probably thousands of years before, this part of the cliff had fallen toward the sea. Moss-covered boulders lay atop an enormous pile of earth. A wide variety of shrubs and trees grew around the rocks. Knowing that the crack he sought was about three hundred paces to the northwest, Akira headed in that direction, counting off his steps.

Though the storm had lessened considerably, rain still assaulted the jungle. Footing was treacherous, and Akira moved with great care. Instead of climbing over slippery boulders, he walked around them and adjusted his course. He hadn't been alone in this jungle, and now that he was, he found himself instinctively scanning for ambush sites and walking in a low crouch. After all, he'd been shot at in such places. Shot at by Filipinos and Thais and Chinese and Americans and Australians. Fortunately, by trying to move through jungles as if he were a fox and not a man, he'd never fallen victim to the kinds of ambushes that killed so many of his comrades.

Akira wanted to think of Annie now that he was alone. He wanted to reflect upon the way she made him feel and how she was able to do so. But being alone in the jungle, and not knowing Roger's whereabouts, he forced himself to be vigilant. He continued to scan the land before him, listening for unusual sounds in the rain. He paused suddenly at unlikely places and peered into the gloom, looking for any sort of movement.

Knowing that he must be close to the crack, Akira started to search for it in earnest. No significant amount of water had been dripping through the opening when they'd seen it earlier, and so he knew that it must be somehow protected. Most likely it lay under a shelf of rock. Looking for such sites, he moved through his environs with increasing care. As he navigated around a decrepit banyan tree, he recalled searching for tunnels in a bamboo forest in China. Sadly, the soldier beside him had set off a trap, and Akira had been able to do no more than pull the man from the sharp stakes that had plunged into various parts of his body.

Pushing the memory away, Akira continued to search. He eased through a gathering of head-high ferns and was surprised to find Nathan sitting atop a massive boulder. Nathan held the airman's dagger and appeared to be etching an image into a wide piece of bamboo. "Hello," Akira said, bowing slightly, as if fearful of interrupting Nathan's work.

Nathan lowered the dagger, peered through the rain and jungle, and smiled when he recognized Akira. "Come on up," he said, gesturing for Akira to climb the boulder.

Akira dropped to his hands and knees and ascended the slippery stone. Moss and small plants grew amid ancient cracks, while other parts of the boulder seemed to have been bleached by the sun. As he rose, Akira wondered why Nathan had climbed the truck-sized rock and why he was sitting alone in the rain. Wordlessly, Akira moved beside Nathan, eyeing the bamboo in his lap.

Nathan lifted the piece of green wood, upon which he'd etched a simple scene from the island—three palm trees standing straight beneath a mighty sun. "It's for my little girl," he said, wiping rain from his brow.

Akira smiled, thinking of Nathan's stash of such treasures, items that he often worked on after finishing his daily duties. "I am sure that she will like it."

"Oh, Peggy likes most everything."

Recalling her face from Nathan's water-stained photo, Akira nodded. "She is your youngest, yes?"

"She's my baby."

"A most beautiful child."

"Thank you," Nathan replied, staring into the jungle, thinking of the distance between himself and his family, as he had so many times before. "You know, it's the simple things . . . I miss the most. If I were home, and it was a Saturday morning, Peggy would be packing a picnic lunch with her mother. And my boy and I would be loading the car."

"And where would you drive?" Akira asked, recalling the Japanese families he'd seen on such picnics, gathered together beneath maple trees along the Kamo River.

"Usually to a pond, or maybe a stream. We like to fish a bit. And if there's grass we'll play some croquet. Then it's time for a big lunch and a spot of shade." Nathan sighed, folding his hands atop his lap, briefly biting his lower lip. "It . . . it seems like a long time ago."

"I am sure that it must. But you will see them again."

"You think so?"

"I think that . . . that you love them too much to not see them again."

Nathan bit his lip once more. He then wiped his eye. "I have to. I just can't imagine . . . not seeing them again."

"You will be home soon. I am sure of this."

Thunder rumbled in the distance. Ferns surrounding the boulder trembled as raindrops fell. "You were forced into the war, weren't you?" Nathan asked.

"Yes. I was handed a rifle and told to fight. Told to fight . . . you. So sorry."

"It's not your fault."

"Still, please accept my apology."

Nathan nodded, and then placed the piece of bamboo in Akira's hand. "When you get back to Japan, please give this to a young girl. And please tell her that it came from an American soldier."

Bowing deeply, Akira replied, "It will be my great honor to do this."

"Thank you."

Akira pocketed the bamboo and bowed again. "You are a good man."

"Maybe one day good men won't have to fight each other."

"I hope we each live long enough to see that day."

"I do too." Nathan eyed the coil of rope around Akira's neck and shoulder. "Well," he said, "I suppose I'll return to the cave. I wouldn't want you . . . to keep anyone waiting."

Akira said good-bye and watched Nathan carefully descend the boulder. As Nathan vanished into the jungle below, Akira again began his search for the opening to the cave. He moved with some haste, for he didn't want Annie to worry about his whereabouts. As he searched, he thought of Nathan, promising himself that he'd do his best to ensure that this lonely father got home safely to his family.

When Akira spied a rock overhang that protected the soil beneath it, he wasn't surprised to discover the crack. His mind shifting to Annie, he began to move more quickly, a sudden urge to caress her face possessing him. He found a stout, healthy tree near the opening and tied one end of the rope around the bottom of the trunk. He was about to climb down through the crack when he stopped and began to tie knots in the rope so that it would be easier for people to ascend. He created simple knots at two-foot intervals. After dropping the coil through the crack, he placed branches over the exposed rope until it was well hidden.

Akira moved under the overhang, putting his feet within the crack.

The area around him didn't feel right for some reason, and he paused to study his surroundings. The opening was larger than he expected and didn't appear to be a natural split in the earth. Perhaps once it had been, but the crack seemed to have been widened at some point. The edges had been smoothed out and didn't look as if they'd once been joined together.

Wondering if the ancient painters had enlarged the crack to give them additional light, Akira began to descend. To ensure that he wouldn't lose his grip, he twisted his left ankle around the wet rope so that it came up between his knees and he was able to apply pressure to it. His legs and torso passed through the crack, and suddenly he plunged into a world of darkness.

"I'm here!" Annie shouted from below.

Akira smiled, imagining her. She'd be moving restlessly, shifting her weight from one leg to the other. It was possible she had a finger in her mouth and was biting a nail. Her eyes were certainly upon him, and he hoped he didn't look too small from so far below. Knot by knot, he descended. He glanced at the ships, though as inspiring as they were, he quickly dropped his gaze to her. The rich light of a fire below bathed her face in amber, and he felt an immediate sense of comfort upon seeing her familiar features.

The rope was about seven feet short of touching the ground, so Akira had to jump when he reached its end. He landed gracefully, bending his knees so that his muscles absorbed the impact instead of his back. Before he could even fully straighten, Annie stepped to him, wrapping her arms about him. She kissed him hungrily, pulling him tight against her. "You've consumed me," she said, running her hands through his wet hair. "I haven't been able to eat or sleep or even talk with Isabelle."

Akira kissed her, stroked the soft line of her jaw, and then pressed his nose into the skin beneath her temple. He inhaled slowly and deeply. "You smell like . . . like you."

She eased her hands into his dripping shirt. "Me?"

"Yes. You have your own smell. A wonderful smell. Something fresh . . . like the sea or perhaps the sun."

She smiled. "It's just me."

He kissed her forehead, delighted to once again be alone with her. "May I . . . may I tell you something?"

"Please."

"It is a little . . . odd."

"That doesn't matter."

He nodded, enjoying the sight of her sapphire-colored eyes. "Aboard the ship, I always watched you. I always listened to you."

"You did? But why?"

"Because you treated me well. Because I liked how your hands felt on my leg."

"On your bullet wound?"

"You washed my face once, yes? When you thought I was sleeping?"

Annie searched her memory. She had always wiped the grime from her patients, believing that if they felt clean, they would feel better. "I did?" she asked.

He gently touched her face. "You took a warm cloth. You pressed it against my skin and you swept away . . . you swept away the mud that had covered me for two days."

She smiled, pulling him closer. "I'm glad I did."

"I had never . . . been touched like that. So gently."

"Never?"

"And when the ship sank, I knew that I could not let you die. That would be like . . . allowing . . . a rare flower to be pulled from the ground."

She kissed his lips softly. "Is that why you taught me about haikus? To give something back to me? To show me how you truly felt?"

"Yes."

"Do you know that I often create them? Even here, waiting for you."

"Please tell it to me."

She kissed him again, longing to touch him as she had before. "Let me feel you first."

Annie, who had known nothing but fast and awkward lovemaking during her time with Ted, began to slowly unbutton Akira's shirt. Her hands renewed their exploration of his flesh. Her mouth moved over his skin in small circles. She felt his naked chest against her breasts, and her body tingled with anticipation. "I'm going to . . . I'm going to write a poem right now . . . with you," she said, somewhat breathlessly, her fingers and lips gliding about him.

After having always had the course of lovemaking dictated to her, Annie felt empowered to be creating the unfolding scene. Knowing that Akira liked the way she'd once touched him aboard *Benevolence*, she touched him again in the same manner. And he responded to her as she hoped he would—his movements graceful and without thought of time.

The ships loomed above them as they began to make love. And as Annie was carried into a magical world that seemed divine in nature, it suddenly occurred to her that Jake had been right. The people aboard the ships did look happy. They did look free.

ROGER PEERED THROUGH the darkness toward the cave. The entrance glowed from the presence of the fire within. The odor of roasting fish filled the wet air. Though hungry, Roger wasn't yet ready to enter the cave. He hated being within its confines, hated having his every movement witnessed by a group of people who seemed sickeningly in love with one another. How foreign he felt within the group. How troubled and clumsy and trapped. A sense of claustrophobia almost overwhelmed him when people gathered within the cave, when their laughter echoed off the damp walls. It was as if they were laughing at him, mocking his entire existence. He'd experienced such mockery before, and having to go through it again was more than he wanted to bear. How much better it would be to kill them all and have the cave to himself. Or at least to himself and Annie. He still craved her, his longing as powerful as his desire to draw smoke into his lungs. And now that he suspected his foe was touching her, this craving was even more acute and wrenching.

Roger blinked the rain away and turned toward the sea, briefly massaging the back of his aching head. From his pocket he removed a smooth, amber-colored snail shell that Ratu had found earlier. "Stupid little runt," Roger muttered, remembering how the boy had excitedly shown the shell to everyone in camp, how he'd told them that his sister would love his discovery. "It sure is beautiful," he said, shaking his head. "But not for much longer." He threw the shell against a barnacle-encrusted rock, smiling when it shattered.

While distant thunder rumbled, Roger remained pleased by the theft and destruction of the shell. Because his parents hadn't been able to afford gifts of any sort, throughout most of his childhood Roger had stolen what he desired. Though he'd secretly filled his pockets in stores and outdoor markets, he'd most enjoyed stealing from other children— taking their treasures and making them his. At first he'd covertly captured what he sought. But as the years passed and his strength and reputation grew, he'd simply hurt or threatened his classmates until they gave him whatever he wanted.

As the storm continued to subject the sky to its groans, memories of plundered toys and treasures kept Roger's headache at bay. But gradually the pain crept forward, expanding once again now that his hands were empty. He cursed the pain, the world, and his empty hands. He ought to hold a cigarette or a woman or a gun. Or, better yet, all three. Instead he sat in the rain and imagined how those in the cave were talking about him, laughing at him.

Forcing himself to think about the future and the good it would bring, Roger wondered when the destroyer would return. Edo should arrive in several days, unless, of course, the storm delayed him. Again massaging his throbbing head, Roger resigned himself to the fact that for the immediate future, he'd have to listen to the bitch's endless musings, the runt's shrill laughter, the captain's infuriating commands. He'd have to endure.

But soon Edo would land and everything would change. The runt and the captain and the Nip would be dead. There would be no more laughter to assault his ears, no more hand-holding to offend his eyes. Yes, once Edo landed, Roger would awaken, sneak into the jungle, and cut the rope that the Jap had dropped into the cave. He'd then meet Edo and lead handpicked men straight to the hiding place. And there would be no escape for his tormentors.

The thought of this future kept Roger somewhat at ease, despite the cold, the other survivors, and the maddening ache within his skull. Drumming his fingers against his thigh, he continued to look out over the sea, continued to wonder where the ships were. They would arrive in force; he knew that much. The Japs always liked to do things in groups, and claiming an island was no different. They'd send five hundred men ashore, and within a week a landing strip, gun emplacements, and living quarters would be erected. The island would be theirs.

"But not the cave," Roger whispered. "The cave will be mine, and if that little bitch so much as looks at me wrong, she'll watch as I paint a ship with her blood."

DAY THIRTEEN

I thought I knew much,
Until I saw a new world.
Songbirds announce dawn.

A Sanctuary No Longer

He saw through the eyes of his father. He recognized his father's hands, which were torn and thick knuckled after years of farming and fishing. Though the hands felt rough, he knew they could also be gentle. They could stroke his brow when needed. They could pull a splinter from his toe. He loved those hands.

In the world in front of his father, the sugarcane field was the only thing that seemed to move. The tall stalks swayed softly in the breeze. The sugarcane was so dense that passing through it was like trying to move while being tied down. Still, a step was taken, a booted foot falling softly on red soil. Somewhere ahead, a bird rose on uncertain winds.

His father lifted his rifle and peered down its barrel, looking for whatever had startled the bird. Only sugarcane filled his vision, however, and though the rifle swept back and forth, he saw nothing. He whistled in three short bursts, each as quiet as the crashes of a very distant surf. This message signified danger. Behind him he heard men who made much more noise than he preparing for a possible confrontation.

His legs trembling, he moved forward into the sugarcane. Squinting so that he could see better, he tried to look for a glint of metal or a shape that should not be in a sugarcane field. He sought anything out of the ordinary. A sound trickled into his ears, and he wondered if the air had stirred, if someone ahead had whispered, or if his mind was playing tricks on him. The sugarcane was slightly taller than his head, and he kept moving forward somewhat blindly. He had tied reeds to his helmet, his rifle, his clothes, and was almost impossible to distinguish from his surroundings. But so, he knew all too well, was the enemy.

The land radiated heat, and sweat rolled down his neck and face like rain on glass. He'd have liked to scratch his back, to pour water from his canteen on his head. But instead he continued to creep forward. A metallic click broke the silence before him and he paused. Someone was hiding; he now knew that for certain. But where? The sugarcane blocked out everything except a cluttered few feet of space ahead.

He managed to repress an almost overpowering urge to step backward, away from the danger. Abruptly, he longed to be home. To sing in church with his wife beside him. To watch her braid their daughters' hair. He wanted to suck on sugarcane with his son instead of creep through it with quivering limbs. He wanted to be anywhere but here, doing anything but this.

He saw a section of the grass move, and his finger squeezed the trigger. He tried to drop to his belly, but before he could do so, a popping noise erupted and he felt as if he'd stepped on a giant nest of hornets. His arms and belly stung fiercely and he fell on his back, his hands clutching at his flesh. The hornets continued to sting his insides, and he found the holes they'd made and desperately tried to pull them out before they bit him again. He screamed at the overwhelming agony. Suddenly, all that mattered was fleeing this place and the hornets that continued to descend upon him. With great effort he rose. He took a step forward. Then a hornet leapt into his head, and suddenly he was looking at a blue sky. A man seemingly made of grass stood above him. Something long and sharp pressed against his throat.

As the bayonet was thrust downward, Ratu finally awoke screaming. He stood up unsteadily and almost ran into the nearby fire. He stumbled past the flames and through the cave's entrance. The vision of the bayonet against his father's throat still fresh in his mind, he fell to his knees on the sand. Weeping, he began to crawl, as if he could somehow find his father, as if he could flee a cruel world that was not of his making.

Ratu hadn't gone far when Jake dropped to the sand beside him. Picking up Ratu as if he were a toddler, Jake gently set him on his lap and rocked him back and forth. Ratu was besieged with fear, and Jake could do little more than hold him tight and tell him that everything would be fine. Ratu shuddered as he sobbed, clinging to Jake as if terrified of being yanked away from him.

"He's dead!" Ratu wailed miserably, pressing his face against Jake's chest.

"It was just a little old dream, Ratu. Nothing more."

"I saw him die! I tell you, I saw—"

"He ain't dead," Jake said, stroking Ratu's head. "I promise you, he ain't—"

"But I saw him! I saw him! They killed him, and he didn't even get to run."

"Shhh, Ratu. You'll see your daddy again. I promise."

"You can't promise a bloody thing! No, no, you can't!"

Jake kissed the top of Ratu's head, hating to see him distraught. Jake was so accustomed to his jokes and laughter that at times he forgot Ratu was so far from his family. "You've had bad dreams before, right?" Jake asked, stroking Ratu's shoulder. In the distance, Jake saw Isabelle and Annie approach. He thought about asking them to help, but decided to politely wave them away. "Ratu, ain't you had bad dreams before?"

"Yes."

"Did people die? People you loved?"

"Yes."

"And when you woke up, were them people really dead?"

"But this dream was different," Ratu replied, continuing to shudder and weep. "I saw him die."

"I saw myself die in a dream once. A darn bus ran me over, and my head popped open like a dropped watermelon. But I ain't dead yet. And sure as sunshine, I ain't been splattered by some old bus."

Ratu shifted against Jake, drawing himself even closer. "I want to go home, Jake."

"Tell me about that home of yours. What's it like?"

"I really want to go home."

"Well, tell me about it. Maybe telling me about it will get you closer to it."

"How?"

"How don't matter. Just tell me and see what happens."

Ratu rubbed his eyes. "It's . . . it's up on stilts, Big Jake. It's wood. There's one . . . big room and we all sleep on the floor."

"It sure sounds nice."

"It is, Big Jake. It is."

Jake squeezed Ratu tightly, then wiped sand from his chin. "Can I tell you something, Ratu?"

"What?"

"If I had a son, if I was so darn lucky to have a son, I'd want him to be just like you."

"You would? But why? I'm not strong or smart. I can't . . . I can't do what other boys can."

"Why, you can tell a good yarn. You can make me laugh. And you taught me to spear big-eyed fish. Whatever else would a daddy need?"

Ratu's tears began again, and Jake continued to cradle him. "I miss them, Jake," Ratu said. "I miss them so bloody much."

"I know."

"Do you really think my father is safe?"

Jake nodded. "A few months ago, I dreamt that I kissed my sister. That don't mean that I did, or that I'm gonna. At least I hope it don't."

"That's disgusting, Big Jake."

"I reckon so. But there I was, kissing her."

A faint smile rose on Ratu's face. "Maybe you should keep that a secret, Big Jake. I tell you, if that was my dream, it would be a secret."

"Well, I trust you."

Ratu shifted his body so that his head rested more comfortably against Jake's chest. For the first time since his dream, he glanced at his surroundings and noticed that it had stopped raining. Though clouds still dominated the sky, like him, they seemed to have shed their tears. "Will you . . . will you sleep next to me tonight?" Ratu asked. "Right next to me, Jake?"

"Ever seen a pair of salamanders sleep?"

"Salamanders?"

"They're like lizards, except they live in the mud."

"No, I haven't seen them."

"Well, them salamanders sleep so close together that their tails get all twisted up. And I reckon that's just how I'll sleep with you."

Ratu wiped his eyes, then leaned back against Jake. "You're my best mate, Jake."

Jake smiled, his thick hands rubbing Ratu's back. "You ain't gonna tell anyone about my sister, are you?"

"I'd be too embarrassed for you, Big Jake, to say such a thing."

Jake chuckled, noting how the sky had lightened. "Let's sit here a spell and wait for first light," he said. "A couple of salamanders on a beach."

THE SEA FELT GOOD against his feet. Akira sat at the edge of a tide pool, his toes creating patterns in the sand beneath them. Dawn had come and gone, and a slate-gray sky hung listlessly above. After two days of wind, rain, and surf, the day was still. The only movement, in fact, seemed to rise from the creatures within the pool at Akira's feet. Black mollusks opened and closed. A pair of trapped fish darted about. Miniature crabs gathered atop a dead starfish, their claws constantly bringing bits of flesh to their mouths.

Akira watched the creatures with interest. He found each to be beautiful in its own way, and he wondered if his appreciation stemmed from the rapture he felt about his relationship with Annie. After all, the thought of her provoked what almost seemed to be a new life within him. Even during his best years, when he'd been a professor and helped guide wonderful minds, he hadn't felt such an abundance of energy and zeal. He'd never realized that the experience of sharing thoughts and feelings with another human being could have such a profound effect upon him. Even in Annie's absence, his mood was buoyant; for he anticipated seeing her the way a child awaits the opening of a special present.

For much of his life, Akira had studied poetry. And poets, especially Western ones, often spoke of love. But until now, Akira had only been able to guess at what such an emotion might actually feel like. And this lack of a real experience had always troubled him, for he knew that guessing about the taste of sugar was entirely different from actually savoring its flavor on his tongue.

As he'd told her, Annie had captured a part of him when she'd wiped his face clean aboard *Benevolence*. He had thought about her for hours afterward, imagining what she might be like. But he'd never fathomed that she could creep deeper and deeper into his heart until it seemed that she belonged there. He'd known her only a short time, and yet, to his amazement, he felt he knew how to make her happy. And she certainly pleased him in ways almost beyond his comprehension.

Though a part of him worried about what would befall them once they left the island, he tried not to think about Annie returning to her fiancé. The hole this event would create in him would be so overwhelming that he forced himself to ignore its eventual possibility. Comprehending his world without her in it was like imagining the sky with no sun. He simply couldn't and wouldn't do it.

Musing over what kind of beauty she saw within him, Akira continued to dangle his feet in the water. So oblivious was he to the realm beyond his thoughts that he didn't sense Roger walk up behind him. Suddenly, Roger's reflection materialized in the tide pool. Though Akira's heart skipped, he turned around slowly. Roger carried a spear in his right hand and was shirtless. Akira quickly noted his muscles, surprised that such a big man could move so quietly.

"How did you do it?" Roger asked, standing just a few feet away.

"Do what?"

"How does a monkey bastard like you get a skirt like her?"

"A skirt?"

"A woman, you stupid Nip. A woman like that little nurse."

Aware of the spear and the precariousness of his position in the tide pool, Akira said, "I did not do anything."

Roger shook his aching head, his fingers whitening upon the spear. "You Japs are such good liars. If you only fought as well as you lied, you'd win the war."

"Why are you—"

"But you won't win the war. You and your stinking kind will be driven back to that piss pot you call a country."

Akira said nothing, keeping his eyes not on Roger's face, but on the spear. Though he didn't think that Roger would attempt to kill him so openly, he wasn't about to take unnecessary risks.

"What's wrong with that little bitch?" Roger asked, leaning forward. "Is she in heat? Does she like to take it like a dog? Isn't that how you Japs do it?"

At these words, Akira's mood began to change. He could ignore taunts against him and even his country. But to hear Annie insulted was more than he was willing to endure. Maintaining his eyes on the spear, he rose slowly. He stood and faced Roger, who was a full head taller than he. "Do you know what five years of war have taught me?" he asked quietly.

"That monkeys can't fight?"

"They taught me that it is men like you, men who pretend to be strong, who always die with the least honor. They are the ones who soil themselves when the fighting becomes fierce."

"What did you say?"

"You understood me."

Roger moved closer to Akira, desperately wanting to kill him but knowing that now wasn't the time. "Do you see your death, monkey man?" he asked, his face inches from Akira's. "Do you look at me and see your death? Because I'm going to kill you. And I'll do it with my own hands. No gun. No knife. I'm going to beat you, you Jap bastard, to death with my own fists. And how do you think that's going to feel?"

Akira's eyes didn't leave Roger's. "I have already died once in this war. Nothing you can do to me would be worse than that. Nothing, so sorry."

"I can do plenty worse."

"You can talk, yes? You can insult a woman who is ten thousand times your better. But you cannot frighten me." Out of the corner of his eye, Akira noticed Jake and Joshua approaching. Switching to Japanese, Akira said, "A coward is all you are, and all you will ever be."

Though Roger understood perfectly well what Akira had said, he managed to somewhat subdue his sudden rage. "What did you say?"

Akira smiled. "Only that it is a beautiful day. And I think that I will take a walk now."

Roger's hand fell upon Akira's shoulder, squeezing it tightly. "I asked what you said."

For a brief moment, Akira thought about slamming the side of his hand into Roger's throat, about watching him die in the tide pool. But he realized that if he killed Roger in such a manner, Joshua would have no choice but to lock him up, and his days with Annie would be over. And so he said, "I am leaving. If you wish to try to beat me with your fists, please do so now."

Roger pulled his hand away from Akira so that his nails left deep scratches on the smaller man's shoulder. "I'll kill you. And then I'll find Annie. I'll make that little bitch wish you hadn't saved her."

"You—"

"And I wonder if you'll hear her screams."

Akira looked at the scratches, felt his flesh sting from rents made by Roger's long nails. He raised his gaze to meet Roger's. "Do you know what seppuku is?" he asked, his voice soft but suddenly quite intense.

"No," Roger replied, lying.

"Seppuku is how Japanese samurai would take their own lives after being disgraced. They would stick a sword in their own belly and make a series of cuts until they died."

"I bet they cried like women."

"When you threatened Annie, when you brought her into our quarrel, you committed seppuku," Akira said, his tone so menacing that he hardly recognized his own voice. "You are still alive, but believe me, you just thrust a sword into your belly. And I will make the cuts." Brushing past Roger as if he didn't exist, Akira walked toward Joshua and Jake. Though he debated telling Joshua about Roger's threats, for the time being he walked in silence, wondering if he could still ponder love and happiness with Roger's blood on his hands.

NOT LONG AFTER Akira's confrontation with Roger, Annie sought out her lover. He had walked far down the rocky beach, trying to determine how to deal with the threat Roger posed without risking everything. Akira now sat atop a massive rock that served as a rampart against the waves. He watched the sea and debated a variety of options at his disposal. He still hadn't made up his mind when Annie stepped to the rock. "Are you looking for ships?" she asked, trying to climb up.

He moved to help her, his hand grasping hers and pulling her up beside him. "I am just thinking," he said.

"Of what?"

"Nothing, really."

Annie saw that his face lacked its usual vigor, and she wondered what troubled him. She sat beside him on the rock, holding his hand and watching the waves break below. She expected him to speak, and when he didn't, she shifted uncomfortably. "Did I do something wrong?"

"No."

A large wave broke violently against the rock, froth rising before them. "Is that the only response I get?" she asked. "A one-word answer?"

He sighed, unsure if he should tell her what happened with Roger. Were he in Japan, he'd have shouldered the situation alone. But Annie wanted to know everything, and he was afraid of betraying her trust by keeping things from her. He also felt that the truth might help protect her. "You must be careful around Roger," he finally replied.

"What does that mean? Akira, what does that mean?"

He looked toward the sky, which was finally starting to clear. "There are men who like to hurt people. And Roger is such a man."

"Did he threaten me? Did he?"

"He threatened us."

"How?"

He shook his head slowly. "I have met such men before. I have seen them kill, and I have killed them."

She sat straighter at this response, surprised at this revelation. "Where?"

"Nanking."

"You were there?"

"For too long, so sorry to say."

Annie had heard rumors of the atrocities. But so many rumors floated about—tales of Hitler's dream to kill every Jew in Europe, stories of Japanese bayoneting thousands of prisoners and civilians, whispers of a secret weapon being built in America that could destroy the world. To Annie, these rumors were too unspeakably awful to be true, even though she feared they might be. "What happened?" she finally asked.

He closed his eyes for a moment. "Remember that first night, when I carried you here?"

"You said that you were reaching for . . . an angel. You said that she saved you."

"She was a young Chinese girl. Perhaps eight or nine years old." Suddenly seeing her battered face, Akira paused, his body going limp, his eyes tearing. "A group of men . . . a group of Japanese soldiers had found her. They had started . . . started to beat her. I . . . I saw them. She looked at me and . . . with her look she begged me to help. At first I tried. But there were too many soldiers and . . . and . . . may she forgive me, I turned away."

Annie reached for his hand, which was unresponsive to her touch. "And what happened?"

He again closed his eyes, prompting a tear to tumble down his face. "And . . . and those men . . . those beasts . . . raped her. And they killed her. And I saw . . . hell that day. Nanking was hell."

She squeezed his hand. She'd seen too many children maimed by war, and the thought of a girl enduring such a heinous fate made her cry. Shuddering quietly, she leaned against him. "And in the water . . . you saw this little girl?" she asked softly, wondering how God could allow such a crime, sad and sickened that such stories had too often reached her ears.

"Yes. She came to me. She . . . she reached out her hand and it seemed that she was well."

Annie watched his tears, watched the breeze ruffle his hair. "How did you survive . . . that?"

Akira sadly shook his head. "The body can survive, yes, while the soul dies?"

"I think so."

"I went back . . . later that day. And I found . . . her body." He released his hand from Annie's and put his fingers against his eyes. "She was . . . no longer was she a little girl," he said, weeping. "And I carried her to a garden . . . to a quiet place. I found a new dress . . . and put it on her. I cleaned her face. I straightened her hair. I . . . I placed a toy horse in her hands. And I prayed. And then I burned her . . . until her ashes could be blown away. Blown away to a far better place."

Annie put her head against his shoulder, her tears cool against her face. "And then?"

He sighed, remembering how he'd wiped the blood from her, how his hands had trembled uncontrollably. "And then," he said, his voice hardening, "I found the beasts who had ruined her and I killed them. Most of them, at least."

"You did?"

"So sorry, but I am good at killing. I have saved only a few, but I have killed many."

"You saved me," she said, aware that his mind was tumbling into the darkest of places and wanting to protect him from that fall. She recaptured his hand within her own. "And you saved Isabelle."

"So few."

"Did you . . . did you know that she's pregnant?"

He looked to her, his eyes bloodshot. "No."

"So you also saved her child."

Akira nodded absently. He watched waves die and be reborn beneath him. "I am glad," he finally said, "to have saved her child."

Annie held his hand, stroking his flesh with her thumb. For a long time they sat together and watched the world before them. A flock of gulls had gathered on the water and rose and fell with the waves. The birds were talkative, their cries carrying over the sea.

"What will we do about Roger?" Annie finally asked. "I'd rather . . . you not kill him."

Akira looked at her. "You are sure, yes?"

"Yes."

"Then I will not kill him. But I will talk to the captain. And later, if Roger comes for you, I will kill him, Annie. I will kill him a thousand times before I let him hurt you."

"Because of what happened in Nanking?"

"Yes," he said quietly, his hand finally stirring within hers. "And also because I cannot imagine the world without you in it. Because you make me . . . you make me understand why the old poets wrote so much of love."

THE SUN FINALLY REAPPEARED, just before dusk. Since they had moved to the east side of the island, they could no longer enjoy sunsets. The clouds above them merely glowed and then slowly darkened, as if the sun was their air supply and without it they suffocated. The wind and sea had almost completely gone still, and the island seemed to stand proudly in the young night, having survived another typhoon. The storm that had sunk ships, toppled buildings, and killed hundreds of humans had done little more than rid the island of its dead and dying trees.

As on the other beach, the survivors had fashioned a fire pit that could be seen from neither air nor sea. Near this pit rose a large, orderly pile of driftwood. In case Scarlet spotted an American ship, Joshua wanted to be ready to light a signal. Around the fire pit, the survivors ate a dinner of dried fish and fresh mango. Though finding fruit on this side of the island had been a pleasant discovery, Ratu and Jake had spent much of the afternoon fishing in the rough waters near the cave and had almost nothing to show for their efforts.

Overall, the mood at camp was upbeat. After two days of being confined to the cave, the fresh air and clear sky were welcome tidings. And though only fruit and dried fish filled their bellies, fewer bugs and other such irritants thrived on this beach than on the other. Also, the typhoon hadn't destroyed their lifeboat or any important supplies. Everything had been carried into the cave and was now secure.

While Roger sat on a distant rock and obsessed over his aching head, the other eight survivors spoke about what they'd do after the war. Most everyone had a clear vision of what such a future would bring.

Nathan wanted to open a deli. Jake spoke of visiting Ratu's village before returning to Missouri. Scarlet was tired of being a nurse, and hoped to attend beauty school. Though Joshua had been in the navy for more than a decade and was weary of the war, he didn't know what he might do were he a civilian. Isabelle decided to keep her pregnancy a secret and spoke of remaining a nurse. Hardly surprising to those who knew her well, Annie wasn't sure what she'd do. Akira hoped to again teach, and Ratu wanted to be taught.

Everyone expected not to remain stranded for long. Joshua had repeatedly told them of the island's strategic importance, of how the battle of the South Pacific was going to be won or lost around the Solomon Islands. He was convinced that if they could hide from the Japanese, they'd be rescued by Americans. All they had to do was wait and signal a passing American warship or aircraft.

After the survivors spoke about returning to their former lives, they continued to plan for how they'd ensure their well-being on the island. Unlike the previous day, when Joshua had done the majority of the talking, most everyone seemed to have an opinion on most every subject. Exchanges were pleasant, though, and ultimately people looked to Joshua to make whatever decisions were necessary.

His faith in himself slightly renewed, Joshua smiled encouragingly at Scarlet when she suggested a means of signaling toward the cave if she spotted something from her perch atop a nearby hill. "I need something shiny," she said, finishing a mango. "It's so bright up there. And we can create some sort of code."

"Like the moose code?" Ratu replied excitedly. "Can't we do that, Captain?"

"Morse code is a bit tricky," Joshua said, gently correcting him. "But I like your idea. What do you have in mind, my first lieutenant?"

Ratu glanced at the distant hill, trying to quickly come up with an answer. "I know!" he said. "What if Miss Scarlet has two shiny things? If she sees an American ship, she can flash both. If she sees the Japanese, she only flashes one. What do you think, Captain?"

Joshua nodded. "I think it's brilliant. All we have to do is—" His words died abruptly as a yellow flash burst over the distant sea. Stepping toward the water, he peered into the growing darkness. Another orb of light flared, illuminating the clouds. Suddenly, the space above the sea was dominated by yellow and orange flashes that appeared like sudden drops of paint on a black canvas.

"What is it?" Isabelle asked, taking Joshua's arm, trying to remember where the binoculars rested but deciding to leave them be.

"A battle," he replied uneasily, the crack and crackle of distant explosions finally traveling to his ears. "Our ships against their ships," he added, inwardly lamenting the confrontation, as he knew that the advanced technology of the Japanese made them better night fighters than his countrymen.

The array of explosions intensified. Entire sections of the sea were inundated with light. The air was rife with the pop of shells being fired and the louder clap of explosions. One area seemed to blaze with light. Several large orange orbs billowed outward from this space.

"What's happening?" Annie asked. "Joshua?"

His unblinking eyes remained fastened to the sight. "A ship is being sunk," he said absently, his fingers moving back and forth as if on a rosary bead. "A big ship."

Like the finale of a fireworks display, the number and size of explosions intensified. Annie moved to Akira's side, thinking of men who were dying, wishing that *Benevolence* was nearby so that some of these men could be saved. Even from miles away she could almost feel the force of the explosions. She'd treated the wounded from battles such as this one—men whose clothes and skin had been burnt away, whose frail bodies had been savaged by almost incomprehensible weaponry. She wanted to turn and hurry back to the cave, but couldn't leave the sight before her.

The battle reached its climax—with a seemingly endless barrage of explosions erupting on each side. Several more ships appeared to catch fire. These burning pyres resembled little more than candle flames atop the water. But Joshua knew that each flame likely represented the death of a ship and hundreds of men. The flames gradually diminished as the mortally wounded ships disappeared into the sea. The frequency of explosions gradually lessened, and the night turned black again.

After the battle, no one moved for some time. Even Roger stood transfixed, watching the distant horizon, his headache and hate temporarily forgotten. He wondered if Edo's ship had been involved in the conflict, and if so, how that would affect his stay on the island. Resolving to make radio contact the next day, he continued to study the scene before him.

After a few minutes, Akira turned to Annie, Isabelle, and Joshua. "It fills the air, yes?" he said quietly.

"What does?" Annie asked.

"The breeze brings it to us," he replied, all too aware of the taint of battle.

Annie breathed deeply and, sure enough, she smelled something foreign in the air—the stench of burning oil and paint and a hundred other such things. After growing accustomed to the sweet scent of the island, she found the odor of battle overwhelming. She realized that the air around *Benevolence* must have smelled the same, but she hadn't been aware of it.

Making the sign of the cross, Joshua began to pray for the dead and dying. Isabelle and Annie followed his lead. Akira lowered his head to honor those who'd fallen. The four of them stood motionless, and all was still but for the waves and the fire.

Nearby, Scarlet and Nathan spoke softly about how they'd seen too many such sights, about how they worried that the war would steal their loved ones. Their words prompted Ratu to think of his father, and he took Jake's hand and walked back to the cave. He felt guilty for being glad that his father wasn't on one of the ships, for his relief that it wasn't his father who was dying. And so he gripped Jake's hand tightly as he glanced behind and saw that Annie, Isabelle, Joshua, and Akira still hadn't moved.

Feeling nauseous and quite tired, Ratu lay on the palm fronds that comprised his bed. Jake moved beside him, placing his arm over Ratu's shoulders. Though they weren't far from the fire, Ratu felt chilled. Closing his eyes, he inched away from the fire and toward the warmth of his friend.

DAY FOURTEEN

Does the bee in fall
Know that a frost is nearing?
Do skies prefer blue?

An Imminent Arrival

After its three-day banishment, the sun returned in earnest. On this side of the island dawn came powerfully, the distant ocean seeming to bleed. Like fire consuming a dry forest, the crimson sky expanded, red tendrils blazing as the color spread westward. Waves lapped feebly at the shoreline, as if they'd exhausted all their energy during the storm and had nothing left to offer.

Akira and Joshua were often the first to rise, and this morning had been no different. Upon seeing the captain tending to the fire, Akira had quietly asked if they might go for a walk. And so they'd left the camp and proceeded north along the coast, circumventing tide pools and crossing small patches of sand. As they walked, Joshua repeatedly looked to the sea, scanning for any ships that survived the battle. Only the ocean's pale face greeted him.

Akira pointed out a marooned sea urchin, taking care to avoid it. He found it interesting that such an outwardly menacing creature could have such a beautiful white structure within. Turning toward Joshua, he said, "I wish to thank you for treating me well."

"Is that why we're here?"

"We are here to take a walk, yes? A walk during a beautiful dawn."

"If you say so."

They took a few more steps, and Akira said, "You have good men, Captain. And women. And you lead them well."

Joshua glanced toward Akira. "Thank you." After a slight pause he asked, "Did you lead men?"

"Yes, though not many. Not nearly enough, so sorry to say."

Believing that ultimately the leaders of the war would decide its outcome, Joshua studied Akira, as he had many times before. Wanting to test him once again, he asked, "What will you do if Japanese land here?"

"I will be honest with you, Captain; I do not want to betray my people. I hope that your countrymen land here rather than mine."

"But if they don't?"

Akira exhaled deeply. "In war, alliances sometimes change, yes? You now fight with the Russians when you could easily be fighting against them."

Joshua thought about the great German armies that had been advancing on Stalingrad when *Benevolence* was sunk. A million men were attacking the city, and a million were defending it. Yes, Joshua thought, we could be fighting the Russians instead of sending them thousands of jeeps, rifles, and tanks. And, God help us, if that were true, we'd almost certainly lose. "Hitler should never have marched east," he agreed. "But what can you expect from a madman?"

"True. But will the Red Army fall?"

"I don't think so. The Russians have too many men. And Stalin doesn't mind sending millions to their deaths to stop the German advance." Joshua spied a flat rock, bent down, and sent it skipping into the sea. "So you're telling me that you're switching alliances?"

"Not from my country to your country."

"What then?"

"From my leaders to you."

Joshua looked for another rock, stalling to give himself time to think. "Why should I believe this?"

Akira spied a suitable stone and handed it to Joshua. "May I tell you a story?"

"Of course."

"It is not quick."

"I'm in no hurry."

Akira nodded, clasping his hands together. "As you must know, one day after Pearl Harbor, we invaded Thailand. I was in southern Thailand. In places like this, near the sea. I led a squad of men, and we occupied a small village. Unlike what we did in China or Korea, we were good to the Thais. We paid them for food. We paid them to work. And most of them did not hate us." Akira paused, wishing that other invasions had been as bloodless. "My squad was in this village for three months. And one of my men . . . he . . . grew close to a Thai woman. He did not tell me this, of course, but I could see what was happening. I liked this man. His grandfather and father had made kimonos, and such should have been his fate. One day, a week before we were to leave the village, this man and woman disappeared. A boat was missing. His gun and uniform and helmet remained on the beach."

"What did you do?"

Akira smiled faintly. "I did nothing."

"Nothing?"

"I never mentioned his disappearance to my men, and I reported to my superior that he had died of malaria."

"You could have been shot for treason."

Akira shrugged, handing Joshua another stone. "In the weeks that followed, I often wondered why this man had left everything, had risked everything, to be with this woman. And I never understood why. If anyone found him, either Thais or Japanese, they would most certainly kill him. And yet he went with her."

Squinting against the young sun, Joshua stopped in his tracks and turned toward Akira. "And this is how you feel?" he asked. "You would risk everything . . . for Annie?"

Akira watched a bird as it stalked a school of fish. "I now understand how the man felt," he said simply.

"Would you . . . could you kill your countrymen for her?" Joshua asked, amazed at what he was hearing.

"Yes," Akira said quietly. "That is why I took the scalpel. To protect her."

"A scalpel against a gun?"

Akira shook his head. "Not every danger is posed by my countrymen."

Joshua started to ask what he meant, but stopped himself. "I'd never let Roger hurt her. I can also see what my men are doing. And if Roger so much as touches Annie, I'll kill him myself."

"She does not want him killed."

"So you've had this talk? A talk of killing him?"

"Yes."

"And you decided not to?"

"She decided."

Joshua nodded. "Well, that sounds like her."

Akira found Joshua's eyes. "If my countrymen land, I will help you hide from them. Will you help me?"

"How?"

"Observe Roger. If I should die, know that he has killed me, and that he will then come for Annie."

"That won't happen."

"If I should die, I ask that you kill him before he hurts her." Akira bowed slightly. "You will do this, yes?"

"Has he threatened her? To you?"

"More than one time."

Joshua looked at the sea, wondering why God had decided to send him this Japanese soldier. What was the purpose of Akira's delivery? "Then I agree to what you say," Joshua replied. "But don't let him kill you. I need you. And . . . and I believe that Annie needs you. And if you're to be with her, then you're to be with me." Joshua stuck out his hand, which Akira took firmly.

"We can . . . be friends, yes?" Akira asked.

"I'd like that," Joshua said, pleased with the handshake, with the partnership. For the first time in months, he thought that perhaps lasting peace was possible. "I'd like that very much."

IN THE JUNGLE near the cave, Isabelle and Annie searched for fruit. The sun mostly failed to penetrate the dense canopy of leaves, and the ground was still quite muddy. Emboldened by the wetness, slugs and snails inched across seemingly every rock and fallen branch. Oddly, there appeared to be far fewer insects than normal, almost as if the typhoon had kindly swept the mosquitoes and flies out to sea.

Annie held the machete, and Isabelle carried a few papayas and breadfruits that they'd found near the cave. The sisters moved slowly, searching for more fruit-bearing trees. The typhoon had certainly left its mark on the island's interior, and Annie and Isabelle constantly circumvented fallen trees or pools of muddy water. The siblings had left with Scarlet, but once they'd reached a large hill, Scarlet had climbed it with the binoculars in hand while Annie and Isabelle had continued onward.

Feeling a large snail crunch underfoot, Annie vowed to watch the ground more carefully. "Did you hear that?" she asked.

"What?"

"I just murdered a snail."

"Where on earth did they all come from?"

"Don't the French eat them? Like popcorn or something? Warm and dripping in butter?"

"Oh, Annie. I'm pregnant, remember? Please don't say such things."

"Let's hope the Germans choke on them," Annie replied, using the machete to push through a series of vines. "Anyway, how are you feeling?"

"Really quite good. Just a bit weak at times. And you?"

"Wonderful, thank you."

"Wonderful?"

"Very much so."

Isabelle kept looking for fruit. "I've seen the way you look at each other. I've seen you holding hands. How else do you feel?"

Annie stepped on a slippery root and almost fell. "Clumsy, I guess," she replied, smiling.

"Well, you've always been that."

Brushing mud from her knee, Annie added, "How did you feel . . . when you fell in love with Joshua?"

"Nervous. Happy. Excited. I think excited mostly. I was so pleased to have found him."

"I feel all those things," Annie said. "But also something else . . . almost like I'm a new person. It's hard to describe and I'm not sure that I even understand it, but I'm . . . I'm more at peace with myself since I've come to know him."

"Why?"

"I don't know exactly. But maybe because I'm not afraid like I used to be. I've always been afraid, Izzy. Ever since Mother slept next to me and I pretended not to notice her cry."

"But these days you're not?"

"These days I'm not."

Isabelle spied a cluster of hanging bananas and pointed it out. Annie rose on her toes and with one deft stroke from the machete cut down the fruit. The cone-shaped mass of bananas tumbled to the ground. "There must be forty of them," Annie said happily, handing Isabelle the machete. Picking up the bunch and placing it on her shoulder, Annie turned and started retracing their steps.

"Can you manage it?" Isabelle asked, surprised at the strength of her little sister.

"I think I love him," Annie said. "I know that I'm engaged, that I've sinned, and that I should be ashamed for what I've done, but to tell you the truth, I don't regret it." She shifted the bananas atop her shoulder. "I . . . I feel terribly guilty about . . . betraying Ted. I really do. But I don't regret what's happened with Akira. I love him, Izzy. He . . . he takes me to a place I've never known. A place I didn't even know existed. He's wise and good and he likes me just the way I am."

"I'm happy for you, Annie, I really am," Isabelle replied, trying to ignore a slight ache in her belly. "But as your older sister, I have a responsibility to tell you—"

"To tell me what? That there's no future with him? That he'll end up in an American prisoner-of-war camp? Don't you think that I know these things? That I think about them every day?"

"I just don't want you to get hurt," Isabelle responded. "And what of Ted? Don't you have a duty to him?"

"And what of me? Don't I owe myself anything? Anything at all? A life with Ted, especially now, after having experienced . . . a taste of love, will be miserable."

"You don't know that."

"You never even liked him that much. And now you're protecting him."

"Well, he's not here to protect himself."

"Protect himself?" Annie asked angrily, walking faster. "What's gotten into you?"

"Love can be blinding," Isabelle said, trying to be patient, knowing that Annie needed to hear these words. "It can blind one to . . . to the realities of life. How do you see a future with Akira? Where would you live? Do you think you could settle in California? How do you think he'd be treated? We have our own camps, you know. The Japanese just don't die in them."

"Why do I have to think so far into the future?" Annie asked. "Just because you followed a perfect little plan doesn't mean I have to. I'm not you, Isabelle. I don't know what I want and how I want to get there. That's not who I am. I want to live for today."

"He—"

"He understands that. He's the first person in my life who hasn't told me what to do."

Isabelle reached out and held Annie's elbow, forcing her to stop. "I'm not trying to tell you what to do. I'm trying to protect you."

"You've protected me all my life, Isabelle! And what has it done for me? I've been alone and afraid, and I'm set to marry a man I don't love."

"I didn't do those things to you. To blame me for them isn't fair."

Annie crossly blew at a large moth that landed on her shoulder. "What do you know about fairness? You with the perfect health. The perfect husband. The perfect life. How can you preach to me about what's fair?"

"Can't you see that I'm just saying what has to be said? If I were making a mistake, wouldn't you talk—"

"You think that falling in love is a mistake? That I'm some kind of fool?" Annie shook off her sister's grip. "What's wrong with you?" she asked, walking as quickly as possible.

"Will you please stop?"

"No!"

"Annie, I don't want to fight. I just want to make sure that you're thinking about what will happen after we leave the island."

"I'm not a child! I can think for myself!" Envisioning being forced to separate from Akira, Annie started to cry. "I can't leave him!" she shouted, dropping the bananas and running into the jungle.

"Wait, Annie, wait! I'm sorry! Please don't go!"

Ignoring Isabelle's protests, Annie hurried through the jungle. For the first time in days, she felt a familiar sense of fear building within her. A part of her knew that Isabelle was right, that fate might make it all but impossible to remain with Akira. And this thought caused her to tremble, to cry as she hurried forward. Fate had stolen so much from her. It had ended her childhood innocence. It had cast a shadow over what should have been some of her fondest moments and memories. And now it threatened to steal the man she loved.

"No!" she shouted, rushing forward so hard and fast that she tripped on a fallen branch and tumbled to the ground. She rolled upon the muddy soil, banging her elbow against a stone. Her body afire with pain, Annie pulled her knees to her chest and wept. The dread of losing Akira, just when she'd found him, overwhelmed her. She felt cold without him, felt more alone than she had in many years. Running her muddy hands through her hair, she tried to gather her wits, but suddenly lacked the strength to do anything but cry.

And so oblivious was she to the world around her that she didn't see Roger standing twenty feet away, leaning against a flowering sandalwood tree. His hands twisted around the shaft of his spear. His face bore a smile.

Her tears made him happy.

THE FOUR JAPANESE WARSHIPS cut through the debris-laden water with the same ease as swans gliding across a pond. At the front of the convoy was one of Japan's newest and most advanced heavy cruisers. Following the zigzagging path of the cruiser were a transport ship and two smaller destroyers. The transport ship carried more than a thousand soldiers, as well as antiaircraft guns, ammunition, armored personnel carriers, and everything necessary to fashion a runway in the middle of a tropical jungle.

From the bow of the cruiser, Katsuo Kawamoto, known to Roger by the code name of Edo, stared through binoculars toward their destination. As he gazed at the sea—which was littered with branches, coconuts, and other debris from the typhoon—Edo speculated as to how the past few days had affected the American spy. Aboard the cruiser, things certainly hadn't been easy. The typhoon had forced every ship in the area to seek calmer waters, and even far from the storm's eye, the seas had been ferocious. Adding to their troubles, two days later the convoy had come upon a similar-sized group of American warships. The resulting battle had been short but intense, not ending until an American light cruiser and a destroyer were sunk. Though Edo's countrymen had been victorious, the ship that carried him and his ten handpicked men was hit by several shells.

Turning around to eye the cruiser's superstructure, Edo was impressed by how much damage had already been repaired. Though some of the buckled and torn metal would remain untouched until they returned to Yokohama, the legacy of the battle was much less than it had been. The cruiser's giant guns were all intact and, even to Edo, looked rather menacing.

Fortunately, none of Edo's men had been harmed during the encounter. He'd selected them himself from a group of elite Imperial Navy paratroopers who'd been aboard the transport ship. Though Edo doubted he'd need so many talented men, the survivors from *Benevolence* had to be dealt with as efficiently as possible. The issue of how to handle the Americans had troubled Edo for the past week, and hadn't been settled until his superior in Tokyo had taken the dilemma away from him, deciding that it would be best if the survivors were eliminated. After all, a handful of Americans telling the world about how their hospital ship was torpedoed wouldn't benefit the emperor— regardless of whether the Americans had broken international law by filling the ship with extra fuel and munitions.

Killing the Americans made Edo's task easier, and he'd been pleased to receive the orders. However, he hadn't been as satisfied with the command to eliminate Ronin. He'd worked with the American spy on several occasions, and while Edo admitted that Ronin was somewhat unstable, the man had served him well enough. Regrettably, the problem of somehow reintroducing Ronin to his countrymen as the sole survivor of *Benevolence* was inherently risky. Too many questions would be asked of such a survivor, and it was possible that the Americans would realize that Ronin had betrayed them and would set about converting him into a double agent. And Edo had to admit that contemplating the future motives of his operative wasn't something he cared to envision.

Putting the field glasses against his eyes once more, Edo looked ahead. Once Ronin contacted him a final time, the particulars of their meeting would be arranged. Then it would be a simple matter to follow Ronin into the jungle and eliminate the survivors. Their bodies would be burned, and after Ronin was killed, no American would ever know for certain what had happened to *Benevolence*. The ship would have simply disappeared.

As Edo scanned the sea, he thought about how he'd directed and manipulated Ronin over the past two years. The man certainly had his talents. He was bright, forward thinking, fearless, and physically formidable. Of course, Edo had always detected a certain kind of madness within him. And this madness ensured that his usefulness would be relatively short-lived. But the destruction of *Benevolence* and its secret cargo had made headquarters happy. Not only had precious supplies been destroyed, but a new American ship had been sunk. Edo didn't care that *Benevolence* had been a hospital ship. In his mind it was an enemy vessel. It took steel and men and time to make. And now that it had been destroyed, the Americans would have to make another—if they wished to draw upon such valuable resources.

Edo had spent much of the war in an underground bunker in Tokyo. He'd created complex schemes that aided the emperor in his early victories. Through secret messages and code-ridden commands, Edo had killed hundreds of men and women. But he'd never killed by his own hand, and a large part of him yearned to do so. After all, wasn't it considered an honor to see an enemy's blood upon one's skin? How could he let the entire war pass without pulling a trigger and watching someone crumple before him?

His fingers tracing the contours of his holstered pistol, Edo debated how he could put himself in the best position to kill. Should he shoot one of the nurses or doctors they were likely to find? Would such a death give him any satisfaction? Or should he kill Ronin? Should he watch the man's face reflect bewilderment, then pain, then peace? Or, better yet, should he shoot several Americans?

Musing over such questions the way a mathematician ponders a complex theorem, Edo continued to create a plan for his arrival on the island. Only much later, when all the details of the next few days had been finalized within his mind, did Edo return to his cramped quarters. There he glanced at a photograph of his wife and children. He cleaned trace amounts of dirt from beneath his fingernails with the tip of a dagger. And he then withdrew his pistol from its holster and pulled slightly and longingly on the trigger.

THE HILLTOP PROVIDED an almost unobstructed view of the entire island. Though three other distant rises were of greater height, these outcroppings only obscured small slices of the sea. After handing the binoculars to Ratu, Scarlet immediately held a giant leaf above her head to shield herself from the sun. "Do you see anything?" she asked, wondering if perhaps his young eyes could discern something she could not.

"I see everything!" Ratu replied excitedly.

Jake smiled and sat down near Scarlet, removing a long blade of grass from his teeth. "I reckon that's what our preacher said once. That God saw everything."

"I'm not God, Big Jake. But I tell you, I see everything."

Jake looked about the hill, curious as to why Scarlet wanted to be alone atop the island. "A nice little day, ain't it, miss?" he asked.

"If you like the sun and heat, yes, I'd say so."

Liking such things, but seeing that she did not, Jake just smiled. "Has anything caught your eye?"

"Some beautiful birds, but that's about it. I look for ships and I look for birds. And I see a lot of birds."

Jake squinted against the sun, his gaze dropping to the trees below. "We don't see many birds on the farm." Then, he added with a grin, "My daddy thinks they're trespassers."

"Trespassers?"

"I'm afraid so."

"Does he shoot them?"

"He did for a time."

"How terrible. Did you?"

Jake scratched his chin, which was filling with whiskers. "I know how to shoot a gun, miss. And on occasion I did eat pheasant and quail and turkey. But I just shot them for dinner, so that my mama had something to fill her pots. Otherwise, I liked watching them. Especially waterfowl."

"I used to feed pigeons with my grandmother," Scarlet said. "In Central Park."

"That sounds real nice."

"It was."

"And now you sit here and watch parrots?"

"It beats sitting in the cave. I can't breathe in that place."

Jake smiled at her and turned to Ratu. "I reckon we should get back. We still got some fish to catch."

"The fish aren't going anywhere, Big Jake," Ratu replied.

"But the day is. Why, sunset ain't but a few hours away. And if we don't catch something for dinner, it'll be like showing up at a barn raising with no hammer."

"What's a barn raising?" Ratu asked, lowering the binoculars. "I tell you, you never make any bloody sense to me, Big Jake. Does he make any sense to you, Miss Scarlet?"

She smiled. "He does."

"Do people just speak differently in America?" Ratu asked. "Do they say things like *barn raising* for no reason?"

"People enjoy using expressions," she answered. "It keeps things from getting boring."

Ratu handed her the binoculars. "Keeps things from being boring? Things like having our ship sunk, a typhoon almost killing us, and planes blowing up? That's crazy, I tell you. You're not making any more sense than Big Jake."

"Can you do me a favor?" Scarlet asked, knowing that Ratu liked such tasks.

"What?"

"Can you tell the captain that I've seen no ships today?"

"But he knows that because you haven't signaled him."

"But you can still tell him. It won't hurt to have you tell him, will it?"

Ratu rose to his feet. "I'll tell him. Should I say anything else? I'll be a good messenger, I promise. I'm his first lieutenant, you know."

She smiled. "That will be fine for now."

"You ain't got a hankering for anything from below, miss?" Jake asked as he stood up.

"I'm fine, Jake. But thank you."

Jake and Ratu said good-bye and started to descend the steep hill. Jake watched Ratu recklessly hurry forward. Several times he stumbled and almost fell. Jake was about to tell him to be careful when Ratu suddenly stopped and turned in his direction. "What's America like?" he asked. "Is it a place I should someday visit?"

Holding Ratu's elbow in an effort to keep him from falling, Jake said, "Well, imagine you was an ant, and you had this here whole island to explore. I reckon you wouldn't see much of it, would you?"

"Not unless I hopped on the back of some bird."

"That's kind of like America. It's so darn big. It ain't easy to see more than just a sliver of it."

"Have you been to the Big Apple Pie?" Ratu asked, his free hand absently fingering the shark's tooth.

"You mean New York City?"

"Of course, Big Jake. What else would I bloody be talking about?"

Jake smiled, wiping his brow. "It's got a heap more skyscrapers than this jungle has trees."

"Skyscrapers?"

"Buildings so tall that they scrape the sky's belly."

Ratu whistled appreciatively. "I can't imagine such a thing."

"And the people. There are so many, and so many different faces. Kind of like all them fish we speared."

Ratu nodded but didn't immediately respond. He leapt over a rock and slid a few feet on the damp soil. They were almost to the bottom of the hill. "Is it good to have black skin in America?" he asked. "I've heard it's not good."

Jake glanced at Ratu's dark face, wondering how such a question should be answered. "In some ways it's just fine. In others it ain't."

"How's it good?"

"It's good because things get better. My daddy owns his land. And it's beautiful land. And as long as it don't rain too much or too little, we'll keep that land." Jake took a sip from his canteen and then offered some water to Ratu. "And there ain't nothing quite like running my fingers through that soil." He smiled at the memory. "I even tasted it once."

"You ate dirt?"

"I sure did."

"Get stuffed, mate. Why?"

"Everything grows in that dirt. And I wanted just a bit of it inside me. Figured it couldn't hurt none."

Ratu reached the bottom of the hill and grabbed a spear that he'd left leaning against a tree. "And the bad part of having black skin in America?"

"I always hold my head real high, Ratu. It's good to be proud, I reckon. But just because I hold my head high don't mean that people will think much of it. A head can be held high, but if that head belongs to a black man, especially a poor black man, people ain't gonna understand that pride."

"What do they think it is?"

"Depends on the person who's doing the thinking, I reckon. Sometimes arrogance, sometimes anger. Sometimes they look at me like they think that I'm running from something. That they should be afraid."

"The captain doesn't look at you that way."

Jake followed Ratu into the jungle, noticing how he continued to hold the shark tooth. "He did once. When we first met. But he ain't done it since, and he's as fine a man as there is."

"Did they laugh at you when you were a boy?"

"A handful of times, I expect. But I tried mighty hard not to give them reasons to laugh."

"How?"

Jake paused, recalling moments from his childhood. "Oh, I'd go through the trash and pull out newspapers. And I'd sit for a spell and read them, try to at least learn how whites spoke. What words they used and such. My brothers and sisters thought I was crazy, reading all them newspapers. But they taught me a lot."

Thinking of his father, of how he was certainly following the orders of white men, Ratu asked, "Why didn't you just stay on your farm? Why come here?"

Jake stepped over a fallen log. "Because . . . because how can I expect the world to be a better place if I ain't gonna try real hard to make it better? I reckon you can't just throw a bunch of seeds on the ground and expect head-high corn. You gotta water and fertilize and pull them weeds. Then you'll get your head-high corn. And that corn will be the sweetest thing that you ever did taste."

"I've never had corn."

"Why is it that you're always touching that tooth?" Jake asked, reaching down to pluck a fresh blade of grass from the ground. "You touch that thing as much as a woman does a baby's fingers."

Ratu slowed his pace, realizing that Jake was right. He had been touching his tooth a lot. "I don't know, Big Jake. I tell you, I bloody well don't. But I think for good luck. My father had a necklace that he always rubbed before we went fishing."

"Well, maybe you'd better rub it a few more times so that we'll catch dinner tonight."

Ratu absently touched the tooth, his mind still awash in their earlier conversation. "Should I hold my head high?" he asked.

Jake wasn't used to giving advice to anyone, let alone to a boy. And so he thought about what words to share. Finally, he said, "Don't let anyone, even me, tell you how to hold your head, Ratu. That'd be like me telling the sun how to shine. You do what makes you happy. Nothing more, nothing less."

"But what if I don't know?"

"Then don't worry. The sun might not know how it shines, but it sure does look pretty."

THE TREE SWAYED like a dancer beneath her. Gripping two branches, Annie sat on a thick limb and watched the jungle stretch and shake. She'd been up in the tree for at least an hour. After she'd finally stopped crying, she'd been angry with herself for getting so upset. She'd felt as if she had taken a step backward, regressing into the old Annie who was forever scared of the world. And so she'd forced herself to do something she'd always feared—to climb a high tree. The way up hadn't been easy, and she'd scraped her arms and legs in several places. In fact, she'd almost fallen when a branch snapped beneath her. But she'd made it to the top, and her head had started to clear.

The motion of the tree had been disconcerting at first, but Annie was now used to the pattern of movement, and it reminded her of being aboard *Benevolence*. After all, the way the tree leaned back and forth was little different from how *Benevolence* had rolled over swells.

Though Annie had originally planned on just climbing up and down the tree, once near its top she hadn't wanted to leave. She wasn't quite ready to face Akira, as well as the questions that had so troubled her after the argument with Isabelle. So even though her stomach rumbled, she remained in the tree, reliving the highlights of the past few days rather than her words with her sister.

The sky was starting to darken when she heard Akira calling her name. Even from a distance she detected urgency in his voice. She responded loudly, and soon he was standing thirty feet below her, looking up with great surprise. "Are you hurt?" he shouted.

"I'm sorry," she said, pleased to see him. "I'm just fine."

"May I climb up?"

"Please."

Akira grabbed a stout branch and pulled himself off the ground. The tree boasted many thick branches and was nearly perfect for climbing. After a few minutes, he reached her spot. He could see the cuts on her arms and legs, and her apparent vulnerability gave him a sudden urge to kiss her brow. He hesitated, but then leaned toward her, and her arms wrapped around him. He pressed his lips against a freckle on her forehead.

"May I ask why you are up here?" he said. "Isabelle is searching for you. She asked me where you were, and I did not know."

"We fought. It was horrible and . . . and I just needed to find somewhere to think."

"So you climbed to the top of a tree?"

"I wanted to escape."

He sat beside her on the limb, one of his hands coming to rest on her leg while he held a branch with the other. A gust of wind penetrated the jungle, and he felt the tree lean to the side. "May I inquire as to why you fought?"

She looked at his face, finding solace in his eyes and lips. "Isabelle was just being my big sister," she answered, gently touching her foot against his.

"She was worried for you, yes?"

"Yes."

"Because . . . because of me?"

"She isn't one to take chances. She has a plan for everything."

"And I am a . . . chance?"

Annie wasn't sure if she detected a new expression on his face. Was it pain? Disappointment? "You're not a chance," she said, turning to kiss him. She had a sudden desire to crawl into his arms, but being unable to do so, she rested her head against his shoulder. Through a thin opening in the canopy before her, she watched the sky. "Thank you for finding me," she said quietly.

"I was missing you."

She smiled at these words, happy to have been missed. "A part of me is afraid, Akira," she admitted, wanting to tell him everything.

"Of the future?"

"Of what might happen to us."

He kissed the top of her head. "You do not have to be afraid."

"But why not? Our countries are at war, and we have no idea what the future might bring."

"We control what happens to us."

"You can't say that."

He nodded, wishing that he could kiss the scratches on her legs. "Some things I can say," he replied. "I can say that . . . that if you want me by your side, I will be by your side. I can say that every war has an end, and that every day has a new beginning."

A bird landed in the tree next to them. The wind blew again, and both trees swayed in tandem. "I'm afraid of losing you," she said, watching the bird, for the briefest of moments avoiding Akira's eyes. "Now that I've finally found you, I can't imagine losing you."

"See how the trees move together?"

"They're beautiful."

"But we cannot see them dance from below. How wonderful it is to see them dance from so high." Akira turned his head so that he could inhale the scent of her.

"Why do you like to do that?" she asked. "To smell me?"

"Because I want . . . each of my senses to feel you. And because I think . . . I think I like the smell of you the best."

"But why?"

"Because . . . that way I can bring you into me."

She kissed his shoulder. "I love you," she said quietly. "Those three words . . . have always been a mystery to me. Like some language I couldn't speak. But now I finally know what they mean."

He smiled, moving on the branch so that he was even closer to her. "I like it here, in these dancing trees. Thank you for showing them to me."

"You're welcome."

The tree continued to sway. The sky darkened. "Your sister is worried," he said. "You should go to her, yes?"

"I'm angry at her."

Akira watched a small green beetle climb across his leg. "I am an only child. So I have never fought with a brother or a sister."

"Sisters fight a lot."

"I think it would be wonderful to have a sister. Or a brother."

She shrugged. "It can be."

"A sibling would be the one person in the whole world who . . . who would be with you from birth until death. At every step, she or he would be there."

"That's true. I've never thought of it like that."

"It would be a beautiful thing, I am sure."

"Are you trying to tell me something?" she asked, familiar with how he liked to give advice through his stories and musings.

He smiled, stroking the skin of her leg. "Tonight, after the others have gone to sleep, will you join me for a swim? The moon is almost full, and I discovered a place where there are no rocks or waves. Just sand and water."

Annie took his free hand within hers. "I have a price."

"A price?"

"I want you to write a poem. In Japanese. In the sand."

He found her eyes. "May I ask why in Japanese?"

"Because that's who you are. And I'd like to watch as you write it. And to listen as you speak it." She kissed him and then carefully moved toward the tree's trunk. She started to descend.

As Akira followed her, he thought about what he would write. He watched the trees sway, wondering how he could bring life to their dance while simultaneously describing his love for her.

Much later, when the right words finally blossomed within him, he could do little more than turn his eyes toward the setting sun and silently beseech it to hasten on its journey.

DAY FIFTEEN

A ballet of wood.
The scent of her within me.
Has spring felt so fresh?

The First to Fall

A talkative gull awoke Joshua and Isabelle just before dawn. They always slept closest to the cave's entrance, for he liked to have a feel for the outside world, and she believed that the fresh air was healthier for their child. And so the gull only spurred the two of them to leave their sandy beds, and they started walking down the beach as the eastern side of the island was painted with a sapphire light.

Isabelle told him about her fight with Annie and their reconciliation at dinner. Joshua had siblings and understood that such confrontations were inevitable. Still, he was pleased to hear that they'd made amends, for while he realized that Isabelle had been trying to do what was right, she'd probably gone too far. He couldn't recall seeing Annie so happy, and as much as he also wondered about her future, he hoped that her relationship with Akira would somehow endure.

The sky continued to lighten as they walked along the rocky shore. All his years on the sea had linked Joshua to the world above, and he often glanced upward to see how the young day was evolving. He realized that it would be a good day for war. Clouds were unseen. Wind was nonexistent. And visibility was limitless. If he were commanding planes or ships, he'd send forth as many as possible to seek and destroy.

Not wanting to think about war, he took Isabelle's hand. She had always walked faster than he, as if she were forever late to her destination. And so he now slowed her down, forcing her to relax as he tried to do the same. She resisted for a moment, pulling him forward. But then she seemed to realize that no reason existed to hurry.

"You're not on *Benevolence*," he said, remembering how she'd constantly rushed about the decks.

She gently squeezed his bandaged hand at the mention of his ship. "Strange how that seems so long ago."

"Maybe because so much has changed."

"Like what?"

"Like you being pregnant. Like Annie falling in love with a Japanese soldier. At this point, I don't think I'd be surprised if I woke up tomorrow and the ocean was purple."

"Well, for the moment it's still blue."

He smiled. "I'd forgotten how nice these walks can be."

She sought his eyes. "On *Benevolence*, did you . . . did you try to forget such things?"

"What do you mean?"

Isabelle suppressed a grimace at a sudden cramp in her belly. "I didn't let myself think about those things at sea," she said. "Things like nice walks. There was just too much else to think about. I mean . . . how could I attend to my patients if I were daydreaming about home?"

"What about at night? Or when you were . . . washing your hair, or something like that?"

She shook her head. "I always thought about my patients. I asked myself who was going to die and who was going to live. And I tried to think of how I could help each person." When he didn't respond, she looked up at his face. "I'm sorry I didn't think about you, Josh. I wanted to. But . . . but I just couldn't. And maybe that's one of the reasons why we drifted apart."

"Don't be sorry. You saved so many of them. And there's still plenty of time to save me."

"I don't think I need to save you anymore. You've saved yourself."

"That's not true. If you weren't here I wouldn't have . . . climbed out of the hole I was in." He inhaled the sea's scent through his nose and deeply into his lungs, enjoying the sensation. "A few days ago you mentioned a little house by the ocean. Can you tell me about it? I'd like to hear more."

She stepped over a bloated jellyfish. "It needs to be old," she replied, speaking slowly, which was unusual for her. "Old so that we can fix it. A once-proud house that's been forgotten."

"And what about the nursery?"

"Oh, I suppose there will have to be ships in it."

"Even if it's a girl?"

"Especially if it's a girl."

Joshua smiled at her response, understanding all that it meant. "And you really want me to teach you how to sail?"

"Why should you get to have all the fun? I can be a captain too."

"You'd run a tight ship. So tight that you'd probably get a few extra knots out of her."

"More than a few, I'd say."

He grinned, glancing from the sea to the sky to her face. "I'm so lucky to have you," he said, his voice growing slightly more serious. "I just don't know how I'd manage without you. I don't even like to think about it."

"You'd manage."

He stopped and turned to her. "That isn't true, Izzy. In fact, nothing could be farther from the truth. And I thought about you a lot," he said, touching the tip of her nose with his forefinger. "All those long hours on the bridge. You were with me more than you knew."

"I was?"

"I wanted us to be like we once were. When we were young."

"Remind me what that was like."

"Like this," he replied, scratching absently at a bug bite. "We took walks. We talked. We laughed a lot."

"I remember laughing."

"So do I."

"Do you think the war changed us," she asked, "or did we change on our own?"

"What do you think?"

Isabelle took his hand and started walking again. "I think . . . I think we let the war change us."

"I—"

"And I don't want anything to change us again. No matter where life takes us. We could have a sick child, or you could be out of work. But even those things shouldn't change us, Josh. Not like the war did. I don't want to keep trying to go back to who we once were. I don't want to feel myself slipping away from you."

Joshua considered her words. "The last thing I took for granted is gone," he said. "And I miss that ship. I really do. And I'm not comparing you to a ship, but for a long time I've taken you for granted, and I'm not going to make that mistake anymore."

"But the war. Even once our child's born you'll still have a war to win."

"And I'll fight that war. For our child. For us. For Poles and Parisians and Jews and Chinese. For people we've never met." He saw a flat rock and skipped it into the surf. "And then one day it will be over. And, God willing, I'll come home that day."

"You'd better come home, Joshua."

He touched her belly. "I won't leave you two alone."

"Promise?"

"I do."

She glanced at their surroundings. "We could wait the war out . . . on this island."

"No," he said, shaking his head. "Not us. That's not who we are."

Isabelle nodded, knowing he was right, surprised at herself for even mentioning it. "Then I want to ask you something," she said.

"What?"

"After we're rescued, give me a week. I want a week of just you. A week in a place like this. Then you can go and do what needs to be done. And I'll have everything ready when you finally come home."

Joshua tried to smile, but having grown so used to her presence, the thought of being separated was suddenly hard for him to ponder. "We'll take two weeks," he said, reaching over to draw her toward him. He held her tightly, kissing her brow, his hand on her belly.

"I think we deserve that."

"I love you, Izzy. I love you, and I won't be pulled away from you. I won't let even this godforsaken war do that to us again."

RATU SCRUTINIZED THE NEARBY beach with immense care. Bordered by tide pools, rocks, and the ocean, the section of sand was about forty feet long and twenty feet wide. Deciding on a course of action, Ratu took a spear, set its point into the sand, and began to walk. Dragging the weapon behind him, he created a rectangle that used most of the available sand. At each end of the rectangle he then placed a pair of coconuts set about five feet apart.

"These are the goals," he said eagerly to Jake. "If you kick the ball through the coconuts, you score a goal."

"And you ain't gonna use your hands?"

"Only a goalie can use his hands."

"So I can?"

"You're not a bloody goalie, Big Jake. In this game, no hands."

Jake looked at the round sponge Ratu had found. Nodding toward it, he said, "So I gotta kick that darn thing?"

"What have I been telling you? Of course you bloody well have to kick that darn thing. If you kick it through my two coconuts, you score a goal."

Picking up the sponge, Jake tossed it up and caught it. He then dropped it and tried to kick it in midair. Missing badly, he lost his balance and had to step sideways to regain it. "How about a larger sponge?" he asked. "I'd rather peel potatoes with a spoon than kick that thing."

"Just kick it, Big Jake. I tell you, it's not hard," Ratu said as he walked toward the middle of his field. Setting the sponge down, he turned toward Jake. "You can have the ball first."

"I reckon we should call it a sponge."

"Bugger off, Big Jake. It's a ball. Now try to kick it by me and into my goal."

Jake stepped toward the sponge. Seeing how Ratu had positioned himself between it and his goal, Jake attempted to kick the sponge around him. However, the kick mainly served to send sand flying into the air. The sponge went almost straight up, and before Jake knew what was happening, Ratu darted forward, kneed the sponge in midair, and sent it sailing over Jake's head. Ratu raced around Jake, shouting triumphantly. He kicked the sponge several times before blasting it through Jake's goal.

"The great Ratu scores first!" Ratu shouted, holding his arms up and spinning around in tight circles.

"That's good," Jake said, "get yourself real nice and dizzy. That ought to help me."

"You need to learn how to kick, Big Jake!" Ratu exclaimed, laughing. "How can someone as big and strong as you not know how to kick?"

"How can someone so little be so darn ornery?"

"Oh, put a sock in it, mate. Do I need to explain the game to you again? I'm happy to do so. It's not hard. I tell you, it's not. Just use that giant foot of yours. If only I had a foot like that! I'd be playing for Fiji in the bloody World Cup!"

Ratu again placed the sponge in the middle of the field. Though Jake managed to kick it forward ten feet, Ratu quickly intercepted the sponge, kicked it around Jake, and scored. "Ha!"

"Ha yourself."

"And another brilliant goal for the great Ratu!" he said, holding his fist before his face, pretending to be a radio announcer. "Fiji leads America two goals to nil! And the crowd is leaping with excitement at this historic match!"

Jake smiled, suddenly remembering what it was like to be a boy and play such games. "The Americans have put in their star player," he added, trying without much success to impersonate another announcer.

"Yes, Jake the Giant has entered the game," Ratu replied, laughing. "His left foot is legendary. He's been known to kick cows from Missouri to the Big Apple Pie!"

"And the ball's in play!" Jake said, trying to kick the sponge around Ratu. To Jake's delight, the sponge rolled over Ratu's outstretched leg. Jake leapt forward, surprising Ratu with his quickness. After catching up to the rolling sponge, Jake kicked it as hard as he could. The sponge sailed into the air, rising above one of the coconuts that marked the edge of the goal.

"A miss!" Ratu shouted, giggling deliriously. "A wide-open goal and a miss!"

"No, no, no," Jake said, still pretending to be an announcer. "A goal. It hit the post and went in!"

"Is that the official ruling, Peter?"

"Yes . . . William . . . that's what the umpire said."

"The umpire?" Ratu repeated, laughing. "He's a referee!"

"A goal! He said it went in."

Continuing to giggle, Ratu retrieved the sponge. "Jake the Giant has put the Yanks on the board," he said, throwing the sponge to Jake.

Jake placed the sponge in the middle of the field and had hardly removed his hands when Ratu kicked it forward. "I ain't ready to—"

"The Fijians have a breakaway!" Ratu shouted, his laughter making it hard for him to run quickly.

Jake hurried to catch Ratu, who was having a tough time kicking the sponge in the furrowed sand. Ratu's giggles were infectious, and suddenly Jake was chuckling as his opponent tried to keep him at bay. "Hey, now!" Jake said, trying to get around Ratu. "No pushing with them hands!"

"Get away from me, Jake the Giant! Get those monster feet away from me!"

"Stop pushing me!"

"Get stuffed!" Ratu said, his hands pressing against Jake's belly. "You're too bloody big!"

Jake made a halfhearted attempt to kick the sponge, and then could only laugh as Ratu sent it sailing between the coconuts. Falling to the sand, Jake watched Ratu collect the sponge. Ratu then threw it against Jake's stomach. Sand went flying in all directions, spraying Jake's face. Ratu laughed while Jake tried to spit out the sand, and Jake reached out and tripped him, sending him sprawling. Jake took the sponge and rubbed it on Ratu's head.

"Stop it!" Ratu shrieked.

"And a fight's started between the Fijians and the Americans!" Jake shouted in his fake accent, pretending to punch Ratu.

"Get off of me, you big, bumbling Yank!"

"Jake the Giant is hammering away at the great Ratu!"

Ratu rose to his knees and dove into Jake's stomach. Jake acted as if the blow stunned him. Grunting loudly, he dropped to the beach and appeared to fall unconscious. Ratu shouted jubilantly, and once more kicked the sponge through Jake's goal. "A four-to-one victory for the Fijians!" he said, his laughter causing his voice to rise in pitch. "It's over. The game is over, and Jake the Giant is done for the day!"

Jake continued to chuckle as Ratu pranced and shouted around him, then leapt upon his back, pretending to hit him repeatedly in the upper body. Throwing his arms behind him, so that they encircled Ratu, Jake stood up and began to run toward the sea.

"No!" Ratu yelled, still laughing. "I don't fancy getting wet!"

"I reckon you don't!"

"No, I tell you! No, Big Jake! Please don't—"

Jake plunged into the sea. When it was up to his waist, he turned around and fell backward so that Ratu was thrust underwater. Ratu immediately surfaced and dove at Jake. Ratu was laughing and shrieking, and Jake caught a glimpse of what it must be like to be a father. He reveled in that glimpse, rejoicing in the simple but perfect pleasure of playing with Ratu. For the first time since he'd been a child, Jake felt like a child. And that feeling of youth, of forgotten memories being reborn, bound him to Ratu with a strength that he hadn't known.

Since he'd become a man, Jake had loved no one beyond his family. While he'd delighted in the land beneath his feet, and once touched a woman's face and felt drawn to her, he'd never met a stranger and had that stranger run into his heart. He hadn't sought such an experience and hadn't expected to celebrate its passage. But now, as he threw Ratu high into the air, Jake realized that he loved this boy. He wanted to protect him, to hear his laugh, to feel his touch. He wanted to watch him grow, and to take pride in his journey.

This was Jake's secret—that he'd discovered a boy who made him feel like a father, made him realize that the greater good didn't solely apply to a nation at war. Perhaps the greater good was also making a boy smile. Perhaps it was ensuring that this wonderful boy returned to his family.

Jake had left his farm to join the fight against fascism. He'd left expecting to see death and pain and misery, and though he'd seen such sights, he hadn't expected his most profound experience to be a simple and unexpected discovery—the realization that his greatest hope was that a boy would survive the war and be reunited with his family.

I'll bring him home, Jake promised himself. Whatever happens on this darn island, ain't nothing gonna stop me from bringing Ratu home.

ROGER KNELT NAKED atop the hill, a cigarette between his lips, his fingers fine-tuning the radio's dial. "Ronin to Edo," he said. "Repeat. Ronin to Edo. Over."

The static that assaulted Roger's ears disappeared. "Edo here. How are the cherry blossoms?"

"Always best under a full moon."

"Agree. How was the storm?"

"Fine. Nothing's changed here."

"Mother coming to roost in two days. Understood?"

"Yes."

"Rendezvous at north side of landing area. At highest ground. Stay hidden. I will find you."

"Understood. What should I expect after rendezvous?"

For a few heartbeats, the static returned. Then Edo said, "You will lead me to the eight chicks. They will be terminated."

"Good."

"I will wear a sword and a pistol. Look for me."

"Understood. Over." Roger waited for a reply, and when one didn't come, he removed his headset. "Two days," he said happily, filling his lungs with the rich, glorious smoke.

Roger closed his eyes, thrilled by the prospect of leading Edo and his men to the survivors, relishing the thought of the resulting confrontation. Such conflicts had been the best part of his life for nearly two decades. He'd gone to great lengths to manufacture them and was rarely disappointed with how they unfolded. In this case, he'd get to witness the deaths of those who so incessantly tormented him—the skirts who scorned him, the Nip who wasn't afraid, the runt who never shut his mouth. He'd even kill one or two such oppressors—surely the Nip and perhaps the maggot captain. And everyone would know, just before they died, that he'd betrayed them, that he was stronger and smarter and more cunning than they'd ever imagined.

Roger sucked hard on his cigarette and started to stow his radio. As he did, he noticed a distant flash of light. The flash came from atop a faraway hill. Recognizing the location as being close to the cave, his heart plummeted as he squinted toward the glare. Almost immediately, he realized that someone, most likely Scarlet, was watching him through the binoculars.

Cursing himself for his appalling carelessness, Roger leapt upward— his cigarette dropping to the ground, his muscles and instincts sprung from the cage that had confined them for so long. His shoes and shorts he swiftly put on; his shirt he left where it lay. He began to hurry down the hill, running in great bounds, moving more like a mountain lion than a man. The land blurred beneath him. The wind tugged at his hair. Jumping over boulders rather than circumventing them, he kept his arms outstretched for balance. Though reeling with misgivings about his recklessness, overconfidence, and stupidity, as the chase unfolded, he became increasingly calm and even happy. It felt good to be running again, exhilarating to be approaching someone who'd soon die at his hands.

Roger entered the jungle as swiftly and precisely as a needle piercing cloth, aware that she'd be running by now, but that she wouldn't be fast enough.

FOR SEVERAL DAYS, Scarlet had enjoyed watching the large bird that nested near the top of the distant hill. Though she hadn't recognized the species, she'd grown to understand the gray-and-white-feathered creature, which liked to dive into the sea, to clasp a fish within its talons, and return to its nest to devour its prey. Scarlet had decided to keep a mental diary of all such birds she'd seen, and upon returning to America, research which species she'd been fortunate enough to study. If she was going to remain stranded in such an awful place, she was determined to leave with at least one positive experience. And that experience would be birds.

With more curiosity than surprise, Scarlet had turned her binoculars from the nesting bird to Roger. Like her, he often seemed to want to escape the confines of the cave and the conversations inside it. So when she had first seen him climbing, she'd thought that he was merely seeking quieter ground. However, she'd been immensely perplexed when he'd taken off his clothes and started to dig; further so when he removed what looked to be a case of some sort. Focusing the binoculars, she'd risen from beneath the shade of a stunted tree and watched as he opened the case. To her surprise, he'd started smoking a cigarette.

It had taken Scarlet some time to comprehend that he was talking on a radio. When she'd finally realized what was happening, she became quite confused. Who was he talking to? And why did he have a secret radio? She had finally come to the awful conclusion that Roger wasn't who he appeared to be, and with trembling hands, she'd watched him remove his headset. She'd then lowered the binoculars to wipe the sweat from her eyes, and when she'd placed them back against her face, she saw that he was looking directly at her. And then he was running, moving like a madman down the hill, his arms and legs swinging to and fro.

Her heart leaping, Scarlet hurried toward the jungle below. The way was littered with loose gravel and large boulders. Grunting, she climbed over the boulders as quickly as she could. The gravel proved treacherous, and several times she slipped and fell. Though the hill wasn't as tall as many on the island, it was steep, and she was forced to occasionally slow lest she tumble to her death.

Even though the cave was fairly distant, Scarlet screamed for help. She knew that Roger was coming to kill her, and she continued to shout in hopes that someone might be nearby. Thinking of her brothers and how they'd always looked after her, she began to cry. She frantically called their names, as if they might somehow protect her again. Her thoughts and movements growing clumsy, she stumbled down the hill. Unable to stop, she ran directly at a boulder, spinning away from it at the last second and twisting her knee in the process. Though her terror was overwhelming, an immense pain suddenly consumed her.

Limping, Scarlet struggled downward. "Joshua!" she screamed, her crushing fear causing her voice to tremble. "Jake! Nathan! Akira! Help me! Please help me!"

Her foot struck an exposed root and she fell. Moaning, she willed herself to get up. Having seen a great deal of death but having never given much thought to her own, she started to sob. She called repeatedly for her brothers, her vision obscured by tears and grit. She tripped again and this time was slower to rise.

"Help!" she shrieked, finally reaching the bottom of the hill. She'd left a spear against a tree and grabbed it as she hurried past. The cave wasn't far now. In a few more minutes she'd be there.

ROGER SWEPT THROUGH the jungle as if it were on fire behind him. He did not waste a single step or second. His path was straight, his legs and arms in constant motion. He leapt over fallen trees, rocks, and even a fairly wide stream. He heard Scarlet screaming not far ahead and her cries served to guide him. He cursed her for the screams, rage boiling within him. The thought of her ruining his carefully laid plans made him long to break her neck. She wouldn't scream then, though she'd be able to watch him kill her. And kill her he would.

A branch grazed his arm hard enough that he winced. Still following her voice, he hurried past trees of all shapes and sizes, briefly reminded of the time that he'd chased a boy through Tokyo's cluttered confines. The terrified boy had finally dashed across a street and directly into the path of a train. Its wheels had cut him in two, as if he'd been no more than a piece of meat beneath a butcher's knife. Mesmerized by the enormous quantity of blood that had pooled from beneath the train, Roger had leaned against a lamppost and waited until the boy's severed body was revealed.

The thrill of the chase propelling him forward as it had so long ago, Roger jumped over a log and suddenly saw his prey. Without hesitating, he launched himself in her direction.

SCARLET STUMBLED FORWARD. She heard a crack, turned around, and suddenly he was there. She screamed, thrusting her spear at him, her tremendous fear giving her a sudden surge of strength. Roger saw her thrust, instinctively spinning his body away from the threat. As the spear rushed past him, he brought his left hand down hard, breaking the weapon in two.

Scarlet shrieked and tried to run. His right hand open, Roger viciously chopped her on the side of the neck, and she crumpled. He then stepped beside her and stood motionless. After waiting for his throbbing lungs to quiet, he listened. He could hear only the distant pounding of the surf and the wind as it wrestled with the trees. Finally convinced that no one had heard her cries, he hid her broken spear under some nearby ferns. He lifted her up and put her over his shoulder. She moaned softly, and angered by the sound, he hit her on the side of the head. "Where the hell were you hiding?" he asked, pulling a fistful of her hair. "How did you pop up like that?"

Scarlet didn't answer, whimpering.

Turning around, Roger walked toward the hill that she'd descended. He hardly felt burdened by her, and his progress was good. Soon he reached the hill. Soon he was climbing.

"Please . . . no," she whispered, her vision and thoughts cloudy.

"Stupid of you to yell," he responded, increasing his speed, attacking the hill as if it were another of his enemies. "You dumb old hag. Your pathetic cries brought me right to you."

"My . . . my family. My little brothers. Please."

"Your family thinks you're dead. Your ship sank, remember?"

"I—"

"Do you know who sank it? Me. I sank it."

"You?"

"I put that bitch on the bottom."

"Please . . . for . . . for the love of God—"

"God has no love," Roger said angrily, reaching the vantage point upon which Scarlet had looked for ships and birds. As she moaned and twisted atop him, he turned about, looking for the steepest section below. After locating what was more than a forty-foot drop, Roger lifted her from his shoulder. He then held her upright, so that her shoes struck the dirt near the precipice. "Are you scared?" he asked, enjoying the feel of her pounding heart.

"Please, don't," she muttered, her face lined with tears.

He lowered her enough so that her feet rested on the ground and he was able to give her belly a firm pinch. "You've been eating too much. Seen any other fat birds out there?"

"Why . . . why are you hurting me? Oh, please stop. Please."

"Think you can fly like them?"

"I won't . . . I won't tell anyone. I . . . I swear it."

"You're right about that, you useless, used-up old hag."

"But why are you . . . doing this?" she asked, shuddering as she wept.

"Because I want to see you pop," he replied, pushing her forward into the abyss below. As she shrieked, he watched her plummet, watched her strike the distant rocks. Blood spread beneath her, and again he was reminded of Tokyo, the memory warming him.

Roger spent the next hour carefully removing all traces of her true fate from the hill. He used a leafy branch to brush away his footprints. He sought out Scarlet's body—wiping the tears from her face and the grime from her hands. He then followed their paths into the jungle, again eliminating all signs of their struggle.

Only when he was certain that the others would deduce that she accidentally fell to her death did he finally return to his radio. Buoyed by the thrill of the chase and kill, he calmly lit a cigarette and then reached into the case, removing his pistol. He caressed the weapon, longing to smell the sweet stench of gunpowder, to feel the heat of the red-hot barrel. The weapon aroused him more than cigarettes or booze or women ever had, for it gave him an ultimate, godlike authority— the ability to destroy anyone who sought to torment him. He also knew that the gun would never betray him and that he could trust it to give him exactly what he wanted. It was his friend.

The gun was a part of his salvation. And he was about to use it.

MUCH LATER, AFTER THE AFTERNOON had arrived and departed, Joshua waded out into the water and looked up at the hill that served as

Scarlet's observation post. Squinting, he tried to catch a glimpse of her, but couldn't see quite clearly enough to discern anything so small. "I don't understand it," he said worriedly to Isabelle. "She's so good at giving her signals. She's as reliable as any sailor I've met."

Isabelle stepped closer to him. "When did she last contact you?"

"As soon as she got up there. Must have been seven or eight hours ago."

"Well, then, we should check on her."

"We?"

"I could use a walk."

Joshua nodded, wading back to the beach. He entered the cave to find and fill a canteen. After doing so, he and Isabelle left the cave and walked along the beach. They hadn't gone far when they saw Annie and Akira, who were talking near a tide pool as they gathered mollusks for dinner.

"Where are you off to?" Annie asked, rising.

"To see Scarlet," Isabelle replied. "She hasn't signaled for hours. And we're worried."

Annie glanced at Akira. "How about joining them for a walk?"

"Of course."

Annie carefully put their findings in a corner of the tide pool. She then stepped toward her sister, immediately noting the concern on Isabelle's face. "Maybe she's following a bird," Annie offered.

Isabelle looked at the hill. "I hope so."

The foursome proceeded down the beach, parts of which were inundated with dead fish. Earlier that morning, the fish had appeared. No one had understood how or why the fish had died until Nathan realized that they'd likely perished during the naval battle—perhaps poisoned by the oil of a sinking ship or killed by exploding shells. The fish, numbering in the hundreds, were now covered in crabs and flies. Joshua had thought about burying them so as to remove the stench, but needn't have bothered—most of the fish were already half-eaten.

Arriving at the end of the cliffs, Joshua turned right and strode into the jungle. Isabelle, Annie, and Akira followed him. The jungle continued to seem quieter than before the typhoon. Only a few mosquitoes harassed them, and with the soil still somewhat damp, seldom did branches crack underfoot. The hill loomed above them and they soon started to climb. The way wasn't easy, and as they struggled up the slippery rise, they called Scarlet's name. No response came.

Reaching the top of the hill, they continued to shout her name and peer into the jungle. Joshua studied the distant surroundings and noted that no ships were present. The sea and sky were little more than two shades of blue that merged at the horizon. Annie and Isabelle were still calling out when Akira suddenly put his hands to his forehead.

"What?" Annie asked anxiously, reaching over to grab his arm. "Akira, what is it?"

He shook his head, biting his lower lip. "She is . . . gone."

"Gone? What do you mean?"

"Below. Look below."

For the first time since they'd been atop the hill, Joshua, Isabelle, and Annie looked nearly straight down. Far below, Scarlet lay motionless on her back. A large amount of blood made the rocks upon which she rested glisten. Her eyes appeared to be open and unmoving, and without question she was dead.

"Scarlet!" Annie screamed. "No, no, no!"

"Oh, Scarlet," Isabelle muttered, stepping next to her sister, instinctively putting an arm around her.

"No!" Annie repeated, shaking her head. "It can't be true! It can't!"

"She must have—"

"But how?" Annie asked in disbelief, interrupting Isabelle. "How could she be gone? She told me that she was careful! She said . . . she said this place was safe!"

Joshua dropped his head in sorrow and frustration. He made a sign of the cross and briefly prayed for her. Only when his prayer was finished did he study the area before him, the spot from which Scarlet must have fallen. A flat, rectangular slab of rock perched atop the precipice. From the edge of the rock, the drop immediately commenced. Noting the loose sand atop the rock and how it tilted toward emptiness, Joshua realized how easily she might have slipped. "That rock's not safe," he said quietly. "She must have been looking through the binoculars, and slipped."

"We should go to her, yes?" Akira asked, wanting to comfort Annie but feeling constrained by the presence of Joshua and Isabelle.

Sniffing, Annie led the way, retracing their steps, her misery causing her to stumble several times. "She was looking out for us," Annie said. "We should have looked out for her. Oh, why didn't we look out for her?"

No one responded, as each of their minds occupied a different realm. Isabelle wondered how they would bury her. Joshua asked himself if he'd made a mistake in granting her wish to search for ships. And Akira scanned the ground before him, believing that Scarlet was too careful and capable to fall from a cliff. However, as thoroughly as Akira looked, as near certain as he was that something was amiss, he saw nothing but their footprints.

After dropping to the approximate height of where Scarlet lay, the four survivors circumvented the hill. "Do you want to . . . see her?" Joshua asked, as Scarlet came into view.

"We're nurses," Isabelle replied. "And she was our friend. Of course we want to see her."

Scarlet lay between two rocks. Her open eyes were bloodshot. Her face was red from being exposed all afternoon to the sun. The rocks below her were covered in blood. Just to be certain, Isabelle felt for a pulse. Finding none, she closed Scarlet's eyes. "She's been dead for hours," Isabelle said softly.

Akira dropped to his knees. Though he felt bad for this woman—whom he hadn't known well, but nonetheless liked—he forced himself not to mourn for her or to console Annie. Instead, his eyes examined Scarlet as quickly as possible, settling upon a bruise on her neck.

"Why are you looking at her like that?" Isabelle asked.

Though tempted to mention the oddity of the bruise, Akira decided that it wasn't the time or the place to discuss such matters. "She was Christian, yes?" he asked, knowing that she was.

"Yes," Isabelle answered. "And we should bury her now. Before Ratu sees her like this."

No additional words were exchanged as Joshua lifted Scarlet. He followed Isabelle down the remainder of the hill and into the jungle. After carefully setting Scarlet upon the ground beneath an old tree, he used his hands to dig in the soft soil. Akira started working beside him.

Annie sniffed, absently wiping her nose. "We'll . . . we'll be back."

"Where are we going?" Isabelle asked.

"Don't bury her yet," Annie said, taking her sister's hand.

Joshua and Akira watched the two women disappear. Then they returned their attention to the hole, widening it between them. "Should I have let Scarlet go?" Joshua asked, pulling a root from the soil. "Maybe it should have been my job to watch the sea."

Akira picked up a flat rock and used it to dig. "She wanted to go, yes?"

"She did."

"Then your choice was correct."

Joshua continued to dig. "Why did you kneel so close to her? I know that Buddhists kneel, but I don't think you were praying."

"I will pray later," Akira replied. "Please look at her neck."

Leaning toward Scarlet, Joshua quickly spied the bruise. "What do you make of it?"

"Something soft hit her there. A rock would scratch, yes? But she has no scratches."

Joshua touched the heavy binoculars that were still draped around her neck and amazingly were unbroken. "These could easily do it."

"Easily? So sorry, but I think not. The bruise is too thin and long."

"But it had to be the binoculars. Nothing else makes sense."

Akira started to dig again, his pulse quickening with the scenes that formed in his mind. "The edge of a hand could leave such a mark."

"A hand? You're saying she was killed? But why? There's no one else on this island. There's—"

"There is Roger. And where was he today?"

"Roger's a brute, and a dangerous one at that, but he wouldn't kill Scarlet. There's just no motive."

Lifting a rock from the soil, Akira continued to dig. "May I tell you something?"

"Please don't ask me that question again. Tell me whatever you'd like."

"When I was interrogating the prisoner, we spoke in Japanese."

"I remember."

"He asked me to fight with him, to attack you while he attacked Roger. And when he asked me this I think . . . I think I saw Roger tense, as if preparing to defend himself."

"You believe that he understood you?" Joshua asked incredulously. "That he speaks Japanese?"

"I am saying that he appeared to understand me. And perhaps he is not who you think he is. Perhaps Scarlet saw something that she was not supposed to."

Joshua didn't immediately respond, though he stopped digging, his face tightening in consternation. "Mother Mary, are you sure?" he asked, wondering if Roger had betrayed them. The mere thought of such treachery nauseated him.

"I am not sure. Perhaps."

"But . . . but could you test him? Could you somehow test him?"

Voices emerged from the jungle, and Akira nodded. "I will test him in the morning. Be ready."

Joshua stared at Scarlet's bruise, reeling at the possibility of Roger being responsible for the sinking of *Benevolence*. Forcing himself to start digging once more, he glanced up at the approaching figures of Isabelle and Annie. "Where did you go?" he asked in an unsteady voice as Isabelle emerged from behind a bush.

She gave him an odd look and then pointed behind her to Annie, who carried several beautiful bird feathers. "She loved birds," Annie said softly, her face wet with tears and sweat. "So it seemed . . . like they should travel with her."

Akira nodded, proud of her for thinking such thoughts, and disappointed in himself for not properly honoring Scarlet. Pushing his conversation with Joshua from his mind, he bowed slightly to Annie. She sat beside him, and for the first time she openly held his hand in the presence of others. He looked into her bloodshot eyes and felt a sudden urge to pull her against him. Instead he squeezed her hand, which caused tears to tumble down her face.

Joshua carefully lifted Scarlet's body into the hole. Annie leaned forward and placed two feathers in each of Scarlet's hands. The feathers were green and red, likely from one of the many parrots that inhabited the island. "She just wanted to go home," Annie said. "To go home to her family."

"Let us hope that she still will," Akira replied.

The four of them knelt on the damp earth and prayed. The Christians prayed that Scarlet was in heaven, and that her family would find the strength to handle her death. The Buddhist prayed that she was being reborn and that her path toward Nirvana was growing short.

After everyone had opened their eyes and it appeared as if each was no longer praying, Joshua said quietly, "I'll bury her." Looking from Isabelle to Annie, he added, "I know that you're her friends, but friends don't . . . they don't need to see everything. So please go back to camp and wait for me."

Akira bowed to Joshua and then rose. Wordlessly, Annie and Isabelle followed him as he stepped away from the old tree, from the spot that would cradle Scarlet forever. Joshua sadly watched his wife depart, wishing that tomorrow he could take her to the house she wanted by the sea. Scooping up handfuls of soil, he began to bury Scarlet. He buried her from the feet upward, because he knew that it would be most difficult to place the dirt on her face. And he was right. When the soil covered her mouth, he knew that at least upon Earth, she would never taste again. When it covered her nose, he knew that whatever scents she held dearest were forever gone to her. And when it covered her eyes, he shook his head in profound sadness, for she'd never again look upon her brothers or her birds, and from what little he knew of her, it seemed that she'd miss these sights the most.

THAT NIGHT THE FIRE burned lower than usual, as if flames were by nature jovial and they too were in mourning. No one bothered to add additional branches or to stir up hot coals. The remnants of dinner sat idle on a large leaf—unusual because such leftovers were always immediately tossed into the sea. Conversation, which had been rare, tended to focus on either Scarlet or a desire to go home. Ratu had taken her death hard and now sat almost motionless on a log, his fingers wrapped around the shark-tooth necklace.

Joshua, who wore the binoculars, occasionally left the cave and searched the moonlit seas for ships. A formation of Zeros had flown over the island not long after he'd buried Scarlet. They'd proceeded due east, several trailing smoke and one flying erratically.

A year earlier, Joshua would have felt guilty about having his duty supersede his desire to quietly reflect upon and pray for a fallen comrade. But he'd since learned that if he didn't adhere to his duty, he'd end up watching others die. And so he alternated between talking quietly with Isabelle and inspecting the seas.

Akira sat away from the fire, near the entrance of the cave. Annie was close by, and though they conversed, she was much less talkative than usual. Not surprised by her desire for silence, and not wanting to intrude upon it, Akira surreptitiously watched Roger and formulated a plan. Though uncertain whether Roger could speak Japanese, Akira's instincts told him that Roger was hiding something.

Akira's plan was almost complete when Annie found his eyes. "Can we go for a walk?" she asked quietly.

He nodded and rose to his feet. Outside, the thick air was warmer than it had been for several days. The night was clear, and the light from the moon and stars faintly illuminated the island and sea. Akira thought about how this part of the world now lay within an infinite shadow, and how in North Africa and in the Soviet Union and in the swells of the Atlantic, men were fighting beneath the bright sun.

"I don't think I'll ever get used to death," Annie said, her voice barely above a whisper. "I've seen hundreds die, but . . . but they all seem to hit me."

He helped her circumvent a tide pool. "That is good."

"Good?"

"That means you are still alive. I have seen men who are used to death, and they are as dead as the people who lay lifeless before them."

She continued to hold his hand after they had rounded the pool. "Nanking, it didn't . . . do that to you? It didn't harden you?"

An image of the little girl flashed before him. "Nanking will always, always be a wound within me. But even though that wound almost killed me, I still live."

She sighed, intertwining her fingers with his. "No one should have such wounds. It's not right. To fight two world wars in twenty years isn't right."

"There cannot be a third."

"With men ruling the world? That seems wishful thinking."

They walked in silence, their feet moving from stone to sand to stone. Akira still wasn't used to holding a woman's hand in the open, as he had never done such a thing; it was frowned upon in his country. But the feel of her palm against his greatly warmed him. "May I tell you something?" he asked, wanting to share his feelings with her, hoping that they might give her solace in her time of need.

"If you want to."

"I would like to tell you that you are . . . my greatest discovery."

"What? What do you mean?"

He glanced at her eyes, which seemed almost too full for her somewhat girlish face. "As a boy, I discovered small worlds within mountains. As a young man, I discovered words. And now I have discovered you. And that discovery has . . . it has made me complete."

Annie sighed, suddenly disbelieving that much good existed in the world. "But, Akira, you've never been around women. Maybe . . . it's like you're on a ship, looking for new land. Maybe I'm just the first land that you've encountered. But beyond me there's probably a much greater place."

He smiled. "I enjoy it when you speak like that."

"Like what?"

"Like you are painting something."

"But how do you know your feelings for me are real when you've never had such feelings before? Maybe you're not experienced enough to know the difference between what's fantasy and what's real."

He spied a sand dollar and handed it to her. "Perhaps I do not want to continue looking for other lands. Perhaps I have found a home that inspires me. Why would I look for something new when I have discovered something beautiful? Something magical?"

"I can be naïve and shortsighted and foolish, and there's really nothing magical about me."

"But that is my choice, yes?"

"What do you mean?"

"To understand my own contentment, and to stay on that land rather than looking for something else."

"Maybe," she answered, stroking the sand dollar. "But my country fights yours, and we don't know what the future will bring. And that frightens me. Scarlet just went to look for some birds, and now she's dead. How do we know what's going to happen tomorrow? I know that I love you. But is that enough? How can that be enough when it can be taken from us?"

Akira continued to walk, searching for the right words. "I am new to love, yes? So I know very little. But a coin, a house, an arm . . . these are things. And things can be taken. But love is a feeling, and how can someone take a feeling?"

"A bullet can take all sorts of things, Akira. I've seen it happen too many times."

He sighed, unsure of how to respond, unsure of how he felt. "A bullet can take a life," he finally said. "It can pull a daughter from a mother or a husband from a wife. And that . . . thievery can cause more pain than we were built to endure. But Buddhists believe . . . I believe that people who find each other in this life will find each other again in the next."

"And love makes that possible?"

"Yes."

"How can you have such faith in a time of such madness?"

"Because I saw her. The little girl. I was dying, and I saw her. And she was happy. She was at peace. And if I am to die, you must think of me as being in this same place."

A tear tumbled down Annie's face. "But I haven't seen this place, Akira. It's not fair for you to expect that of me. You can't . . . leave me and expect that."

He stopped, turning to her, watching a tear drop from her chin, gently tracing the tear's trail with his forefinger. "You are right," he said softly, understanding and sharing her fear. "And I am so sorry."

"Don't be sorry. I know what you're trying to do." She put her arms around him and pulled him close, squeezing him even tighter when she heard him smell her skin. "I think a feeling can be taken," she said, her voice growing more resolute. "And I don't want . . . to experience that. I don't want Isabelle to either. So whatever you have to do to keep that from happening, will you do it? Will you please do it?"

Akira closed his eyes, aware of her body against his and the comfort that this encounter generated. "You will see another side of me," he said, worried that such a sight might drive her from him.

"I'm not afraid of that side. I know it's not who you really are."

He kissed her temple. "Thank you . . . for being you."

She turned to him, pressing her lips against his. "And thank you for not sailing on."

He smiled. "Only a fool would sail on, Annie. Who but a fool would find such land and sail on?"

DAY SIXTEEN

There is no finding
Like the first feeling of love.
Crickets feast on song.

Paths Diverge

After finishing a breakfast of mango, when he knew that Roger's eyes were surreptitiously upon him, Akira asked Joshua if he could borrow the machete. Joshua, realizing that Akira's plan was unfolding, pretended to weigh his decision. Several awkward heartbeats passed before he reluctantly nodded. Akira bowed and then strode to where the weapon rose from the sand. Pulling it free, he walked from the cave and into the jungle.

Believing that his actions would prompt Roger's interest, Akira forced Annie out of his thoughts. He couldn't be distracted by her, even as pleasant as that distraction was. And so he focused on the task at hand. His field of vision sweeping the jungle, he headed toward a bamboo grove that he'd earlier discovered. In a few minutes, he found the spot and studied the uniform stalks of bamboo that rose like oversized green pipes from the moist soil. The stalks rubbed against each other, creating a discordant and somewhat eerie series of low groans.

Finally settling on a stalk that was about as thick as a woman's wrist, Akira chopped hard with the machete, quickly creating a three-foot pole. Sweat gathering on his brow, he walked back to the cave, depositing the machete in the same spot as he'd found it. Glancing about, he saw that Annie and Isabelle had disappeared. Roger was pretending to fill a canteen, but his stare darted to Akira the way a snake's tongue inspects the air.

Reminding himself of the American's quickness, Akira carried his crude sword outside. Though he hadn't held such a weapon since Nanking, memories of a real sword's weight and feel flooded into him. Before he could push the thought aside, an image of practicing swordplay with his father flashed before him. His father's face was unlined and untroubled and slightly bemused by the growing strength of his son's thrusts.

Akira moved north along the beach, the sand leaving a temporary vestige of his passing. After a hundred or so paces, he turned toward the sea. Closing his eyes for a moment, he tried to bring the world into him, opening his mind to a kind of meditation—a process of purging and purifying thoughts, something that his father had taught him over many months. Akira heard, but didn't see, a group of gulls far above. He smelled the salt, the decay, the scents that the wind bore to him from distant places. He felt the sun on his face and then on his back as he slowly turned from the sea to the island.

Though Akira would have liked to set the makeshift sword down and to properly meditate, he felt that a violent man would be drawn to violent acts. His experience had certainly taught him as much. During his years of war, he'd watched men seek out carnage almost as if it were an element, like air or water, that had to be brought into them so that they could live. And so he viciously swung his sword in a series of classic and complex attacks, the bamboo pole humming in his hands as it parted the space before it.

Though Akira hadn't much liked to train with a katana, he'd known that doing so pleased his father, and he'd done it. And as the years had passed, he'd gotten quite good at it. He'd never been a brilliant pupil, for brilliance stems from joy, but he'd been fast and sure, and his father had often smiled at his feats.

As soon as Akira noticed Roger walking in his direction, he pretended to be slightly less skilled than was true. He brought his feet too close together. His cuts and blocks were a quarter heartbeat too slow. He even dropped the pole once, quickly picking it up and continuing with his thrusts.

Roger followed Akira's footsteps. When the American was ten feet away, Akira lowered his weapon. "Fancy yourself a samurai?" Roger asked, smirking. Suddenly longing to throw Akira from a cliff in the same way that he'd killed Scarlet, Roger stepped closer. "The samurai are a lie," he said. "Monkeys aren't brave. They aren't honorable."

"But samurai were both," Akira replied, his stance seemingly relaxed.

"You swing that stick like a girl trying to hit a bug."

"Why are you here?"

"To learn how girls fight."

"I wish you would leave."

"Know what I wish, you goddamn Nip?" Roger asked, stepping closer, the need to bloody his adversary's face suddenly dominating him. "I wish I could taste what you're tasting."

"I am tasting nothing."

"How does the little bitch taste anyway? She looks so sweet. I'll have to try her myself."

Hating Roger's words and wanting to be free of them, Akira started to respond, and then pretended to abruptly stop himself. "Do you . . . do you hear that?" he asked, furrowing his brow, feigning bewilderment.

"Hear what?"

"Can you hear them?"

"What? What are you talking about?"

"So many!"

"What the hell are you—"

"Planes," Akira answered quickly in Japanese.

Roger's eyes unconsciously darted upward. He saw a slice of blue and almost immediately realized that he'd been tricked. "Clever little monkey," he replied, lunging for his adversary.

Akira had been expecting such an attack and stepped backward, simultaneously swinging his pole with all his strength. Though Roger was quick, Akira was quicker. His weapon struck hard against Roger's unprotected side, breaking a rib. Most men would have doubled over and fallen at such a blow, but Roger merely grunted and let his momentum carry him into Akira. His rage at being tricked and then struck overwhelmed him, and Roger smashed his open palms into the sides of Akira's head. Having extended himself in his attack, Akira was temporarily defenseless. Both men toppled backward. Akira was beneath his assailant and gasped when the air was hammered from his lungs by the force of Roger's knee.

Akira struggled to breathe and fight, disbelieving Roger's strength. He saw his adversary raise an open hand as he prepared to strike, but then Roger turned and realized that Joshua and Jake were running toward him. Still enraged, but not blinded by that rage, Roger rolled off Akira and began to run. Akira leapt from the sand and started after him. Though Akira knew that Roger moved like a deer, he'd been wounded, and even a deer can't run well with an injured rib. And so Akira hurried after him, paying little heed to his throbbing head. Understanding that Roger had somehow betrayed the Americans and that Annie's life was at risk, Akira ran as he never had. The sand and sea swept past him as if cars on a busy street. Soon Roger entered the jungle, and Akira rushed into the foliage, leaping over rocks and logs. Behind, Joshua and Jake struggled to keep up.

Cursing, Roger held his side with his right arm and swept deeper into the jungle, following a trail he'd secretly marked two days before. Small piles of rocks led him forward and, rounding a corner and recognizing two dead trees that he'd leaned against each other, Roger reached a smooth boulder and leapt forward as far as possible, hitting the ground hard, rolling to minimize the impact.

Akira hurried ahead, catching only glimpses of Roger, but following the sound of his ragged breaths. Roger's tracks curved to the right, and suddenly his damp footprints disappeared. Somehow, despite his pain and fear and exhaustion, Akira realized that he was in danger. He tried to stop, his right foot sliding on firm ground and then going through the branches and leaves that Roger had placed above his trap. Feeling himself tilting toward and falling into the hole, Akira leapt off his left foot, propelling himself sideways. He managed to grab the trunk of a slender tree as the trap's roof collapsed. The sapling bent and slowly broke, providing Akira the time to carefully drop into the pit. A spike scraped his calf, but he wasn't impaled.

Akira shouted at Joshua and Jake to stop. They appeared in a few seconds, both sweating profusely. When Joshua saw Akira at the bottom of the stake-lined pit, he fell to his knees, pounded the ground with his fist, and shouted Roger's name. Knowing that Roger had escaped, and that he was surely the reason for *Benevolence's* sinking, Joshua screamed again in rage. He cursed Roger so loudly that his words seemed to reverberate throughout the jungle.

After kicking over the stakes, Akira climbed from the pit, reaching upward to take Jake's hands. "Damn that man to hell," Joshua muttered, dismayed that he'd let Roger escape.

"He can speak Japanese," Akira said, his head aching from Roger's blows.

Jake's brow furrowed at these words. "But . . . I reckon that means—"

"That he betrayed us," Joshua said. "He told them about a secret cargo that *Benevolence* was carrying. And he sank our ship, God help him."

"If my countrymen land here, he will lead them to the cave," Akira added, wiping blood from his calf. "And they will want to eliminate the survivors."

Joshua thought of Isabelle and their unborn child. A sudden fear of their getting hurt caused an intense sense of panic to surge within him. "We'll have to move again," he heard himself say. "But where to? He knows the island better than any of us."

An unseen bird squawked in the distance. Jake shifted a spear from one hand to the other, musing over a plan that had occurred to him several days ago. "I expect this soil's used up," he said, his mind surprisingly clear. "As used up as an old mule."

"The soil?" Joshua asked. "What do you mean?"

Jake dug the butt of his spear into the ground. "You see, Captain, on a farm it don't pay to stay put. Instead, you move your crops around, so that you raise wheat, then corn, then barley on the same spot of ground. You plant a new crop each season. Every darn one. That way you ain't letting crops make the same demands on soil year after year. That way you get a healthy crop."

"You're saying . . . we should move? But where?"

"Move islands, Captain. Surprise that snake and put everyone on the lifeboat and move islands."

"Roger could see us move. He'd just tell the Japanese."

"Not if we left at night," Akira interjected.

"But he'll figure it out," Joshua countered. "It just buys us time."

"Better to buy time, yes, than nothing at all?" Akira asked.

Joshua tried to think, hating the feeling of helplessness that had suddenly swept into him. He worried about whether they could make a night passage of probably ten miles, knowing facts about boats and currents and patrols that neither Jake nor Akira understood. "Is there any chance of us catching up to him in the jungle?" he asked Akira.

Though a part of him wanted to continue along Roger's trail, Akira couldn't fathom leaving Annie so unprotected. "If we do, we leave the cave, yes?"

"Yes," Joshua answered.

"And we might . . . we might regret that until our very last breath."

Joshua found Akira's eyes and nodded. "Then we'll go back. And maybe we'll find some new soil. And maybe this godforsaken war will at some point leave us alone."

The three men hurried back toward the cave, their speed increasing as they neared the ones they loved.

As IT ALWAYS HAD, pain propelled Roger forward. The ache in his side, though it raged as if a row of nails had been hammered into his rib, only served to further motivate him. Since he was eleven years old, Roger had used pain as a tool. During his childhood days in Tokyo and years later in Philadelphia, his enemies had often feared hurting him, for they knew that if he were bloodied his vengeance would be even more resolute.

As a boy, Roger had also feared pain. And the memory of this fear was one of his worst, as it reminded him of his tears, his misery, and, above all else, of the laughter that so belittled him. Hiding in *pachinko* parlors, under bridges, on trains, he'd been able to shut the laughter from his ears, but not from his mind.

And so Roger now exploited the pain in his side to remind him of the beatings and humiliations he'd once commonly endured, and this reminder served to drive him forward, to push him beyond the limits of what other people could do. He hadn't been wounded in such a manner for many years, and his hatred toward Akira seemed to double with the passage of each aching step. As he climbed, he envisioned what torments he'd cast upon his foe the next day. Though the Japanese would certainly want to interrogate the traitor, Roger would ask Edo for that privilege.

In Tokyo, Roger's cinder block home hadn't been far from a polluted and concrete-bound creek. He had often sought refuge beneath nearby underpasses, and once his pursuers had vanished, he'd expend his anger on the creatures that dwelled there. Frogs were blinded. Turtles hurled into rocks. Snakes tied in tight knots.

Thinking of his afternoons alongside the creek, Roger wondered how the monkey would fare without his eyes or feet or tongue. Or with each of his ribs broken. Such thoughts warmed Roger like wine. They allowed him to repress the demons of his past, for each horror that he inflicted upon Akira would be a new memory to carry forward, a memory that would further obscure his recollections of misery.

Finally reaching the summit, Roger quickly uncovered his box. Immediately, he lit and sucked on two cigarettes, drawing the dense smoke deeply into his lungs. His broken rib protested this sudden movement and he grunted in pain. Cursing vehemently, he inhaled again, but more carefully.

With the cigarettes held between his lips, Roger focused on his supplies. He didn't touch the radio. Instead he grabbed the pistol. The cool steel felt natural within his grasp, like a mere extension of his arm. He gripped the weapon tightly. He then pointed it at his throbbing side and pretended to shoot the rib that was so bent on torturing him.

Knowing that the ships must be close, Roger looked out at the sea. Nothing broke the flat horizon save a splattering of distant islands. Suddenly wanting the others to fear him, and hoping to trick them into believing that he'd remain far away, he held his weapon skyward and fired a single bullet. The crack of the gun seemed unusually loud, and in the jungle below birds took flight, seeking refuge from the foreign noise.

Wishing that he could see their anxious, pathetic faces, Roger rested the warm barrel of the gun against his aching side. He then set the pistol down and buried the box. Suspecting that his enemies would assume that he'd stay far removed from them, and realizing that they'd certainly change positions, Roger began the long walk back to the cave. His plan was to watch the others move and to follow them to whatever new hiding place they discovered. Tomorrow he'd bring Edo and his men directly to them.

Content with his plan and eager for the coming day, Roger hurried down the hill. With almost every painful stride, he violently cursed those on the other side of the island. He cursed them individually. He cursed them as one. And though his side throbbed, his mind remained clear enough to explore the intricate and delightful possibilities of what dawn would bring.

THE DISTANT GUNSHOT surprised everyone. On the beach outside the cave, they'd been talking about Roger's betrayal, about what to do in the remaining hours of daylight. The gunshot had stopped such talk. People looked westward, simultaneously fearful that Roger wielded a gun and pleased that he was so far away.

"I can't believe he has a gun," Ratu said, shaking his head and stepping closer to Jake. "I tell you, I just bloody can't believe it."

"If he has a gun, he has a radio," Joshua replied, trying to act calm. "We have to assume that. We have to assume he's communicating with the Japanese. That they're coming here. They torpedoed a hospital ship, and they won't want survivors talking about it. Now, all of that might not be true, but we have to assume it is and prepare for the worst."

"I think Jake's idea is a good one," Nathan said, the fear that he wouldn't see his family again causing his side to ache, his face and neck to perspire. "We could leave tonight for another island."

Joshua glanced to the east. "That's riskier than it sounds. The new island might not have water. Also, the currents and winds here are strong, and rowing into them, we might not even reach landfall. Or we could be captured at sea. Or we could arrive at an island that's already swarming with Japs. We could go from a bad position to an even worse one."

As the others spoke, Akira worriedly watched Annie. He felt as if events were pulling him from her, conspiring to forever yank them apart. And though as a Buddhist he was supposed to accept suffering as a part of life, he couldn't imagine his life without her. Better to strip me of my senses than of her, he thought. "We have no good choices," he said quietly, "but another choice exists."

"What?" Joshua asked, turning toward him.

Akira shielded his eyes from the sun as he looked up at Joshua. "If he is dead, he can tell no one where we are hiding."

"That's not true," Joshua said. "He could have told them already over a radio."

Akira shook his head. "So sorry, but I do not think he would do this. Then they would not need him. No, a man like Roger would rather show them himself."

"That's a big, risky assumption," Isabelle interjected, feeling slightly nauseated, wishing they were anywhere but here.

"Again, so sorry, but not with men like Roger," Akira replied. "He will want to lead them to us."

"I agree," Annie said.

"Oh, Annie," Isabelle countered, and then stopped herself from immediately continuing. Taking a deep breath, she said, "He has a gun, Akira. How would we kill him anyway?"

"I'd like to know that too," Joshua added.

"If my countrymen arrive, they will land in the harbor, yes?" When Joshua nodded, Akira continued. "Roger will wait for them there. If I arrive at the beach tonight, under the protection of darkness, I can hide. I can watch for him. At some point he will reveal himself. And then . . . then I will kill him."

Joshua again looked at the distant islands, wishing that a strong wind was coming from the west instead of the northeast. Rowing into that wind would be hard. The lifeboat, overloaded with seven passengers and various supplies, would be extremely heavy. Lifeboats were designed to float rather than to travel great distances, and Joshua wondered if they could even reach land. He suspected that they could, but worried about encountering the Japanese at sea or on another island.

"We're going to take the boat," he said suddenly, feeling that the island was like a noose drawing about their necks. "God willing, we'll leave tonight. We'll pack only the most critical supplies. I can navigate by the stars, and with luck we'll reach landfall a few hours before dawn. We can't just sit here and hope that we're not found. That's just not good enough."

"May I say one other thing?" Akira asked.

"Of course."

"If I followed him and I found his radio, we could call for help. Yes?" Nathan turned to Akira. "Now, that's a thought."

"But you can't do all that, Akira," Annie said worriedly, changing her earlier position now that she realized how dangerous it would be for Akira to go after Roger. "He's got a gun. He knows the ground. You've got nothing."

"So sorry, but he expects us to run."

"Bloody hell. I think we should run," Ratu said anxiously. Tugging on Jake's arm, he added, "I tell you, Big Jake's idea is the best. Let's do what the captain says. Let's get off this island. Let's run."

Joshua turned the pros and cons of each plan over in his mind. As Akira had said earlier, they didn't have any good choices. Just choices. "He's like a cat in that jungle," Joshua finally replied. "I just don't see how you're going to sneak up on him. You'll just end up getting shot. So we're going to take the boat. We'll take it tonight."

Akira nodded. "Then we will take the boat."

"Good," Joshua said. "I think it's the least risky proposition. So now let's plan our trip. Why don't—"

Jake, who was on the westward side of their circle and was facing the sea, suddenly pointed over Joshua's head. "Look, Captain."

Joshua often carried the binoculars, and this moment was no exception. He found a distant smudge with his unaided eyes and then brought the field glasses to bear. "Mother Mary," he whispered as a group of warships came into focus. Squinting, he looked for identifying marks, and felt his heart drop when he saw strange white characters slightly below the bows. A heavy cruiser led the convoy, followed by a transport ship and two destroyers. The ships were heading due west, directly toward the island.

"Are they ours?" Annie asked, biting a nail, afraid of the answer.

"Unfortunately, no. And they're headed this way." Joshua glanced at Isabelle and said a quick prayer, knowing that the transport ship could carry more than a thousand soldiers. He saw fear in the faces before him and tried to control his own dread. "They're not going to find us," he said, looking from person to person.

Ratu took Jake's hand. "But we're trapped. And they're coming . . . coming for us. Oh, what are we going to bloody do?"

"If Roger fails to meet them," Akira said, "they will waste time looking for him and us on the island. They most likely will not know of the lifeboat, yes? And so if we are on another island at that point, they will never know it. And if I can find the radio, we can take it with us."

Annie shook her head. "But Joshua's right. Roger is like a cat in the jungle. How would you sneak up on him? It's impossible. It's too much for you to do alone. You just can't go and do that."

Akira sighed, believing that his course of action was the best. "Then I will not go alone. If he would like, Jake can join me."

"Jake's not a soldier," Joshua said.

Jake, who until this point in the war had only fixed engines, had never expected to actually fight. Though he'd felt no compulsion to do so, he did experience a sense of pride at being asked. Also, he was terribly worried about what might happen to Ratu if the Japanese discovered that his father was leading Americans against them. Because of this fear, several days earlier, Jake had decided that he'd do whatever possible to protect him. And now, as Jake looked into Ratu's frightened eyes, he felt compelled to accompany Akira. If the two of them could keep the Japanese at bay, Ratu would never be alone in a room full of hostile men who didn't care about the tears of a boy.

"I'll go, Captain," Jake finally said. "I reckon I can be of use."

Joshua considered his options. Removing Roger would certainly improve their chances of staying unharmed. But was it fair to risk the lives of two good men? "I should go with Akira," Joshua said.

"So sorry, Captain," Akira replied. "But I do not agree. If something should happen to us, you will be needed for the lifeboat. None of us know the sea like you do."

"We should stick together," Annie said. "We need to—"

"Annie," Akira said, interrupting her for the first time since they'd met, "please remember what you told me. What you asked of me. I am doing what needs to be done."

She started to reply but forced herself to stop, turning away from him. Knowing that he was right but suddenly overwhelmed by the thought of him getting killed, she wasn't certain what to do. How could she let him go when he might not return?

"What do you think, Captain?" Akira asked. "A good plan, yes?"

Joshua nodded. "Only if you two return alive."

"We will return."

"We'll have to move a bit up the coast, just in case he comes back here," Joshua said, hating to risk their lives but deciding that Akira's plan was the best option. "We'll take the boat. We'll head straight north, along the beach. But we won't go far. When you're done, just walk up the beach and you'll find us. And then we'll get off this godforsaken island together."

"Thank you," Akira said, bowing slightly. "Jake and I will leave at dusk."

Additional strategies were discussed. The group then disbanded, each member having been assigned an important task. In the distance, the four Japanese warships loomed larger. To the unaided eye, they looked like nothing much more than four gray ducks on a lake. To the aided eye, however, they bristled with guns and men, and were immense steel beasts that couldn't have seemed more out of place on the warm waters.

SEVERAL HOURS LATER, after all preparations had been made and the crucial cloak of darkness had not yet fallen, Annie and Akira sat within the secondary cave. They waited miserably for the inevitable passage of time, though the sun seemed to have stuck in the unseen sky. The shaft of light angled downward, illuminating airborne dust. The ancient boats glowed and faded as a small fire flickered in the cave's corner.

Annie and Akira sat opposite the ships, watching them as they seemed to move upon invisible waves.

"I know that I told you to do whatever was necessary, but I still don't want you to go," Annie said quietly.

Akira didn't respond, knowing that she'd have to hear the right words to grasp the wisdom of his plan. Finally he said, "Do you want to see me off this island?"

"Yes. You know I do."

He stroked the back of her hand with his thumb, watching how her skin moved beneath his. "Please describe where you want to see me."

Her face tightened in bewilderment. "But why?"

"Just tell me, please."

She shrugged tiredly. "Well, I would . . . I'd want to show you California. A lot of Japanese are there, and I don't think it would be a big problem."

"What would we do in California?"

"We would . . . walk the streets."

"Holding hands, as Americans do?"

"Yes," she said, smiling fleetingly at the thought.

"Can you please tell me more? Much more?"

"We'd . . . we'd hold hands and we'd explore new places together. We'd visit parks and museums, and we could go to the sea."

"And at night?"

"Nights would be the best," she answered slowly, contemplating evenings spent with him. "We'd read so many books and poems. I could teach you to paint. And we'd talk, but not always. I don't think we'd need to talk constantly, like so many couples do." She paused, seeking his eyes. "And you? How do you see us?"

"How does one see a dream?" he asked. "For that is what it would be."

"Try. Try to . . . see it."

He kept his gaze on her face, loving her, hopeful that he'd have endless chances to talk with her again, but also dreadfully worried that these words would be the last between them. "Some say that love grows old," he replied, his voice hardly more than a whisper. "Like a child's once-treasured kite, it becomes less joyful. But I think our love would simply grow."

"I think so too."

"Perhaps, if many years passed, some things would slow. Would the thrill of our touch lessen? Perhaps yes. Perhaps no. Could we teach each other as much? I am not certain. But I do think that one day . . . if we grew old together . . . one day we would truly understand the treasure of our love. Because that child, once she grows old, will look upon that kite and be reminded of all that is good in the world, of all that was good in her life. And that kite will make her smile, will make her life seem complete. And that is how it would be for us. I would look at you, and I would know that I have been a lucky man."

"Do you feel lucky now? Despite Nanking? The long years at war?"

"I feel that I have just been given that kite. That I am watching it fly for the first time."

Annie squeezed his hand. "That's why I don't want you to go tonight. I can't imagine . . . losing so much. Won't you please stay?"

"That is why I have to go tonight. For such a future will never exist if we do not survive to leave this island."

She brought his hand to her lips and kissed his fingers. "Could I go with you? I'm not afraid. As long as I'm with you, I'm not afraid."

"I want that future, Annie," he said, completely aware of the meeting of their flesh. "I have never wanted anything nearly so much. And so you will have to trust me. Do you trust me? Yes?"

"I do."

"Then know that this is the best way, the best road for us to walk. I will do what must be done and then I will be yours until you tire of me."

She kissed his forefinger again, trying to be strong, but terribly afraid for him all the same. "I won't tire of you, Akira," she said, wanting to tell him exactly how she felt, and unsure how to proceed. "And though I loved your words about the kite, you're not a kite. And I won't ever stick you in a closet and not look lovingly at you again until I'm an old woman."

"You will never be old to me."

Annie briefly closed her eyes, pleasantly surprised by his compliment. "I won't ignore you," she promised. "Instead I'll . . . I'll treasure you every day that I have you. For I've known what life was like before you and . . . and since you, and as far as I'm concerned, these are two different lives. And one makes me so very much happier than the other."

He smiled at her, kissing her gently. He was always surprised at the softness of her lips, and this moment was no exception. She felt almost impossibly tender and warm. "Thank you," he said quietly, "for telling me of those two lives."

"You're welcome."

Akira kissed her again, savoring the feel of her. His whole life he had enjoyed opening his senses to the world. As a boy he had listened to cicadas, and savored the sweets his mother brought him. As a young man he had marveled at the sights of ancient temples and gardens. And as a man he had touched a great many things. But he'd never felt anything that gave him as much pleasure as Annie's lips.

And so Akira used all of his senses to revel in her extraordinary company. He removed her clothes and found her to be a greater beauty than he had seen. He listened to her whisper his name and believed her voice to be the most intimate and alluring sound he'd heard. He felt her eyelashes against his neck and delighted in the unexpected discovery of this intimate sensation. He smelled and tasted the soft curves of her flesh.

And the combination of these wonderful sensations so overwhelmed him that he felt as if he'd left one world and entered another that was almost entirely unknown to him.

LATER, WHEN THE SUN WAS ONLY AN HOUR or so from setting, Akira and Jake left camp. They carried a canteen, the machete, the pilot's dagger, and some dried fish. Knowing that they'd spend the night hiding in the jungle and that mosquitoes would assault them, they had stood near the campfire for some time, inundating themselves in smoke. Akira had used some old coals from the fire to darken his flesh and clothes. Jake had done the same to his shirt and pants.

After they passed deeper into the jungle, away from the tearful and reluctant good-byes of Annie and Ratu, they paused near a stream. Akira had suggested that they talk for a few minutes, because once they neared the harbor, any further conversation would likely result in their deaths.

"I will always lead," Akira said softly. "Please watch what I do, and little else. If I stop, you stop. If I go, you go. Kindly stay ten steps behind me and imagine . . . imagine that you are a mouse and that a very hungry snake is nearby. You must be as quiet as a mouse if we are to live. You can do that, yes?"

Jake nodded. "What best we do if the snake sees us?"

"If he sees us, we run. At least, you run. I will try to surprise him as he chases you."

"And when we get to that harbor?"

"We will arrive after the sun has set. In the darkness we will hide. And when the morning comes, we will wait for him to reveal himself. And when he is distracted, when he is defecating or drinking or talking on his radio, we will strike."

"Why me and not Nathan?" Jake asked suddenly. "I ain't a soldier. I spend my days killing weeds and grasshoppers and varmints. And though Roger is a varmint, he's an awfully big one, I reckon."

Glancing toward the shrouded sun, Akira said, "Annie told me once . . . of how you wished to fight for freedom. Of how that fight is important to you. I want such a man beside me. Such a man will do anything . . . to be free."

Jake nodded slowly, wishing that his mother could see him. She would be proud. She wouldn't say a thing to anyone, but her eyes would tell him everything. "You fight for the same?" he asked.

"Yes, I now fight for the same. For years, I have fought because I was told to. But no longer. Now I fight to be free." Akira looked again at the sun, which clung stubbornly to the sky. "Do you have . . . freedom on your farm?"

"It's my family's land. And it's fine land. And I reckon that's got some freedom to it." Jake watched a hermit crab shuffle toward a dead tree. "But my people to the south, they often live in shanties, places not fit to house my darn pigs. And to them, freedom ain't but a word with no meaning. So I expect that I'm really fighting this war for them."

"I am glad that you are with me, Jake," Akira replied, bowing. "I am honored to have you with me."

Jake shook his head. "That honor's mine." When Akira smiled and turned to leave, Jake reached out. "If something . . . something ill happens to me, will you see that Ratu gets home? He needs to get home in an awful bad way."

Akira nodded. "But, Jake, do not think of Ratu now. Think only of being a mouse. We each . . . have people to think about. But not again until Roger is dead."

Picking up a long blade of grass and placing it between his teeth, Jake tried to suppress thoughts of Ratu as well as his own nervousness. "Well, as they say, the early bird gets the worm. We'd best get going."

And so they went, past logs and streams and millions of creatures that didn't care whether they lived or died. For the first few minutes, Akira was painfully aware of Jake behind him. The big man stepped on twigs, slid down rocks, and even breathed too loudly. But as they continued, a remarkable metamorphosis happened, for more than anything in life, Jake understood the land. He'd never tried to be quiet on his farm, but he understood the farm's silent ways. He'd glimpsed such workings, and he soon mimicked the silence that he had so often appreciated within his crops.

As much as Jake would have enjoyed thinking about his mother or Ratu or the search for freedom that might claim his life, he focused only on the jungle. He became a part of it, and he felt empowered and enlightened by the merging of himself and the land. And though his heart quickened when they finally neared the harbor, and though he didn't want to die, he felt as if a thousand friends were beside him. In their company, his fear didn't dominate him. And so he was able to crawl forward in the darkness, glance at the sparkling sky, and hope.

DAY SEVENTEEN

I will give my life
So my second heart endures.
Spring survives winter.

For Love and Honor

In the utter blackness of night, dawn came slowly, rising like a tide of distant and muted color. Lying within clusters of ferns, Akira watched the edge of his world gradually lighten. He knew that it would possibly be the last sunrise he saw, and its simple and timeless beauty caused his eyes to dampen. He'd been thinking for the past several hours of Annie, and for the first time in days, musings of her hadn't been dominated by joyous emotions. On the contrary, a profound sadness consumed him. This sadness was different than the despair that had haunted him after Nanking, but was an equally powerful emotion also centered on loss.

Akira knew that disarming Roger would be an exceedingly difficult task. The man was capable, cunning, and carried a gun. All Akira possessed was the element of surprise. And even with this advantage, sneaking up on Roger would be fraught with danger. If Roger saw him coming, Akira would throw the dagger and hope for the best. He could do little else.

Though the unseen sun dimly illuminated the western sky, the night was still dark. Knowing that he had only a few more minutes until he must completely focus on Roger, Akira allowed himself to ponder Annie. Thinking of her, after all, was one of the greatest pleasures he'd ever known. She made him want to write poems, to reflect upon won-drous sights, to run like the boy he once was. She emanated joy and grace and beauty, and he loved more things about her than he did about himself.

Akira longed to lie beside her and listen to nothing more than the sound of her lungs filling with air, to see her face change with time, to help deepen the laugh lines about her mouth, to explore and learn and grow with her. And yet he might have already looked upon her for the last time. If Roger killed him, he'd only be able to try to pull a sliver of her along with him as he began the journey toward rebirth. And the thought of perhaps not even being able to hold on to that sliver pro-duced a nearly unbearable sadness within him. With his death she would be stolen from him. Moreover, her sadness at his passing would be acute. And he did not want to think of her as broken. For to him, she was like a white-winged crane, and she would not soar with shattered wings.

The sunrise strengthened, and Akira cautiously wiped his eyes of tears. Annie lingered in his mind, and, knowing that he had to force her from him, he bit a knuckle on his thumb until it bled. The resulting pain helped to direct his thoughts, and he studied the jungle, which was still remarkably quiet. Though Jake was just seven or eight feet away, Akira was almost completely unaware of him.

Akira felt the dagger's hilt in his hand. He inhaled deeply through his nose, thinking that perhaps he could smell the campfire smoke that so often dominated Roger's clothing. However, he could only detect the scent of the moist soil—the acute combination of decay and new life. Knowing that he'd have to be patient, Akira listened for any sound out of the ordinary.

When the earth twisted enough so that the sea was faintly illumi-nated, Akira saw the silhouettes of the four warships. They were an-chored a mile offshore. Surprised that he'd heard or seen nothing from them during the night, he scrutinized the vast swaths of gray, discerning movement on the long decks. The ships' guns were pointed defensively toward deeper waters, and he suddenly wished that they'd be attacked.

A whistle carried over the water to where Akira hid. Not long afterward, he realized that a flotilla of landing craft was headed directly toward the beach. These vessels were about fifty feet long—highlighted by a double bow that bordered a raised ramp. To Akira, they looked and sounded like approaching dragons. Certain that the familiar boats carried everything from light tanks to artillery pieces to men, he tried to keep his heart from speeding forward. He breathed deeply, searching through the jungle for Roger. Once the Japanese landed, there would be little he could do. His entire plan, after all, depended on catching Roger as he waited for the approaching force.

Cursing silently, he continued to scan the jungle. Where could Roger be? Why wouldn't he show himself? Akira resisted the powerful urge to rise and look for his adversary. He reminded himself that in war, plans were most often useless, and the people who didn't panic when plans failed were the people who tended to survive. "Patience," he whispered to Jake in a voice so low that he barely heard himself.

The landing craft, of which there were four, didn't slow until they struck the island. Immediately, the raised ramps dropped and scores of soldiers jumped into the shallow water. Hearing the familiar and terse shouts of his countrymen, Akira watched as formations of soldiers secured the beach. The soldiers fanned out, spreading across the beach, settling into the sand. A few heartbeats later, an undersized tank rolled forth from one of the boats. Belching black smoke, the tank climbed the beach as if some sort of monstrous crab. The tank's turret swayed to and fro as its crew searched for possible threats.

The landing crafts' drivers put the powerful engines into reverse, and the boats yanked themselves from the shallows. Understanding that the vessels would make many trips to and from the transport ship, Akira briefly closed his eyes in frustration. Already, more than a hundred soldiers occupied the beach. While most of the men remained in a defensive perimeter about the landing site, others began to dig trenches. Akira watched one soldier plant a pole that bore the Japanese flag. The image of the rising sun on a white background caused memories to leap

to the forefront of Akira's mind. Forcing them aside, he continued to
scan the area, hoping that Roger would reveal himself.

Several sets of binoculars studied the jungle. Akira steadied himself,
for a moment not even breathing. Discovery now would mean death.
The binoculars continued sweeping. As he lay motionless, he listened
to familiar orders being issued in his native tongue. Having spoken
little Japanese in several weeks, he felt disconcerted listening to it once
again, as the sounds seemed slightly foreign to him.

The binoculars finally dropped, and Akira was again able to breathe
and blink. In the distance, a second wave of landing craft was headed
toward the beach. Suspecting that his countrymen would likely cut
down a section of the jungle near the beach, Akira tried to slow his
heart. He and Jake wouldn't have much more time here. If they lingered
too long, they'd be discovered.

As much as Akira's instincts screamed at him to leave, he resisted the
urge. If he left now, he left with nothing but the knowledge that he'd
soon die. Roger would lead a strong force into the jungle, and protecting Annie and the others from such a force would be impossible. Realizing that he had no choice but to steal some weapons, Akira studied
the scene as it unfolded. The landing craft were again throwing themselves onto the beach. More men and arms and supplies were offloaded.
The Japanese appeared unduly nervous, for they acted with immense
haste, dragging artillery pieces from landing craft and setting them up
around the beach. Do they expect to be attacked? Akira wondered,
thinking such an occurrence would be too good to be true.

A giant centipede, longer than Akira's hand, crawled across his arm.
The creature stopped on his elbow, its head swaying back and forth like
a cobra's. To take his mind off the hideous-looking thing, he watched
his countrymen perform their tasks with discipline and efficiency. As he
watched, he thought of Annie. He asked himself if he'd willingly die for
her, and knew that the answer was yes.

Two weeks earlier, Akira would not have minded dying. In fact, he'd
have found immense peace in the process, for it would have rescued

him from his demons. But since then, Annie had rescued him. And even though he'd give his life for her if necessary, he'd never wanted to live as much as he did at that moment.

ON A HILL overlooking the beach, Roger shielded his eyes from the sun and awaited Edo. Sitting atop a boulder with his pistol on his lap, he studied the metamorphosis of the beach. In a matter of minutes it transformed from an idyllic, unspoiled stretch of sand into a mass of men and machines. As a young boy, Roger had stuck sticks into the openings of anthills, removing the twigs after a few minutes. Hundreds of ants had often then poured forth, and the Japanese below reminded him of those ants. The soldiers swarmed over the beach and started moving into the jungle. Roger heard the dull thud of axes striking wood. Several large palm trees swayed and fell.

Despite the awful pain in his side, Roger was pleased with himself, for late yesterday afternoon he'd traveled back to the cave and watched his enemies pack up the lifeboat and head to sea. Though he'd been tempted to shoot Joshua and Nathan, Edo's instructions had been specific on that matter. And so Roger had stayed still, watching the lifeboat as it struggled into the waves and then headed north. Akira and Jake, oddly enough, had been nowhere to be seen. Believing that they'd come for him, Roger studied the jungle near the beach. Were the maggots there? Did they know that they'd soon scream for an end?

Glancing at his side, Roger was surprised to see significant redness and swelling around his wound. Perhaps all his running about the island had further damaged his rib. In any case, shutting out the pain was becoming increasingly difficult. Each breath sent a jolt of agony through his system, starting at his side and traveling up his spine. Cursing, he wondered if movement was causing the broken rib to tear at his flesh from within.

Having decided that he'd tie Akira down, break each of his ribs, and leave him alone to die, Roger tried to escape his pain by imagining his foe's cries. Maybe I'll let the little bitch save her monkey by sacrificing herself, he thought. Maybe she'll see his agony and do anything to make his suffering stop.

Yes, Roger decided, I'll test their love. I'll see how far down it reaches. Her actions will let me know.

THE PREVIOUS EVENING, Joshua had rowed them north for almost an hour. In the dim light, they'd spotted some vegetation near the beach that would provide good cover for the lifeboat. After dragging the craft across the beach and hiding it beneath palm fronds, they'd erased the deep groove its keel had cut in the sand. Sleep had been fitful for some and nonexistent for others.

The following morning, they'd located various outposts from which they could watch anyone who might approach. Joshua and Isabelle had split up near the shore, their eyes scanning the sea and beach. Annie, Ratu, and Nathan were posted at the edge of the jungle so that they'd be aware of any approach from the rear.

Annie now sat atop a log and tried to be still, tried to study the land before her. But her mind was wholly fixated on Akira's absence. She felt naked without him, as if unable to awake from a dream in which she saw herself run unclothed down a street thick with gawking bystanders. The thought of Akira facing death out in the jungle caused her to tremble, to beg God for his safe return.

Throughout the morning, Annie had dreaded hearing the sound of a gunshot, for she feared that if she did, Akira would be dead. If she heard such a sound, she knew that she'd run to him. He could be wounded or dying, and leaving him to suffer alone was something she couldn't do— regardless of the price she might pay. Better to endure whatever Roger might do to her than to let Akira bleed to death in the jungle.

Suddenly, Annie heard Ratu sniff, despite the fact that he was posted more than twenty feet away. Though Joshua had told them not to make unnecessary movements, Annie immediately rose and hurried to where Ratu sat crying. He had his arms around a slender tree and his face was streaked with tears. Wordlessly, Annie hugged him, squeezing him tight, pressing her cheek against the top of his head. As she rubbed his arm, she noticed that he was trembling.

"He'll come back," she whispered, trying to be strong. "I promise he'll come back."

Ratu shuddered against her, his fingers wrapped about his necklace. "He can't die. I tell you, Big Jake can't die. He's my mate. My very best mate in the whole world."

"Let's rest," Annie said, lowering him to the ground, placing his head on her lap. She began to stroke his face, and he moved even closer against her. She used her thumb to gently close his eyes. "Tell me . . . tell me about your home," she said. "What makes it special?"

"I'm so bloody worried about Big Jake, Miss Annie. I just don't know what to do."

"I know you're worried. I am too. I feel sick about them being gone. But . . . but they're going to be fine." She squeezed him tighter, fighting her misery, willing herself to attend to Ratu. "Now let's talk about . . . about something else for a moment. I'd love . . . I'd love to know what kind of home produces such a wonderful boy. What makes your home so special?"

Ratu continued to tremble, moaning quietly. "My family," he finally replied, his words barely more than a whisper.

"What about them? Can you tell me one thing about each of them?"

Ratu thought about his loved ones, more tears seeping forth. "My mother . . . she likes to laugh."

"Is that who taught you? To laugh?"

He nodded. "She's always laughing. I tell you, she's so much funnier than me."

"And your father?"

"My father . . . my father wants to be with me. Not with his friends. But with me."

"He must love you very much."

"He does."

Annie continued to stroke his face. As much as she tried, she couldn't help but think of Akira, and tears dropped to her cheeks. She wiped them away, not wanting Ratu to know that she was crying. Her despair was suddenly so overwhelming that it took all her might to keep from sobbing.

Ratu's eyes opened. He studied her for a moment as she tried to collect herself. "You . . . you love him?" he asked.

She hesitated only a moment. "Very much."

Ratu nodded. "Does it make you . . . feel warm?"

"Yes."

"I don't want them to die," he said, starting to cry again. "I don't want anyone to die."

"We're going to . . . to go home soon," she replied. "We're each going to go home. You to your laughing mother and to your . . . your loving father. And to your five sisters. And they'll hold you and love you and all of this will just seem like a bad dream."

He shuddered against her. "You promise?"

"You'll be a boy again," she said, her tears fresh and numerous. "And . . . as Akira might say, you'll be reborn."

"Reborn?"

"Because you're going to be so very happy, Ratu. You're going to laugh and fish, and you're never going to feel like this again."

UPWARDS OF FIVE HUNDRED soldiers occupied the beach when Akira noticed a group of eleven men head straight into the jungle. They walked with a sense of purpose and were heavily armed and supplied. Believing them to be the team that Roger would rendezvous with, Akira felt as if he were watching Annie's death unfold. And this horrific sensation prompted him to immediate action.

Not far from Akira's location, a group of soldiers busily chopped down trees. He hoped, somewhat desperately, that they'd set their weapons aside and he could steal some arms. With his belly and legs pressed against the soil, Akira started to crawl, using only his elbows to propel himself forward. Fortunately, the vegetation was thick, and now that the Japanese had secured the area, no one seemed to be paying attention to the jungle. During the night, Akira had woven reeds into his hair and clothes, and he wondered if he looked as much like a bush as he thought he did.

Despite his fear of the eleven soldiers and the death that might follow in their wake, Akira moved slowly, perhaps ten feet a minute. He felt rather than heard Jake behind him. Not far ahead, Akira listened to men talking and working. Axes rhythmically thumped into wood, and trees swayed and toppled. Someone was complaining of the heat and bugs. A terse voice reminded everyone of their duty to the emperor and demanded they double their efforts. More trees fell.

When Akira was perhaps two dozen paces from the work crew, he paused again. Though bushes obscured much of his view, he saw eight men. Seven were laboring with axes and saws while an officer, who had a sword at his side, gave endless instructions. To Akira's delight, he noticed rifles leaning against several trees. A light machine gun was also present, but sat in the midst of the men. Deciding that he'd try to steal the two rifles that were set deepest in the jungle, Akira crept forward, glad for the swinging axes, the orders, and the conversation of the men. Even so, he moved with extraordinary care, eyeing the ground ahead before settling himself upon it.

As Akira neared the guns, his heart pounded with increasing vigor. Though sweat stung his eyes and dampened his clothes, his mouth felt dry and stale. Trying to slow his breathing, he edged closer. The guns were only five feet from him, and the nearest man thrice that distance. Akira inched ahead. The distant drone of aircraft then found his ears, and he stopped. Around him the soldiers chatted excitedly, talking about a squadron of Japanese bombers that was returning from what they assumed to be a successful mission. The approaching planes sounded unusually low, and the officer ordered his men to return to the beach and bow to honor their victorious comrades. At first, Akira was dismayed by this request, for he knew that the men would take their guns. And they did, each grabbing a weapon and then hurrying to the beach. However, extra guns must have been present, for a trio of rifles was forgotten next to a fallen tree. Not believing his luck, Akira waited for the men to vanish and then crawled to the guns. He grabbed the rifles and, crouched over, ran away from the beach.

Suddenly, Jake was beside him, and Akira handed his companion a rifle. They moved silently through the jungle, hurrying as fast as they dared. Finally, when they were far from the beach, Akira said in a low voice, "Did you see the eleven?"

"Sure did. And that pack of wolves ain't nothing but trouble."

"They will come for us."

"I reckon so."

"With Roger, they will have twelve. And these rifles each contain five rounds. That means fifteen bullets for twelve men. We will have to shoot very straight and very fast." Akira launched himself over a fallen tree. Turning to Jake, he said, "Are you ready to run? Yes?"

"I ain't never been so ready."

"Good," Akira said simply, his legs churning beneath him, his mind now focused solely on getting back to Annie as quickly as possible.

Trying to hide his pain, Roger made his way down the hill toward the eleven approaching soldiers. Though not surprised, he was pleased to see that they were heavily armed and appeared well trained. The soldiers moved not as individuals but as a single unit. A small man led the group, his movements much less fluid than those of his comrades. He seemed more concerned with making his way up the steep slope than with his surroundings. Were he in battle, Roger knew, he'd die quickly.

Believing that the small man was Edo, Roger called out a password and approached the group. Edo told his men to remain still, and he continued upward alone. Unlike many desk-bound soldiers who longed for the field, Edo possessed no such temperament—even if he yearned to kill at least once during the war. Though he pretended otherwise, Edo despised the island's smells and flies, heat and sun. A part of him wished that he was back in his bunker in Tokyo, or at the very least in his room aboard the cruiser. The actual fighting in a war was best left to the young and stupid, he had long believed.

But having been ordered to terminate Roger, Edo felt compelled to be on the ground to ensure that the deed was done. Moreover, as much as he hated the field, he relished the prospect of using his gun. He knew that regardless of how important his work was, his duty would never be considered truly honorable until he had killed. That was a simple fact of the war.

And so complicated and somewhat contradictory feelings coursed through Edo as he approached the big American. Certainly Edo was pleased that he'd fire his pistol for the first time in the war. But he also wanted the bloodshed to happen sooner rather than later. He felt out of his element on the island, and was afraid that his men would detect his inexperience and discomfort with his surroundings. They'd never witness his desk-bound brilliance, he knew, but they might see his field-bound shortcomings.

Edo and Roger met on an outcropping that was mostly devoid of trees and foliage. Neither man spoke, as the two had worked together for some time but never met in person, and now they quickly assessed each other. Edo broke the stillness, pointing at Roger's side. "What happened?" he asked roughly in Japanese.

Roger noted the harsh undercurrent in the other's words. "There was a complication," he replied, the effort to talk worsening the pain in his side.

"A complication? Describe this unfortunate complication."

"After sixteen days on this rock, they discovered who I was. That was yesterday. We fought, and I retreated here."

"How many did you kill?"

"One."

"Just one? Why?"

"I was outnumbered."

"You were a fool to get caught," Edo said. "Unforgivable to get caught."

If anyone else had so disdainfully called him a fool, Roger would have killed him immediately. But with ten of Edo's men standing nearby, Roger stifled an urge to break the little man's neck. "It changes nothing," Roger finally replied. "I know where they've gone. And they don't know this."

"Then why are we talking?"

"Fine. Follow me."

"No," Edo said, shaking his head. "You will stay at the rear. You will tell my men where to go."

Though surprised by the command, Roger merely shrugged. He then said, "There's a Japanese officer with the Americans."

"With them?"

"He's betrayed the emperor."

Edo's eyes narrowed, as if he didn't believe such a thing possible. "And?" he said, swatting futilely at a fly.

"And I'd like to kill him."

"You are paid to kill Americans, not Japanese," Edo said, glancing at Roger's side. "Is he the one who gave you this complication?"

"With your permission, I'd like to interrogate him. Him and his American lover."

Edo's face tightened. He found this revelation to be almost as disgusting as the man's betrayal of the emperor. "I will give you . . . some time with them," Edo replied. "But I will finish what you begin."

"And I will watch."

Edo grunted, wondering how anyone could find an American woman attractive. He'd seen pictures of them and found their noses and shoulders and waists to be enormous. Why anyone would want to bed such a monster was beyond him. "Is she repulsive?" he asked, starting to descend the hill.

Though Roger was surprised by the question, his answer came quickly enough. "You'll want to squash them both. Like a couple of fleas."

"Fleas don't break ribs."

Roger bristled at this remark, suddenly hating Edo. But he suppressed an angry reply, for the little man had promised to give him Akira and Annie, and for such a gift, Roger could surely endure a few insults. After all, such a gift would keep him warm on cold nights, entertain him years from now, and set him free.

THE BEACH FELT MARVELOUS against Akira's feet. Though his lungs and legs ached, he ran without slowing his pace. The sand meant that he was drawing closer to Annie, that he'd see her once again. "You can continue, yes?" he asked Jake.

Jake struggled to keep pace, but nodded. "I . . . I wasn't . . . born to run," he said between intense gasps of air, sweat dropping like rain from his cheeks and nose. "But neither . . . was the turtle . . . who won that race."

Akira didn't understand Jake's response but asked for no clarification. His mind was set only on rejoining the group. He wanted to get to them as quickly as possible, for he believed that Roger's force wasn't far behind. And though Akira feared that he'd still die soon, the thought of once again holding Annie in his eyes and arms gave him immense strength. He ran as if he'd just escaped from prison and was returning to her after many years of separation.

A part of him hadn't expected to survive the morning, and despite the fact that his plan had failed, Akira felt almost as much hope as he did dread. If he and Jake could lead the approaching force in the wrong direction, Annie and the others might be able to escape in the lifeboat. And perhaps fate would be so kind as to let Jake and him swim after the

boat. Stranger things happened in war. The will of the few could overcome the strength of the many. Akira had seen it happen before. How
else had Japan dominated China?

Running at the edge of the sea, so that the water covered their tracks,
Akira led Jake to the north. They passed the cave and only slightly
slowed to glance inside. Hurrying around rocks and tide pools, they left
little trace of their passage. Akira was careful to keep the rifles free of
sand and sea. The guns, after all, were as important to him as the beat
of his own heart. Without them, everyone would die.

"You . . . run . . . like you're on . . . fire or something," Jake said haltingly, trying to keep up. "You ain't gonna . . . explode . . . are you?"

Akira leapt over a mound of kelp. "I have never . . . run like this."

"She must . . . be awfully . . . special."

"Like the sun."

Jake smiled at Akira's response. Though Jake was still scared, he also
ran with hope. He'd watched Akira in the jungle and had been in awe
of the man's cunning and courage. With Akira leading them, maybe
they stood a chance. Maybe Jake would return Ratu to his village and
then journey home to Missouri. Maybe no one else would get hurt.
Might they be so darn lucky?

They had traveled another half mile or so up the shoreline when a
sudden shout caused them to stop. Joshua and Isabelle emerged from
the edge of the jungle, followed not far behind by Annie, Ratu, and
Nathan. Annie stumbled as she hit the beach, regained her balance, and
pressed forward. Akira moved toward her, laughing as she leapt into his
arms, holding her and the rifles above the sand.

She started to speak but kissed him instead. They'd never so openly
touched, but for the moment nothing but the joy of their reunion mattered. She squeezed him tight, her arms and legs wrapped about him.

"I am going to fall," he finally said, smiling.

"Oh, of course!" she replied, dropping from him.

A few feet away, Ratu slapped Jake on the back. "You did it, Big
Jake! I tell you, you bloody did it!"

Jake tussled the boy's hair. "Remind me . . . never . . . to run with him again."

Joshua smiled and, glancing skyward, said a quick prayer of gratitude. He then took the heavy guns from Akira and Jake. "What happened?" he asked eagerly, leading them back toward the jungle.

Akira explained what had occurred during the night and early morning. Only when he mentioned the eleven soldiers did people worriedly look into the jungle. "They will find us," Akira said. "They are professionals, and they will find us."

"How soon?" Joshua asked, his euphoria abruptly gone, his eyes glancing at Isabelle. She hadn't been looking well for the past several days, and earlier that morning, several drops of blood had spotted her underwear.

"A few hours," Akira replied.

Joshua groaned. "We've no choice. We'll get in the lifeboat and take our chances at sea."

"Yes," Akira said. "That is what you will do. But Jake and I will not."

"Why not?"

"We will take the three guns and lead the soldiers in the wrong direction. And when we have confused them enough, we will swim to you."

"Swim?" Nathan asked incredulously, shaking his head, worried for them. "How would you ever find us?"

"We once swam from your ship, yes? We can do it a second time."

Isabelle saw the sudden fear and hurt in her sister's eyes, and stepped closer to Akira. "You've already risked everything. It isn't right to do that again."

"But the plan did not work," Akira replied, not wanting to return to the jungle but knowing that he had no choice. "Roger is still alive. And he will bring them to us." Akira nodded toward the rifles. "I am an expert shot. I will shoot Roger first. Then Jake and I will run to the sea. Without Roger, they will never find us."

"He's as right as rain," Jake said, his arm around Ratu. "They ain't gonna get us. Not with that devil dead."

"And you want to go with him?" Joshua asked. "Again?"

"Better two of us than one, I reckon."

Joshua bit his bottom lip. His prayers for Akira and Jake's safe return had been answered, and now that the group was reunited, he loathed the thought of breaking it up again. But what Akira had said made sense, even if his plan wasn't perfect. "Don't fully engage them," he said, trying to sound confident. "Fire a few shots from a far distance. Hit Roger, then lead them deep into the island, lose them there, and head for the eastern beach. Grab a branch and start swimming. We'll be a mile offshore, waiting for you. Once we're a mile offshore, the naked eye shouldn't be able to see us."

Annie started to protest, but Akira looked at her and shook his head. She paused for a moment and said, "Two against twelve doesn't seem right. I don't care what any of you say; it's not right."

Aware of the pain on her sister's face, and finally understanding the depth of her love for Akira, Isabelle added, "I agree completely. For goodness' sake, there just has to be a better way."

Akira glanced at Isabelle and then at Annie. "Your mother must be strong and wise," he replied, "to create such daughters." Before either sister could answer, he added, "This way will set us free."

Knowing that time was precious, Joshua nodded, handing a rifle to Akira and another to Jake. "I'll go with you," he said. "Three of us will fare better."

"So sorry, but you must lead the lifeboat, Captain," Akira said, reaching forward to take the other gun. He smiled and added, "When we catch up to you, you can row the boat, yes?"

Joshua reluctantly released the gun. He reached out to shake Akira's and Jake's hands. "You're good men," he said. "Damn fine men."

Emotional farewells were exchanged, and the group scattered. Holding the two guns, Akira followed Annie a few paces deeper into the jungle. She leaned against a tree and slowly shook her head, tears descending her face. "You don't . . . you don't have to do this."

Akira set the guns down. He placed his palms gently against her damp cheeks. "I do not want to die," he replied, trying to keep his eyes from tearing, to hide the despair that threatened to engulf him. "More than anything, I want to live."

"So why? Why go?"

"I go . . . so that we will all live. So that . . . my days with you will have just begun."

She leaned into him, resting her forehead on his shoulder. "Please come back to me," she whispered.

He inhaled deeply, once again bringing the scent of her into him. Closing his eyes, he tried to lock this part of her within him, so that he could carry her wherever he traveled. "May I ask you a favor?" he asked softly.

"What?"

"Write one poem each day."

"What do you mean?" she asked, her face awash with tears.

"Write about something that touches you. A flower. A child, perhaps. A climb in the trees."

"Why are you telling me this?"

His eyes glistened. "If I . . . should fall, know that . . . that I will still be beside you. I will—"

"You won't fall. You can't fall, Akira. Please, please don't fall."

"So sorry," he whispered, stroking the back of her head. "I love you," he said, holding her tight. "You have been the greatest gift of my life."

She looked up, pressing her lips against his. "You run," she said, her voice cracking, but resolute. "You run like you've never run before. And then you swim like you've never swum before. And then we won't ever have to say good-bye again."

He kissed her forehead, her closed eyes, her tears. "I first . . . found you in the sea," he said quietly. "And I will return to you in the sea." He kissed her lips, savoring their fullness and warmth. "I must go," he said, reluctantly pulling away from her.

"This isn't . . . a good-bye," she replied, weeping.

"How can you say good-bye to someone . . . who . . . who is a part of you?" he asked, turning as his voice broke, as his world collapsed. Snatching the two guns, he took one last look at her and stumbled toward Jake.

SLIGHTLY DEEPER IN THE JUNGLE, Ratu held his necklace in his right hand. Scanning the dense foliage, he awaited Jake's arrival. He'd wanted to hug Jake on the beach, to tell him that he loved him, but Joshua had been instructing his friend, and, frustrated, Ratu had decided to delay his good-bye until a time when Jake could freely speak to him.

Ratu planned on giving his shark's tooth necklace to Jake. The necklace, Ratu believed, brought good luck to whoever carried it. And he desperately wanted to pass such luck to Jake, for he worried greatly about what would happen to his friend once the Japanese saw him.

"You're too bloody big," Ratu whispered to himself, nervously fingering the shark's tooth. "And they'll see you. I tell you, they'll see you." Ratu groaned, his stomach aching, his mind spinning in a hundred different directions. "Where are you? Please, Big Jake, tell me where you are."

Unseen birds screeched in the distance. Ants carried chunks of bright leaves. The day was hotter than most, and sweat rolled down Ratu's face and back. Turning about in a circle, he looked for his friend. "Did you already get lost? Oh, Big Jake, you shouldn't be doing this. You're only a farmer."

Ratu's heart began to quicken its beat. The jungle abruptly seemed too thick, too quiet. Suddenly frantic with worry over Jake, he ran back toward the beach. As he broke into the open, he saw Joshua and Nathan removing foliage from the hidden lifeboat. "Where's Jake?" he asked, hurrying forward.

Joshua turned to him. "Jake? Jake's gone."

"What do you mean? I didn't see him go!"

"He and Akira left five minutes ago. They ran down the beach."

"The beach?" Ratu replied, panicking. "Not the jungle?"

"No."

"But I didn't get to say good-bye!" Ratu said, crying. "I didn't give him my necklace!"

Isabelle, who'd been trying to help with the lifeboat as much as her fatigued body permitted, stepped toward Ratu and dropped to her knees before him. "He called for you. He was looking for you, Ratu."

"But I didn't bloody hear him! Why . . . why didn't someone get me?"

"We tried to—"

"Why didn't someone call?"

"We did."

"But I didn't give him my lucky necklace!"

Isabelle put her arms around him, drawing him close. He was shaking, and she tried to soothe him. "He's going to be fine, Ratu. You'll see him in a few hours."

"But he doesn't have my necklace!"

Nathan knelt beside them, hating to see Ratu so distraught. "You'll give it to him soon," he said, putting his hand on Ratu's back. "And that smile of his—"

"No, you don't understand. Not a bloody bit. He's not going to be fine without my necklace! He's too big! They'll—"

Suddenly, distant gunfire and explosions interrupted Ratu's words. A few seconds later, a large number of fighter planes flew almost directly over them, then circled back toward the other side of the island. The planes bore a single propeller and a bright white star.

"They're Hellcats!" Joshua shouted.

Isabelle's brow furrowed. "Hellcats?"

"American!"

The planes disappeared behind the trees. Again the repeating crack of machine-gun fire filled the air. Louder thumps responded as Japanese antiaircraft guns opened up. Several large explosions seemed to shake the island.

"We've got to go!" Joshua shouted. "Now, while they're distracted!"

He hurried to the rear of the lifeboat and pushed with all his might. Nathan moved beside him and the two men thrust the heavy boat forward. Fortunately, the beach tilted toward the sea and the craft slid ahead. The air crackled with small-arms and machine-gun fire. Planes circled above and headed back toward the fray. One smoking Hellcat suddenly lost a wing and cartwheeled into the sea.

"Hurry!" Joshua yelled, aware that the Japanese were being hit very hard. He helped Isabelle into the boat. He saw Annie emerge from the jungle. Once Isabelle was settled, Annie, Nathan, and Ratu prepared to climb in. Then a massive explosion erupted on the far side of the island, the blast so large that a fireball reached above the treetops.

Leaping into the boat, Joshua glanced once more at the planes and began to row. His knuckles whitened on the oars, and he propelled the lifeboat into the waves, which smashed against the bow and inundated everyone with spray. The chaos became even more intense as the sky thickened with smoke. Hellcats continued to strafe the faraway beach, and antiaircraft guns boomed.

Realizing that the attack was a miracle that could save them, Joshua rowed with all his might. His injured hands once again split open. His will forced the lifeboat beyond the surf and into the sea. And his mind was so bent on saving everyone that he wasn't aware that Ratu hadn't gotten on the boat after all, but was running down the beach, chasing Jake's deep footsteps.

THE NOISE OF THE DISTANT explosions and gunfire seemed louder, as if a typhoon of burning steel was churning forward to consume them. Though pleased by the presence of the American planes, Akira almost immediately forced the battle from his mind. He needed to focus like never before on the task at hand, and neither Annie nor the nearby conflict was going to interfere with his thinking.

Akira didn't believe it would be hard to locate the approaching group of his countrymen. A large ravine tended to funnel everything from one side of the island to the other, and all he and Jake had to do was locate some suitable high ground and wait. Holding a rifle in each arm, Akira ran steadily. "Fire when I fire," he told Jake. "Roger will be leading them. We shoot for him. We shoot and we run."

Jake winced as a branch cut into his arm. Though he sought to remain as focused as Akira, he couldn't help but think about his mother and father, as well as Ratu. Faces flashed before him, faces he wanted to see again but didn't know if he would. "I wish you . . . weren't so fast," he said, trying to smile.

"After Roger is down, follow me. We will lead them away from the beach, and then we will circle back and swim."

"You sure . . . you didn't see Ratu wave good-bye?"

"Do not think about him, Jake! Not now!"

Jake had never heard Akira raise his voice and was surprised by his tone. Though Jake tried to follow Akira's advice, Ratu kept returning to his mind, like a dream that one cannot fully awaken from. Was he escaping? Jake wondered. Does he know how darn much I love him? Why didn't we say good-bye?

No answers presented themselves, and all Jake could do was run. The heavy gun pulled him toward the ground, and the thought of Ratu pulled his mind in directions that it should not go.

TEN MINUTES BEHIND Jake and Akira, Ratu hurried forward. He followed their footprints from the sand into the jungle. Though tempted to call out their names, he ran quietly, gripping his necklace. "Where are you, Big Jake?" he whispered. "Don't run so fast. Please don't run so bloody fast."

He stumbled ahead, his lungs heaving. Unseen planes roared overhead, the frightening screams of their propellers and guns forcing him to crouch as he ran. "Why didn't you wait?" he muttered, weeping.

Ratu shuddered, feeling more alone than he ever had. "Oh, Big Jake, please wait for me!"

AT THE REAR OF THE COLUMN, trying to focus on anything but his tremendous pain, Roger watched the troops in front of him. They continued to move as one unit, slithering through the jungle like a serpent.
They were hard men, Roger knew, for not a single figure had cowered
when the explosions started. No questions had been asked, no wordless
exchanges of expressions. The men had merely paused for a moment
and then started forward again.

The pain in Roger's side had become a living thing, expanding and
contracting with each breath he took. The agony was like a monster
within him, its claws and fangs biting deeply into his side. He tasted
blood at the back of his throat. And the taste of his own mortality filled
him with an anxiety he'd never known. Suddenly, all he wanted was to
crush out the lives of Akira and Annie as if they were cigarettes to be
extinguished. He wanted to obliterate these lives, and then find a medic
who could save him from the taste of his own blood.

"Follow . . . follow that stream," he whispered to Edo, his thoughts
slow and muddled. "That stream," he added, "will lead us to . . . to the
white woman . . . and the yellow . . . the yellow traitor." He tapped Edo
on the shoulder, breaking customs and protocols that he'd understood
for years. "I . . . I want to taste their blood," he said, somewhat deliriously. "Let me taste their blood."

Edo paused, noting the feverish glaze that consumed Roger's face
and eyes. "You want . . . to taste their blood?"

Roger nodded slowly, as if his head was of unbearable weight. "I
want . . . to taste their deaths." As Edo remained motionless, Roger
raised his pistol, his finger on the trigger, the monster within him
screaming for revenge.

AKIRA AND JAKE LAY STILL, covered in leaves and branches. The two
were about fifteen feet apart, close enough that they could communi-
cate, but not in such proximity that a grenade blast could easily kill

them both. Akira had selected the ambush site with immense care. Perched atop a gentle, thirty-foot rise, they overlooked the ravine that ran from one side of the island to the other. Akira was fairly certain that Roger would select this route, as it was the fastest way to reach the eastern shore.

The foliage surrounding Akira and Jake was thick. Lying in it, they were almost invisible from below. Only their faces and the black barrels of their rifles were unobscured by ferns, giant leaves, and branches. "Strike Roger," Akira whispered, his finger tight against the rifle's trigger. "Strike him and then follow me."

Jake, who had only shot birds before, nervously licked his lips. His heartbeat seemed to travel and shudder from his chest to his eardrums. Sweat rolled down his nose. Ants crawled about him. "What if they see us?" he whispered.

To the west, a parrot flew above the trail, screeching loudly. Akira closed his fist, signaling silence. Except for the sounds of distant gunfire and explosions, suddenly the jungle seemed eerily still. Hooting insects and frogs had gone quiet. Animals of any sort were nowhere to be seen. Akira slowed his breathing as much as possible, not wanting the branches atop him to move with his lungs. About a hundred paces before him, the trail rounded a bend and followed the ravine in his direction. Akira kept his gaze fastened on the bend, unaware of a mosquito drawing blood from his neck.

The trail was still for perhaps another minute. Then Akira saw a soldier step cautiously into view. The man, who wore a khaki-colored uniform, carried a light machine gun. Akira had assumed that Roger would lead the assault, and closed his eyes briefly in frustration. The soldier moved like a shadow passing through the jungle. He was extremely cautious, his movements so refined that Akira's chest tightened in fear.

Ten feet behind the man on point, another soldier appeared. He carried a rifle and also moved like a seasoned veteran. More men materialized around the bend. The leader was slowly but surely approaching the spot directly beneath Akira and Jake. Where is Roger? Akira frantically asked himself, trying to somehow see beyond the distant bend. Abruptly, the point man paused, as if sensing that he was being watched. He dropped to one knee, his gun held in a firing position, his head twisting left, then right. He looked up, eyeing the ridge above him.

Akira, who had kept the man within his gun sight, held his breath. The soldier's gaze appeared to sweep past him. However, the point man then frowned, his eyes narrowing as he noticed the rifle's barrel. The soldier was remarkably fast, swinging his machine gun upward, sending a burst of bullets in Akira's direction. Despite the stream of bullets rising toward him, Akira didn't move, his finger pulling on the trigger, his eye re-aiming the gun even as the point man fell. Jake fired a heartbeat later, and the second soldier in the column spun to his left as the bullet struck his shoulder.

Akira fired another shot, hitting a third man, and then rolled to his left, away from the soldiers below. Jake did the same, closing his eyes as bullets thudded into the soil around him. He twisted over the top of the hill and was momentarily safe.

"Run!" Akira shouted, heading down the other side.

Jake stumbled after Akira, the explosion of a hand grenade almost knocking him off his feet but miraculously not wounding him. Hearing the Japanese shout below, and knowing that they were clambering up the hill, Jake moved in vast strides, running through bushes rather than going around them.

Understanding all too well that Jake would provide a target almost impossible to miss, Akira urged him forward. Suddenly desperate, trying to give their pursuers a moment's pause, Akira screamed, "Banzai!" The Japanese war cry reverberated eerily in the jungle.

After a few seconds passed, angry replies reached Akira's ears. His countrymen called him a traitor, and without question their hearts were filled with rage and hate. And Akira knew that were he and Jake to fall, their deaths would not come nearly fast enough.

WHEN THOSE ABOARD THE LIFEBOAT had been at sea for no more than a minute, two extraordinary discoveries were made almost simultaneously. First, with the binoculars pressed tight against his forehead, Nathan spied a strike force of American warships. The vessels were several miles due east and were headed full speed toward the other side of the island. Then, equally stunning, while Nathan spoke about the looming naval battle, Annie realized to her horror that Ratu wasn't on board.

"Where's Ratu?" she shouted, frantically looking about, standing so quickly that she rocked the lifeboat.

Isabelle left her seat as well, scanning the water. "He was with us! I saw him get in!"

"He's not with us!" Annie shrieked, putting her hands to her head. "He must not have—"

Not very far from where they'd left the beach, the unmistakable sound of machine-gun fire suddenly split the silence. A heartbeat later, explosions belched mushroom clouds up through the jungle's canopy. Small-arms fire filled the gaps between the explosions, scores of streaking bullets announced with brief outbursts of sound.

"Akira," Annie muttered. "They're . . . they're chasing him!" More explosions and gunfire dominated this side of the island. Suddenly, Annie found it hard to breathe. The world seemed to tip and sway about her. "I . . . I have to go," she said haltingly, the fear of her own death suddenly inconsequential when compared with thoughts of what might happen to Akira or Ratu.

Isabelle reached for her sister. "Annie, you don't—"

"I love you," Annie said, then jumped off the lifeboat.

"Annie!" Isabelle screamed, dropping to her knees, trying to grab her sibling's arm.

Annie kicked away from the boat as if she'd been born to do nothing but swim. Her hands and feet tore through the water, propelling her forward. Her terror over Akira's possible death gave her a strength she'd never known. She didn't care about what pain she might endure or what limbs she might lose, or dying alone in the jungle. All that mattered was that she find Akira. That she'd be there for him as he'd been for her.

So intent was Annie on reaching the shore that she didn't hear Isabelle and Joshua screaming for her to come back. She didn't see the life jacket that Nathan had thrown near her. And so Isabelle grabbed Joshua's arm. "We have to turn around!"

Joshua placed his free hand over hers. "Are you willing to risk everything?"

She bit her lip at the thought of losing their child. Her vision blurred. Her stomach threatened to heave. Still, she nodded. "We can't . . . we just can't leave her alone out there."

Nathan picked up the machete, silently telling his wife that he was sorry for whatever might happen, that he would always love her and be with her. "Let's go get Annie," he said, his limbs weak with fear.

Joshua started to fiercely row his left and right oars in opposite directions. The lifeboat began to turn. A smoking plane roared overhead and crashed into the sea. Watching Isabelle weep and hold her belly, Joshua was filled with a sudden and seemingly infinite sense of pride. "I love you," he whispered, wondering if this would be their last day together, praying that it would not.

"Please hurry, Josh," she said, her voice quivering, her face streaked with tears. She rocked back and forth on the bench, a profound feeling of helplessness overwhelming her. Though her time aboard *Benevolence* had been often defined by tragedy, at least she'd been able to subdue her patients' suffering. At least she'd helped. But now, much to her horror, when Annie most needed her, Isabelle could feel the distance between them increasing. She could do nothing.

As Joshua's hands bled upon the oars and he felt a muscle give way in his back, he tried to comfort her, for he could see that she was at the extreme limits of her endurance. "I bet it's a girl," he said, his eyes growing moist.

"A girl?" she replied, surprised by his words.

He nodded, grunting against the oars, biting his lower lip as he thought of their child. "With big . . . blue eyes and a heart . . . a heart like her mother's."

Isabelle watched Annie drag herself through the shallows and then start running down the beach. "Look at her go," she whispered, shuddering as she wept.

As Joshua watched Annie, he prayed for her safe return, pleading with God to deliver everyone unharmed. "Where did the frightened little girl go?" he asked, awed by the change in Annie's character. "When did she get so brave?"

"When she fell in love," Isabelle replied, her trembling hands reaching for the medical kit. "I think Annie . . . she just needed to fall in love."

WHEN RATU HAD FIRST heard the gunfire, he stopped running. Leaning against a tree, he wept, clinging to his necklace as if only it could save him from drowning. When the sound of death had suddenly stopped, he started running again. Darting around trees, he quietly called out Jake's name, repeating it over and over in the same determined manner that a baby wails for its mother from a crib.

The deeper Ratu moved into the jungle, the more anxious he became. "Where are you, Big Jake?" he half spoke, half cried into the endless trees. "Big Jake, please tell me where you are! Please!"

Several gunshots rang out not far away. An explosion and additional gunfire seemed to answer. Believing that Jake and Akira were still alive, Ratu hurried ahead. He cried as he ran, his small frame wracked by sobs. Ratu had never felt so alone. Not when he first stowed away on *Benevolence*. Not when his father left. The terrible noises, the jungle, and the absence of his friend overwhelmed him. Suddenly, nothing mattered but finding the man who he'd grown to love.

And so Ratu charged blindly through the jungle, calling for Jake. As he crossed a stream, he thought he heard shouts in the distance. "Big Jake!" he screamed. "Big Jake, I'm here!"

Twenty paces away, bushes suddenly parted and Akira and Jake burst forth. Jake grabbed Ratu with his left hand, sweeping him over his shoulder. Ratu looked up and saw a handful of soldiers running forward. Gun muzzles flashed and bullets thudded into nearby trees. Akira paused briefly to fire, and a soldier cried out and fell.

Beneath Ratu, Jake hurtled over logs and rocks and seemed as strong as ten men. Ratu tried to wrap his arms about Jake's torso, but his friend's giant leaps caused Ratu to bounce and groan. More gunfire rang forth, and suddenly Jake grunted and stumbled forward. Ratu almost immediately saw the wound in Jake's leg. Blood spurted from an ugly hole, and Ratu tried to press his hands against the torn flesh. A crushing explosion then threw Jake from his feet, tossing him against a tree as if he were no more than a leaf in a gale.

Akira screamed when he saw the grenade detonate so close to Jake and Ratu. Jake crumpled against a tree, his rifle spinning end over end into the jungle. Ratu was thrown into nearby foliage. Knowing that his countrymen would bayonet Jake and Ratu if he left them alone, Akira dropped to one knee and fired his rifle. His bullet struck a soldier in the neck and he died instantly. Even before the soldier's body hit the ground, Akira was running toward it. He dove for the man's light machine gun and, grasping it, rolled and fired in practically one motion. Another two soldiers fell and then an explosion lifted Akira off his feet. The world spun around him. He twisted through the air like a tossed toy, landing hard on his back. He tried to stand but his legs betrayed him. His ears rang. His thoughts weren't connected. Time expanded, wobbled, and burst. To his immense surprise, he noticed that two fingers from his left hand were missing. He then saw Annie smile, and he reached for her.

Roger knocked Akira's outstretched arm aside. Still on his knees, Akira started to mumble something, and Roger slammed the butt of his gun into Akira's ribs. Pinpricks of light dominating his vision, Akira toppled face forward onto the ground.

"Don't kill him, you fool!" Edo snapped. "I need to—"

Roger thrust his pistol into Edo's open mouth and pulled the trigger.

The back of Edo's head disintegrated, and he fell lifeless at Roger's feet. "Goddamn . . . monkey," Roger muttered, swaying unsteadily.

At the sound of Roger's voice, Akira groaned and rolled to his back. Blinking, he tried to bring his enemy into focus. But Roger noticed Akira's wound, stepped on his injured hand, and ground his heel upon the bloody stumps that had once been fingers. Akira screamed. He tried to beat Roger's leg with his other hand, but the world still spun and his blows were almost powerless.

Roger laughed deliriously, gripping his side. "Where . . . where's that little bitch?" he asked, finally removing his foot from the wound.

Akira sought to gather his thoughts, to properly wield his mind and strength. Blood poured from his wound, and he knew that his world would soon go black unless he bandaged his hand. "Free," he finally replied.

"Free?"

"From the . . . the ugliness of you."

Roger wiped his sweaty brow, tried to steady himself, and again smashed his heel upon Akira's wound. Akira screamed as pain nearly overwhelmed him. "I'm going . . . to drink her blood," Roger said, spitting out the taste of himself. "Yours too."

Akira closed his eyes, aware that he was fading, desperate to see Annie again. "Are you . . . a coward . . . or a man?" he asked in Japanese. The pain on his hand came again, darkening the nearby jungle, threatening to send him into oblivion. "I—"

"Get up," Roger suddenly yelled, kicking him in the ribs.

Akira clawed back from the blackness. He opened his eyes and saw a plane burst into flames through a gap in the canopy. An image of Annie atop a tree then flashed before him, and he made no effort to force her away, as he needed her now. How he loved her. How she brought a sense of wonder into him that he'd never known. Thinking of this wonder, and of how Roger wanted to steal it from the world, Akira stood unsteadily and faced his adversary.

Roger spat out more of his own blood. "You'll never . . . touch that little whore again," he said, raising his pistol in one motion, pressing its warm muzzle against Akira's nose.

"But you see," Akira said, closing his eyes, keeping the image of Annie locked within him, "I am . . . touching her now."

"Now?" Roger laughed, putting slight pressure on the trigger. "Did you say now?"

"You would not . . . understand. So sorry."

"She'll be next. And she's going to—"

Akira suddenly twisted to his left, knocking the gun aside with his uninjured hand. Roger reflexively yanked on the trigger, and Akira felt a searing pain in the side of his neck. But his world didn't immediately darken, and so he slammed his knee into Roger's broken rib. And as Roger shrieked in pain, Akira dropped to the ground, grabbed Edo's fallen pistol, and sent a trio of bullets straight up and into Roger's groin and chest.

And then Akira started to fade away. Thinking of Annie, and of how he wasn't nearly ready to leave her, he forced his injured hand beneath Roger's shuddering body so that the weight of his dying enemy would stop his own blood from departing.

FIFTY FEET AWAY, the gunshots reverberated within Jake's mind. With immense effort, he opened his eyes. Ratu lay motionless nearby. His head was bleeding profusely, and the sight of such blood caused Jake to weep. "No," he whispered, trying to move, besieged with grief. "Please . . . no."

Ratu blinked, grimacing at the pain within him. "Big . . . Jake?"

Jake attempted to rise to his elbows, but his body barely responded. His tattered legs were immobile, as if he were a snail and they his lifeless shell. Still, he slowly dragged himself toward Ratu. Moaning at the agony his movements brought, Ratu clawed to his friend. Their hands met, and Jake rolled over and pulled Ratu closer. Ratu managed to put his head on Jake's chest. Lying on his back, Jake pressed his hand against the wound on Ratu's forehead.

"Thank you . . . for . . . for finding me," Jake whispered, the edges of his vision darkening.

Ratu began to tremble. "Big . . . Big Jake?"

"Yes?"

"I'm . . . afraid . . . of dying," Ratu whispered, the mere effort of speaking making him dizzy.

Jake felt himself fading, and with all of his will, pulled himself into the present. "You . . . you ain't alone. I'm here . . . with you."

"You are?"

"Can't . . . you . . . feel me?"

"I'm . . . cold. So cold."

"Think of . . . all them fish . . . we caught," Jake whispered, his thumb moving slowly against Ratu's wet eyelashes.

"I'm . . . tired."

"Me too."

"Will . . . we . . . travel to heaven . . . together?"

"We . . . surely will," Jake replied quietly, fighting the darkness with all his remaining strength, wanting to be with Ratu for as long as possible. "Like . . . two salamanders."

"Will you . . . hold my hand . . . on the way?" Ratu asked, shivering.

Jake could no longer move his head, but felt tears roll down his face. "Yes," he whispered, unable to open his eyes. "And we'll . . . we'll fish. And . . . and laugh."

"Please . . . please hold my . . . hand, Big Jake. Along . . . the way."

In the blackness that nearly consumed him, Jake managed to lower his hand from Ratu's face. He searched for Ratu's fingers and, finding them, squeezed them with his own. "You . . . feel that?" Jake asked, unsure if he'd said the words aloud.

"Is that . . . your hand?"

"I reckon." Jake wanted to say more, but an enormous weariness was overcoming him, as if he hadn't slept for years. Finally, he whispered, "I . . . love you, Ratu. You're . . . my son. My boy."

"I . . . I am?"

"Sure as . . . rain's wet. Good . . . sweet rain."

Upon hearing these words, Ratu wanted to hug Jake but was powerless to do so. "Do you . . . still have my hand?"

Jake saw his farm. The day was hot and long. Ratu was beside him. "I'll . . . always . . . always have . . . your hand."

"I . . . love you too," Ratu said softly, closing his eyes.

"A . . . fine . . . son," Jake whispered. "Such a . . . fine son." He tried to say more, but he could no longer speak. And so he squeezed Ratu's hand once more. And then he felt himself moving, felt the days of his youth merging with the memories of middle age. He saw knee-high corn, his mother's face, a dirty arrowhead held by his small fingers. And then he saw Ratu. And he held Ratu's hand and didn't let go, even as he felt himself being carried somewhere distant, even as the colors of new worlds washed over him like waves.

DESPITE THE CLAMOR of the distant battle on the beach, the three gunshots reverberated in the jungle, causing Annie to stop and listen. Her heart thudding wildly, she hurried to her left, her wet clothes covered in mud and grime from the many falls she'd taken. Though Annie had been afraid for most of her life, she wasn't afraid now. At least not of her own death.

And so she ran, trying not to panic at the thought of what the gunfire meant, wondering why the nearby jungle was once again silent. She prayed for Akira, Ratu, and Jake, hoping that a miracle would befall her, and that they'd all be fine. She promised God that such a miracle would prompt her to dedicate the rest of her life to a noble cause.

The first body she came across was a Japanese soldier who'd been shot in the chest. He hadn't died instantly, and thinking of Akira, she started to weep when she saw the agonized look on the man's face. Twenty more paces brought her to two more dead soldiers. She spun around, peering through the foliage. "Akira!" she yelled, no longer caring if anyone else heard her. "Akira! Where are you? Jake! Ratu!"

No answer emerged from the jungle. The silence terrified her, for it meant that they might all be dead. Running forward, she tripped over another body. "Akira!" she shouted. "Tell me where you are! Please!"

Annie came to the crest of a small hill and saw Ratu and Jake, saw how they were holding each other. "No!" she shrieked, running forward, sliding to her knees as she neared them. She frantically felt for Ratu's pulse. Finding it, she searched for wounds. He had a nasty cut on his forehead, and, screaming with effort, she ripped part of his shirt off and wrapped it around his head, binding the wound as tightly as possible. Her hands then searched the rest of him. His left arm was broken, but she couldn't locate any other significant wounds. Carefully, she laid him down and propped his head up.

To her dismay, Annie couldn't find Jake's pulse. His flesh was still, and his legs were bloody and ruined. Trying and failing to hold back her sobs, she leaned down, pressed her mouth against his, and desperately sought to bring him back to life. "Don't go, Jake," she whispered, pushing rhythmically on his chest. "Please . . . please don't leave us."

She tried to awaken his heart until her shoulders ached. She looked once more for a sign of life. Seeing none, she leaned down, kissed his brow, longingly touched his face, and said good-bye. Then she rose and stumbled through the nearby foliage, shouting Akira's name.

She found him tangled with Roger and a small Japanese soldier. Weeping, she searched for his pulse and cried out when she felt its beat. Though a plane suddenly crashed into the jungle not far from her, and antiaircraft guns continued to boom, she barely heard the explosions. Her years of training and service took over, and she inspected Akira with trembling hands. She moaned at the sight of his two missing fingers. Ripping a strip from his shirt, she bandaged his wound as best as possible. She then focused on his neck, which bore the rut of a passing bullet. Her tears dropped like rain upon him as she worked.

Suddenly realizing that Ratu was unattended, Annie groaned in frustration. About to leave Akira in order to help Ratu, she heard her sister calling for her. "Izzy!" she screamed, disbelieving her ears. "Izzy, where are you?"

The bushes near her parted and Isabelle, Joshua, and Nathan rushed forth. The two men held rifles, and Isabelle carried the medical kit. Isabelle dropped to her knees beside Akira. Quickly Annie removed bandages and other supplies from the kit. "Ratu," Annie said, pointing toward a tree. "Go to him, Izzy!"

Isabelle and Joshua ran into the bushes while Nathan remained. "What can I do?" he asked, setting his rifle aside.

Annie looked at Akira's wounds, which she'd almost finished dressing. "Can you carry him?" she asked, her voice cracking.

Nathan nodded. "I'm sorry, Annie. I'm so sorry."

Having finished with Akira's wounds, Annie brought his uninjured hand to her lips, kissing it. Shuddering, she then hurried toward Ratu. "How's he doing?" she asked Isabelle, pulling anxiously at her own hair with bloody fingers.

"He'll be fine," Isabelle answered, glancing sadly at Jake.

"It's going to be hard . . . oh, Jake's death is going to be so hard on him."

"I know," Isabelle replied as she fashioned a sling for Ratu's broken arm.

Louder explosions suddenly thundered on the other side of the island. "It's the ships," Joshua said, helping Isabelle with the sling. "They're engaging."

"Should we stay or go?" Isabelle asked, trying to deny the weariness that threatened to overcome her.

Joshua put his arms beneath Ratu. "It's time to go."

"We can't leave Jake," Annie said. "I'll carry Ratu. Josh, can you get Jake?"

"Let's . . . let's take him home."

Annie picked up Ratu as carefully as she could, holding him like a baby in her arms. Stepping unsteadily, she headed back to Akira. Annie saw her lover's bloodied hand and neck, and her tears began anew. But she also began to walk toward the shore, and she didn't stop until her feet touched the sand.

SIX HOURS LATER, after the giant guns of the ships had gone silent, after dusk had swelled and then darkened the sky, Joshua finally stopped rowing. He carefully eased the oars into the boat with bleeding hands that were closed tight by the memory of the wood. Sitting on the bench before him, sheltered within Isabelle's arms, was Ratu. He stared blankly into the distance—his mind dulled by morphine. Fresh stitches dominated his forehead, and his arm was in a sling. He'd said almost nothing since he awoke.

At the front of the lifeboat, Nathan peered into the binoculars, seeking to make sense of the darkness. On the bench nearest to Nathan's perch, Akira and Annie also sat quietly. She'd stitched up the wounds on his hand and neck. The hole that had once held his two fingers had been extremely difficult to close in the rocking boat, but she'd finally finished. When Akira had opened his eyes, she gave him a dose of morphine and leaned his head against her shoulder.

At the bottom of the boat, Jake lay in a fetal position. He looked to be sleeping. Joshua had thought about burying him on the beach, but realizing that Ratu would want to say good-bye, Joshua had gently placed Jake in the boat and then collected a few fist-sized rocks, setting them next to him. Now, as Joshua sat beneath the shimmering sky, he thought about the heat of the coming day, and how Jake would have to be buried at sea. He also pondered how he should mention such a burial to Ratu.

Finally reaching a decision, Joshua carefully stepped over Jake and sat next to Ratu, patting his shoulder, noting how his eyes were fixed on the endless waves. "May I tell you a story?" Joshua asked quietly.

Ratu turned to him as if waking from a dream. "What?" he whispered.

"A story. I'd like to tell you one."

"Tell . . . tell Big Jake too."

Joshua sighed, cradling Ratu's hand within his own, already missing the twang and joy of Jake's voice. "Ever since people sailed the seas," he said, "it's been considered a great . . . the highest honor to . . . to be buried at sea." Joshua spoke slowly, giving Ratu time to comprehend his words. "There's . . . there's a sense of peace found at sea. And unlike a grave on land, which can only be visited in one spot, a grave at sea . . . well, the entire ocean becomes the grave. So the deceased . . . so Jake could be visited from almost anywhere."

A tear rolled down Ratu's face and dropped to Isabelle's wrist. He nodded but said nothing.

"Is this . . . what you want, Ratu?" Isabelle asked, stroking his cheek.

Ratu nodded again. Annie rose to kiss him on the top of the head. Nathan gently squeezed his shoulder. Akira bowed deeply to him, almost passing out in the process. Quietly and carefully, Joshua put the rocks he'd found into Jake's pockets. "Would you like me to say a prayer?" he asked Ratu.

Instead of answering, Ratu awkwardly removed his necklace with his uninjured arm and, with Isabelle's help, placed it around Jake's head, and then leaned down and held Jake tight. While Ratu cried and shuddered, everyone else comforted him with their touch and words. Meanwhile, the sea rocked the lifeboat as if it were a cradle.

When Ratu clearly began to weaken, Annie and Isabelle helped him back to the bench. They tenderly held him as Joshua began to pray. "The Lord is my shepherd," he said softly. "I shall not want. He maketh me to lie down in green pastures. He leadeth me beside the still waters. He restoreth my soul."

Joshua continued the prayer until its conclusion. Silence descended swiftly, only the sounds of Ratu's quiet moans and the restless waves reaching their ears. Joshua nodded to Nathan, and the two men lifted Jake. They then eased him into the water. As he started to sink, Ratu moved to the side of the boat, his fingers darting into the water to grasp

Jake's hand. "I love you . . . Big Jake," he whispered, his tears dropping to the sea. "I love you so bloody much."

Ratu held Jake's hand for so long that it seemed he was unwilling or unable to let go. The lifeboat swayed. The stars slowly moved as the earth twisted. And only when Ratu slipped into unconsciousness did his grip finally loosen.

DAY EIGHTEEN

They say all things end,
But I say all things begin.
Warm winds carry seeds.

Rebirth

S everal hours after dawn, the remaining six survivors from *Benevolence* were plucked from the sea by eager sailors aboard a heavy cruiser of the U.S. Navy. The survivors were given fresh clothes, additional medical care, and hot food. Joshua provided the executive officers with an account of the past weeks, starting with the attack on his ship. Though normally a detailed man, he rushed through his story so that he could return to Isabelle and Ratu. Still, the questions posed to him were many—questions of Roger and Akira, of the Japanese battle group, of *Benevolence*. And though Joshua started to dread the endless inquires, a series of unlikely comments and musings suddenly caused his heart to pound.

As soon as protocol allowed, Joshua rose from the long table, saluting the officers about him. He then hurried through the innards of the ship, running when empty spaces confronted him. He found Isabelle and Ratu exactly where he'd left them—in a small, cramped room containing a cot and a desk. Isabelle sat on the cot, cradling Ratu's head, which now bore a proper bandage. Joshua moved beside her. "I've got wonderful news," he said, so excited that his voice trembled.

"What news?" Isabelle asked, as she gently cleaned Ratu's face with a warm rag.

"Ratu's going home."

"Home?" Ratu asked, his bloodshot eyes widening and filling with tears.

"It's all being arranged," Joshua replied. "I told the captain that my first lieutenant was due some shore leave. And he agreed."

Ratu rose from Isabelle's lap. "When, Captain? Soon?"

"Well, we have to sail here and there, and then catch a plane. But we'll get you home."

"You'll . . . get me?"

"Yes."

"You're going with me?" Ratu asked, not believing what he'd heard. "You're going to take me to my family?"

Joshua nodded, glancing at Isabelle. "I promised my wife two weeks on a beach, Ratu. I told her that I'd teach her to sail. You've got sailboats in Fiji, right? Sailboats and beaches?"

"Oh, of course, Captain," Ratu replied, his voice regaining a bit of its old speed. "I tell you, we have very beautiful beaches and very fast sailboats."

Isabelle kissed the top of Ratu's head. "Maybe you could join us for an afternoon on the water."

"Could my sisters come? All five of them?"

"The more the merrier," Joshua said.

Ratu smiled for the first time in what seemed an eternity. "Can we leave now? Today?"

Joshua patted Ratu's knee. "We'll leave soon, I promise."

"Soon?"

"And . . . and that's not all, Ratu," Joshua said, his eyes glistening. "Not by a long shot. The best is yet to come."

"The best? What do you mean, Captain? Tell me."

"There's a story . . . a wonderful story being told. I just heard it."

"What story?"

Joshua smiled, and to Isabelle his face suddenly looked a decade younger. "I was told of a Fijian man looking for his son," he said. "This man serves with Americans and for weeks has been visiting about every ship and port and base in the South Pacific. He's even asked about *Benevolence*. They say that he won't rest, that he's done so well in the field that the brass support his search. He's seen every captain from here to—"

"My father?" Ratu asked, suddenly weeping with joy.

"I think so. I don't know who else it could be."

"Oh, Captain!" Ratu replied, wrapping his arms around Joshua, squeezing him as tightly as possible. "Thank you! Oh, thank you so bloody much! I know it's him! I tell you, it sounds just like him. It just has to be him!"

"You're going to be with him soon, Ratu," Isabelle said, rubbing the back of his head, her tears almost as numerous as his. "Imagine how happy he'll be to see you."

At her words, Ratu's euphoria seemed to overwhelm him, and for once he was speechless. His lips trembled. His damp eyelids pressed tightly together, sending tears tumbling. He clung to Isabelle and Joshua and continued to hug them. And as the ship gently swayed, the three companions leaned against each other, holding each other. They cried and smiled and even laughed. Finally, when Isabelle said that it was time for Ratu to rest, they laid him gently upon the cot. "Now, may I borrow my lovely wife for a moment?" Joshua asked.

"Just one, Captain," Ratu replied. "Please just one."

Joshua took Isabelle's hand and stepped out of the room. The narrow passageway was empty, and he drew her toward him. "Can you believe it?" he asked. "Apparently, his father is a bit of a legend by now. They say he doesn't sleep. He's got half the Pacific fleet looking for his boy. Looking for . . . for Ratu."

"What a miracle, Josh. What a . . . marvelous miracle. Are you sure? It's almost too good to be true."

"I'm sure."

Isabelle wiped her eyes, so relieved for Ratu that her legs suddenly felt weak. She leaned unsteadily against a nearby bulkhead.

Joshua worriedly moved closer and held her shoulders. "What's wrong?"

"Nothing. Nothing whatsoever."

"Are you sure? You look pale."

"Everything's fine, Joshua. You were there. You heard what the ship's doctor said."

"And the cramps?"

"Nothing to worry about. I just need to rest."

"You, resting?"

"I'm going to try," she said. "You know, I can learn new things."

His bandaged hand slid to her belly. He kissed her briefly. "Do you know what?"

"What?"

"I'm a lucky man, Izzy. Lucky to have you. And I'm sorry if I didn't always realize that, but I realize it now. And I'm not going to forget it again."

"And?" she asked, smiling faintly.

"And . . . and when this war . . . when this world stops fighting with itself, I'm going to come home. Come home for good. And I probably won't give you everything you want, but I'll try to give you plenty."

Isabelle leaned forward, kissing him, pulling him against her. "I just want you, Josh. That's all I want. That's all I need. Just you and the baby and a run-down house that we can fix up and call home. Nothing else much matters."

He kissed her again. "We'd better get back to Ratu. I'd like the two of you to rest. Lay beside him and go to sleep."

"Will you find me tonight?"

"I'm always going to find you, Izzy," he replied, stroking her brow. "Us old sea captains, we know where to look for the best waters."

THE HEAVY CRUISER, having survived the battle almost unscathed, escorted a pair of damaged destroyers toward safer seas. The smaller ships trailed oil and smoke but were taking on no more water than their pumps could clear. Aboard the cruiser, sailors welded torn steel, watched the sky for Zeros, and caught up on some much-needed rest. At the bow, Akira and Annie stood close enough that the rise and fall of the ship often brought their shoulders together. Below, several dolphins leapt in front of the froth and spray created by the bow slicing through the water. The dolphins seemed to delight in the thrust of the iron beast behind them, catapulting themselves high into the air.

"The morphine is leaving me," Akira said, grasping the rail before him with his good hand.

"I should give you something else for the pain," Annie replied. "Let's go belowdecks. You shouldn't be up here anyway. And I want to see how everyone is doing."

"It can wait a moment, yes?" he asked, studying her face, not used to seeing her in unspoiled clothes.

"It can."

Akira watched the dolphins, remembering how he'd encouraged Annie to swim in their company. The creatures below were sleek and smart and beautiful. He felt oddly linked to them, as if he were in their debt for helping him place a bridge between himself and the woman he'd grown to love. "Such freedom," he said, nodding toward the dolphins.

"I'll never forget my swim with them."

The dolphins continued to leap. Akira edged even closer to her side, pleased that her face bore a faint smile. "My hand hurts," he said. "And Jake, a good and noble man, is gone. And I have seen too much death. But still . . . no words, no music, no sight or poem, can describe how I feel now."

"Can you try?"

"It would be easier to swim like those dolphins," he said, looking below. "How do you describe . . . a combination of hope and peace and love? Is there such a word? Such a feeling?"

Though Annie ached because of the loss of Jake, she understood what Akira meant. She knew that life was long, and she felt that for

Isabelle, and for Ratu and Joshua and Nathan and Akira and herself, the best years lay ahead. "Just try," she finally replied. "You can try to describe it, can't you?"

Akira felt the sun on his back, smelled the fragrance of the sea. "Once," he said reflectively, "when I was a boy, I rode my bicycle to the top of a mountain range near my home. It took me almost all day to reach the top. The leaves of the maple trees were turning to gold, to scarlet, to orange. And so the mountains looked . . . they looked as if they had been painted below the blue sky. And a wind blew, and when I rolled down the mountains, the leaves fell on me, fell like little orange blankets. I seemed to descend forever, as if I were a river twisting down that mountain. And I felt such joy and freedom and hope. And I have always thought that was the one pure and perfect moment of my life, a moment that showed me how the suffering and sorrow of life could be eclipsed." Akira looked to the dolphins, and then again to Annie's face. "I now have two such moments. Because I feel this same joy and hope right now."

She placed her arm around his back, drawing him closer, suddenly indifferent to the stares of distant sailors. "For me," she said, "that moment was the night you first made love to me. I knew then that my search was finally over."

"Your search ended then? Not before? Not on the beach?"

"No, not like that. That night changed me forever."

"How?"

"It showed me what was possible. And I'd never seen that before. Never known . . . that . . . that there weren't limits to how I could feel."

Akira looked at her face, loving each precious part as much as the whole. "I feel as if I am once again riding down those mountains. In those leaves. But it is even better now, for I have you beside me, and the ride does not end when I reach the bottom, but continues. And I know that it will go on and on and on. And though it may rain, it may get cold, I may puncture a tire, such things will . . . they will ultimately make our journey better. And when the twilight of that ride is finally upon us, we will look at the trail we have taken and at the signs of our passage. And though our tears will be many, we will know that great lives have been lived, and that our memories will forever bind us together."

ACKNOWLEDGMENTS

Without question, writing a novel is one of the hardest and most enjoyable processes that I have experienced. The joy stems from a profound sense of discovery and creation. The struggle is akin to being lost and alone in a forest and trying to emerge into a light that exists miles away.

I think most novelists would say that writing is a solitary affair. Characters and themes are constant musings that are rarely shared. Not surprising, the struggle to breathe life into such elements is often void of the camaraderie found in so many other occupations.

And yet writers wouldn't be able to write if not for the support of family, friends, readers, and colleagues. I certainly couldn't.

My parents, Patsy and John, inspired my love of reading and travel, for which I will be forever grateful. Equally significant, they taught me of the importance of giving and goodwill. My brothers, Tom, Matt, and Luke, are a wonderful source of pride and happiness. My wife, Allison, has always believed in my dreams and has done her best to make those dreams become realities. And our children, Sophie and Jack, remind me of why the world remains a beautiful place.

My sincere thanks go out to my fantastic editor, Kara Cesare, and everyone else at Penguin. I'm delighted and honored to have such a fine publishing house behind my works. My agent, Laura Dail, has been a marvelous blessing and, as far as I'm concerned, is the best in the business.

In one way or another, the following people have been of immense support: Mary and Doug Barakat, Bruce McPherson, Laura Love, Tracey Zeeck, Pete Kotz, Denise McNamee, Marjorie Weber, Eriq La-Salle, Terri Lubaroff, Pennie Clark Ianniciello, Amy Tan, Wendy Artman, Sandra Dallas, Kara Welsh, Dustin O'Regan, Hank Nerwin, and Donna Gritzo.

And, of course, I would be terribly remiss not to thank all of the readers, librarians, reviewers, and booksellers who have been so kind as to champion *Beneath a Marble Sky* and *Beside a Burning Sea*. I'm forever indebted to such friends.

DEAR READER

When my first novel, *Beneath a Marble Sky*, was published as a paperback in 2006, I decided that I wanted to try and give something back to readers. After all, if people were going to buy my novel, tell their friends about it, and lend me their support, the least I could do was to be supportive in return. I opted to place a letter at the end of *Beneath a Marble Sky* that invited book clubs to invite me to participate in their discussions. I included my e-mail address. To be honest, I wasn't quite sure how my proposal would be received, though I had a hunch that readers wished for such interaction.

I was fortunate in that over the following few months, *Newsweek* magazine and the *CBS Evening News* did stories on my book club program. And as a result of this publicity, I was inundated with requests to talk with book clubs. In fact, over the course of the ensuing year, I spoke (usually via speakerphone) with more than one thousand book clubs. Most of these clubs were based in the United States, though I spoke with groups from Canada to Zambia. And while most clubs were fairly traditional in their approach, others decided to wear saris, cook Indian food, hire henna painters—thereby getting into the spirit of *Beneath a Marble Sky*.

Chatting with more than one thousand book clubs gave me a true appreciation for how carefully people read books. Time and time again, readers greatly impressed me with their insightful questions. As a result, I learned to never take the reader for granted. If people are going to invest hard-earned money into a book, and then take the time to read it, they deserve to experience something memorable.

I hope that *Beside a Burning Sea* moved you. I certainly tried to create a lasting story. I remain delighted to receive and respond to e-mail. Just drop me a line at shors@aol.com.

I'd like to end this note by expressing my profound gratitude to readers. Thank you for all of your support and encouragement.

Beside
A Burning Sea

JOHN SHORS

AN INTERVIEW WITH
JOHN SHORS

❖

Q. During your conversations with more than one thousand book clubs, what have been some of your more memorable moments?

A. The conversations were fantastic, of course. But even more so have been the letters and e-mails that I received afterward. These contained wonderful messages, as well as photos of the groups (oftentimes with members wearing saris and covered in henna paintings).

Q. What's something that you learned about book clubs during your many visits with them?

A. I was quite surprised at the diversity of the book clubs I encountered. Not in terms of race or religion or political orientation, but in their approach to discussing *Beneath a Marble Sky*. For instance, some book clubs would take a rather studious approach, and come prepared with a variety of insightful questions. Other groups would be well into their third round of margaritas. I was never really sure what kind of group I'd be talking with.

Q. Why did you decide to write a novel set in World War II?

A. I've always been fascinated by World War II. And I've felt that in the West we've tended to focus on the war in Europe. Having lived in

Asia for several years, I've been intrigued by the intricacies of the war in that part of the world.

Q. Was it hard to go from writing about the Taj Mahal in Beneath a Marble Sky *to World War II in* Beside a Burning Sea?

A. I think that transitioning from one book to another is a difficult process. After spending such a long time writing *Beneath a Marble Sky*, I became quite connected to its characters. And having to create a batch of new characters for *Beside a Burning Sea* felt somewhat like learning a new language. The voices in both novels are fairly unique, I believe, and giving life to such voices was a time-consuming process.

Q. Your first novel took place in India, and your second novel occurred in the South Pacific. Why do you like to write novels set overseas?

A. I was lucky enough to grow up reading, and have consumed a couple of books a week for most of my life. I have always most enjoyed novels that took me to a new place, and that taught me something. Such novels prompted me to explore much of the world, in fact. And after visiting so many wonderful places, I decided that I wanted to share such locales with my readers.

Q. To that end, where will your next novel be set?

A. It will take place in modern-day Saigon, and will involve a variety of characters from different parts of the world. The story is quite close to my heart, and I'm excited to see it unfold.

Q. What did you most enjoy about writing Beside a Burning Sea?

A. The challenge of creating a setting—of fashioning a time and place of my own design—is immensely gratifying to me. I want my readers to feel as if they've visited the environs that I describe, and giving my novels the necessary richness to achieve that goal is a rewarding challenge. Of course, I also greatly enjoy the process of creating the overall story, and then of sitting down and actually bringing that story to life.

Q. *For you, what is the hardest thing about writing?*

A. I tend to edit my novels a lot, as I want them to be as good as possible. And sometimes it takes a great deal of willpower to try and focus on rereading my novel for, say, the twentieth time. I console myself with the knowledge that each edit makes the book better, but that doesn't make each edit any easier.

Q. *Poetry plays a prominent role in* Beside a Burning Sea. *Why did you decide to add this element to your novel?*

A. Having lived in Japan, I've long had an appreciation for the simple beauty of haikus. Starting each chapter of *Beside a Burning Sea* with a haiku (written from Akira's perspective) was fun for me as a writer. I hope readers enjoy these musings. Additionally, I felt that poetry—or a love of such inward exploration—was a thread that could be used to connect Annie and Akira.

Q. *How much of your success do you attribute to the book club program that you launched with your first novel?*

A. Publishing is an extremely competitive industry. A great number of good books exist, but many simply don't sell. The fact that *Beneath a Marble Sky* is available in fifteen languages and is selling briskly throughout much of the world is due in large part to all of the wonderful book clubs that I spoke with. These clubs (as well as individual readers, of course) have been tremendously supportive of me, and have really championed my novel.

Q. *Are there any other thoughts that you'd like to share with your readers?*

A. Simply that I continue to be grateful for their support.

DISCUSSION QUESTIONS

❈

1. Discuss the significance of the title *Beside a Burning Sea*. Additionally, the original title was *The Poet Makers*. Which title do you prefer? Why?

2. Did *Beside a Burning Sea* provide you with a better understanding of World War II? If so, how?

3. Would you consider *Beside a Burning Sea* an antiwar novel?

4. Who was your favorite character and why?

5. Are you interested in learning more about haikus?

6. Is this a novel that would lend itself well to the silver screen? If so, who would you imagine playing the various characters?

7. Are you more interested in reading a novel set somewhere you haven't been, or would you prefer a locale that you're familiar with?

8. What do you think was the biggest challenge that John Shors faced when writing *Beside a Burning Sea*?

9. Did you connect more with Annie or Isabelle? Why?

10. Of the three main relationships in the novel (Annie and Akira, Isabelle and Joshua, Ratu and Jake), which did you most enjoy? For what reasons?

11. How effective was the character Roger as a villain?

12. What was your favorite scene within *Beside a Burning Sea*?

Watch for the next poignant, provocative novel from
bestselling author John Shors

In the Footsteps of Dragons

Coming from New American Library in September 2009

Set in modern-day Vietnam, *In the Footsteps of Dragons* tells the
tale of two Americans who, as a way of healing their own painful
pasts, open a center to support and educate Vietnamese street
children. Learning from the poorest of the poor, the most silent
of the unheard, the Americans find themselves reborn in an ex-
otic land filled with corruption and chaos, sacrifice and beauty.
Resounding with powerful themes of suffering, love, and re-
demption, *In the Footsteps of Dragons* brings together East and
West, war and peace, and celebrates the resilience of the human
spirit.

Photo by Jim Barbour

After graduating from Colorado College, **John Shors** lived for several years in Kyoto, Japan, where he taught English. On a shoestring budget, he later trekked across Asia, visiting ten countries and climbing the Himalayas. After returning to the United States, he became a newspaper reporter in his hometown, Des Moines, Iowa, winning several statewide awards in journalism. John then moved to Boulder, Colorado, and helped launch GroundFloor Media, now one of the state's largest public-relations firms. John's first novel, *Beneath a Marble Sky*, was a *ForeWord* magazine "Book of the Year" and is available in fifteen languages.

John has been lucky enough to spend much of his life abroad, traveling in Asia, the South Pacific, Europe, Africa, and North America. Recently achieving his lifelong dream of becoming a full-time novelist, John spends his days writing and going on family outings with his wife, Allison, and their two young children, Sophie and Jack. *Beside a Burning Sea* is his second novel.

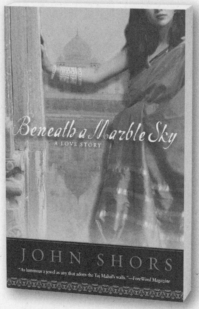